THE EX-BOYFRIEND'S FAVORITE RECIPE FUNERAL COMMITTEE

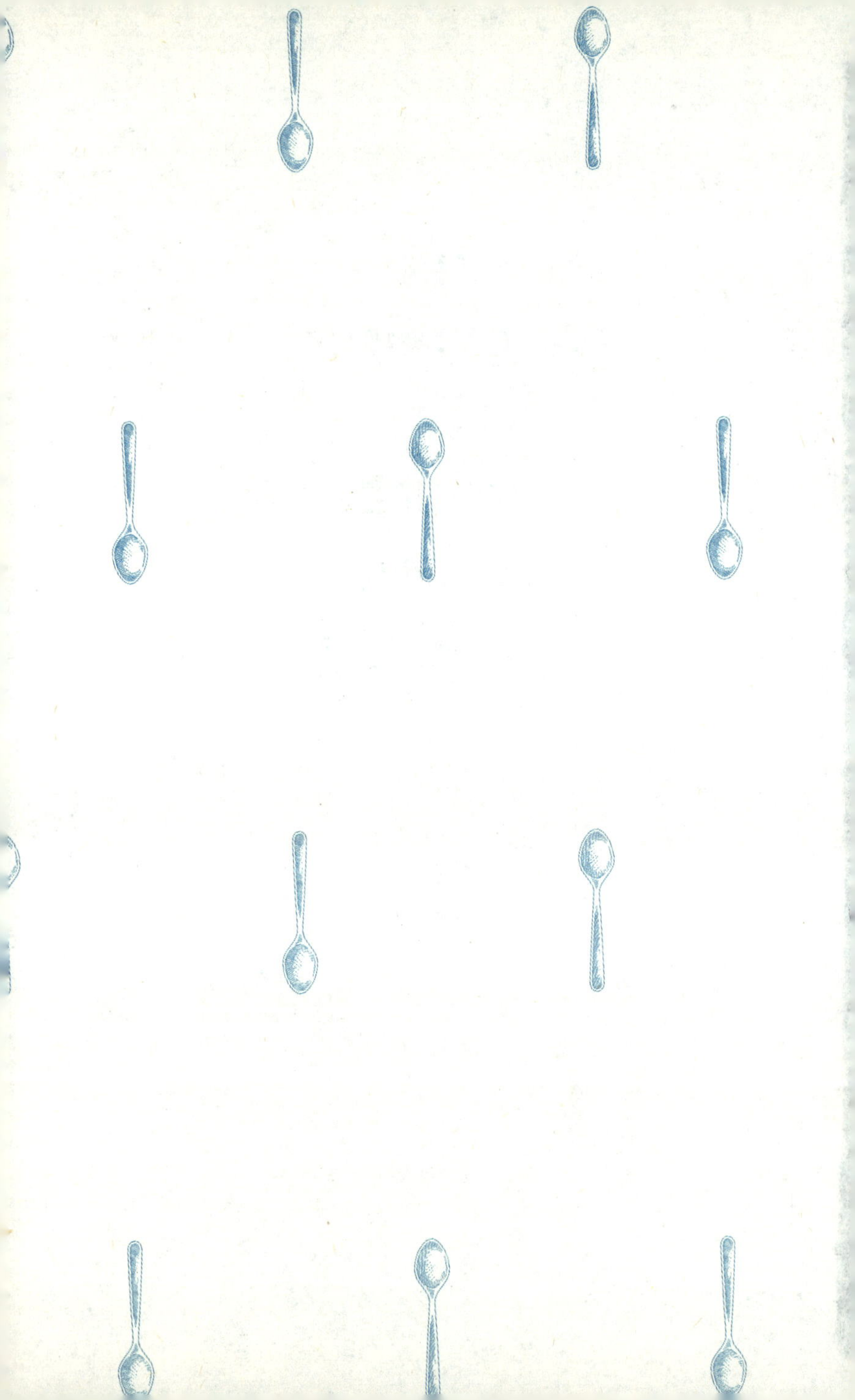

THE EX-BOYFRIEND'S FAVORITE RECIPE FUNERAL COMMITTEE

A Novel

SAKI KAWASHIRO

TRANSLATED FROM JAPANESE BY YUKA MAENO

CROWN
NEW YORK

Crown
An imprint of the Crown Publishing Group
A division of Penguin Random House LLC
1745 Broadway
New York, NY 10019
crownpublishing.com
penguinrandomhouse.com

Translation copyright © 2025 by Yuka Maeno
Copyright © 2023 by Saki Kawashiro

Penguin Random House values and supports copyright. Copyright fuels creativity, encourages diverse voices, promotes free speech, and creates a vibrant culture. Thank you for buying an authorized edition of this book and for complying with copyright laws by not reproducing, scanning, or distributing any part of it in any form without permission. You are supporting writers and allowing Penguin Random House to continue to publish books for every reader. Please note that no part of this book may be used or reproduced in any manner for the purpose of training artificial intelligence technologies or systems.

Crown and the Crown colophon are registered trademarks of
Penguin Random House LLC.

Originally published in Japan as MOTO-KARE GOHAN MAISOU IINKAI by
Sunmark Publishing, Inc., Tokyo, Japan, in 2023.

Translated from Japanese by Yuka Maeno/Arranged by TranNet KK.
This translation published in the United Kingdom by Simon & Schuster UK.

Library of Congress Cataloging-in-Publication Data is available.

Hardcover ISBN 978-0-593-80109-3
International edition ISBN 979-8-217-08818-8
Ebook ISBN 978-0-593-80110-9

Editors: Amy Einhorn and Lori Kusatzky | Production editor: Serena Wang
Text designer: Amani Shakrah | Production: Jessica Heim
Copy editor: Ethan Campbell | Proofreaders: Lorie Young, Katy Miller
Publicist: Lindsay Cook | Marketers: Hannah Perrin, Allyson Coy

Spoon illustration by Shutterstock.com/avni design
Bowl illustration by Shutterstock.com/Net Vector
Hamburger steak illustration by Shutterstock.com/LadadikArt
Plate illustration by Shutterstock.com/mamaruru
Potato illustration by Shutterstock.com/Epine
Plum illustration by Shutterstock.com/aniok
Carrot illustration by Shutterstock.com/Evgenii Doljenkov
Chocolate illustration by Shutterstock.com/Pinchuk Oleksandra
Pizza slice illustration by Shutterstock.com/logaryphmic
Osechi illustration by Shutterstock.com/Foontntd

Manufactured in the United States of America

1st Printing

First US Edition

The authorized representative in the EU for product safety and compliance is
Penguin Random House Ireland, Morrison Chambers, 32 Nassau Street,
Dublin D02 YH68, Ireland, https://eu-contact.penguin.ie.

TABLE OF CONTENTS

THE EX-BOYFRIEND'S FAVORITE RECIPE FUNERAL COMMITTEE

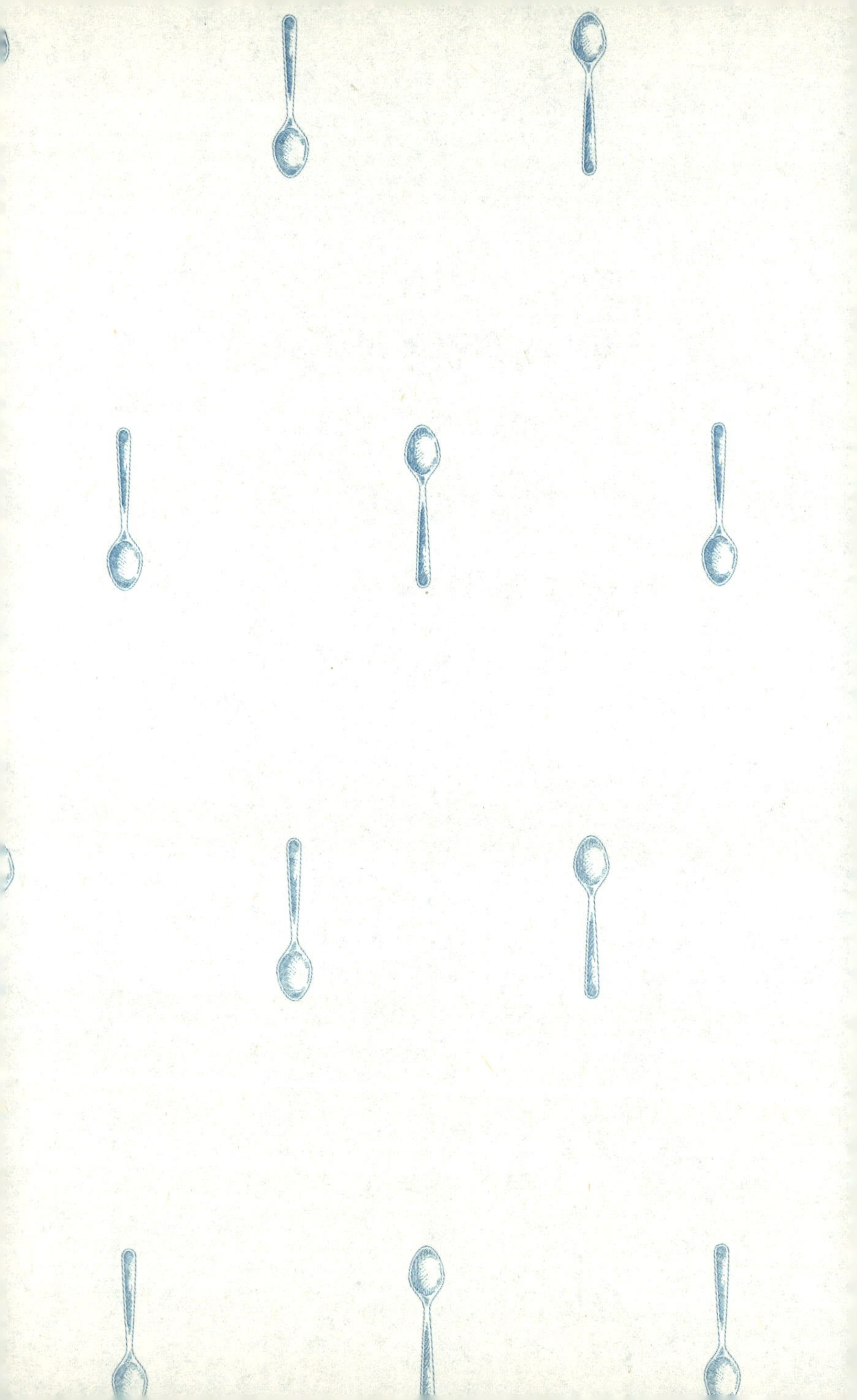

CHAPTER 1

MY EX-BOYFRIEND'S FAVORITE BUTTER CHICKEN CURRY

Of all places he could've dumped me, he chose to do it in a love hotel. A love hotel!

Lying down in bed, I struggled to stifle a sob.

I didn't want to hold back. I wanted to bawl my eyes out. I wanted to howl and wail and let out every sound I had inside of me with so much intensity that you would be able to *actually* see the emotions pouring out of my mouth. But instead, I bit my lip. I had to save what was left of my dignity.

And that was because Kyohei Takanashi—the jerk who'd just broken up with me—was lying on the other side of the bed, purposefully leaving enough space so that an adult could have fit between us. He was facing away, so I couldn't tell if he was fully asleep. There was no way I could let him know that he had broken my heart. Whatever I did, I wasn't going to let him feel sorry for me.

Grabbing the charging cable by my pillow, I drew my phone toward me and checked the time under the covers. My eyes were burning from the tears, and the blue light didn't help. It was already two in the morning. I had been in bed for at least thirty minutes, but I was never going to sleep. Instead, my nose began to run as a new flood of tears spilled from my eyes.

Taking care not to disturb Kyohei, I gently stretched my arm over to put my phone back. At that moment, my fingers touched a plastic wrapper. It was an unused condom.

Had he planned on it? He must have put it there for us. If only I had known. If only . . .

I felt a surge of emotion I couldn't decipher: Regret? Shame? Whatever it was, it welled up inside of me, as the tears kept coming.

It wasn't that I *really* wanted to sleep with him and was frustrated we hadn't. It wasn't that. I just . . . I'd just thought that he was the one I'd marry. That there would be no one else for me. But our love, which had lasted four years, had come to an abrupt and humiliating end. On a hotel bed far bigger than necessary, our relationship shattered to pieces and vanished entirely.

It smelled like a mix of spices, and I thought of the time I had made butter chicken curry for Kyohei. He'd put away three whole bowls of it in one sitting, and I'd called it the "Kyohei curry" ever since.

I guess I won't be making that ever again. But wait . . . why am I smelling curry right now?

I opened my eyes. I could see the grain pattern of a wooden table and realized I had been sleeping with my face down. I groaned in pain as I struggled to lift my head and get my bearings. I noticed I was sitting on a comfortable sofa, and that I had a splitting headache. It felt as though my head was being crushed and ground up in a stone mill. My vision was blurry, and bits of mascara fell off my lashes as I rubbed my eyelids.

Where am I?

There was nothing familiar about the place. It looked as if it might be a café. There was an antique cuckoo clock and a small TV to my left. Coffee cups and books, as well as a snow globe, were mixed among a collection of antique items on the display shelves. A dusty smell—that smell you can only find inside old buildings—and the subtle scent of curry filled the air.

Looking around, there was only one other customer. The place was small, with four seats at the counter and a few tables with their own sofas, which allowed for seating another eight people.

"You're awake."

A crisp male voice came from behind me. I cradled my aching head with my hands as I finally sat upright.

"I'm sorry, I can't remember—wow, you are gorgeous! Oh, I didn't mean to say that out loud." Embarrassed, I covered my mouth.

The man's well-defined nose was as sharp as a right-angled triangle, and he had big double-lidded eyes. His facial features worked in perfect harmony, neither too close nor too far apart from one another. It was like all the qualities of every good-looking man on the planet had been brought together to create the epitome of beauty. The navy blue sweater he wore even complemented his skin tone.

"Actually, it's not the first time you've called me gorgeous." He laughed.

"What? Are you sure it was me?"

"You really don't remember?"

I really didn't remember any conversation I'd had with this man. I did have a slight recollection of leaving the hotel at eight in the morning. I was going to get the train, but changed my mind after seeing too many happy couples on board. Since I had taken the day off to spend it with Kyohei, I didn't want to go home and do nothing. So, deciding that it was a good idea to drink it all away, I went into a twenty-four-hour izakaya bar, ordered a shochu on the rocks, and downed it. And that was the last thing I remembered . . .

I reached into my pocket to get my phone.

"Why is my phone screen smashed?"

"Again, you said that exact same thing earlier," the man said.

He radiated so much charisma, it hurt my eyes to look at him. I felt a little dizzy as his dazzling smile pierced through my cocktail headache like a laser beam. The way he smiled was so incredibly charming that, if he had been born a few centuries ago, he would have been some kind of legend. A mural would've been painted in his honor and named *The Secret Treasure of the East.*

I tapped my phone, relieved to find it still working despite the big crack on the screen. It was noon.

Noon?! Has it been that long?

There were apparently more blanks to fill in than I'd hoped.

"Excuse me," I called out to the man, "where exactly am I?"

"You're in Sangenjaya."

"Are you kidding?" I stood up and stepped outside.

Please tell me he's joking.

"Wait, where are you going?"

It was not a neighborhood I recognized. I glanced over to a poster on a utility pole that showed the address: *Taishido, Setagaya.*

I was indeed in the Sangenjaya area.

Seriously? I walked all the way from Shibuya to Sangenjaya?

It explained why the bottoms of my feet were hurting so much. I gazed down and scanned myself, suddenly realizing how messy I looked. There was a patch of soy sauce on my dress, and a tear in my tights ran from my toe to my thigh. A Hello Kitty bandage covered my grazed knee (I obviously didn't remember how that happened). I had splurged on a new pair of pumps for my date night with Kyohei—spending precisely 39,800 yen—but the heels on them were now completely worn out.

Wondering what it was that had made me come to this place, I turned around to take a good look at the café.

Its name was Amayadori—"taking shelter from rain." Although ironically, judging from the run-down exterior of the building, I was pretty sure that the roof would leak. The name of the café printed on the awning had faded so much that it was barely legible. The door, the front step, and frankly everything else about the building was thoroughly worn out. As I stared at the tired, tatty wall, something about it reminded me of my great-grandfather in Kagoshima—an image of the age spots on his skin floated into my mind. A chalkboard sign near the entrance read: **OUR MOST POPULAR DISH! LUNCHTIME SPECIAL CURRY–1,000 YEN**, which explained the smell inside.

The good-looking guy joined me outside.

"You walked through the door shouting, 'This shabby little place is exactly what I need right now! I'm in no state to go anywhere fancy!' Then you yelled, 'Hey, gorgeous! Bring me a beer, please!' You seemed to be having a great time, but then you fell asleep with your head down on the table pretty quickly. Not that I minded . . . we didn't have any other customers anyway."

"I am so sorry," I said, completely mortified. Not only had I barged in drunk, I had demanded a beer in a café. I bowed repeatedly to express my apology.

"Really, I am so sorry—wait, I think I'm going to be sick . . ."

"Take it easy, don't move your head so much. Why don't you go back inside and rest a little longer?"

This man was a national treasure. If this was a normal day, I would've been thrilled to encounter a man this hot who was actually nice to me, but under the circumstances, the whole situation made me feel all the more ashamed. I desperately wanted to crawl into a hole.

"You should eat. Let me make you something."

"Thank you for being so nice to me."

I learned that the handsome man's name was Iori Amamiya and that he was the manager of the café. As I sobered up, I noticed how tranquil the place was, and it dawned on me that I was single-handedly responsible for ruining the café's serene atmosphere. I felt terrible.

Noticing the customer sitting at the end of the counter, I silently apologized, picturing myself kneeling down and bowing to him. The man was well-built, had a shaved head, and wore glasses. He was dressed in a samue, so I wondered if he was a Buddhist monk. He was eating a plate of curry, oddly pairing it with an ice cream soda—a green, melon-flavored drink topped with ice cream—while reading a paperback book.

I gulped my water down to wash away my misery and nausea. A melting piece of ice slid down the back of my throat like a flattened marble.

I sighed.

My thoughts drifted to Kyohei. *Did he have water when he got home?* He was never good at keeping himself hydrated—he would easily go the whole day without drinking water unless I reminded him. Then I remembered about the Contrex mineral water subscription I'd signed up for after he told me that the results of his annual health checkup showed some concerns.

He'll be fine; he has that water at home. But maybe I should message him and tell him just in case . . .

I reached for my phone. As if on cue, a notification popped up on the screen. It was a message from Kyohei, and I jumped up in panic as my phone vibrated in my hand.

Sensing that the man with the shaved head was staring at me from the counter, I quickly sat back down.

Taking a deep breath, I opened the message.

I've packed up your things. I'll post them to you later.
I'd appreciate it if you could cancel all subscriptions
under your name ASAP.

After this businesslike message, he sent a sticker—the one of a bear with beads of sweat dripping from its downcast face.

"What is this?"

Why would you send me that sticker? You're not even the sticker-sending type.

We had sent numerous messages to each other over the last four years, so I knew all about his style. Most of the time, he opted for an exclamation point. When I suggested that we both purchase one of those paid stickers so that we could match, he said no. He said he was too embarrassed, and he never changed his mind about it.

Anyway, I knew that I wasn't supposed to worry about his health. I wasn't part of his life in that way anymore. But . . . didn't we just break up yesterday? No—it happened in the early hours of the morning, so technically, it was today. We even ended up sleeping in the same bed because we both missed the last train. It had only been a few hours since we parted ways.

Were you that desperate to break up with me?

Did he hate me so much that he wanted all my stuff gone, as soon as our relationship ended? As he packed my things into cardboard boxes, did he not think about getting back together? Not once? Not even a little bit?

It felt as though the apologetic bear sticker was some kind of official stamp that announced he was "Never Coming Back." My crying had subsided as I slept, but now a wave of fresh tears came flooding back.

I knew that there was no point in me crying, but I had no control over it. It was as if my emotional brakes were broken.

Oh, God. Everything in my view was filtered through Kyohei: the coffee cups, the bathroom sign, the plants outside the window. I had gained the ability to link the most random things in the world to a memory with Kyohei.

Don't do it, I chided myself. I had already come into the café drunk and passed out. If I burst into tears now, it would just make me weirder. I didn't want to cause any more inconvenience.

I opened my eyes wide to stop them from welling up. I knew that if I blinked, my eyelashes would push the teardrops out like a windshield wiper, so I stretched my eyes as open as they would go. My plan was to stay like that until my tears dried up.

"Oh."

The shaved-headed man and I locked eyes. He looked frightened, and I suspected this was due to my eyes. The paperback he was holding slipped out of his hand and hit the floor with a flop.

I felt the need to apologize immediately. "I'm sorry. You must be creeped out by me."

"Excuse me?"

"First, I caused a disturbance by walking in drunk. And now I've suddenly gotten all teary. I've never even come to this café before. You think I'm a freak, don't you?"

"Oh, umm . . . I never said that."

"I've always been like this. I get all emotional and lose control. My boyfriend used to tell me off for it. Is this why people think I'm needy? What do you think?"

"I'm not really in the position to—"

I hauled myself onto the barstool next to him and picked up the man's book.

"Hold on, why are you sitting down?"

I handed it back to him.

"He used to take me out to classy restaurants almost every week," I continued, barely taking a breath. "He sent me chat messages daily and told me I was pretty and that he loved me. But recently, he hadn't said any of those things. At first, I thought he was having a tough time at work—he's a salesman and has targets to hit. I thought, well, I want to be the one who's there for him, you know? So I started leaving meals for him in his fridge and surprised him with full-course dinners even if it wasn't a special occasion. I made a huge effort, even mentioning three nice things about him every day, but do men consider this kind of behavior a nuisance?"

"Umm . . . are you still drunk?"

Crap. Talking about it made me well up again. I pressed my eyes with a tissue.

"Was everything I did in vain?" I said between sobs. "Was I just being clingy?"

"How should I know? Iori, this lady is—hey, will you help me out here?"

A thought occurred to me, and I retrieved the agnès b. paper bag that I had been lugging around with my handbag. Something about this man had put me at ease. Perhaps it was his monk-like look. I suddenly felt the urge to let out the resentment that had built up inside of me.

"Please, look at this," I said, as I pulled out a gift-wrapped box from the bag and presented it to him.

"Umm, okay . . ."

"I got these for Kyohei's birthday. It's a pair of couple's watches. Is it clingy, do you think? The set cost me sixty-seven thousand yen. Does that make me seem needy? I did consider splashing out on a pair of Cartier watches, but I didn't want to overwhelm him with such an expensive gift. So I held back, you know? It's not exactly extravagant, considering we'd been together four years, don't you think? Is there something wrong with my perception of things? What does the Buddha say?"

"I don't believe the Buddha would ever gift couple's watches."

"Right. Well, if the Buddha doesn't even know . . . I guess it is what it is."

"But—" The monk-like man scratched his bushy eyebrows uncomfortably and muttered, "Generally speaking, that is not an inexpensive gift. And the fact that they are a matching set . . . well, I suppose that would probably put you in clingy territory."

"I knew it!" I scratched my head vigorously. What part of our relationship *had* I done right? Where had I failed? I was getting more and more confused. The man tried to take back his words, telling me not to listen to him, but the sound of his mumbling now seemed far off.

All I could think about was the fact that I had spent four whole years—no, it was much longer than that. Twenty-nine years . . . I had lived twenty-nine years thinking the way I behaved was the best way to keep a man, and that was just . . .

"Nwaahhhh!" I exclaimed in frustration.

"Hozumi, go easy on her, will you?"

I looked up. It was Iori. I guess the man I had been moaning to was called Hozumi.

"You should never drink on an empty stomach. Sorry to serve you leftovers." In graceful gestures, Iori laid down a plate of a classic chicken curry on the table.

As soon as I saw it, my heart dropped. Unwanted images came rushing back.

Crap.

I had an extensive collection of Kyohei's expressions stored in my brain, and so many of them were curry related. That face as he gleefully filled his cheeks with curry. Him telling me, *It has a real kick to it today!* with beads of sweat forming on his temples. His bed hair as he had his second serving of morning curry. I could simultaneously play back hundreds of different Kyoheis in my mind.

"Is everything okay? Do you not like curry?"

"Oh, no, that's not it. It looks delicious."

Calm down, I told myself, and gripped the spoon.

You just got dumped in a love hotel. You are drunk. You still have a throbbing pain in your head. You are not calm right now. You are the opposite of calm. You know more than anyone that nothing good can come of a situation like this.

I was reminded of the time when I found myself rejected by the hundredth company I interviewed with during my shukatsu, that grueling period of job-hunting for soon-to-be graduates. The next thing I knew, I had dumped my phone and flown to India. Thinking that I had gone missing, my brother filed a report with the police. It was total chaos.

I weighed my options. I could be heartbroken and hungry, or heartbroken and not hungry. Neither of them was going to take away my pain, so I decided to go with the less unpleasant one. The latter was still the lesser evil. At least on a physical level, I would feel better if I ate something.

Scooping up a heaped spoonful of curry and rice, I swallowed it in one bite.

"Huh?" I choked out.

"Is something wrong?"

"Oh, no. It's just . . . maybe my stomach is upset."

Dodging the nice manager's gaze, I poured myself a cup of water from the pitcher and downed it. Then I chugged another cup.

I attempted another bite.

What . . . is this?

Watery and tasteless. I couldn't smell the slightest bit of spice. I wondered if I could even call it curry—it was more like hot water with a little bit of flavor.

To put it simply, it was disgusting.

I had made a disastrous curry once. Kyohei was going to come over to my place, so I had gotten all worked up and prepared it the day before, but I miscalculated the seasoning ratio. I had to remake the whole thing in a hurry, and— *I'm doing it again! Stop thinking about Kyohei!* I willed my brain to turn Kyohei autoplay off.

"Do you not like it?"

"Oh, no! It tastes . . . wonderful!"

"Really? I'm glad to hear that."

Oh, no. Now he thinks I like it.

But what other choice did I have? He had been an angel to me. It wasn't as if I could stare into his smiling face and say, "Actually, it's disgusting."

Glancing over to my left, I saw that Hozumi had finished his glass of ice cream soda. He had also polished off his plate of curry. In fact, he had tucked into it as if it were a perfectly normal thing to do. I recalled the chalkboard sign outside, which confidently advertised the curry as their "most popular dish."

I took a deep breath in an effort to compose myself as the world around me began to spin, my heart racing faster and faster.

Then a dark thought rose up in my mind.

What if it's me and not the curry? It can't be my palate . . . can it?

After thoroughly blowing my nose out into a tissue, I tried another mouthful. It still tasted strange.

Seriously? Are my taste buds having a meltdown?

My dad used to run an izakaya bar back home in Kagoshima. As a young child, I helped out, and often did the cooking at home, too. Naturally, I became pretty confident in the kitchen. Give me thirty seconds, and I will have sliced half a cabbage end to end into perfectly julienned strips.

But come to think of it . . .

When I was in my third year of elementary school, our izakaya went out of business. It was my dad who'd shown me the ropes. I'd lived my entire life believing everything he taught me about cooking.

What if Dad's palate couldn't be trusted in the first place?

What if . . . both my dad and I had driven the izakaya out of business with our poor palates and bad cooking? Then, still under the guise of ignorance, I invented my own signature curry, and served it to Kyohei with so much confidence that he felt compelled to say that he enjoyed it even though it was horrible.

Kyohei's words from last night mixed with the smell of the curry and clung to my skin.

"To be honest, I've known for a long time that I needed to have this conversation with you. But when I looked at your face, I could see how hard you were trying for me. I couldn't bring myself to do it. I'm sorry."

When he'd said "delicious," had he really meant it?

Was he really "having fun" when he told me so?

What about his "I love you"s?

As my thoughts spiraled, memories flooded over me, the what-ifs and maybes multiplying and sticking clammily to my body. I wished that I could escape to India. I wished that I could pass out again.

"I couldn't help but overhear your conversation earlier. Are you going through a bad breakup?"

As I lifted my head, Iori settled down next to me. Crossing his long limbs, he sipped his coffee elegantly.

"Could you be any more direct?" Hozumi said scoldingly.

"Well, at a time like this, the best course of action is to let it all out to someone."

"Let it all out?"

"After all, only three things can heal a broken heart: empathy, time, and revenge," Iori said, holding up three fingers.

"Empathy, time, and revenge . . ."

"Uh-huh. They say 'time is the greatest healer,' which I guess isn't untrue. In my experience, though, it takes at least six months to get over the person who dumped you."

"Did you just say six months?!"

I have to live with this pain for six whole months?

My headache worsened immediately.

"The question is, how will you get through those six months? To be able to fight pain, you need the empathy of others. Once you start believing that there are other people who share the same emotions as you, that's when you finally start to feel like maybe you can move forward. So, tell me your love story."

Iori rested his cheeks in his hands and smiled softly.

"Your words are as beautiful as your face," I said.

With Iori's kindness, my heart began to feel a little soothed. I wondered what I'd be doing if I hadn't found this café. I imagined myself holed up at home, alone and weeping.

"Well . . . I'm pretty sure once I start talking, I won't stop. And I will very likely bawl my eyes out. Are you sure about this?"

Iori let out a chuckle. "Sure. Why not?"

Suddenly, a smell that reminded me of smearing ink came wafting over, and it began to drizzle quietly.

At least the sound of rain will mask some of my sniffling, I thought.

I normally hate the rain. But at that moment, I felt a little grateful that it was there.

"So you were together for four whole years, and then you got dumped at twenty-nine? Well, that explains the drinking."

Iori was a great listener, and I had practically given him my entire life story.

He now knew that my full name was Momoko Yuuki, and that I was from Kagoshima. I told him that I worked for a company that operates a restaurant chain, and how its culture was so toxic that employees were always leaving. To make up for the worker shortage, I had to take over the manager role for multiple restaurants. This made taking the weekends off almost impossible, but as it was Kyohei's birthday yesterday, I'd played every card I had in my deck to get myself out of the shift for two days. Because of the unexpected turn of events, my weekend was now wide open.

"I think the number of I-forgots is proportionate to how uninterested a person is," I said as I choked down the curry. I had started to get used to the flavor and had almost persuaded myself that it was growing on me. "I forgot to call. I forgot our anniversary. I forgot Christmas. I forgot your birthday."

"Birthday is a tough one."

"Right? Gradually, the number of I-forgots increased, and his excuses got less and less convincing. Then, over time, he just stopped making excuses."

And I got better and better at saying, "Well, there's nothing you can do about that," as if I really meant it.

"Birthdays, I can take. I can't blame someone for forgetting my birthday if they were completely snowed under at work. Forgetting birthdays is forgivable—let's just say so. But how . . . how on earth does someone forget New Year's?" I struck the table with my fist.

Just a few months ago, as we drew closer to the end of the year, I tried to get ahold of Kyohei, but no matter how many times I contacted him, he didn't reply. I was worried sick that something had happened to him. Then on New Year's Day, he wrote back, "Sorry. I didn't realize that it was New Year's Eve." He had the nerve to use *that* as an excuse.

"How could anyone living in Japan possibly forget New Year's?" I asked.

"True. You'd have to be living under a rock." Iori gave a dry grin.

"Maybe he was working overnight on New Year's Eve?" Hozumi suggested.

"But I saw that he had liked a post by a pizza place announcing a New Year's deal. It wasn't that he had forgotten New Year's itself."

This seemed to startle Hozumi, and he fell off his chair.

"Are you okay?" Iori asked.

"Other people can see your likes?"

"Of course they can," I responded.

Hozumi's glasses had slid down his face. Pushing them back up, he continued his questioning. "Is that because you are an especially clingy person, and therefore you know a special trick that gives you the power to check other people's likes?"

"How rude! Anyone can see other people's likes!"

I showed him how to check the likes and Hozumi's face turned pale; he started to tremble and scrolled furiously on his phone, mumbling something to himself.

"Hozumi, are you—"

"Let's just leave him be," Iori cut in. "Please continue."

Ignoring the awkwardness that now filled the air, I carried on.

"Anyway, stuff like that kept happening, but I couldn't bring myself to say anything about it. And then yesterday, on Kyohei's birthday, we were finally able to get together after a month of not seeing each other."

We had a dinner date at a fancy restaurant, and we both got a little tipsy. I was relieved, thinking that nothing had changed between us after all. I accidentally-on-purpose missed the last train, which then led us to spending the night in a hotel.

As I remembered, I felt a deep pain in my chest.

There was a huge bed in the hotel room. I went to wash first. I put on my emergency skincare and lingerie I had thrown into my bag "just in case." I had also packed an atomizer containing my Chloé perfume, but I thought better of it. I didn't want to come across as desperate.

After bathing, Kyohei sat down on the bed with his legs crossed, rubbing his hair dry with a towel. I threw my arms around him and kissed him gently.

The spark has not faded, I thought.

My heart was beating faster and faster.

Kyohei sighed quietly.

"But then he said to me, 'Can it wait till tomorrow?' "

It was the moment my intuition told me everything I needed to know.

"Oh . . ." Iori covered his face with his slender hands. "That must have hurt. That must have really hurt."

"To be honest, I kind of thought last night would be our chance to get back on track. I was hopeful that he had planned on doing it, too."

"Sorry, what do you mean by 'doing it'?"

"You know . . ."

It seemed that Hozumi wasn't following. Iori began to whisper something into his ear. Furrowing his brow, Hozumi looked dead serious as he listened. Eventually, his cheeks turned pink.

"Oh, right," he said bashfully, and pushed his glasses up with his finger.

"It wasn't like I was sexually dissatisfied. That wasn't the point."

This isn't about sex. It's not about sex at all.

"I took it as a direct sign that he didn't love me anymore. We hadn't seen each other for a whole month, yet he didn't even try to touch me. A healthy man in his twenties who hadn't slept with his girlfriend for a whole month wanted to wait 'until tomorrow.' I lost all hope at that moment. It felt like I was now officially worthless as a woman."

I wondered if I had overshared, given that we'd only just met, but they were such generous listeners that the words kept pouring out.

"I didn't know what was going on in his mind—he didn't say he wanted to break up or tell me if there was any part of me that needed to change. I didn't have the slightest clue as to how to make things better. I couldn't cope with the pain of being neglected without any answers. I thought that if he told me straight what he wanted, it would end my suffering."

A teardrop fell into my spoon and formed a tiny puddle.

"I couldn't take it any longer, so I said, 'If you don't love me anymore, maybe it's better to end things.' I told him I didn't want to waste any more time on someone who wasn't interested in me."

It was an ultimatum. I had vowed never to declare the words that I had held back, even though they had been on the tip of my tongue for the last four years.

"Did you want him to say it wasn't true?" Iori asked gently.

I had wanted Kyohei to say, "Don't be silly, I love you, I'm just tired today." I'd wished he would pat my head and squeeze my hand. That was all I had wanted.

Was it, though?

"I admit there was a part of me that wanted him to feel hurt, at least a little."

I set my spoon down and pressed my eyelids with a tissue. I had wanted to look immaculate on my last morning with Kyohei. All of my carefully applied makeup was now melting away.

"He knew I was hurting but pretended not to notice. We never had a real conversation about it—he evaded the topic, and that bothered me constantly. I was far from a perfect communicator myself, though. When Kyohei was busy, I played the role of the independent girl—the solitude-embracing woman I wished I was. I was too proud to tell him how I really felt."

So, no matter how disinterested Kyohei behaved, I acted grown-up all the time. Even when he was being cold or turned me down.

But as we fell into this pattern of unspoken issues, anger started to boil up inside of me.

The stuff that I'm angry about concerns both of us, so why are you acting like that, like you seem to think that showing emotion is a childish thing to do? This is about us! Of course we should get emotional! How can you look at me like this has nothing to do with you?

Why is it that I can never cause you any pain?

"I suggested breaking up, hoping to see the pain in his face. For once, I wanted to be the cause of *his* anguish. I thought, if I could see him like that . . ."

It was a one-sided relationship. He would ignore my messages, leaving me on read for three days. When he finally did reply, it would just be a sticker.

I'd wait another three days before sending a harmless message like: *It's freezing today! Don't catch a cold.*

Even if he kept treating me this way, I would have been okay with it, if I could catch even the smallest glimpse of pain in his eyes. "I'm awful, aren't I?"

It seemed that they were at a loss for words, and we all fell silent for a moment.

"That's pretty normal, actually." Iori took a sip of his coffee and said quietly, "What did he say after you laid down that ultimatum?"

"He told me that he had been trying to get me to dump him. He wanted me to break up with him, because he couldn't bring himself to talk to me about it. He said he ignored my messages on purpose, pretended to forget important occasions so that I'd get the hint."

Kyohei proceeded to apologize. In a feeble voice, he told me how sorry he was for all the mixed messages. He kept his head lowered, didn't even look me in the eye. I wanted him to cry, at least a little, but he didn't. I never saw a single tear.

"No part of him looked hurt. He was emotionless, calm. That was hard to take."

"How can I say this . . . he's not exactly a player, is he?" Iori said.

"That's what I liked about him."

Kyohei was a live-in-the-moment kind of guy, taking each day as it came. Like an innocent child, he was oblivious to his surroundings. He wasn't the romantic type, but there were times when he tried to do something sweet, just to make me happy. I wanted to feel those butterflies again. I kept holding on, waiting for that version of Kyohei to come back.

"Suddenly, it was two in the morning. I would have preferred to keep arguing until sunrise, but we ran out of things to say to each other. In the end, we slept on opposite sides of the bed and parted ways at around eight o'clock."

When I rolled over, I saw that Kyohei's back was about two feet away from me. Until a moment ago, I could have reached out and touched his back. But now, he wasn't mine to hold anymore.

If I hadn't said, "Do you not love me anymore?"

If only I had said, "You're tired, I understand."

Then maybe I would be running my hand over his back right now.

A million could-haves floated above the bed, going round and round in circles all through the night.

"I can't stop thinking about what I did wrong. Did he think I was needy? I tried not to seem like it. I made sure I waited at least an hour before replying to his messages, even if I was dying to write him back. I really, really tried. I would have liked to tell him I loved him more often, but I held back so as not to scare him."

I thought about all the unsent *I love you*s I had deleted.

Even this morning, when I knew that we weren't going to see each other again, I still couldn't look him in the eyes and tell him I loved him. Instead of telling him how I felt, I waited and waited for him to suggest starting over.

"I love him. I'm in love with him."

I felt a cold sensation on my cheeks. Droplets of tears trickled down my jaw and merged with my curry.

"I *loved* him. I loved everything about him. If things were going to end like this, I should have said it more."

If I had, would I have no regrets?

I was scared—terrified—of being myself. I constantly thought about what it meant to be the perfect woman that he would desire. I wanted to be the good girlfriend. I spent all my effort trying, and this was where I ended up. I had turned into an overthinking idiot.

Kyohei never truly opened up to me, because I was so concerned with covering up my own flaws.

I struggled to control myself. Belatedly feeling embarrassed, I wiped my under-eyes with the sleeve of my dress and forced down the remaining flavorless curry.

When Kyohei said that my curry was delicious, he was probably just being polite. Maybe he had already been trying to find the right time to break up with me.

My hand gripping the spoon paused.

An image of his face appeared before me.

"This is the best curry I've ever had in my life!"

He ate a second helping, then another—he kept going until there was nothing left in the stockpot. When he realized he had demolished several days' worth of curry in one night, he smiled as though he didn't have a care in the world.

Had his smile been genuine, though?

"Maybe some ice cream will cheer you up," Iori offered.

I needed to find out.

"Umm . . . My curry . . ."

"Huh?"

Of our four-year relationship, how much was true? How much was a lie? How much of it did I get right? How much of it did I get wrong?

I can't trust anything anymore.

The question came blurting out: "Will you try Kyohei's favorite curry?"

"Who?" Iori asked.

"You."

"Me?"

"And him, the gentleman who looks like he belongs in a temple . . . it's Hozumi, right?"

This seemed to catch Hozumi off guard. He spat out his water and sent himself into a coughing fit.

"Me as well?"

"I need more than one tester for the result to be credible."

"Oh, well, I do have to get back to my training . . ."

Wiping his cheeks dry with a handkerchief, Hozumi slowly got up from his chair.

Iori grabbed him by the shoulders.

"Hozumi." He smiled, bringing his face close to the tip of Hozumi's nose. Iori's delicate lips formed the most perfect curve, as if they belonged in a makeup ad. "You wouldn't leave me here alone now, would you? That would be bad karma, wouldn't it?"

Hozumi wrestled out of Iori's grip and adjusted the collar on his samue.

"I'm just a customer here . . ."

"Please." I bowed to them. Not only had they let me take a rest here, but they had also let me go on and on about my breakup. And now I was demanding that they try my curry recipe. I knew I was asking a lot.

"Please. I promise to pay you both back for this. I'll come back to apologize properly. I'll bring a box of sweets with me, too. Oh, and money. I have plenty of cash. I even have a fixed-term deposit account—"

I need this.

"Okay, okay. Tell me what you need." Iori let out a sigh and made his way to the kitchen.

Pulling the fridge door open, he checked its contents.

"We have chicken and onions. Write me a list of anything you're missing. I'll run to the store."

He handed me an apron and a notepad.

"Are you sure?" I asked.

"It's too late to turn back now; I might as well see it through. Besides," Iori said with a somewhat lonesome grin, "you need to let your heart break completely when the opportunity arises, or else you'll lose your chance to heal properly forever."

Three plates of curry were neatly arranged on the table. A creamy, buttery curry infused with spices. As a finishing touch, I topped the dish with a sprinkling of dried parsley.

"P-please, go ahead," I said. I swallowed hard, fixing my gaze on Iori and Hozumi.

They said, "Itadakimasu," to show their appreciation before reaching for their spoons.

I watched them dig into the curry and rice as I rubbed my sweaty palms on my dress. When I tasted it earlier, it was good. *I* liked it for sure. The question was, would they?

Once Iori had swallowed his mouthful, he widened his eyes. "It's amazing!"

"It is?"

"It's really good. It's pretty spicy, but it's somehow still mellow. I love the flavor." The corners of his eyes crinkled as he smiled.

"I can tell you spent a lot of time perfecting the recipe for your boyfriend. Hozumi, didn't you already have my curry earlier? You must have been really hungry to devour a second plate."

Hozumi, who had been shoveling the curry into his mouth, stopped momentarily. "To be honest . . . I am trying to get rid of the aftertaste from your curry, Iori."

"Eh? That's not nice."

"Did you try tasting your curry today?" Hozumi asked.

"Oh . . . no."

"I think you added too much water. It was really runny."

Iori darted into the kitchen and tasted his curry. A look of disgust appeared on his face. He put the lid back on the pot. "I thought I had properly followed the recipe. The one I made yesterday was fine."

"Maybe you got careless because I would be the only customer eating it?"

The two continued to argue nonchalantly.

So . . . Iori made an error when making the curry? There's nothing wrong with my taste buds?

I drew my interrogative gaze closer to them.

"So it's good?"

"Yeah."

"It's delicious."

"You're not just saying that because you feel sorry for me, are you?"

Showing me his near-empty plate, Iori asked, "Does it look like we feel bad?"

"Well, that's a relief . . ."

My cooking isn't bad!

I stared at the ceiling and exhaled. The tension that had built up inside of me dissolved.

"I am so, so glad."

Feeling a wave of relief, I flopped onto the counter.

"Were you that worried?" asked Hozumi.

"I had started to think that everything about the last four years was a lie."

My doubts had made me wonder whether every time Kyohei smiled, said he loved me, or told me he was having fun, it was because he felt that he had to.

"I don't know what the truth is anymore," I said. "What I do know is that I was running around in circles the whole time, like an idiot. But I can now believe that there were times when he was honest with me."

I was on the verge of tears again. Worried that the two men were fed up with my crying, I wiped my eyes on the sleeves of my dress.

"It's Momoko, right?" Hearing a quiet voice, I lifted my gaze. It was Hozumi, who had finished eating. Dabbing his mouth with a napkin, he continued, "Have you heard of shikuhakku?"

"Shiku . . . hakku . . . Do you mean the idiom?"

My mind went blank at the unexpected question. *Where is he going with this?*

"It's originally a Buddhist term," Hozumi explained.

Iori exclaimed, "Look at you, showing off your Buddhist knowledge! You know, he doesn't just look like monk, he *is* a monk. And believe it or not, he went to the University of Tokyo. He used to work for a corporate trading house, you know."

"Please shut up."

Iori smirked and carried on teasing him. He explained that Hozumi was a trainee monk at a nearby temple called Seizanji and that he had become a regular at Amayadori, where he got his daily fix of ice cream soda.

Hozumi cleared his throat and continued bashfully.

"*Anyway,* I was saying, in life, we encounter many kinds of suffering, like disease, aging, or having to be with someone you dislike. In Buddhism, these unavoidable sufferings experienced by humans are categorized as shikuhakku, or the four sufferings and eight sufferings."

I had never heard about the origins of the idiom.

"The reason I decided to become a monk is because I learned that life itself is one of these sufferings. In other words, living life is also a suffering."

"Life itself is a suffering?"

"Yes. Life is difficult as it is. Everything you go through in life, like trying to avoid being hated or getting hurt, is a struggle. But you threw yourself into a relationship and put everything you had into getting the person you loved to love you back. You even perfected your own signature curry."

Hozumi gently placed his hand on the rim of his empty plate.

"You're doing something extraordinary. You're fighting shikkuhakku. You said that you were going round in circles like an idiot, but there's no need to beat yourself up like that."

"Hozumi . . ." I said.

"What a nice thing to say," Iori added.

I *did* struggle. I was always thinking of Kyohei. I couldn't push him out of my head, that was how much I loved him. It was proof that the love was real. Even if I wasn't great at it, and things didn't go as I wanted, I had faced the battle. I had faced life.

Just then, a sudden burst of energy filled up my body, and I felt the urge to get on my feet.

"I feel like . . ." Blood rushed through my veins, shuttling back and forth between my heart and my brain. "I've reached nirvana."

"Huh?"

"All my resentment is melting away, like I'm . . . enlightened!"

I rose from my chair.

Iori and Hozumi stared up at me with their mouths wide open.

"Hozumi, would you mind doing a little Buddhist chant now? Like 'Namu Amida Butsu' or something?"

I knelt down and presented my hands before him. *I'm ready!*

"Actually, that chant belongs to a different sect than mine, so I can't help. Besides, that's not how Buddhist chants work."

"Right, okay. Then can you say something like 'Rest in peace, ex-boyfriend'?"

"That would make it seem like your ex-boyfriend is dead."

"You've ruined it now. I was so close to getting rid of my resentment . . ."

"What exactly do you think Buddhism is?"

Dammit.

I had thought that if I kept the momentum going, I'd feel better about everything, and I wouldn't have to suffer anymore. I'd wake up tomorrow morning and be completely over Kyohei. Imagine that! But it wasn't going to be that straightforward.

Iori, who had been silently observing the conversation, suddenly spoke. "Recovering from a breakup isn't that easy. But listen, Momo-chan, I have a better idea."

"Oh! What is your idea?"

"To get back at your ex."

"Get back at him . . ."

I recalled his words from earlier, that the three rules of healing a heartbreak were empathy, time, and revenge.

"You mean to take revenge?"

"Exactly. You were so passionately in love that you even invented the most authentic, delicious curry. Yet your ex couldn't accept your love. Isn't that kind of annoying?"

"It . . . it is."

"So," he said enthusiastically, lifting the corners of his mouth into a bright boyish grin, "why don't we add your curry to our menu?"

"Huh? Add it to the menu . . . ?"

"Here's what's going to happen," Iori theorized, raising his forefinger. "Your curry is going to be the new dish on our menu. And it's going to become so famous that people are going to wait hours in line for it."

Iori winked, as if to say, *You know what's going to happen next, don't you?*

My curry will get famous . . . and then . . .

"Kyohei might hear about it!"

Iori nodded.

"The curry will become legendary," I continued, "and it'll be featured on TV as 'the number-one dish in Sangenjaya'! And then it will turn into a collab with 7-Eleven, and be sold as one of those boil-in-a-bag curries all over the country. Right?"

"I wouldn't go that far, actually," Iori conceded.

"And six years later . . . Kyohei will walk into a store and purchase it unknowingly."

I had gotten so animated, I thought my heart was going to leap out of my chest.

"She sounds like she's preaching," Iori directed to Hozumi.

"The 'six years' part makes it oddly realistic," Hozumi commented.

"Kyohei will take one bite of the curry and gasp. He recognizes the flavor! He will examine the package and is astonished when he sees a certain name printed on the bag. And that is because the name belongs to his ex-girlfriend from six years ago!"

Iori chuckled. "Has she completely lost it?"

"Manager Iori! Please let me work here!" Rising to my feet, I offered him my hand.

"That's what I've been trying to tell you," Iori replied.

I felt a cool sensation on my palm as Iori shook my hand. It was a deal.

Hozumi watched us with a cold look on his face. "Iori, does this have anything to do with the kitchen staff position you've been trying to fill?"

"I—I don't know what you're talking about. Of course not!"

"I heard you saying on the phone that your sales were not great."

"Were you eavesdropping? Now, that's a dirty habit," Iori said. "As soon as I tasted her curry, I knew Momo-chan was a talented chef. Besides . . ."

"What?" I asked.

"I have another interesting idea."

One month had passed.

"What is this, Manager Iori?"

"Do you like it? I made it myself. Pretty impressive, right?"

"You're missing my point. What on earth is 'The Ex-Boyfriend's Favorite Recipe Funeral Committee,' and why is my name on it—as the president?"

Having successfully resigned from my company, I had been looking forward to making a fresh start during my first day at the café. But when I arrived, I was taken aback to see a prominent poster pasted onto a chalkboard at the front of the café:

THE EX-BOYFRIEND'S FAVORITE RECIPE FUNERAL COMMITTEE
HEARTBREAK STORIES AND MEMORY-FILLED
EX-BOYFRIEND (OR EX-GIRLFRIEND) RECIPES WANTED!

"Since you're now officially a member of the staff here, I want to be honest with you." Iori looked dead serious as he spoke. "Modestly speaking, I have an incredibly good-looking face, do you agree?"

"Umm . . ."

Was he like this before?

"With a man as beautiful as me running this café, it should attract more customers, don't you think?"

"I wish I could deny your theory, but I have to agree. I would expect it to attract lots of women."

As usual, Amayadori was dead silent. Its backstreet location wasn't exactly ideal for attracting passersby.

Once you were inside, it had a lovely atmosphere. Its vintage charm was certainly appealing, so why wasn't it getting more customers?

"So *that* is where the problem started!" Squeezing his fists, Iori spoke fervently. "The women start to become regulars. All of them. Some come to lunch every single day, and others sip ice cream sodas at the counter while spilling out their relationship troubles to me."

"That sounds great."

"But then, the more I listen, genuinely trying to help, their interests start to shift . . . toward me. They turn to me and say affectionately, 'If you were my boyfriend, I would never need to feel this way . . .' "

Right.

Everything made sense now. It explained how he had become such a good listener.

"That's a nice problem to have."

The bell on the door made a dull sound, and Hozumi entered, mumbling angrily to himself.

"They don't even know what this greedy guy is thinking. They're better off coming to Seizanji temple. I could offer them much better advice . . ." He headed straight to the far end of the counter and sat himself down.

Iori glanced at him and continued. "Once they've opened up to me about their relationship troubles, ninety-nine percent of the women fall in love with me. I always turn them down—it wouldn't be right to date customers. It normally ends with them screaming at me, 'You led me on!' before storming out of the café crying. And that's how I ended up with *this*."

Iori removed his phone from his pocket and held it out. Hozumi and I peered into the screen, which showed Google reviews of Amayadori: *The manager is a jerk. I'm never going back. Don't let this man deceive you!*

A stream of insults followed. They were hands down the worst reviews I had ever seen.

"Wow," I said. "The average rating is 1.8. How did you get one hundred and five one-star reviews? Even a rural dentist with a bad reputation can do better."

"I never intended to lead them on. I was just offering my best hospitality."

"I didn't know handsome men had these problems."

"Well, I can see that you're definitely still hung up on your ex, and you're a bit of an oddball, so I don't need to worry about you falling in love with me."

"Did you just call me an oddball?"

"And, oh!" Iori beamed. "Your name has been added too, Hozumi!" He pointed to the poster.

"Huh?" Leaping out of his chair, Hozumi took a closer look.

"I'm relieved that you're so willing to be involved," Iori said. "I can't thank you enough."

I also took a good look at the poster. "Oh! He's being serious. It says: *President—Momoko Yuuki; Burial—Hozumi Kuroda.*"

"But I don't want to be involved," Hozumi objected.

"That won't be possible. I've already handed out the flyers, and it starts at ten o'clock on Friday night." Iori picked up a flyer and waved it around. The same logo from the poster was proudly displayed.

"Ten o'clock on Friday? But it's Friday today! We can't start today!" I cried.

"I'm sorry, but this will determine the survival of this café. My role in the Ex-Boyfriend's Favorite Recipe Funeral Committee is to listen to people's stories. Momo-chan, yours is to empathize with them. Hozumi, your duty, since it's kind of your line of business, is to 'bury' their resentment for good. We'll get the customers to share their heartbreak recipes, and we'll add them to our menu. We'll be killing two birds with one stone."

It felt a little bit as if we were being coerced into the whole thing, but I supposed it made sense. Kind of.

"If our café becomes famous, *Brutus* might even want to do a feature on us," Iori whispered into my ear.

Brutus magazine? Well, well . . . that didn't sound too bad.

Iori drew himself closer to Hozumi's ear and muttered something. Knitting his brows, Hozumi paused for a while. Then he let out a sigh, as though he had relented.

"Two glasses a day, and we have a deal."

"You want two free drinks a day?"

"No, two free ice cream sodas."

"That's a lot of ice cream soda."

"I can't help it. Training as a monk requires an inordinate amount of energy."

"That's your excuse?"

Watching their exchange, I burst into laughter.

Gentle drops of rain began to fall. I stepped outside to lay out the doormat for wet weather. In doing so, I noticed that the chalkboard sign had been rewritten.

On the front, it read:

NEW DISH!
MY EX-BOYFRIEND'S FAVORITE BUTTER CHICKEN CURRY

On the other side, it said:

NOW OPEN
THE EX-BOYFRIEND'S FAVORITE RECIPE FUNERAL COMMITTEE

The wound in my heart was still open and painful, and I regularly thought about Kyohei. But over the past month, little by little—and I mean teeny tiny steps—I was starting to feel more ready to live with my scar.

I turned the sign so that customers could see the committee's details. The first gathering would be held that night.

MY EX-BOYFRIEND'S FAVORITE BUTTER CHICKEN CURRY

Serves 4

PREP

18 ounces (500 g) boneless, skinless chicken thighs

1 medium onion, thinly sliced

1/4 cup (50 g) butter

1 clove garlic, peeled and chopped

One (2-inch / 5 cm) piece fresh ginger, peeled and chopped

One 14 1/2-ounce can whole tomatoes

1 teaspoon salt

1 teaspoon sugar

1 teaspoon soy sauce

1/4 cup (50 ml) heavy cream or milk (optional)

FOR MARINATING THE MEAT

1 teaspoon salt

1 teaspoon ground turmeric

1 clove garlic, peeled and ground into paste

One (2-inch / 5 cm) piece fresh ginger, peeled and ground into paste

1/2 cup (130 g) plain yogurt

FOR THE SPICE MIXTURE

1/2 teaspoon ground cardamom

1 teaspoon ground cumin

1 teaspoon ground turmeric

2 teaspoons ground coriander

1 teaspoon garam masala

1 1/2 teaspoons ground paprika

1/2 teaspoon chili powder

METHOD

Cut the chicken thighs into bite-sized pieces.

Put the chicken, salt, turmeric, garlic paste, ginger paste, and plain yogurt in a resealable plastic bag or suitable alternative, and massage the marinade into the chicken. Leave to marinate for two hours.

Mix the spices together well.

Put the butter, garlic, and ginger in a pan and cook on low heat until you start to smell the aroma.

Once the aroma spreads around the room, add the sliced onion and fry for 5 minutes.

When the onion turns translucent, add in the spice mixture. Mix it well with the onion and fry for another 5 minutes.

Add the whole tomatoes. Cook on medium heat. Squish the tomatoes and simmer for 5 minutes. (Make sure you properly squish the tomatoes, or they'll be too prominent later!)

Add the chicken to the pan. (Don't be afraid to pour in the marinade sauce—the yogurt, turmeric, and everything else will blend in nicely to create a lovely aroma!)

Add the salt, sugar, and soy sauce, and simmer for 15 minutes on medium heat (Stir regularly. It will burn easily, so do not neglect it!).

Try tasting it at this point. If you feel that it's missing something, add a little more salt to your liking. If you want to make it milder, add the cream, and simmer for another 10 minutes to let it thicken. (If you don't have cream, you can use milk!) Sprinkle dried parsley over the rice. Pour the curry into the same plate and enjoy!

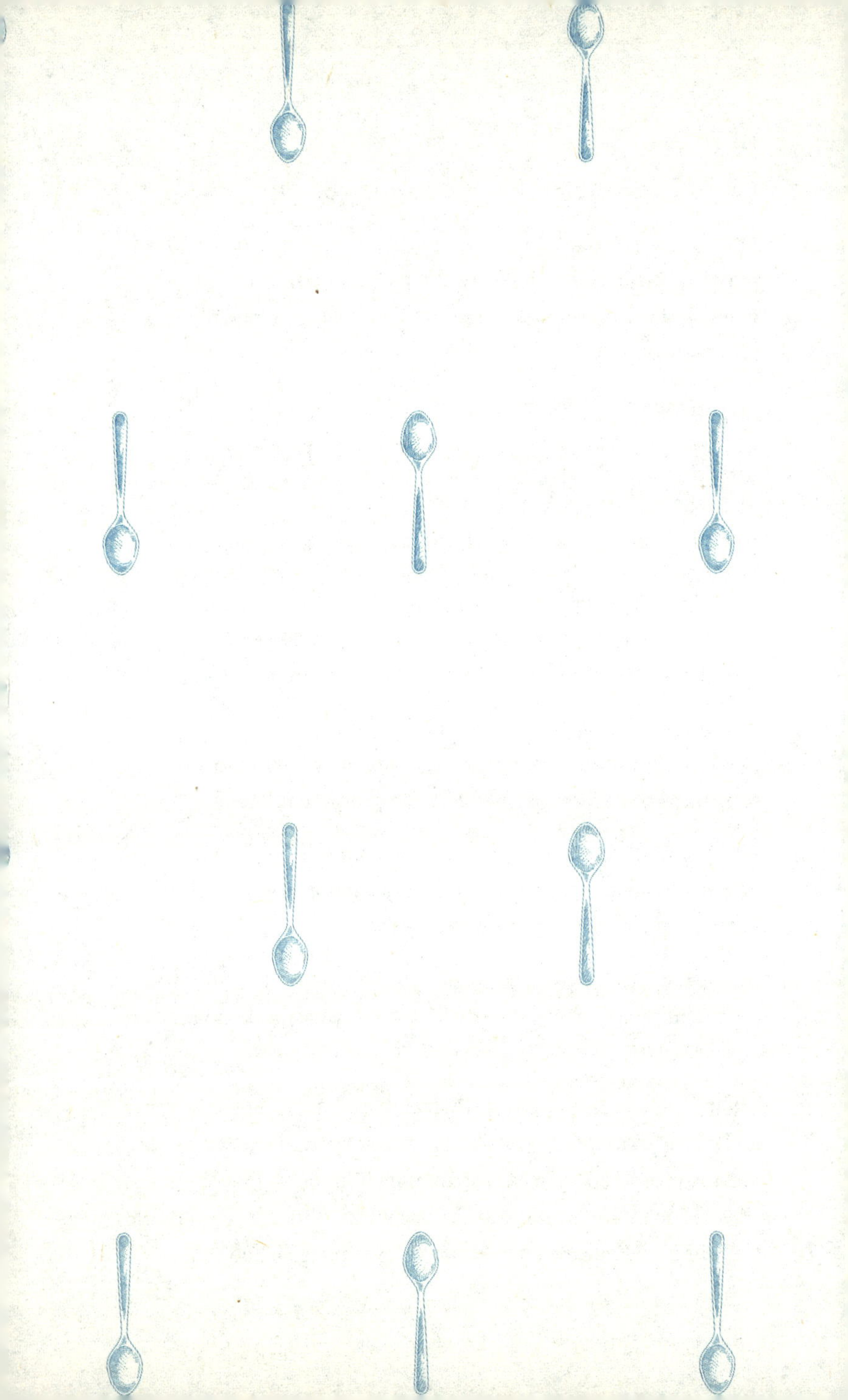

CHAPTER 2

THE RED FLAGS MEGASTORE HAMBURGER STEAK

The month was February. I'd been working at the café for several weeks. And on a bitterly cold Friday, I found myself in a predicament.

"We've had no customers today," I said.

Iori looked completely unbothered no matter how intensely I glared at him. Sipping his coffee under the dim light, he tapped away on his keyboard graciously.

"Kimura from the bookstore came, remember? So did Adachi the butcher."

"You mean *only* Kimura and Adachi."

"I guess you could say so."

"Plus, those middle-aged men stayed for three whole hours. They only ordered one cup of coffee each."

"Men in their prime have lots to talk about."

"The coffee is five hundred fifty yen per cup," I said, "which would make sales for the day . . ."

"Don't be silly, Momo-chan," Iori broke in. "Kimura and Adachi have a big stash of those free drink coupons from ages ago. They paid nothing!"

No.

No, no, no, no, no.

Unable to suppress my irritation, I found myself standing up. "Iori! Will you stop being so handsome? I can't be mad at you because you're too hot!"

"What kind of complaint is that?" Hozumi said mockingly as I cradled my head and let out a groan. He was sitting next to me, taking small bites of the ice cream floating on his melon-flavored soda.

"I burned all my bridges when I quit my job. And yet Kimura and Adachi are the only customers I've seen. And no one came to our first Funeral Committee meeting. It's been the same story every single day since I started."

"Don't forget Takamura who owns the fruit parlor," Iori said.

"Takamura also belongs to the coupon tribe!" I howled in frustration. "Plus, we don't even charge Hozumi for his ice cream sodas because it's supposed to be his pay for the Funeral Committee . . ."

"Now you've made me feel guilty," Hozumi said, clearly not feeling enough guilt to stop eating his ice cream.

"This café is going to go bankrupt at any moment . . ."

Thanks to the restaurant management experience I gained at my previous job, my brain had already done the math, even though I didn't really want to know. We had almost no sales all week because the café had given out a bunch of free drink coupons in the past. There was a female customer who had come in for a solo lunch, but she was the only new customer that had walked through the door. Our reputation on Google was getting worse and worse, with more complaints about Iori appearing every day. The situation was dire.

If things don't improve, we won't be making enough to pay my salary.

I had braced myself for instability when I quit my company, but I hadn't expected things to be this bad. To reduce costs, we had switched off all the lights except the ceiling, but it hardly made a difference.

"We'll somehow get through it, Momo-chan," Iori said. "Your curry is popular among those who have tried it. Now, we just need the Funeral Committee to take off, and all our problems will be solved."

Seemingly finished with his admin work, Iori finally glanced up from his computer and removed his glasses. "Oh, look, we have a customer."

I turned around, remembering that it was the Funeral Committee tonight.

Taking its time, the wooden door made a groaning sound as it creaked open, the bell ringing faintly.

I could make out the silhouette of a woman by the doorway. Long hair covered her eyes. She wore a face mask. A faint image of her face floated in the dimly lit room.

"E-excuse me," the lady whispered, "I'm here for the burial."

She held out her hand. There was something odd about her, but I had to go and greet our customer.

"Good evening. It's a cold night, isn't it? Please, come in."

"Wait a second, Momoko."

The moment I stood up from the sofa, I felt a forceful tug. It was Hozumi, pulling at the hem of my apron.

"What is it?" I asked.

"Something is off. She's holding . . . something."

"Holding what?"

"Momo-chan! Look at her hand!"

"Huh? Hand? What's the matter with you—"

Straining my eyes under the dim light, I finally saw what it was that she had in her hand and gulped. It looked like a lump of raw meat. I felt my throat tightening. My whole body froze up and a chill ran down my spine.

It was definitely meat. Some kind of ground flesh.

"The sign at the front said that you were hosting the Ex-Boyfriend's Funeral Committee?"

At that moment, the lady tripped over the front step, falling to her knees. Her hair, which grew down to her waist, draped over her. The flesh slithered out of her hand and landed on the aging wooden floor. It shone eerily, reflecting the dim light.

"Oh, no . . ." The lady groaned, awkwardly twisting her body as she raked up the sticky fragments of meat strewn across the floor.

I stared at it.

She turned around. Giving us a fierce glare, she murmured, "You bury ex-boyfriends, don't you?"

Don't tell me that is her ex-boyfriend!

"Ahhh!"

I backed away, hitting the wall behind me. A sharp pain ran all over my body, but I had bigger problems to deal with.

"I . . . I think you misunderstood! Yes, we are the Funeral Committee, but it doesn't involve an actual burial!"

How did we end up here? I did want customers, but not this!

Not knowing what to do, I panicked. I wanted to escape, but I was so petrified, my legs wouldn't move. Just as I was about to ask Iori and Hozumi for their help, I found them uselessly trembling in the corner, seemingly paralyzed.

Come on, guys, help me out here!

Her hands gleamed with the sticky raw flesh as they drew closer and closer to me.

Bracing for the last moments of my life, I closed my eyes.

Looking back, I couldn't say that I knew what I wanted from life. I burned myself out working for a toxic company. Even my boyfriend, whom I thought I'd marry, dumped me. But then I found Amayadori. I was determined to change my life. I had been so excited about finally starting a life that I enjoyed. And yet—

"Excuse me."

"Huh?"

When I opened my eyes, the lady, who now had her mask pulled down, was peering at me with an apologetic expression.

"Would it be okay if I go and wash my hands? And I'm sorry I dropped my hamburger steak all over the floor."

"Hamburger steak?"

"Yes. I was in the middle of making them for Sho and myself, when I suddenly ran out of my house." The lady pointed to the meat on the floor.

Coming back to my senses, I flicked more lights on. Iori and Hozumi, who had been glued to the wall, now seemed to feel safe enough to come closer.

Iori kneeled down and observed the meat. "That is . . . hamburger steak."

"There's onion in it, too," Hozumi said.

Indeed, it was an uncooked hamburger steak patty.

"The bathroom is that way."

My body eased in relief. I started to wonder if the three of us were fit to lead this committee.

Had I jumped the gun when I handed in my notice?

The lady tied her hair back into a ponytail, revealing her big doe-eyes. That's when it clicked for me.

"You were here the other day!"

Something about her baby-faced features and rounded forehead reminded me of a young bird. Now that I could see her face clearly, she looked familiar, and I realized she was the same young woman who had recently come in for a meal during lunch hours.

"I did mention it earlier," she told us.

"Huh?"

"I'm sorry, you probably couldn't hear me. I speak so quietly, and I'm wearing a face mask."

"It's not your fault! We should get our ears checked, really."

It looked as though she was having a particularly rough day. She seemed like a different person than the one I had met previously. Her face was free of makeup, and she was dressed in what looked like loungewear—a sweatshirt and a pair of jeans. What concerned me the most was the gloomy air that surrounded her. It was as though she had been sent to the underworld against her will.

"My name is Nagi Kojima. . . . I'm twenty-four years old," she said. "I am an assistant at an accountant's office. In my free time, I like to manage my savings."

"Please, come sit down and let us hear about your ex." I motioned for her to sit down.

The four of us settled on the sofa at the table near the back of the café. Iori made us coffee, and we drank it while we listened to Nagi's story.

Nagi wasn't kidding about saving money being her hobby. We learned that she enjoyed spending her weekends at a café, writing in her kakeibo, a private budget planner. She had been walking through the neighborhood a few weeks ago, hoping to find a suitable place for her favorite pastime, when she chanced upon Amayadori. It was then that she saw our poster and learned of the Funeral Committee.

"Oh, it's The Ex-Boyfriend's *Favorite Recipe* Funeral Committee, not The Ex-Boyfriend's Funeral Committee!" Nagi said. "How embarrassing. You must have thought I was some kind of psychopath."

"Oh, no, it's not your fault at all. We completely misjudged the situation. Didn't we?"

"Th-that's right," Iori stuttered. "I'm glad you came to us, though. You must have been going through a really difficult moment, to have burst out of your house in the middle of making hamburger patties like that?"

As Iori smiled at her, Nagi looked away sheepishly and gave a faint nod.

"Something happened just before I came here. I couldn't take it anymore, and I just stormed out in a rage while cooking for him. I had always known that I needed to leave him, but this is the first time I did anything about it. In the past, even when I'd decided to dump him, I couldn't follow through. I kept thinking that he wouldn't be able to live without me. I do love him, though. I love him, but . . ." She trailed off, pausing to think. "Maybe . . . I should just go home."

"Just hold on a second, Nagi," I said.

"There is so much disconnect between reason and emotion that you've broken your mental equilibrium," Hozumi observed.

"Stop analyzing her like that," I commanded.

Flustered, Nagi kept standing up then sitting back down again. I swapped places with her, hastily pushing her back onto the sofa, putting her in the window seat. This way, I didn't have to worry about her running off.

I exhaled. "Why don't you have some coffee first? Let's take it slowly, untangle things one by one."

"Y-yes, sorry."

What. The. Hell.

This was so much harder than I'd anticipated. I felt my body heating up. Rolling up the sleeves of my sweater, I brought my cup to my lips. I took a deep breath, prepared to dive into everything slowly.

"I'm sorry if this is out of line, but are you dating a toxic man?" Iori asked bluntly.

Startled, I nearly spilled my coffee. He was definitely out of line.

Nagi widened her big eyes and said, "How did you know?"

"Just a hunch. You seem like the type who falls for the wrong guys. There's something about you that tells me you attract people like struggling musicians, for example?"

"Don't be ridiculous," I said to Iori.

That would be too typical. It can't possibly be true.

"Do you follow my secret Twitter account or something?" To my disbelief, Nagi's face turned completely pale as she spoke.

"Wait, are you dating a musician for real?" I asked.

"Here." Nagi timidly held out her phone and showed us a slew of resentful tweets.

Arrgh. It's not working, is it?
Give me my money back!
What am I gaining from doing so much for him?
My life ended the day I started dating a musician.
Does anyone have any answers for me?

She didn't exactly come across as mentally stable, with messages posted every hour.

"My friends tell me that I'm a toxic boyfriend magnet," Nagi said, as she slid her phone back into her pocket. "I have to always be doing something for my partner. If I'm not, it makes me feel as though the relationship isn't equal, like I'm not worth going out with."

"I can kind of relate to that. I'm that type, too." I thought of my relationship with Kyohei. Whenever I spent the night at his place, I would wake up early to make him breakfast and iron his shirts before hanging them in his closet. "It might seem like I'm doing it out of love, but it's more like unless I do this, the relationship isn't even. It's that kind of feeling."

As Nagi blew on her coffee, I noticed that her lips were like the beak of a tiny bird.

"I've been a groupie for six years now," she continued. "I got so used to doing things for him that it became the norm. I brought him gifts at the end of his gigs, and whenever his band didn't sell enough tickets—they had to hit a certain target—I would do my best to buy the unsold ones. Sometimes I even covered their studio rental. For superfans, this kind of thing is pretty common. My relationship with him was an extension of that."

Huh? She pays his studio costs? Surely that's excessive, even for a superfan.

Although her statements filled my head with a flurry of questions, we decided to watch a video of the band.

It was a rock band of four. Despite being indie, they seemed to have a solid following. We watched as alternating lights of purple and red illuminated the stage. Guided by the upbeat rhythm of the song, the crowd threw their arms in the air, raising their index fingers upward. When the band was finished with the chorus, the guitarist, who had been playing on the right-hand side, came out to the center and performed a phenomenal solo.

"This is him." Nagi pointed at the guitarist bashfully.

Of course it is, I thought to myself. The guy emitted an inordinate level of charisma.

He had enigmatic eyes, which peered through his hair. His loosely worn T-shirt and jeans showed off his slim figure, enhanced by his pared-back style. Strumming his guitar in a trancelike state, he looked as though he believed that the only things remaining in the world were him and his music.

From time to time, he lowered his guitar, tilting its head downward. The way in which he slid the tips of his slender fingers across its neck was just . . .

"So erotic, isn't he?" Iori said with a deadpan expression.

"I wish you'd warn us before you come up with these inappropriate remarks," I retorted.

"Well, I can tell that the guy on the guitar gets the most attention in this band," Iori continued matter-of-factly. "The bassist is pretty popular, too, I imagine. The guitar-playing vocalist, as well as the drummer, have probably been with their girlfriends for about three years, if not already married. Nagi-chan, it seems that you've gotten yourself into a rather tricky relationship."

"I doubt any of that is true," Hozumi remarked, shooting Iori a skeptical look.

Nagi's mouth was open. "Are you . . . psychic?"

"Don't tell me he's right?" I gasped.

Nagi started to rub her arms nervously, as though she had just witnessed something truly terrifying. What was it with Iori and his laser-sharp intuition? I wish he would utilize it more in improving sales.

"Everything you just said is right. Sho—oh, that's short for Shogo—he's incredibly popular with the girls. People say that he has slept with every woman in Machida city."

"I was pretty accurate, then," Iori said. "Just so you know, in *my* backpacking days, I gained something of a cult following, too, and *their* saying was 'Women on Earth fall in love with Amamiya twice.' "

"This is not the time to get competitive!" I said. "What does that even mean?"

As we continued to quarrel, someone's stomach rumbled. Without intending to, I glanced at Hozumi.

"It wasn't me."

"Iori . . . ?"

"Of course not. I'm too handsome for stomach growling."

"How is being handsome relevant . . ."

Just then, someone raised a tentative right hand.

"I'm sorry, it was me."

It was Nagi.

"Oh, are you hungry? You haven't had dinner yet, have you?" I asked.

I stepped into the kitchen and opened the fridge to see if I could cook her something to eat.

"We have ground meat, onions, and breadcrumbs, so I could make you a hamburger steak. Would you like that? Oh, I suppose you're not in the mood for that. . . . I could do a soup or—"

"I would! I would love a hamburger steak, please! I was in the mood for it earlier."

Bouncing off the sofa, Nagi got to her feet.

"Oh, sorry," she apologized, "I didn't mean to be so ill-mannered."

As Nagi spoke, her stomach made loud growling noises. Her cheeks turned bright red. *I'm starving!* She silently pleaded with her puppy-dog eyes.

"I'll get right to it." I chuckled. "Sit tight."

Nagi nodded enthusiastically. She looked as if nothing in the world had ever made her so happy.

Once I had made vertical and horizontal cuts, I chopped down, listening to the rhythmic beat of the knife hitting the chopping board. A mound of finely minced onions began to form. There are few things I enjoy more than the sound of a fresh onion being sliced.

An impressed Nagi peered into the kitchen. "Wow, you're like a food processor."

I asked the three of them to move to the counter seats so that they could keep me company while I cooked. We continued chatting while I prepared the hamburger steak.

This is nice, I thought to myself.

My mom passed away during my fifth year of elementary school. I took over the housework, and that included preparing meals every day. My brother, who is three years younger, ate with me. My dad rarely made it home before dawn, so I never got the chance to ask what he thought of my cooking. The kitchen in my house was always dead silent. No one was there to taste-test my food or to cry "I'm starving!" to me.

"By the way, why did you storm out of your home today? What was the thing that you couldn't take anymore?" Iori asked as he sipped the red wine he'd just opened to pair with the hamburger steak.

"About that . . ."

I poured some oil into the frying pan as I listened, then started to fry the minced onions with a wooden spatula.

"To tell you the truth, I had just lent Sho some money."

"You gave him money?" I blurted out. Nagi made this shocking revelation just as I shook the frying pan. The pieces of onion flew out of the pan, landing all around the sink and on my hand. "Ah, that's hot!"

Realizing that Nagi's story needed my undivided attention, I turned the cooker off and wiped down the worktop.

"How much money did you lend him?"

Curling her shoulders like a puppy caught red-handed, she slowly held up three fingers.

"Three? Thirty thousand yen? Or three hundred thousand?"

"Three million."

"Three million yen?" I yelled.

I was speechless.

She's only twenty-four! How did she manage to save up so much—stop. Focus.

"Did he need the money to buy instruments?" Hozumi wondered. "Guitars can be very expensive."

"That has happened a few times before, but this time it wasn't that."

Although I was taken aback by the "a few times before" part, I decided to let it go for the moment. I willed myself to keep my composure. *Must stay calm must stay calm must stay calm . . .*

"Sho's second girlfriend was married, but when her husband found out about the affair, he sued Sho. He needed to find three million yen by the end of today. He's taken out enough high-interest loans as it is, so I decided to pay on his behalf for the time being."

"That is way more information than I can comprehend." I was in disbelief.

Second girlfriend? Married? Sued? High-interest loans?

"What is he, the Red Flags Megastore?" I yelped.

"All right, everyone, take a deep breath." While the rest of us sat in astonishment, Iori swirled his glass of wine elegantly. "Let's break down the facts. How many girlfriends does Sho have?"

"Well, it depends, but usually five or six. For your information, I am number three."

"You say that like it's your student number at school," Hozumi commented, rubbing his eyes as though to confirm he wasn't dreaming. "Why are you giving him so much? If you're going to concede so much, you should at least do it for a better boyfriend."

"We know! We don't need you to tell us that, Hozumi!" I said.

"I wasn't asking you, Momoko," he countered.

Why would Nagi do such a thing? I actually couldn't find a rationale.

Why couldn't girls like Nagi and me find a guy who would spoil his girlfriend, call her all the time, and never fail to surprise her on her birthday? A guy who cared about us deeply? "The secret to a woman's happiness is being loved rather than loving" is the saying, isn't it? At least according to my girlfriends and the internet.

I knew. I knew in my head I'd be happier with a man like that.

And yet I was somehow incapable of loving someone who loved me. I always fell for the ones who couldn't reciprocate. Kyohei was still imprinted on my heart and refused to disappear. Kyohei, who was so terrible at breaking up.

"I guess it's because . . . I love the songs he writes."

Nagi pulled out her phone and opened a music app. A variety of songs showed up on the screen, all by the band Sho played in. Nagi tapped on one of them. Completely different from the song in the video we'd watched earlier, it was slow in tempo and had a somber feel to it.

The sound of the guitar evoked a melancholy mood. The song was a confession of loneliness. Though the lyrics were dark, something about it resonated with me.

When it finished playing, we all let out a big sigh.

"That was amazing," I said.

"Right?" said Nagi. It was the loudest I had heard her speak all night.

Seeing her beaming face, I suddenly felt that I understood. In Nagi's eyes, Sho was her oshi, her sacred idol, who deserved her utmost respect. His boyfriend status was secondary to that.

"I came across the band when I first moved to Tokyo. I was having a tough time keeping up with university assignments, and I felt like I didn't fit in. I had no friends. Then I happened to walk into a music venue, where Sho was playing this song. It was the first time I felt like I wasn't alone in the big city. I thought, *This song is about me.* He's singing about *me*. I might not have made it through my university days if not for this song."

When I heard that she had lent the guy three million yen, I had thought that we had caught her in a "love is blind" kind of moment. But I was wrong. It wasn't that simple. It's not easy to fall out of love with a superhero who had pulled you out of the darkest period of your life.

Respect can outweigh everything. One truly admirable quality and, boom, you're in love. Just like that, everything you'd looked for in a guy, whether it's good looks, or not taking you for granted, or having great taste in picking restaurants, goes right out the window.

"What makes Sho's music special is that he draws from his flaws. As his girlfriend, it's been rough, but as a fan of his music, I couldn't reject him. There was a part of me that wanted him to be flawed. I admired him in his struggles and the music that came out of that."

"I think I know what you mean," Iori said emphatically, and crossed his arms. "I'm more drawn to songs written by someone who isn't perfect. They give us the validation that we need, that we're not the only ones living with pain."

Hozumi offered, "Is it like 'The words of an apprentice are wiser than the words of the Buddha'?"

"Sorry, Hozumi, I can't relate to that in any way," I replied.

"This was before I joined the temple, when I was working for the trading house. I was going through a difficult time, and I turned to books. I found the words of people who were in the middle of their struggles more meaningful than those of people who had already made it through to the other side of the tunnel."

I had forgotten that Hozumi used to work in corporate Japan.

"Yes, that's it." Nagi spoke with passion, waving her finger back and forth. "I loved him for the struggles he was going through. He would show up at three o'clock in the morning and wrap his arms around me. He wouldn't say what was wrong or anything. Instead, he would ask me 'You love me, don't you?' over and over again. He's that kind of guy."

"But he had multiple girlfriends?" asked Hozumi.

"Yes, he was dating a million other girls. But I think that's what I liked about him. He has a huge hole in his heart that cannot be filled no matter what. I yearned to become a means of filling that hole."

Yearned to become a means of filling that hole.

That, I could relate to. I knew exactly what she meant.

"Like 'Others might think that you're a bad guy. That you're just a jerk. But I know that deep down, you're not that guy.' "

When I said this, Nagi looked up, as though she was having a moment of realization.

"You want to be able to say 'I'm not like other girls.' It gives you a sense of superiority. That's part of the reason you want to accept his flaws."

"Momoko . . ." Nagi said.

"I'm sorry, I'm talking about myself. That's how *I* used to be."

"But I'm the same! I wanted to be the girl who can say 'You don't need to be perfect.' And that's why I was okay with being number three. I acted as though I was the girl who had infinite patience—you don't need to fix your flaws; you don't need to grow; you are beautiful as you are. In a true sense, I'm the only person in the world who feels this way. I told myself, *He just hasn't realized yet that I'm the only one who really gets him.*"

I felt a stab of pain in my chest, as though someone were trying to tear my heart out.

One day, he'll grow up and realize that I'm the one. I just have to wait it out. I'll be okay; I can wait. I'm a woman of infinite patience.

I thought about the times when Kyohei didn't reply to my messages and how I turned to a fortune teller each time. One of them, who had a good reputation for her ability to see the before-life, told me, "His soul is still young. Be patient, and he'll catch up with you."

I pinned all my hopes on those words and carried them with me like a good luck charm. So what if I wasn't at the top of his list of priorities? I was fine with that. I thought I would be, at least *one* day. After all, fate had brought us together, and it was just a matter of him not having realized that yet. I happened to get there before he did, as the fortune teller said, and it was my *duty* to wait patiently until he caught up to the same level as me.

Maybe I was looking down on him all along, even if I made it seem as though he had the upper hand in the relationship. Or maybe it was the convenient explanation I needed, because I was too afraid of facing the truth, that he would never love me the same way I loved him.

"Perhaps . . ." Nagi said thoughtfully, bringing her hand to her chin. "Perhaps it wasn't just him that I lost interest in today. I lost interest in this version of myself, too. I think I got sick of pretending to be the girl with infinite patience."

Hozumi was listening thoughtfully to all of this and finally said, "You have been patient for sure. You've given up a lot for someone else. That's not an easy thing to do."

Instead of replying, Nagi smiled gently and took a sip of her coffee.

My ears perked up at the sound of a car splashing past.

"The forecast said it would stay sunny today," Iori muttered, shifting his gaze to outside the door. Rain seemed to follow me everywhere I went, but it felt as if there had been a lot more rainfall since joining Amayadori. Was Iori a "rainmaker" like me?

"Have you heard from Sho? What did you tell him when you left?" I asked.

"Oh, I told him I was going to the supermarket. He probably thinks I'm just taking my time."

Nagi glanced at her phone. He hadn't called or messaged.

"It was Sho who requested hamburger steak. This morning, after he told me about the money he needed, I took the day off from work. I went from bank to bank, withdrawing all my savings. I didn't have enough, so I sold off the expensive guitar and equipment I'd paid for in the past. I even called my parents to borrow some money from them."

"Wow," was all Iori could say.

Hozumi looked confused. "But you said you liked to save money? You didn't have enough?"

"Well . . . I was always squeezing out money to lend to Sho. It's sort of why I have a budget planner . . ."

"Ah."

"Sorry for asking. Please continue."

Thanks to Hozumi, the atmosphere had grown somber, and it now looked as if we were in the middle of a wake.

I tried to reset the mood.

"Anyway, what happened after that?"

"When I finally had the three million yen, he said to me, 'After all that running around, I'm drained. Aren't you? Let's have something nice to eat. I'd love a hamburger steak.' "

I returned to my cooking as I listened to her story unfold. Transferring the fried onions and ground meat into a bowl, I mixed them firmly with my hand so that the mixture would become sticky.

"As I stood in my kitchen, kneading the meat, I suddenly thought, *Wait a second, it was me who did all the running around, not him. Why does he look like he's just accomplished something?* It was like I snapped to my senses."

"I bet you wanted to be like '*You* do the damn cooking!' " I said.

"But I kept telling myself that it was *my* decision to lend him the money, so I couldn't be resentful. Suddenly I had an urge. After everything that happened today, I deserved a treat. I thought, *I'm going to have cheese.* No holding back today. Maybe I would feel a little bit better if I had a little bit of something I loved. Just as I was about to fold the cheese into the patty, he said something—can you guess what he came out with?"

Nagi balled her small hands as she readied herself to say what had happened next.

"He said, 'Hey, what do you think you're doing? Leave the cheese out. I don't want it to be heavy on my stomach. Make it light, will you?' I couldn't believe my ears!"

"What?" I reflexively squashed the patty I had been shaping. "He borrows three million yen. Then he asks for a specific meal to be cooked for him. He does nothing himself and makes his girlfriend do all the work. And then he says he doesn't want the cheese? What the . . ."

"Wow . . ."

Even Iori's and Hozumi's faces stiffened.

"I said, 'I'm sorry, you like it with grated daikon radish, don't you, Sho?' And he said, 'That's my girl! You know what I like. Why didn't you do that from the start?' "

"What a misogynistic little—"

Iori butted in. "Easy, Momo-chan. Why don't you step away from the bowl for a second?"

I was enraged. "Hey, listen! Hamburger steak is hard labor! It's not simple to make. It's not the kind of thing you want to be doing after you've spent the day trying to source three million yen! It's a lengthy process as it is. To think that he asked for grated daikon radish is just . . ."

The more I spoke, the more infuriated I became. I felt my face getting hot. For Nagi, who had been completely burned out both mentally and physically, a cheesy hamburger steak was her last hope of salvation. She needed as many calories as possible to heal her wounds. And yet!

"Don't tell me he expects you to grate his fucking daikon radish."

"Of course he does. He didn't stop there! Because I hadn't planned on the radish, I didn't have any. I told him I would need to run to the store, and he said, 'That's okay, I can wait, no problem. But don't forget the shiso leaves!' "

"What the . . ."

"At this rate, he's going to have a horrendous afterlife," Hozumi remarked.

"True. He can't complain if he ends up in the animal realm."

I put down the patty and gave my hands a wash. Leaving the kitchen, I walked up to Nagi.

"Listen, Nagi."

"Y-yes?"

I grabbed her shoulders. "We will have a cheesy hamburger steak."

"Oh?"

"You absolutely *have to* have your hamburger steak with cheese—you need to eat an unbelievable amount of cheese. Do you understand?"

Nagi shook her head. "But I feel bad. I wouldn't want to impose any more than I already—"

"You don't need to feel bad," I cut in. "Eating isn't just good for your body. It nourishes the soul. Nagi, you worked harder than anyone else today. You must have used up all the mental energy you possessed. So you need to fill yourself with anything and everything that you love. Would you like me to add anything else to it?"

"But do you even have cheese?" she asked Iori.

"Don't worry. Hozumi and I will run to the late-night supermarket." Flinging his coat on, Iori gave Nagi a pop idol–like wink.

Turning back to Nagi, I asked her a tough question. "Why don't you try being the one who asks for something for a change?"

When you're the one who's always giving, the one who's constantly supporting others, you forget that you're allowed to ask for help.

When someone lends you a hand, you feel a sense of guilt. It makes you feel as if you're being selfish.

When guilt becomes an ingrained habit, it's not easily removed.

Before you know it, you begin to think that you need to give the other person something of value in order to have an equal relationship with them. Once that way of thinking gets stuck in your mind, it doesn't let you go.

Of course, helping others is a wonderful way of life. But at least while she was here at Amayadori, I wanted *Nagi* to be the one asking for help.

She fidgeted in her chair, playing with the edge of her sweatshirt. Suddenly she made up her mind and said, "I would like the cheese inside the patty, as well as on top of it, and a soft-boiled egg on the side. Oh, and a big grilled sausage, too."

She was almost shouting. Her eyes looked like two glass marbles as she gazed into me.

There's no better feeling than satisfying someone's food cravings after they've made it through a really long day.

"Coming right up!"

As Iori burst back through the door proudly proffering the cheese, Nagi's face broke out into a smile. After I quickly melted the cheese, the steaks, as well as some accompaniments, were ready. I served them with rice and bowls of soup.

I sank my knife into the meal, letting the cheesy center ooze out and spill onto the sizzling hot plate. I lifted it to my mouth along with the cheddar cheese topping. The hot juices from the meat filled every corner of my mouth.

"I've been craving this for a really long time!" Nagi blew on her hamburger steak before taking an enormous bite.

As she chewed, her hands cradled her cheeks, and she squeezed her eyes shut. She let out an enormous sigh.

"This is heavenly! Wow . . . it's been a long day."

Nagi let her arms go limp and sank into the sofa with her eyes closed. She looked as though she had realized just how exhausted she was.

As requested by Nagi, I had topped each patty with lashings of cheese and had also garnished it with crunchy cheese crisps. Heavy on our stomachs? Damn right it was! Coupled with the rice and soup, she was going to be happily well-fed.

I figured it was time to ask the hardest question.

"Do you think you'll be able to finally end things once you get back home?"

Nagi gulped down a mouthful of sizzling-hot sausage before answering.

"Yes. I feel like I can finally do it, thanks to this food."

"The food?"

"It made me realize that I hadn't eaten what I wanted in a really, *really* long time."

Nagi sighed. She explained that, because Sho was dating several girlfriends at a time, she never knew when he would turn up to see her. He would contact her out of the blue, telling her he was on his way. For years, she constantly kept her kitchen well stocked with the ingredients needed to make Sho's favorite dishes, so that in case he did show, she could offer him the best hospitality possible.

"Also . . . when he told me that he wanted something lighter, that wasn't too heavy on his stomach, I was like *This guy cares about his stomach?* It was a total buzzkill. He had an affair with a married woman and wrecked her family. He was completely fine with his girlfriend giving him all her life savings. Yet he cares about his *stomach* getting upset? That was the biggest shock of all, more than the money and the affair."

"So true!" I giggled.

Sometimes the flame burns out when we least expect it.

As Iori wrapped a generous amount of melting cheese around his hamburger steak, he said, "I guess the stresses of the relationship had been accumulating inside of you, so when he mentioned his stomach, that became the last straw. It probably turned off your maternal affections."

Nagi sighed. "Maybe you're right. I think I was trying to get him to live up to my expectations of the 'ideal bad guy' while pretending to accept him for who he was. The cheating, the affair, and the pain he carried made him seem all edgy and musician-y. But the upset stomach thing was too human. I didn't want to see that side of him. It's been six years of this, so I can't remember exactly how it all started, but I think the original dynamic was more like organized girl versus sloppy guy in the beginning."

Nagi gave a self-conscious laugh.

"Did things change gradually?" I asked.

"I started to pretend like I was the girl with infinite patience, and he became the guy who carried pain. We both continued playing those roles. I think we gave it our biggest shot to make it work. We really did."

Having made that statement, Nagi ate the remaining food I had made for her. She shoveled the rice into her mouth, finished every drop of her soup, and polished off her plate of hamburger steak. She demolished everything, clearing all of the broccoli and every grain of corn. She ate with so much enthusiasm, it felt good just to watch her.

"Thank you for the meal. For everything. I feel much better now. I'm going to go home and properly break up with him."

She tightened her long ponytail as if to say, *I'm ready now.*

I smiled at her. "If you get tired of being the girl with infinite patience again, whether in romance or at work, you know where to find us. I'll make you a cheesy hamburger steak anytime."

Nagi suddenly remembered something. "Oh! And according to the poster, I'm supposed to give you the recipe of my ex-boyfriend's favorite dish?"

"Doesn't matter! *Your* favorite recipe, forgotten because of a toxic partner, can work, too! Right, Iori?"

"As you wish, President." Iori opened his hand toward me.

With that, I winked at Hozumi, signaling that it was time for him to play his part. Straightening his back, he cleared his throat.

We all pressed our palms together and said, "Our condolences."

I prayed that Nagi's six-year love—a complicated relationship that had twisted itself out of shape—would rest in peace. That the quiet Nagi, who had been hiding inside her own heart, would be able to come out fully, even if it takes her a long time.

And one more thing.

That she would not hesitate to say "I want that," whenever she craved a cheesy hamburger steak.

As Nagi walked out the door, Iori turned to me with a twinkle in his eye. "I have an idea . . ."

"Cheesy hamburger steak for Adachi, Takamura, and Kimura, please!"

"Got it! Oh, Iori, these are for the customers on the sofa. Two lunch sets."

Amayadori, which had been practically deserted seven days a week, was now starting to see more customers after the cheesy hamburger steak gained some fans in the neighborhood. Although we only had twelve seats, when there was a constant stream of orders, it was hard to keep up.

After the lunchtime rush, I took a break and drank some water. I had just let out a big sigh when the bell rang.

"Momoko! Iori! Hozumi!"

I glanced over to find Nagi standing by the entrance. Her hair had been cut into a short blunt bob.

"Wow! I didn't even recognize you! You have a gorgeous forehead."

Nagi giggled sheepishly at my compliment.

"Did you manage to break up with Sho?"

"Absolutely. In fact, I got him to prepare a letter pledging to pay his debts. He's even signed it with his thumbprint."

Nagi gave me a thumbs-up. It appeared that, thanks to her accounting knowledge, she had formally sorted out the money and paperwork side of things.

"By the way, I'm dying for a cheesy hamburger steak today. Could you make me one?"

"Of course! But first, its official name is . . ." I handed her a copy of the recently printed menu. "The Red Flags Megastore Hamburger Steak!"

"Pretty direct!" Nagi chuckled.

"I suggested 'Hamburger Steak of Love and Desire,'" Iori chimed in.

"I told him no, because it sounds weird. And erotic."

Iori's suggestion made Nagi grow all fidgety.

"I wouldn't mind it if Iori wants to call it that," she said, her cheeks flushing.

"Oh, no. Nagi, do *not* fall for this man! It will not end well. Anyway, let's eat first, shall we?"

We chatted, we cooked a delicious meal, and we ate. What do I hope to achieve at Amayadori? That, I still don't know, but for now I'll do the things I can do.

A warm breeze slowly drifted inside.

Spring was nearing.

THE RED FLAGS MEGASTORE HAMBURGER STEAK

Serves 2

1 small onion (approx. 200 g)
$^1/_4$ cup (25 g) fine dry breadcrumbs
$^1/_4$ cup (60 ml) milk
10 ounces (300 g) ground meat (beef, or a mixture of pork and beef)
1 teaspoon nutmeg
Salt and pepper

AS MUCH AS YOU LIKE OF:

Any cheese suitable for melting
Cheddar cheese
Crunchy cheese crisps
Sausages
Rice

METHOD

Finely chop the onion and sauté in a frying pan. Remove from the pan and allow it to cool. While the onion cools, combine breadcrumbs and milk in a small bowl.

Put the sautéed onion, ground meat, breadcrumbs soaked in milk, nutmeg, and salt and pepper into a bowl, and knead.

Shape the patties with your hands, filling each patty with the cheese for melting. Top the patties with cheddar cheese and fry them in a frying pan.

Serve with crunchy cheese crisps, grilled sausage(s) topped with plenty of cheese, and rice, then eat to your heart's content!

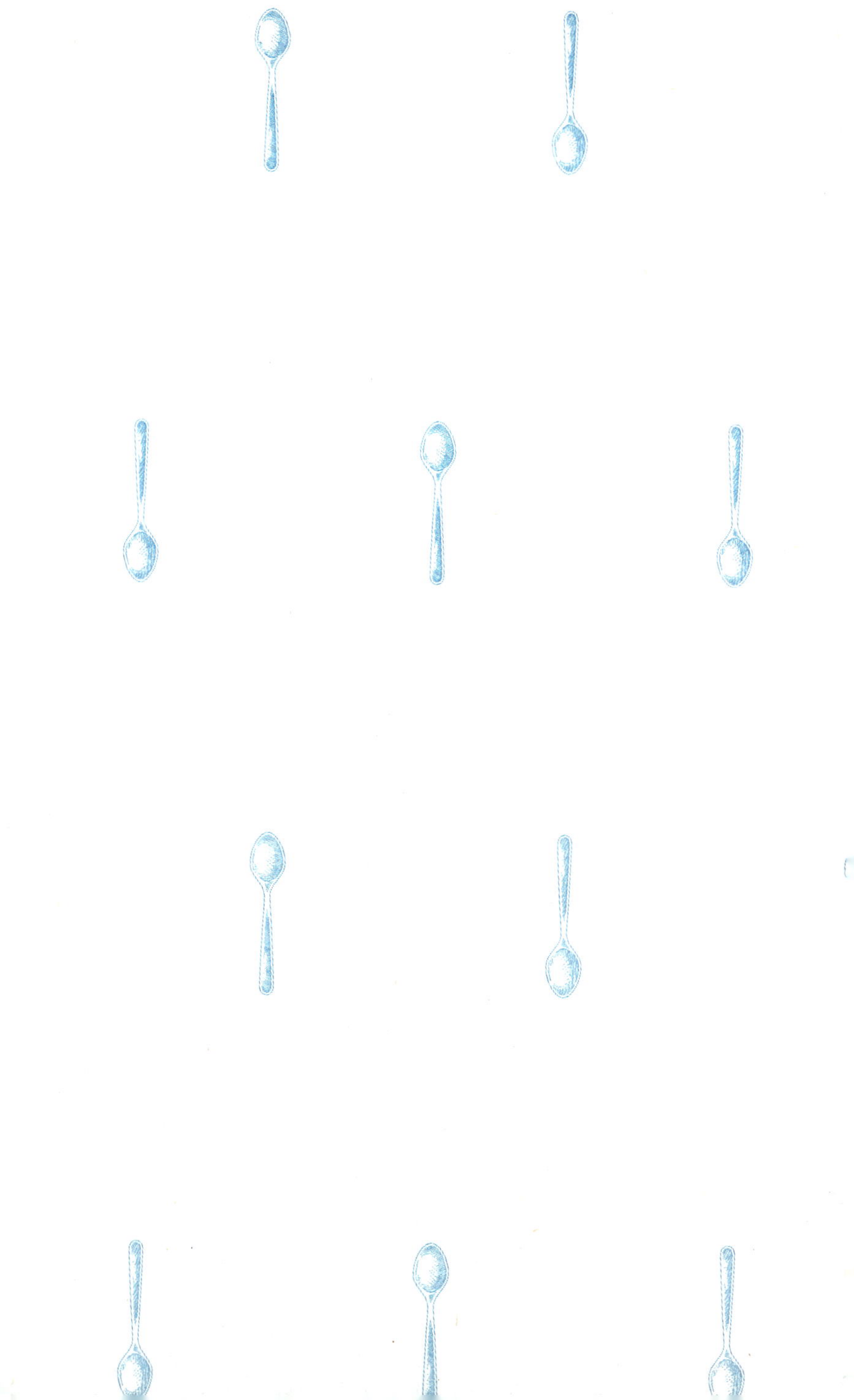

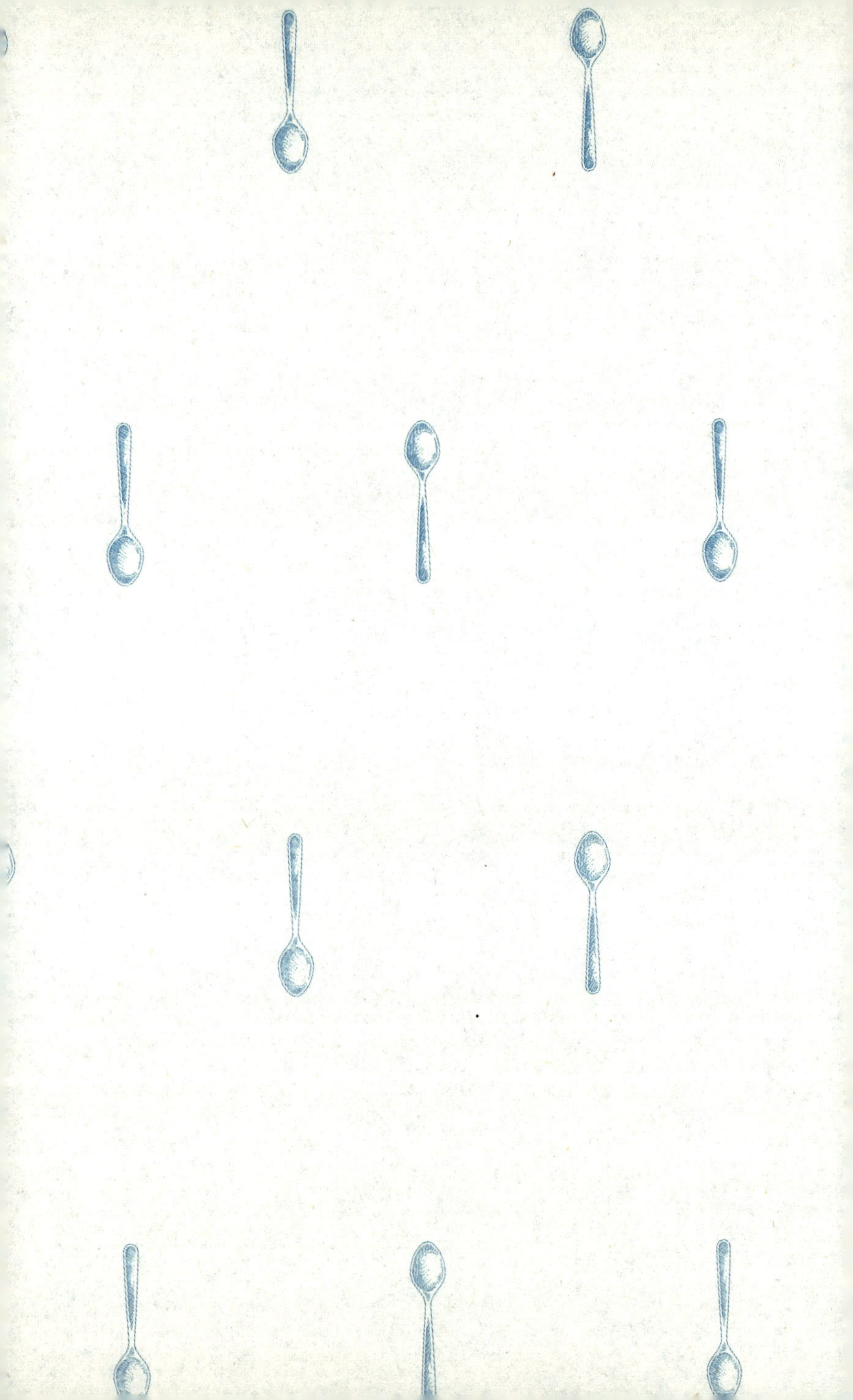

CHAPTER 3

SO WHAT IF I'M HIGH-MAINTENANCE POTATO SALAD

With all the memory-evoking stuff your ex-boyfriend has left behind (birthday letters, matching mugs, old tickets from that trip to Disneyland), do you:

A) Throw everything out as soon as the relationship ends, or . . .
B) Keep everything that's functional because stuff is just stuff, or . . .

"What are you mumbling about? It'd be nice if you got some work done." The undisguised irritation in Hozumi's voice interrupted my sojourn in denial land.

"I would say I'm the 'I live on other people's hand-me-downs so throwing stuff away isn't an option for me' type," said Iori, answering the question I didn't realize he'd heard.

"No one's asking you," Hozumi retorted.

"Guys, please. I'm trying to have an emotional moment here."

"This was your idea, Momoko. You're the one who couldn't get rid of this stuff on your own."

True. Hozumi had made a very good point, and I couldn't say anything in reply. Suppressing my emotional anguish, I put my hand back into the cardboard box and resumed sorting through the items.

No matter how hard I had tried the last few months, I couldn't part with the things that reminded me of Kyohei. Bagging everything up and taking it out to the garbage felt as if Kyohei and I were *officially* over, so I held on to every little thing: his toothbrush, his hair gel, presents he'd given me. Some part of me was trying to keep alive the hope that Kyohei and I were going to get back together.

But Amayadori was starting to draw in more customers, and the more time I spent listening to people's stories at our Friday-night Funeral Committee meetings, the more I started to feel that maybe it was time for me to move on.

Not that I could just put everything behind me and march on—my personality is way too obsessive for that. But I needed to do *something* and decided to start by getting rid of this box of stuff. Thus commenced my spring cleaning idea.

But when I started at home, I couldn't bear to throw anything away. I made absolutely no progress. Even my own bottle of perfume made me think things like *Kyohei said I smelled nice when I spritzed this on my dress.* I knew I was doomed when a pack of pocket-sized tissues—one of those marketing freebies distributed on the streets—made me well up because I thought it might have been given to me while Kyohei and I were out together in Shinjuku. Too overwhelmed to continue, I tossed all the stuff around me that had memories into a cardboard box and lugged it to Amayadori, where I was met with the usual reactions: Iori found the whole thing hilarious and Hozumi found it ridiculous.

"When you hold on to things, you hold on to the past. Right now, you're being dragged back to the past, Momoko."

Hozumi made a very good point.

Biting my lip, I threw an old movie ticket (Kyohei had slept through the whole thing) into the trash.

"Yes, sir, you are right."

"Come on, let's get to work."

I felt grateful. Sorting through the items swiftly and decisively, Hozumi seemed more dependable than ever.

In the meantime, Iori kept prattling on about this and that, barely lifting a finger to clear things out.

"You're trying to hold us back on purpose, aren't you, Iori?" Hozumi finally snapped.

"I was just thinking I might as well keep this stuff, since it's free and everything. How does this look?"

Iori held an *I Love NY* T-shirt to his chest. It was the shirt Kyohei used as loungewear when he was at my place, a souvenir from a trip to the U.S. It was the cheesiest, most typically tourist thing ever, yet once it had Iori's face attached to it, it somehow looked incredibly stylish.

"I can take anything that I want, right?"

"Sure. I can't think why you'd want to keep stuff that belonged to someone's ex, though."

"Well, I'm broke, so I'm not really in the position to be picky."

Iori looked pleased as he folded up the T-shirt and slid it inside a paper bag.

Of course. Two months had passed since I started working at Amayadori. If I'd learned anything about Iori, it was that the man was stingy with a capital *S*. I couldn't even get him to approve my requests to order new cooking utensils. He loved collecting coupons and loyalty cards—his wallet was constantly stuffed with them, which had led me to the conclusion that the real reason he insisted on giving away coupons to his customers so generously (when he obviously couldn't afford it financially) was because couponing was his true passion.

So here the three of us were, on a Friday night in March, waiting for our Funeral Committee client to arrive, working away at organizing my emotional (and physical) baggage.

Our guest tonight was to be Makiko Nishino, a regular customer of Amayadori.

Makiko, who ran Kisaragi, a small bar about a three-minute walk from our café, was something of a local celebrity in the shopping district. Apparently, her regular visits to the café started when Iori first opened its doors, so the two of them went back a long way. She had called Iori earlier in the week and without elaborating told him that she "absolutely needed to vent." All we knew was that she was going to come over to the café as soon as she closed up the bar for the night. I wondered what her heartbreak story was going to be like.

The hands on the clock showed that it was thirty minutes to Kisaragi's closing time. I had been thinking about talking to Makiko about my "to dispose or not to dispose" dilemma concerning Kyohei's stuff, when:

"Iori, come quick!"

Adachi, one of the Three Couponeers—the loving nickname I had gifted the ragtag group of businessmen who were our regulars—and the local butcher, burst in to the café. He was followed by Kimura the bookseller and Takamura the fruit parlor owner. Adachi and Takamura didn't seem too worn out—they were sturdy men and still in their sixties—but if I remembered correctly, Kimura was seventy-four. He sounded like a dying goat as he leaned against the door, struggling to catch his breath.

"Wh-what's going on?" I stammered out. "Are you all okay?"

Jumping to his feet, Iori tried to help them into chairs. I rushed to fetch some water for them, but Kimura stopped me before I could do so.

"M-Momo-chan, don't worry about us. It's Makiko . . ." He tugged at my arm.

"Momo-chan, you're good friends with her as well, aren't you?" Adachi joined in, wiping the sweat off his face with his shirt.

We all looked at one another.

"Has something happened to Makiko?" Hozumi asked.

Holding his round belly, Adachi took a deep breath.

"We were having a drink at Kisaragi, but Makiko wasn't her usual self. She said something like 'I can't get through this without getting drunk.' She kept on drinking, and we couldn't get her to stop."

I was shocked. "You mean she drank even more than usual?"

"At least twice as much as her normal amount."

Twice as much!

Makiko liked to laugh heartily and drink generously, and she talked like a machine gun. In all my life, I had never met anyone who could hold a drink as well as she could. She always made me drink an unbelievable amount (Iori likes to drink at his own pace, and Hozumi is intolerant to alcohol, so that role constantly landed on me), and I often found myself waking up at Kisaragi the next morning after passing out. Just the thought of her drinking double her usual amount sent shivers down my spine.

"Then out of nowhere, she yelled, 'I'm going to take revenge on that jerk!' and stormed off," Kimura said with hunched shoulders, making his small frame look even smaller.

Something was going on, likely related to a heartbreak. Perhaps she was going to wait until the Funeral Committee to pour it all out but had gotten herself drunk prematurely and couldn't wait. Whatever it was, we needed to go and find her.

"I've heard the stories about . . ." Iori said, his expression turning solemn as he brought his hand to his chin, ". . . Makiko the Destroyer."

"Makiko the Destroyer?" the rest of us repeated in unison.

"What is that?" I said. "It sounds like a pro wrestling name."

I thought he was joking, but the serious look on his face told me otherwise.

"Makiko has high professional standards," Iori said. "She's not the type of person who shows others her weaknesses, right? No matter what is going on, she wants to keep laughing and wants others to enjoy a drink with her. Even if she is upset, or she's physically exhausted, she never takes time off. But because of that she doesn't allow herself an outlet for stress. And once in a blue moon, she hits her limit. When she drinks excessively after her stress level reaches a breaking point, she turns into . . ."

I finished his sentence for him: ". . . Makiko the Destroyer?"

Iori gave a silent nod.

Looking back, I couldn't think of a single moment when Makiko seemed to be having a difficult time. The only image of her that appeared in my mind was the one of her flirtatiously raking her hair back with her fingers, breaking into raucous laughter, which showed off her perfect white teeth. It was hard to picture Makiko without a smile.

"So what happens when she turns into Makiko the Destroyer?"

"I heard that she goes around destroying everything in her path. According to rumors, Makiko the Destroyer once annihilated an entire shopping district."

The Three Couponeers bunched together, vibrating in fear.

"Oh, dear . . ." Kimura said, his skinny arms shaking helplessly like small branches rattling in a storm.

"That sounds too extreme for it to be true," Hozumi said calmly.

I guessed that it was one of those exaggerated rumors that had grown into something of an urban legend. In any case, we knew for certain that she had gotten terribly intoxicated after drinking over her limit.

Having regained his composure, Iori decided to take action. "We'll start searching the places she could have gone." Turning to the three men, he continued, "It looks like you're all a little drunk, so it's probably best if you went home. We'll deal with this."

After walking the tipsy men back to the shopping district, the three of us split up to search. An hour had passed when the news came from Hozumi.

"I found her. We'll be at her bar."

Iori and I hurried back. Wherever she had been, she was now plopped down outside, barefoot.

"What a relief. How did you find her, Hozumi?" I asked.

She had lost her shoes, and her makeup was melting down her face, but she didn't look injured in any way.

"I remembered that thing people say about drunks always finding their way back."

"Impressive detective work."

"She *has* turned into the Destroyer, though," Hozumi said. "Look."

I glanced at Makiko to see her scraping at Kisaragi's signboard. I watched her strip off the black paint bit by bit, going from corner to corner. Like a child peeling a sticker off a chest of drawers, she dug her nails into the paint and scratched away.

"Her destruction methods aren't as harmful as I imagined," Iori said with a sigh of relief.

I tried to get her to look at me a few times, softly saying her name and offering to get her a bottle of water, but Makiko showed no signs of moving from the stoop. Perplexed, Iori gave a shrug.

"Come on, Makiko, I was looking forward to hearing your story," I coaxed.

As I crouched down next to her, she finally seemed to acknowledge my presence and raised her eyebrows, as though she was genuinely surprised to see me.

Ugh, her breath! Exactly how much did she have to drink?

"Why don't we go inside?"

"Momo-kichi, you're here! Momo-kichi."

"It's Momoko, not Momo-kichi."

Momo-kichi was a nickname she had once drunkenly given me.

Her normally lively eyes looked dull and tired, as if someone had colored them in with a black crayon. Although I was staring directly at her, it seemed impossible to lock eyes with her.

"Men," she said. "All men are just jerks. Aren't they? Don't you think they're jerks?"

Makiko grabbed me by the collar of my sweatshirt, swaying me back and forth. Then, distracted, she promptly turned back to her signboard and resumed destroying it. Uprooting her was going to take some effort—it didn't help that she was pretty tall.

What are we to do?

We stood by the bar entrance debating our options. The worst-case scenario would be utilizing Hozumi's muscles to haul her off the ground and push her inside.

Suddenly, Makiko spoke. "You guys are pros at breakups, right? So tell me something."

"Yes?" I asked.

"What do you think were his intentions?"

Despite her beautifully gel-manicured nails, Makiko continued to scratch the signboard recklessly. Bits of picked-off paint descended to the ground.

"What do you mean 'his intentions'?"

"The guy that I lived with for a year suddenly stopped coming home. Then one day he contacted me and said, 'Could you mail me my stuff? Don't worry, I'll pay for the cost of delivery.' And the addressee he gave me was the name of a woman."

I felt a chill.

Did she just say the addressee was a woman?

"Then I googled the name and a young, cute girl comes up. Tell me, does that mean . . ."

Makiko stopped destroying the signboard.

". . . that we were not even *in* a relationship? Is that what this means?"

Bending down to sit next to her, Iori quietly handed her a glass of water.

"What emotion am I supposed to feel as I'm writing that name on the address label? Tell me, what is the correct emotion to feel when I'm sending off the belongings of the person I love to the house of another woman?"

Makiko's shoulders were shaking, just a little.

"Go inside and make yourselves some drinks," Makiko said. "I'll be right there."

With her back still turned to us, Makiko waved her hands exaggeratedly as she spoke.

Is she crying? She must be crying.

Droplets must have been trickling from her eyes and hitting the ground. I couldn't be certain, though, because Makiko kept her head lowered.

She was totally hammered. She'd been betrayed by the person she loved. Seeing her like this, I felt my chest squeeze, as if my heart were shriveling up. I wished that she would let herself have a real cry. What was pushing her to play the role of a woman who never shows her feelings?

After somehow carrying her inside, we relaxed a little. Makiko locked herself in the bathroom for a moment, but when she reappeared, her face looked fresh, as though she'd returned to her usual self, and she joined us where we were sitting at the bar.

"I'm so sorry for all the trouble. I'm the worst bartender, aren't I?"

She's trying to revert to the bubbly and high-spirited Makiko, I thought to myself.

The emotional mask that she'd been wearing had started to peel off, and she had fixed it up behind that bathroom door. I noticed that her hair, which had become all disheveled, was now neatly gathered with a hair clip, and the black mascara smeared below her eyes had been wiped clean. Her wrists and the cuffs on her shirt were damp, probably from splashing water on her face.

"I'm fine now. You can go home. God, I'm sorry you had to see me in such a state."

Makiko let out an embarrassed laugh and started to clear the bar counter, pretending the last hour hadn't happened.

"Do you want to talk more about what you were telling us earlier?" I asked her softly.

"Oh, sorry, it's nothing worth talking about. I thought I'd taken a feral cat in, but it turns out it had an owner all along! It's the kind of thing you hear all the time, which makes you go, 'I can't believe I considered letting that cat live with me for good—am I an idiot or what?' "

"Isn't that what you wanted to vent about?"

Without stopping her hands from rinsing a glass, she replied, "Don't worry about it. It's past midnight already. Sorry again; it's my fault."

She must have done this over and over again. Whatever life threw at her, she must have prioritized not worrying others and instead busied herself with work.

I need to stop her, my intuition told me.

If she doesn't vent the feelings that she's bottling up now, her thick skin that makes her the Makiko that people love will grow even thicker. Though she has the ability to live life without showing her weaknesses, and sometimes I find myself aspiring to be like her, I need to make this a night where she doesn't play the role of "Strong Makiko."

"Makiko."

I grabbed her wrist as she reached out to wipe down the bar countertop.

"Why don't you stop acting like the low-maintenance woman? Just this one day—no, this one night."

Makiko turned to look at me.

"Once in a while, you've got to embarrass yourself and let yourself be the needy, high-maintenance woman."

She smiled slowly, sighing.

"All right, Momo-chan. Can I get anyone a drink?"

Makiko's story went like this.

About a year and a half ago, a young man walked into Kisaragi and soon became a regular customer. He was a memorable client because of his distinctive looks—he wore head-to-toe black and a pair of round sunglasses. He would arrive just after ten o'clock at night and would always sit at the end of the counter. The man would then spend an hour drawing in his sketchbook while sipping a gin and tonic.

Printed on the business card in rustic type was his name, *AKIRA*

NAGAYAMA, and profession, *Artist*. Still in his twenties, he was an exciting up-and-comer with a number of well-received exhibitions already under his belt.

Akira began to spend more and more time at the bar, gradually seeping into Makiko's life and eventually moving in. She and Akira cohabited for about a year until one day, suddenly, he stopped coming home. Makiko worried that he had been involved in an accident, but two weeks later, she heard from him.

"So that's when he said, 'Post my stuff to my girlfriend, I'll pay for delivery'? What the hell is that?"

I was so infuriated, it took all my energy to keep my hands from shaking.

"He hadn't even talked to you about breaking up! That is *not* okay. What kind of jerk 'offers' to pay for delivery when he hasn't even apologized to you yet?"

"Well, Makiko has always been a compassionate person," Iori said with a bitter smile. "Certain types of men take advantage of that."

"You think so? Do I seem like the type that men take advantage of?"

Makiko covered her blushing face with her hands.

"I guess . . ." Makiko began, ". . . Akira never thought of me as his lover or anything of the sort."

Hozumi took a sip of his tomato juice and asked, "How did you two become a couple in the first place?"

"I was hoping that question wouldn't come up." Makiko furrowed her brow and let out a long groan.

"Makiko?"

Biting her lips, Makiko was motionless.

"Did he ever say 'Will you be my girlfriend?' or anything along those lines?"

"No . . . he didn't."

"Then did you ask him?"

"I . . . didn't." Makiko's voice had grown so hoarse, she sounded as though she was in excruciating pain, as if her arm was being squeezed and twisted by a gigantic humanoid or something.

She got up, and with the speed of a ninja, she lifted a bottle of whiskey from the shelf.

"Makiko, wh-what are you—you can't have any more to drink!" I shouted.

"No! Let me! Please! I can't deal with this without drinking!"

With practiced hands, she pulled the lid off the bottle, swiftly filled a glass with ice, and poured whiskey over it before garnishing it with a wedge of lemon. I gazed in awe at her bartending technique, but this was no time to be impressed.

"Stop right there!" Iori grabbed Makiko's arm just before her first sip and took her glass away. In exchange, he produced a bottle of soda water from the refrigerator.

"You have this, Makiko, and *I'll* enjoy the whiskey."

"Iori, brutal as always," she said.

A crestfallen Makiko came out from behind the bar, joined us, and sipped her fizzy water. She gave a long and depressing sigh, as if we were in the middle of an apocalypse.

"To be honest, the reason I didn't want to give you all the details was because I knew that it was all my fault. I deserved it."

"What do you mean, it was all your fault?" I asked.

"What I mean is . . ."

Makiko mussed her long bangs with her fingers, working up the courage.

"I was scared to know the truth. Scared of being told to my face that we were just friends with benefits. I wanted to take a chance on the possibility that we were on the same page—that we were a couple—without saying the words out loud."

"Makiko . . ."

I know what you mean. Finding out how someone feels about you can be terrifying.

But wait. Something doesn't feel right.

I couldn't shake the feeling that there was more to the story.

"Akira basically crashed at your place, then ended up moving in, right?"

"Yes."

"When a woman lets you live at her place for a whole year, isn't it pretty obvious that she has feelings for you? It doesn't take a genius to work that out. Or is he hopelessly obtuse?"

"No, no. It's really not like that." Makiko gripped the bottle of soda water so tightly, it made a crackling sound. "It was me who suggested to Akira that he move in with me."

"Wait, *you* asked *him*?"

"I told you, it's all my fault!" Makiko covered her face and groaned into her hands.

This was going to be a long night.

Swaying his now-empty glass lazily back and forth, Iori began a piece-by-piece summary of the facts.

"So basically . . . Akira is someone who is sorely lacking in basic life skills. The more you got to know him, the more concerned you became for him."

Here were all the facts we'd gathered from Makiko: He only ate once a day (and it wasn't unusual for him to not eat at all). His phone would be turned off for days. His mailbox at home was constantly overflowing with unread mail, and when he did open it (once in a blue moon), he would put all the letters straight in the trash without properly checking for bills or other important documents. It came to a point where Makiko was concerned about just how it was that Akira kept himself alive.

"I think his artistic talent swallowed up all of his energy." Makiko sighed.

"And then, what did you say again?" Iori continued. "Akira had completely forgotten that the renewal of his apartment contract was due, and he was practically evicted? He had to couch-surf while he looked for a new place to live. You learned that he kept showing up at Kisaragi because it was where he could kill time until he found a place to stay that night. Is that right?"

"Well, yeah. Which is why you can't blame me for asking him if he wanted to stay with me!"

"We hadn't blamed you . . . yet," I said.

"Momo-chan, if you were in my position, you wouldn't be able to leave him alone. And you, too, Hozumi!"

"Actually, I can't stand the thought of another human entering my home," Hozumi replied.

"He hadn't even found anywhere to live, yet he would say to me apathetically that it was all just 'part of life.' I started to worry that one day he would just die without me knowing."

"And that's how you ended up letting him live with you?"

Makiko frowned, answering Hozumi's question with a nod.

"I couldn't just sit there and watch him live so recklessly. The next thing I knew, I was saying to him, 'You can stay with me until you find somewhere to live.' And from then on, things spiraled . . . I found myself cooking for him and helping him out with organizing his affairs whenever I had a chance."

That is so—how can I put it? It's typical Makiko behavior.

She had been like this with me when I first met her. I went to introduce myself to her as the new kitchen manager at Amayadori, and without even being asked, she started telling me who the most cost-efficient fresh food suppliers were and even wrote me a list of everyone in Sangenjaya whom I should go and pay my respects to.

Makiko was simply incapable of being a bystander in any situation. If she could do something about whatever was happening in front of her, she couldn't ignore it. Whether she'd benefit from it or not was never a concern. If she could help, she would, and she would never forgive herself if she didn't.

"Shall we have a snack?" Makiko said. "I'm starting to feel a little hungry."

"No more drinking," I warned.

"I *know.*" Makiko rolled her neck and shoulders, making cracking noises as she opened the fridge door. She paused. "Oh, yeah, I forgot that I'd cooked my ex-boyfriend's favorite recipe for tonight."

"You did?"

"Want to try some? Might as well."

Makiko brought out a container filled with potato salad made with crispy bacon pieces, boiled egg, and black pepper. I could see that the potatoes were broken up roughly, and I wondered if she had deliberately kept them chunky.

"He ate like a bird. Once he started painting, he wouldn't stop. He would keep working for days, looking emaciated. He rarely touched the food I'd kept for him in the fridge, but this was the one dish he ate well."

"Normally we cook the dishes together as you tell us your story, but we're happy to do it this way, too!" I proclaimed.

I spooned the salad onto small plates. We all put our hands together and said, "Itadakimasu," and dug in. It was like a classic potato salad, but from time to time, a creamy taste spread through my mouth.

Could this be . . .

"Smoked cheese?"

"You're spot-on, Momo-chan! I add pieces of smoked cheese to the potatoes while they're still hot so that it melts."

Right. What an idea.

The smokiness and the bacon made a wonderful combination. Apparently very fond of potatoes, Makiko had tested the recipe over and over again until she finally came up with this version. Since Akira was basically only interested in food that went well with alcohol, she seasoned it generously.

"True, the flavor pairs irresistibly well with alcohol," Iori said, and let out a satisfied sigh. He deftly opened the bottle of Heineken that he'd grabbed from the fridge earlier and took a gulp of it with great relish.

"Are you doing that to torment me, Iori?"

"Not at all. I'm genuinely impressed, Makiko." Iori recrossed his legs and stared into her eyes as he asked, "When was the first time you did it with Akira?"

"You mean . . . when did we start a physical relationship?"

"Yeah. Did it happen straight after he moved in with you or before?"

The quick change in conversation made Hozumi clear his throat awkwardly.

"Probably . . ." Raising her gaze to the ceiling, Makiko searched her mind. ". . . about two months after we started living together."

"How did it happen? Did you initiate it? Or did he?" Iori continued, maintaining a serious look on his face.

What? Why would he want to know that?

Makiko, scratching the lid of the plastic bottle, replied, "From the beginning, we slept in the same bed because I didn't have a futon for guests."

"You slept in the same bed?" I gasped.

"Yeah, but for a long time nothing happened. I assumed he didn't see me in that way, and thought of me like a roommate, or a housemother or something. I would lie next to him like I would do with a friend. But one day, he reached out to touch me . . . and it wasn't like I wanted to push him away, so we kept going."

"Did you fall in love with him after you slept with him?"

Makiko moved her head in agreement, as though she had finally relented.

"I . . . guess so. I fell in love with him, yes. I think it sped things up for me."

I released a sigh. *I know that feeling.* I'd had that experience, where I found myself in love with a man after sleeping with him, even though I initially didn't have strong feelings for him. A lot of men lose interest in women after sleeping with them, but it's usually the opposite for women. Unfortunately.

Iori wouldn't stop. "I know I asked you already, Makiko, but are you sure you never tried to find out how he felt? Not even indirectly?"

Makiko's fingers froze at his words. She sat for a while, apparently lost in thought, but eventually gave a sigh, as though she had given up.

"Iori, you creep me out," she said. "I've always felt that way about you."

"Oh, thanks."

"I did try. Just once."

Makiko expelled a breath, as though she was about to make a confession.

"I think he'd been living with me for some time at that point. We were lying on the bed after sex one time, talking. He was twirling my hair around his finger, looking a little sleepy. It felt so much like we were a couple. I thought it was my only chance to ask him. So I did, in a way that didn't sound too interrogative."

"What did you say?"

"I said, 'Akira, what are your intentions?' "

I felt a pain in my heart, as though it was being pressed down.

They lived under the same roof. They were comfortable around each other. They enjoyed being together. They were having sex. But he'd never defined their relationship, at least not out loud. The uneasy, unbearable feelings that Makiko must have felt sprang up inside me, as if they were my own.

"And? What did Akira say?"

Makiko rubbed the inner corners of her eyes, then glanced back at Iori with a determined look.

"He said, 'Of course I have intentions.' "

We sat there, too stunned to speak, waiting for more.

"He didn't say anything else. Then he hugged me. I didn't have the strength to question him any further, so I just went to sleep."

"Oh, no." Iori cradled his head with his hands.

He had intentions? What intentions?

I pounded my knees with my fists. "What a bastard!"

It was the perfect evasion, a cunning response that guaranteed him an escape route should he need one. How was it possible for someone who supposedly lacked basic life skills to be so sharp-minded when it came to something like this?

"Sorry, do you mind if I smoke?" Makiko, seemingly unable to fight the urge, got up and fumbled a pack of cigarettes from behind the counter. She brushed off the dust from the plastic wrapper before pulling the tear strip and drawing a cigarette out of the pack.

"Want one?" She tilted the pack toward Iori, but he shook his head in silence. She knew neither Hozumi nor I smoked.

Makiko lit her cigarette with a disposable lighter in a confident, practiced way. A sweet scent of raspberries mixed with the smell of burning tobacco.

"I'd quit because Akira said that the smell of cigarettes distracted him from his work, but I guess I can start again now."

How could this happen to someone as nice as Makiko?

Some people in this world are impossibly generous. They're the kind of people who sacrifice themselves to keep giving to someone else. People like that deserve to be rewarded. I *so* wanted them to be rewarded. Why did the world have to be so unfair?

The four of us fell into silence. We each found something to gaze at—a hangnail, the ashes in the stainless steel ashtray, random marks staining the wall. We quietly tried to suppress our unbearable emotions.

I felt somewhat restless and decided to step outside for a moment.

A cold sensation hit my head. Seeing that it had started to sprinkle, I quickly took shelter under the awning.

It always seems to rain on the Ex-Boyfriend's Favorite Recipe Funeral Committee nights.

Hozumi had once muttered these words. Now that I thought about it, it did seem that Fridays were always enveloped in the earthy smell of rain. I supposed it was only fitting that the air was so damp.

My phone screen told me it was almost two in the morning. I hadn't realized how late it was. The night felt awfully long.

Akira, what are your intentions?

It must have taken Makiko so much courage to say those words. She must have been driven to the point where she felt her suffering would become intolerable unless she had an answer.

And even if his answer was that he didn't intend on having a committed relationship with her, at least she would *have* a clear answer. And yet Akira didn't even . . .

"How can he be so cruel?" I said out loud.

I knew I had no reason to cry. But the more I thought about it, the more my nose started to burn. I lifted my head, fanning my watering eyes with my hands.

A thought crossed my mind and I pulled out my phone. I started typing *Akira Nagayama* in a search engine app, but before I could finish, his name autofilled, and that fact infuriated me even more.

Akira Nagayama. Age 25. Painter. From Fukuoka prefecture. Debuted as a modern artist after winning the 51st Taiyo Arts and Culture Award as a student. In addition to holding solo exhibitions, he has been involved in the art direction of TV commercials and package branding.

His profile came up straightaway. I found some interview articles, and in all of them, he was dressed in black and wore round sunglasses. The reason he wore head-to-toe black was apparently because "black makes paint stains less noticeable," and the reason he wore sunglasses was because he's "a shy person lol" and he's "not good at making eye contact with others." He gave ambiguous responses to every question asked, and my stomach tightened with more rage.

"The ones that claim to be 'shy' are never that shy," I muttered to myself.

An overwhelming smell of rain-soaked concrete rose up from the ground.

What should I do? How can we let her love rest in peace?

As the Ex-Boyfriend's Favorite Recipe Funeral Committee, our duty was to listen to our client's story, eat a memory-filled dish, and most importantly, give their smoldering feelings a proper burial.

But however much we try, no matter how many words of consolation we offer to Makiko, without knowing Akira's true feelings, we won't be able to lay her feelings to rest.

As these thoughts went through my mind, the bar door opened quietly. Makiko popped her head out.

"I thought I'd smoke outside—oh, it's raining."

She came out anyway and put a fresh cigarette between her lips.

She must have caught a glimpse of what was on my phone screen because she gently took it from me and started to scroll through the articles about Akira.

"He's saying pretty cool things, isn't he?"

"Hey, Makiko."

"Hmm?"

Makiko took a long drag on her cigarette and exhaled. The smoke turned the air murky, then faded into the drizzle.

"I think it's unfair," I said.

"What is?"

"Akira was well aware that you were in love with him, and he used that to his advantage. And the fact that he said he 'had intentions'—by saying something that could mean a million different things—he was allowing himself plausible deniability. He avoided facing you properly because he knew that would make him the bad guy."

Makiko said nothing.

"He hurt you, and treated you unfairly, and once everything started to become inconvenient for him, he moved on to a new nest. And here he is going around saying all this pretentious bullshit, like 'My art is born from time spent in complete solitude,' and doing exhibitions of his so-called masterpieces."

"Momo-chan . . ."

Before I knew it, my eyes were filling up. Only a moment ago, I had been able to hold back my crying, but now the floodgates had opened. I couldn't stop the tears from streaming down my face.

Makiko went back inside, brought out a box of tissues for me, and rubbed her hand against my back.

I'm the one who should be comforting her, not the other way around!

"Someone has even said 'Nagayama-san's work has expressed the pain I'd been carrying all alone.' How is it fair, that a guy like that is getting all the praise? I want to say to him: Stop running away. Before you talk about your *own* pain, why don't you face the fact that you have hurt someone?" I said.

Right.

My vision turned blurry, warping the view before me. I replayed the scene of my breakup with Kyohei in my mind—that love hotel, that bleak winter day.

I realized that Kyohei hurting my feelings wasn't what angered me.

"I was trying to get you to break up with me. I did things on purpose, so that you would initiate the conversation."

Kyohei had uttered these words awkwardly. Though he seemed mostly apologetic, I couldn't help but notice that part of him—maybe about twenty percent—wanted the whole ordeal done and over with.

It wasn't that I didn't want to get hurt. I was fine with that part. To find love, you need to risk getting your heart broken, and I was prepared for that. What impacted me the most was that he had let four years pass by without ever being prepared to get hurt or to hurt me. The stakes were so low for him.

If we had confronted each other, if we had fought a fair fight, and if it still didn't work out, then I could have accepted that.

But it turned out that I had been the only one who was serious, and I didn't realize until the very end that I was the only person in the relationship who had loved with so much passion.

What was I supposed to do with myself now?

How was I supposed to lay my smoldering feelings to rest?

"I was the same, though . . ."

I raised my head toward Makiko's whispery voice. She gave a faint smile and threw down her cigarette, stubbing it out before speaking.

"I didn't want him to think that I was a high-maintenance woman. The fact that I'm thirty-six and single automatically puts me in that category. It doesn't matter if nothing about me has changed or if I wasn't interested in marriage. If I want to have a romantic relationship with someone, the weight of being in the 'high-maintenance woman' category keeps growing, whether I like it or not. It gets so heavy. Gives me knots in my shoulders."

"Makiko . . ."

"To be honest, I kind of knew that Akira wanted a low-maintenance relationship, and that was why I kept pretending like I didn't need much attention, as if I wasn't serious, as if I was a no-strings-attached kind of woman."

Makiko stared into me intently. It looked as though she was forcing a smile to hide her emotions.

"Akira didn't run away. There was nothing to run from. Nothing had started in the first place. I was the one putting on a performance, making it look like an easygoing, casual relationship. But anyway . . ."

As she spoke, Makiko's mask gradually peeled away. Her features contorted, her eyes and cheeks tensed up. The corners of her tight-lipped mouth lowered.

Makiko was crying.

"When you put off getting hurt for so long, it really stings when it finally hits you."

Makiko's face became even more contorted as she forced a smile. Instinctively, I embraced her.

Makiko said, "Thank you," and nothing more as she cried quietly. I cried with her.

Our sniffles disappeared into the patter of the rain.

One week later, Makiko called to let me know that she had met up with Akira to have a proper talk. I quickly stopped her, and suggested we do another Funeral Committee meeting, this time the right way, at Amayadori. I told her to be prepared to make her potato salad.

Makiko and I started in the kitchen and instructed Hozumi to peel the boiled eggs. Iori, who had an inventory deadline at the end of March, sat glued to his computer with deep bags under his eyes.

I watched as Makiko effortlessly cut the smoked cheese into the thinnest slices.

"So, what did you do with Akira's stuff? Did you send it to him in the end?"

Makiko chuckled at my question. "I delivered it to him."

"You delivered it? You mean you took it to him yourself?"

"Yes. I took it to his *exhibition*."

"What?"

Makiko nonchalantly mashed the potatoes and drank her beer.

"Oh, and his real girlfriend was there, standing right next to him. It seems that the whole industry knows that they're a couple. They were bowing together and everything."

I imagined the girlfriend acting all proprietorial and bit down on my lip. We knew next to nothing about the girl, but the image hit a nerve.

"Did you mention that you and Akira had been together?" Hozumi leaned in and asked.

"I considered doing that as I was getting ready, but I thought of a better way to get my revenge."

Makiko gave a chuckle and held her phone out to us with a triumphant smile.

"You look stunning!"

What I saw on her phone screen was the most beautiful sight of Makiko I had ever seen. Tastefully dressed in a blazer, white shirt, and a pair of jeans, her understated style complemented her features.

And next to her was . . .

"Is that Akira?" It was the famous artist, wearing a stiff smile on his face. "What exactly am I looking at? I can see that you look gorgeous, but . . ."

"Aren't I? I was a big hit with the people Akira works with."

"You talked to them?"

"Of course. I gave them my business card. In fact, I did a lot of networking with potential customers. There were some big names there, so maybe my bar's sales will go up."

"You're one tough cookie," commented Hozumi.

Akira would have had to tread very carefully in that situation. Makiko had seized the opportunity and promoted her bar. I was so impressed. Picturing the scene, a giggle escaped me.

"And what did you do with his things?"

"I got a big Sembikiya bag and filled it with all his belongings. I handed it to him and said, 'Here you go, Nagayama-san. Please take a look later.' "

Makiko pulled her lips into a mischievous grin.

"So the people who work with him must have thought . . ."

"Who knows? I went straight home, so I don't know what happened after that. But it must have just looked like I had brought some fancy cake from Sembikiya for everyone there. While they were all happily saying things like 'Wow, Sembikiya? You're spoiling us!' Akira just stood there, completely frozen. When I saw him like that, I wondered if I had gone a little too far."

Makiko's shoulders dropped for a moment, but she quickly shook her head.

"But," she added, "it wasn't like I lied to him. So we're kind of even, aren't we?"

Adachi the butcher looked over the menu for the umpteenth time.

"When will you add Makiko's potato salad?"

The windows at Amayadori were bathed in the warmth of the afternoon sun. As usual, the Three Couponeers were here. All wearing T-shirts, the gentlemen now appeared to have switched over to their spring closets.

"I decided to make it a seasonal dish. You have to be patient and wait until the Destroyer potatoes are in season."

"Destroyer? You mean Makiko's other name?"

"No, actually. It turns out that the meaning of 'Makiko the Destroyer' wasn't so literal. It was referring to the name of a potato variety."

When she taught me the recipe, Makiko told me that her potato salad tasted the best when you used a potato variety called Destroyer. As implied by its name, these potatoes have a sinister look to them. They are marked with red patches, reminiscent of a pro wrestler's mask, hence the name. After comparing many different varieties, Makiko fell in love with the rich, full-bodied flavor, so much so that for a while she even contemplated growing them on her veranda.

In the Kanto region, Destroyer potatoes aren't a common variety. Unlike Danshaku or May Queen potatoes, they're rarely distributed in the markets unless it's early summer. One night, after Makiko kept on shouting "I want some Destroyer potatoes!" at the bar, one of her customers drunkenly started to call her "Makiko the Destroyer." From then on, the nickname took on a life of its own, and that was apparently how rumors of "Makiko the Destroyer of Sangenjaya" began to spread.

"I suppose we'll have to wait until the summer then," Adachi said resignedly.

"It just means we have one more thing to look forward to," said Kimura.

His skinny arms reminded me of a willow tree as he unrolled his hot hand towel and used it to wipe his face.

"I've already decided on the name of the dish, though," I said, setting down their coffees. At that moment, the bell rang out dimly.

"I'm back. I made the deadline!"

It was Iori. Earlier, he had left the café in a hurry after telling us that he needed to get to the public office to submit the financial paperwork he'd pulled an all-nighter working on. It seemed that he had made the deadline just under the wire. His attire was clearly the last thing on his mind—he was dressed in that worn-out *I Love NY* T-shirt and sweatpants, and his bangs were swept back with one of those hair clips you use to section hair.

Seriously? He went to the public office looking like this . . . ?

Sure, Iori had a good face, and that gave him the power to pull off most looks, but this was not one of them.

Iori collapsed into the sofa. I poured him a glass of cold water and handed it to him.

"You must be tired."

Iori drank the water in one go.

"That's better! There was extra paperwork this year, what with Momo-chan joining, there was insurance and stuff that needed—" Iori stopped mid-sentence, noticing something. He stared at the Three Couponeers in wide-eyed astonishment.

"What are you wearing? I mean, your T-shirts . . ." Iori said. "Are they the same as mine?"

"They're from Momo-chan. Very good, aren't they?" Adachi boasted, showing off the *I Love NY* logo printed across his chest.

"Wait, yours are in a better condition than mine."

Pulling the bottom edge of Adachi's T-shirt, Iori compared it with the one he was wearing and became indignant.

I had forgotten that I'd bought more than one T-shirt while in the U.S. I discovered them deep in my closet, still sealed inside the plastic packaging they came in.

In the end, I decided to throw away all things related to Kyohei. The letters, the photo albums. I even deleted the pictures and videos saved on my phone. Once I had removed all traces of Kyohei, it felt as if a part of me had disappeared.

"Wait, is *that* how I look? Do I really look that tacky?"

Iori seemed to have realized for the first time just how tacky he looked. He started to throw a tantrum about it. It didn't help that he hadn't slept all night.

I remembered the last thing Makiko had said to me that night:

"Thank you, Momo-chan. I'm glad. I'm glad that I am letting myself be a 'high-maintenance woman.' I'm glad I let myself break down into tears, and that I got to act immature and take revenge. I realized that, whatever your age, there are times when you have to let yourself be needy."

One day, I might remember how I howled and wailed over one little breakup. I might look back and think how foolish I had been, and say "I was young then."

Even if I do become adept at handling the things life throws at me, when I do get my heart broken, or if I break someone else's heart, I'll remember to howl and wail. To go through the pain. To ask for help.

Watching Iori and the men continue to argue in my peripheral vision, I pulled out a pen and wrote on a sticky note:

NEW DISH!! SO WHAT IF I'M HIGH-MAINTENANCE POTATO SALAD

I attached the note to the calendar hanging next to me.

The warm sun shone over the four men dressed in super-tacky T-shirts. Just the sight of them made me crack up.

The bell over the door tinkled.

"Hello . . . a glass of ice cream soda, please."

"Hi there, Hozumi. You won't believe what Momo-chan did—huh? Are you seriously wearing that? Momo-chan, you set us up, didn't you?!"

Oops. Now there were five.

SO WHAT IF I'M HIGH-MAINTENANCE POTATO SALAD

Serves 2

4 medium potatoes
4 or 5 bite-sized cubes smoked cheese
$1^1/_2$ ounces (40 g) thin-cut bacon
4 tablespoons (60 g) mayonnaise
Salt and pepper
3 shakes MSG
2 eggs
Enough black pepper to satisfy your soul

METHOD

Peel the potatoes and remove the eyes (sprouts). Roughly chop up the potatoes. After soaking them in water, cook them in a microwave oven (approximately 6 minutes in a 900W microwave oven).

Tear up the smoked cheese cubes into pinkie-nail-sized pieces and add them to the potatoes while they are still hot.

Cut the bacon into $^1/_4$-inch (5-mm) strips and cook them in a frying pan until crispy.

Add the bacon, mayonnaise, salt and pepper, and MSG to the potatoes and mix well.

Soft-boil the eggs: Bring water to a boil, then add the eggs and boil them for 7 minutes. Then place the eggs in an ice bath.

Peel and add the soft-boiled eggs to the potato mixture, roughly breaking them apart.

Place on a dish and top with as much black pepper as it takes to satisfy your soul.

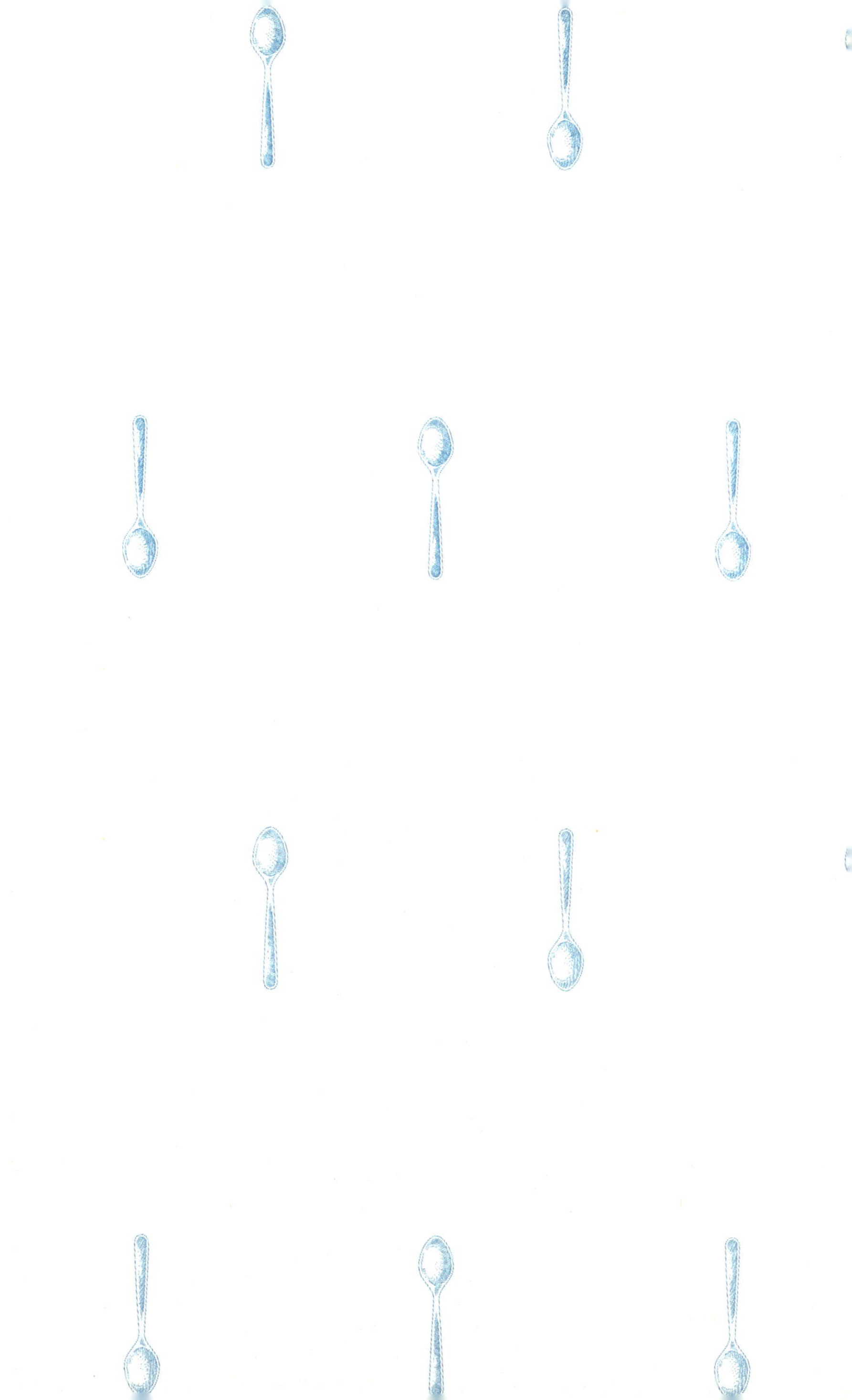

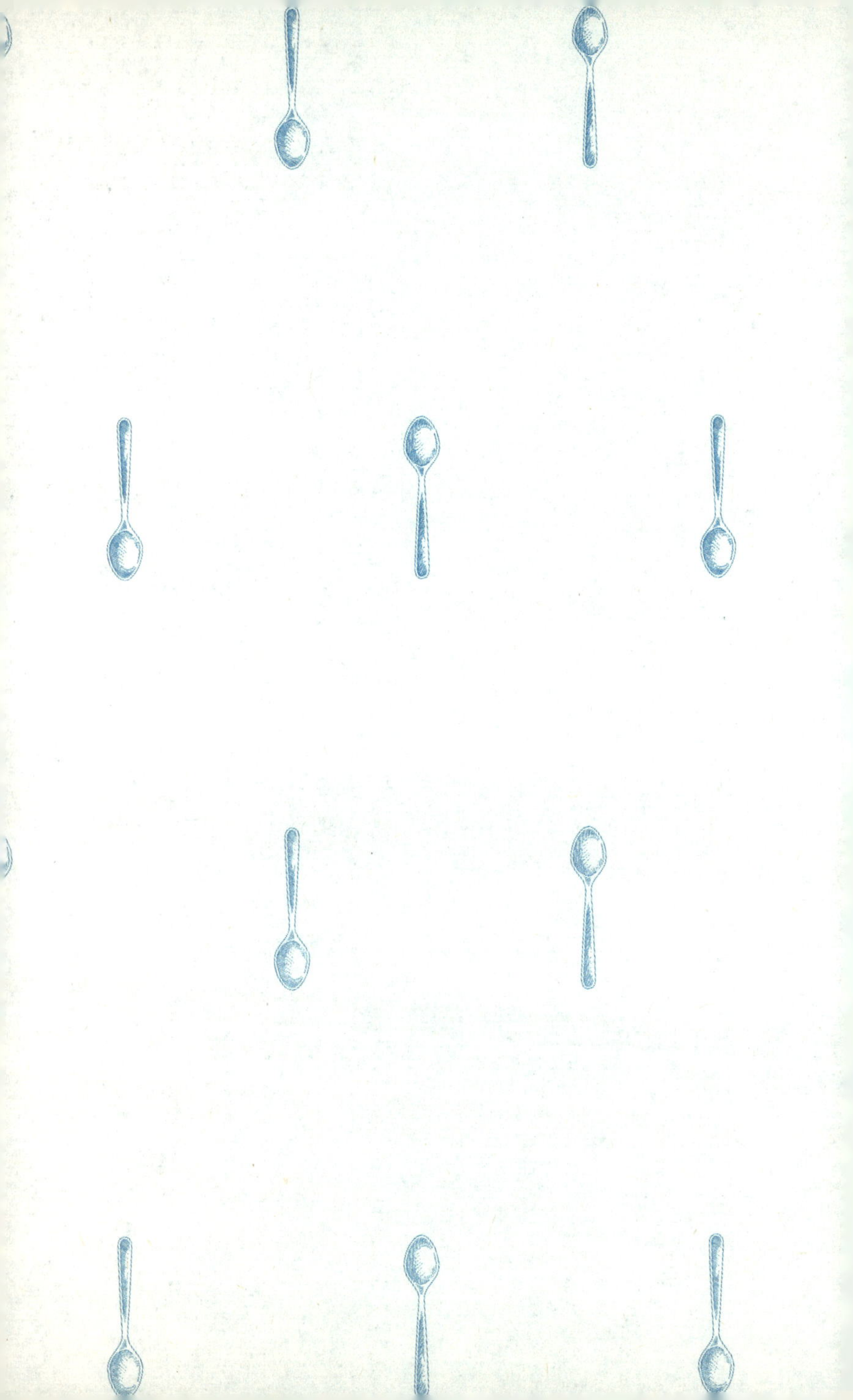

CHAPTER 4

GRANDMA'S SECRET UMEBOSHI

"Are you sure you can re-create the flavor? The last time he tasted it was three years ago, right?" Hozumi said, deftly pressing the rice together in his palms to form an onigiri.

"What was I supposed to do? He said I was his last hope. Don't you want to help him out?"

"I do, but . . ."

After shaping the rice into a perfect triangle, Hozumi wrapped a sheet of nori around it as the final touch, then got started on his next onigiri straightaway. I watched his skillful hands in awe.

"What?"

"I was just thinking how perfect your onigiri looks. You're like a pro."

"Oh, it's because I make my own packed lunch all the time. What's next?"

"Umm . . . a Tawara-shaped onigiri, please—you know, the cylindrical ones," I said. "After that, I'd like ball-shaped ones."

Laid out on the counter at Amayadori was an array of onigiri in different shapes, each filled with a different variety of umeboshi. I felt dizzy at the thought of having to find the right onigiri shape and umeboshi out of an infinite number of combinations.

It had all started two weeks ago.

The Three Couponeers of Amayadori were having their usual chats, catching up on the latest gossip about corrupt politicians and whatnot. They happily ate their soft-serve ice cream, commenting on how much hotter the days had become. Having lingered for a good two hours, the men finally rose from their seats and made their way to the till.

"Momo-chan." Kimura, who had been waiting for his turn to pay, suddenly turned toward the kitchen where I was standing. "What do you call that funny thing you do . . . you know, where you talk to a customer and re-create their dish?"

"Do you mean the Ex-Boyfriend's Favorite Recipe Funeral Committee?"

Glancing nervously at Adachi and Takamura as they settled their bills, he quickly leaned close to my ear. It was obvious that he didn't want them to hear.

"I don't suppose you could . . . re-create a flavor from the past? That would be a bit of a stretch, wouldn't it?"

The flavor that Kimura longed to taste was the onigiri that his late wife, Matsuko, used to make.

Yasunari Kimura was the owner of Kimura Shoten, a bookstore about a six-minute walk from Amayadori. Ever since he was a young man, he had spent most of his time working, rarely taking a day off.

He told me that Matsuko used to pack him a homemade lunch every day, and that was what had gotten him through the day.

"I've been having the same dream almost every night as of late," said Kimura, letting out a deep sigh. "In it, Matsuko hands me my lunch, telling me not to forget it. As usual, I take it from her. At the shop, I go to eat it . . . I unwrap the furoshiki and lift the onigiri to my mouth. But then I realize, I can't taste anything. *I can't remember how it tasted.* I've never forgotten before, but now . . ."

How could I say no to that plea? I suddenly clutched Kimura's fragile shoulders, promising him that I would find a way to re-create Matsuko's onigiri.

And so, every day since, I found myself making different flavors and getting Kimura to taste-test them.

It seemed that Hozumi was skeptical.

"This flavor of Matsuko's . . . how do we know if we're getting anywhere near it?"

"Kimura said it's been a really long time since he had one, so he doesn't remember it that well, but I hear that taste and smell can trigger all kinds of memories. He'll probably know it as soon as he tastes it."

I tried to sound as convincing as possible, but inside, I was starting to feel more and more anxious. Normally, the clients of the Funeral Committee would give us a recipe, and if not, they'd make the dish and we'd watch how they made it. But things were different this time. The only information we had about the dish was that it was an onigiri and that its filling was umeboshi.

"I wonder if she really didn't leave a recipe," Hozumi said.

"Kimura said he looked for it but couldn't find anything. I suppose onigiri are so simple to make that it would be unusual for someone to write down the recipe."

Kimura was due to come to Amayadori once he closed his store for the day. I'd ordered several types of umeboshi online and had made onigiri of different shapes. I hoped that we were getting closer.

Iori, who had been working on his computer, peered into the kitchen.

"Maybe he's tried too many varieties, and now he's confused? Why don't you give it a break for a while."

Just then, the door flung open.

"I—I remember!"

It was Kimura. Leaning against the counter, he breathed heavily with his shoulders. He removed his gilet and wiped off the sweat dripping down his neck. His stooped back was trembling.

"Easy now, are you okay?"

"I *just* remembered, Momo-chan. It's the plums!"

He sipped the glass of water that Iori had poured for him. Once his breathing had calmed, he spoke again.

"The umeboshi inside Matsuko's onigiri—they were terribly sour. Today, I had a recollection of eating them. My face would get scrunched up because they were so sour."

Her umeboshi was so sour that it made him squirm in his seat.

"Oh! Why don't you try this one first, then?"

I handed him an onigiri filled with the sourest umeboshi I had sourced. After taking several bites of it, Kimura shook his head.

"No, it was sourer than this."

"Really? This one features the sourest plums I could find. Do you know which brand she used?"

There is a huge variety of umeboshi all over Japan. Looking for the specific one Matsuko bought would be like looking for a needle in a haystack.

I had another thought. Nowadays people like to cut down on salt.

If her umeboshi were so sour, they would have to have been *extremely* salty—it was unlikely for such umeboshi to be sold in stores anymore.

That must mean . . .

"Could it be that Matsuko made her own umeboshi?"

Kimura stared at me with widened eyes. I watched his veiny hands as he rubbed his forehead. A look of realization swept across his face.

"Come to think of it, we used to receive a box of yellow-colored plums every year . . ."

"Bingo!"

"I always assumed that the plums were for making plum wine."

"A lot of people make plum wine and umeboshi together. That must be it! Did Matsuko spend a day in July or August working on something outdoors for a long time, like on your veranda or in your backyard?"

"Yes—yes! Every year. And I always wondered why she had to choose such a hot day for it."

Aha! That is definitely it!

"Matsuko must have made her own umeboshi and used them in her onigiri!"

"Right . . . but I don't have any of that umeboshi left."

A gloomy expression came over Kimura's face as he let out a sigh, realizing it might not be possible to re-create them. Sliding off his glasses, he rubbed the sweat off his eyelids.

There must be a way.

Biting my lip, I racked my brain for ideas.

I cast a glance at my phone screen as a thought bloomed.

June 20th . . . we might make it just in time if we start now.

"We'll make umeboshi ourselves!" I declared, pumping my fists.

"But, Momo-chan, do you even know how?" Kimura asked.

"Don't worry! Back home in the countryside, I used to help my grandma make them. And thanks to the Funeral Committee, I've gotten pretty good at re-creating recipes. I'm sure I can do it with umeboshi, too."

Hozumi's suspicious glare pierced through me as he asked me silently, *Are you really sure?*

What the hell—if I don't do it, then who will?

Kimura quietly rose from his chair and took my hand with both of his hands.

"Please. At this rate, I will—"

He stopped mid-sentence.

Then he said, "Thank you. I know I can count on you, dear."

Kimura's home was a cozy two-story house. Its entryway was lined with pots and planters full of dry soil and no flowers.

We were led to the back of the living room. Makiko's kitchen, where she had spent most of her life, was behind a curtain made of wooden beads.

"Wow. It's . . . amazing," I said, goose bumps popping up all over my arms.

"It feels like stepping into the past," Hozumi commented.

"It's like something out of a drama," Iori added.

There was a well-worn kettle in red enamel, and all sorts of condiments were arranged tightly next to one another. Handwritten recipes were attached to the fridge door by magnets, her beautiful penmanship catching my eye. The dates on the recipes indicated that they were all from four years ago. She must have noted down the recipes from a TV program, because some of them had the words "from NHK" scribbled next to them. While she had made good use of the small space available, keeping her items neatly organized, it didn't lead to a minimalist approach; it was obvious that she liked to stock up on things. There were five or six unused boxes of rubber bands and Saran Wrap and countless pairs of chopsticks.

"I try to keep everything exactly as she left it," Kimura explained.

On closer inspection, I could see that most of the condiments were past their use-by dates. When I touched them, my hand felt sticky with dust. It was a reminder that, although the space looked as if Matsuko could walk in at any minute, it hadn't been in proper use for three whole years. It was as though the room was stuck in the past.

"Feel free to search anywhere you like. I believe my wife kept the cookbooks on the bookshelf opposite the back door," said Kimura. He glanced at his watch. "I do have to get to my store now."

I tapped my heart with my hand, hoping that the gesture would put him at ease.

"Don't you worry about anything. Leave it with me! I'm sure I'll find the recipe in no time. Call it chef's intuition."

"Are—are you sure?"

"Absolutely! You go over to your store now."

Although Kimura looked a little worried—actually, he looked really, really worried—he thanked us and headed out.

Two hours later, we had found nothing. Absolutely nothing.

"How? Why?"

Surely we should have found it by now.

"My eyes are getting blurry." Removing his glasses, Iori gave his right eye a rub.

Although he was still in his thirties, he was always complaining that he couldn't see small print clearly. He seemed to be having a hard time sifting through all the recipes.

Matsuko's bookshelf was packed tightly with cookbooks. Scanning the books, I counted roughly three hundred. She even had folders filled with cuttings from newspapers and cooking magazines.

I was pretty certain that we had gone through everything. I even got Hozumi—he was tall enough for it—to check the top of the bookshelf, to make sure nothing had been shoved away, but all we found were some old cans of vegetable juice covered in dust.

"Maybe she didn't keep a recipe of her umeboshi," Iori said, shrugging.

"It's possible. She made it every year, so she could have memorized it. Or maybe she threw it away?" Hozumi suggested.

"Should we take a break and go talk to Kimura, Momo-chan?"

Something didn't add up. A strange sensation swept through me; I felt that I was overlooking something very important.

I grabbed one of the cookbooks that was within my reach and flicked through the pages.

Most of the books had sticky notes in them. She had also marked the text with a pink highlighter, and sometimes made her own edits to the recipes—she neatly crossed out certain measurements and added comments like *make this two teaspoons.*

She was really passionate about cooking.

Her approach was comparable to that of a diligent researcher, sparing no effort in her cooking. The Matsuko that I imagined was the kind of person who put all her energy in every little thing she made.

Could it really be true that she didn't have a recipe for umeboshi? She had kept detailed notes of how to make nukazuke, jam, yuzu kosho seasoning, and even koji miso, so why not umeboshi?

Every day, Matsuko made umeboshi-filled onigiri for her husband, who worked tirelessly without ever taking time off. No matter the weather, he went into his shop, opened up the heavy boxes, and put the books up on the shelf. That umeboshi must have meant a lot to both of them.

"Isn't it unusual that the recipe for something so special is missing?" I asked. "Why would she keep a detailed record of everything except umeboshi? It doesn't make any sense. Umeboshi requires meticulous attention . . . I mean, I've never made them myself, but my grandma always said that the smallest difference in the amount of salt, or drying time, can change the flavor completely."

"So." Iori brought his hand to his chin and deliberated for a moment. "Are you saying that she wanted to keep it a secret from her family?"

I nodded my head in reply.

If it was me, where would I hide a recipe?

Suddenly, a memory I had long forgotten came back to me. Around the time I started getting into cooking, Grandma had said these words to me:

"Listen, Momoko. No matter how much you love spending time in the kitchen, make sure you set aside one drawer to yourself. And don't forget—that's your space. Don't you let anyone find it, all right?"

"I remember . . ."

My body started to move as if of its own accord. I walked over to the filing cabinet in the living room and, starting from the top, pulled each drawer open.

Probiotics, bandages, pens, nail clippers, ear pick. No, this isn't the one.

"There she goes again," Hozumi said.

"Err, Momo-chan, would you mind explaining to us what you're doing?" Iori asked.

I spoke as I opened another drawer.

"I once heard that for many women, privacy becomes a foreign concept once they have kids. They share their bedroom with their family. Even if the kids have their own rooms, and the husbands have their own office, there's no such thing as a mother's room. It's hard for women to create a private space for themselves. Eventually, even the mother *herself* becomes a thing that is shared. And the portion of her time and energy that's allocated for herself becomes smaller and smaller. It's important for women to try and consciously create a space that's not shared with anyone else, no matter how small."

"It's like that time when she told me she didn't need her own room because she'd be spending most of her time with her kid anyway . . ." Iori said out of nowhere, mumbling to himself.

I turned toward him. "Huh?"

Snapping back to reality, Iori clapped his hands.

"Right! Hozumi, let's help her look for the recipe."

He rolled up the sleeves on his shirt and resumed searching for the recipe beside me.

It appeared that Kimura had been spending a lot of his time at the dining table. On it were piles of books as well as his ledger, and a contact book listing publishers' phone numbers. I opened up a box file containing documents, though it was unlikely the recipe was going to be there. It was full of thin strips of paper folded in half.

"What are these?"

There was text printed on each strip: the title of a book, the name of a publisher, and the price. They were the size of a bookmark. I was pretty sure I had seen them at the till of a bookstore.

"They're what you call 'slips,'" Hozumi said, poking his head out from behind me. "You can find them inserted in most newly published books. They're used to tally up the number of copies sold. Whenever someone buys a book, the bookseller removes the slip from it and holds on to it. It's a handy way of tracking the books you've sold and how many."

"You sound like you're a bookseller yourself."

"Didn't I tell you? I worked in a bookstore when I was a university student."

"Ohhhhhh!"

"What?"

"It's just very fitting. You're *exactly* that type of guy."

"What is that supposed to mean?" Hozumi retorted.

He picked up the slips and flicked through them.

"I used to write notes on them," he said. "Whenever I couldn't find a notepad, I would use the slips instead."

"Are you allowed to do that?"

"Technically, no. But sometimes I needed to quickly jot something down while on the phone, and there was usually a slip or two around."

Iori called out abruptly. "Momo-chan. Hozumi. Come here!"

I looked up but couldn't see him anywhere. The living room door was open.

"This way," he shouted again.

Just outside the living room were traditional sliding doors. Iori popped his head out through the doors.

"Did you find it?" I asked.

"I haven't checked yet."

Iori told me to come in, and I entered the room. It was a square Japanese-style room of four and a half tatami mats. My nose started to tickle as soon as I walked in. Judging from the musty smell, the room hadn't been used in a while. A thick layer of dust covered an ancient-looking massage chair. There was a glass display case, and in it was a stuffed bird. I accidentally locked eyes with it and shuddered.

"I thought this might be the secret place that she didn't share with anyone else," Iori explained.

I shifted my gaze to the direction he was pointing to find a traditional dressing table. It was pretty compact in size, slightly bigger than the width of my shoulders. It had a mirror and a few drawers. In front of it was an upholstered square stool covered in velour.

"A woman's dressing table is something of a special place, isn't it? Kimura would probably never go anywhere near it, either. What do you think? A good place to check for the recipe?" Iori posed hopefully.

Of course. How did I not think of this before?

A dressing table was where women would sit in front of the mirror, put on makeup, and switch themselves on. Then, once the children were asleep, they would sit here again, this time to unwind.

I brought my hand to the drawer.

This must be it. The recipe is here. My intuition is telling me so.

My throat was drying up. I swallowed, but I couldn't feel anything. It was as if the back of my throat was closing up.

"I'm opening it."

Tightly gripping the drawer, I tugged it toward me.

Just like in the kitchen, it was packed with stuff. A retractable lipstick, face powder, eyebrow pencil . . . but there was nothing that resembled a recipe.

"What about those?" Iori pointed to some smaller drawers.

I opened up all of the ones on the right-hand side. Still nothing.

"Damn, I thought this was a pretty good guess. Now we're back to square one," Iori said, vigorously scratching the back of his head as he set himself down on the stool. "What should we do now, Momo-chan?"

I thought for a moment, staring at Iori shrugging his shoulders.

I could have sworn that we were on to something. It even felt as though Matsuko was calling me.

So much for that "intuition" of mine. But I guess her children could have opened these drawers. She would have needed something better, a kind of secret storage.

Secret storage . . .

Secret storage?

"That . . ."

"Huh?"

Walking on my knees, I moved closer to Iori.

"What is it, Momo—"

"That!" I pointed at the square stool Iori was sitting on.

"Move over," I said to him. "Some of these stools have storage space inside them."

I grabbed the upholstered seat and lifted it. It was hollow.

"Aha. There's something inside!"

"It looked just like a normal stool."

I pushed the stool directly under the light and peered into the newly discovered square hole. I rubbed my sweaty palms on the thighs of my jeans.

Slowly, I slid my hand inside.

A notebook.

On its cover was a title, inscribed in that same beautiful handwriting I had seen on the fridge.

"It says *Yasu . . . nari . . .*"

Hozumi said, "I think it says *Yasunari Notes.*"

"Yasunari . . ." I said, exchanging glances with Iori and Hozumi. "That's Kimura's first name, isn't it?"

I took a breath and looked upward.

"Matsuko, please excuse us for taking a peek. I just want to see if you've left the umeboshi recipe in here."

I pressed my palms together and bowed to the notebook before swiftly turning the cover.

"This is . . ."

H15. 11.15

HOW TO MAKE KARAAGE LIKE A PROFESSIONAL

"H15? Like year fifteen of the Heisei era? That's 2003!" I said.

"She started this notebook a long time ago."

I could now see how old it was. The edge of the pages had browned. A tiny silverfish crawled across the page, just above the word "karaage."

"There's something on the other side."

I suddenly noticed a small bump on the other side of the page with the karaage recipe. Turning the page, I found the same strip of paper we saw earlier on the dining table.

"What do you call these again, Hozumi?"

"Slips. We call them sales slips."

For some reason, the piece of paper was neatly taped to the page. The book title on the slip was *Junior High School English Vocabulary (Advanced).*

She had kept it safely tucked away in her notebook. But why?

"Was she studying English or something?" I pondered.

"Hang on," Hozumi said, and reached his hand out, lifting up the upper corner of the slip.

My heart skipped a beat.

Something was written on the back in thick black marker.

Dear Matsuko

Thank you for lunch
Your delicious karaage brightened my day
Thank you, as always

Yours sincerely
Yasunari

I covered my mouth with my hand reflexively.

"Oh my God. It's a love letter."

There was no doubt the message inside the narrow piece of paper was a letter from Kimura to Matsuko. His penmanship was even neater than Matsuko's.

She had also written a note on the page.

Iori, putting his glasses back on, read the words out loud.

"Let's see. 'It was chilly today, so I made karaage, Yasunari's favorite. Pleased to hear that it brightened his day. The children loved it also. Thank you, my dearest Yasunari.' "

"Such a nice couple," Hozumi said.

"Yeah. Look at all the other pages—they all have slips taped to them. Who knew Kimura was such a romantic, right, Momo-chan? Wait, Momo-chan, are you . . ."

"You're crying already?" Hozumi interjected.

"I can't help it!"

I tilted my head back so as not to ruin the notebook with my dripping tears and mucus.

Stop making me cry, Kimura!

Going through the notebook, we realized that the slips were taped to a compilation of Kimura's favorite recipes. It became clear that the division of labor worked like this: Kimura took responsibility of running the bookselling business, while Matsuko was in charge of running the household and raising the children. With their lives being so busy, the couple probably didn't get much chance to have a proper conversation with each other.

I imagined Kimura returning his empty lunch box to the kitchen at the end of each long day, leaving with it a message written on the back of a slip just for Matsuko's eyes.

Matsuko had kept every message. The ones she didn't manage to put in her notebook were tucked away in bundles inside the stool.

I turned to the very last page of the notebook, and there it was.

"It's here. We found it!"

"Finally," Iori said.

"This was probably the most challenging request we took on as the Funeral Committee," Hozumi added.

"We haven't finished yet! We now have to make the umeboshi!" I said.

How are you, Grandma? How are things in heaven?

It's Friday, July 29th. It's a beautiful sunny day in Tokyo. The sky is so blue that it's almost unreal. If I were to make a painting of it and submit it to an art competition, the judge would probably make a sneering comment like "The colors of the sky are more complex than this." It's absolutely scorching, but it's the perfect weather for sun-drying the umeboshi outside. I couldn't have asked for a better day for it.

It's been one month since we visited Kimura's house.

I had no idea how arduous umeboshi-making is! As you probably know, I had to pickle the plums with salt first, then with red shiso leaves. I then laid them out on strainers made of bamboo and took them to the rooftop of Amayadori's building, leaving them to sun-dry. When it was time to turn them over, Iori and Hozumi came out to help. It was so much fun (except for the part where Hozumi's scalp got red from the sun).

Today is the final day. When we bring the umeboshi inside tonight, they should be ready. I can't wait. I think Kimura can finally be at peace.

I wish you could have some, too, Grandma.

Actually, it would've been nice if you had been here to help me make them.

In fact, I'd love to hire you, Grandma.

You worked so fast, you would have been a great help. If you were here, I'm sure you would have had all these orders ready in no time.

I'll tell you what, Grandma, why don't you send your résumé to Amayadori from heaven and—

"—chan! Are you listening? Momo-chan! Another plate of curry and a cheesy hamburger steak, please. And the customer wants potato salad with their curry. Hello? Can you hear me? Momo-chan. Momoko-san. Momoko Yuuki!"

Iori stood in front of me, wearing a worried expression. The café was absolutely packed—all the tables and every seat at the counter were occupied. A never-ending line of customers had formed outside the window.

Iori clapped his palms together in my face. *Smack.*

"Are you all right, Momo-chan? You don't have heatstroke, do you?"

Reflexively, Iori tried to feel my forehead with his palm, and I snapped back to my senses.

I've had no time to use blotting paper on my face today. If I let Iori touch my greasy forehead, a part of me will die.

"I'm sorry, Iori. I'm fine! It's just been so busy. I got lost daydreaming."

I turned my head away from him just in time and got started on the curry order.

I need to regain my sanity.

I'd been working nonstop since the morning. The inside of my T-shirt was damp with sweat, but I couldn't even find the time to get changed. Considering how empty this place was six months ago, it was a nice problem to have. I just had to focus on getting through the busy hours.

"I don't blame you. I never imagined we'd get so popular."

Opening the fridge door, Iori promptly filled two glasses with ice.

Amayadori was having its busiest day ever.

The café had appeared on television—a comedian visited Amayadori as part of a prime-time variety show featuring hidden spots around the city, and that show had aired the night before. I was hopeful that it would draw in more customers, but I never imagined so many people would turn up. I'd asked Hozumi to give us a hand, busing tables and taking orders, and though he agreed to join us later in the evening and on Saturday and Sunday, he couldn't come any earlier because he had some chanting to do. Which meant it was going to be just Iori and me for a while.

But hey, we can do this!

"I know it feels like we're in hell right now," I said, casting a glance at Iori while flipping over a hamburger patty, "but we're going to make our biggest total sales today. And the umeboshi drying outside is almost ready. We'll be able to try them in the evening. I can finally make that onigiri for Kimura. Today is going to be an amazing day. That glass of beer we're going to have tonight is going to taste so good!"

"Only you can say something so positive at a time like this."

Iori flashed a wary smile as he ladled the soup and dished out the salad for a lunch set order.

"I'm just pre-celebrating that it-was-worth-it feeling we're going to experience later."

Iori let out a chuckle. "I like how your mind works. I always have."

I was flattered and surprised by the compliment.

"Have I said something like this before?"

"Maybe not, but you do always seem to have a turn-lemons-into-lemonade attitude about life."

"Well, just like in cooking, you need all kinds of flavors in life, even the bitter or astringent ones. Otherwise your repertoire is going to be very limited." Looking back on my life, I'd always managed to overcome hurdles in this way.

As I opened the rice cooker, I wondered if I had sounded like I was trying to act cool, and felt a wave of embarrassment.

But the tide of customers showed no sign of receding, and I couldn't dwell on it. We would need to use the ingredients stocked up for the weekend, but that should just about cover it, I calculated in my head. My hands were moving on autopilot.

"Oh, Momo-chan?" Iori uttered, as if he'd just remembered something. He placed empty glasses and dishes in the sink. "Didn't Hozumi say something about it always raining on days we have the Funeral Committee meetings?"

I was about to sprinkle cheese over the hamburger steak, but my hand stopped short.

"D-don't say that. You're going to jinx it."

"Well, it's kind of true, isn't it? It always rains."

No. No, no, no.

But he was right. On the days we had the Funeral Committee meetings, it rained at least once during the day. It was as though the gods were expected to hit some sort of quota, and they were going out of their way to make sure we got some form of rain, whether it was a downpour or a bit of drizzle.

"The umeboshi on the rooftop will be ruined if they get wet, won't they?" he worried.

In umeboshi-making, there is a custom known as doyo-boshi, the airing out of umeboshi during the period of "summer doyo," which starts around July 20th and ends around August 6th every year. It is said that this is the best time for it, as drying the plums under the hot sun after the humidity of the rainy season has passed is the key to making the most delicious and storable umeboshi. In one of her notes, Matsuko had written with heavy pressure, *Oh, dear, I'm running behind this year. Must have them dried before the end of July!!*

I had planned on putting the plums outside as soon as we entered the doyo period, but oddly, the sky remained cloudy, and on some days it even sprinkled. There hadn't been a single day that I could call sunny until three days ago, when I was finally able to place the plums outside.

"I-I'm sure it was just a coincidence! I mean, it's scorching outside. I checked the forecast earlier, too. I know that the rain seems to follow me everywhere, but I really don't think that's going to happen *today*."

"Okay then." Iori shrugged, then went to attend the next customer in line.

But I couldn't stop thinking about what Iori had said and grew more worried. Even the hot bubbles of cheese melting on the hot plate reminded me of raindrops hitting the concrete.

I'll check, just in case. Really, I can't stress enough how unnecessary this is, but I'll do it, just for peace of mind. You know, just in case.

I placed the plate of cheesy hamburger steak on the counter. Then, before a new order could come in, I quickly pulled my phone out and tapped on the weather app.

"The forecast in Setagaya . . ." I mumbled to myself as I scrolled.

There's no way it's going to rain.

"Sunny with . . . scattered rain."

Huh? This can't be. I swear, it said it would be sunny—and only sunny—when I checked this morning!

Weather forecasters get it wrong all the time. I'm sure they got this one wrong, too . . .

A voice called out.

"Excuse me, do you have a spare umbrella I could borrow?"

And just like that, I was in hell.

"It's started raining out of nowhere. None of us have umbrellas," another customer added, clearly unhappy.

I don't believe this!

When I turned around, I saw that the customers who had left just a few minutes before were poking their faces through the door. One of them pressed a handkerchief to her bangs, and I could see that the tips of her hair were slightly wet.

It was true.

Rain. Big drops of rain.

I could see it through the window. I could see the needles of rain falling to the ground.

My phone slipped out of my hand, and I heard it hit the kitchen floor.

Calm down. You have to get it together and quickly bring the plums inside.

Another customer: "Is that rain?"

"Oh, dear, I've left the laundry outside!"

The first group to get up were local ladies, who had been lingering and chatting away, even *after* they'd finished their lunch and coffee.

"So sudden."

"Oh, gosh, it's really coming down!"

One after another, the ladies spoke loudly, causing other customers who had finished eating to also get up in a hurry.

"Please wait your turn to pay, thank you!" I shouted, attempting to control the chaos.

This can't be happening!

Please, not now. Let me get to my umeboshi!

My prayers were in vain. Thanks to the ladies, a long line formed by the till, people eager to pay and get out before the rain became worse.

Although the ladies were beloved regulars of Amayadori—they visited the café at least four times a week to see Iori—at that very moment, I wanted to kill them.

I mean, the fate of our umeboshi was hanging by a thread.

Please, I just need to slip away for a moment to go and save them . . .

But I couldn't do it. Despite the sudden rain, the customers in the line that had spilled outside were still waiting. They'd gone out of their way to come to Amayadori. There was no way I could just leave them.

It was over.

Our umeboshi. Our precious umeboshi!

Everything that had happened in the last month flashed before my eyes.

I pictured the three of us plucking the stems off the plums one by one. Because we would be spending long stretches of time on the rooftop, we had borrowed camping equipment from the café owner and used it to build a small workspace. It took us all night to put up the tent. My poor skin even got badly sunburned.

My God, it was arduous. Of all the dishes I had cooked in my life, umeboshi-making was hands down the most exhausting.

Is this how artists feel when the sculpture they've put their heart into gets smashed to pieces?

I'm sorry, Kimura. I'm so sorry.

Even though I was drowning in tears inside, my body moved seamlessly around the café, my energetic voice ringing out as I served the customers. It seemed that whatever happened, I was always going to be well-suited for this job. That was one thing I could be sure of.

"Why don't you go up already?" Iori asked after the rush hour had settled.

"I don't want to see it."

"I thought you said life was better with the bitter and astringent flavors."

"Oh, I didn't actually mean that," I replied. "I just got carried away."

"What is this depressing creature, and what have you done with Momoko?"

Hozumi walked in. "Don't tell me you—"

"Yes, the umeboshi got wet from the rain . . ." Iori whispered to him. "We haven't gone to see them yet."

Hozumi's eyes filled with pity as he looked at me.

"The rain follows me everywhere," I said. "I'm a failure. I'm not good at anything."

Had things gone to plan, we would be checking in on the umeboshi right now. I could be saying fun things like "They're nearly ready!" and could have pinched one to try. We could have taken bowls of rice with us and sampled the umeboshi and shiso leaves on the rooftop.

And the Funeral Committee meeting could have gone on as planned.

Iori, seemingly tired of waiting, sighed.

"Hozumi, could you take her up? I'll stay here and mind the café."

"I guess I have no choice," Hozumi replied. "Come on, let's go."

"Ugh . . ."

With Hozumi's help, I somehow managed to drag myself out of my seat. Taking my time, I followed him outside to the staircase next to the café door. I trudged up the stairs.

Each time I lifted my foot, my mind brought back a memory.

"You can make them again," Hozumi said without turning around.

"I can't anymore. Not this year. The plums are out of season now."

"Make them next year, then."

"We're going to make Kimura wait another year?"

"It will just give him another thing to look forward to. Motivate him even more to live a long life."

His words made me shed yet another tear.

I know that I have to accept it. Stuff like this happens all the time.

If anything, things had been going too well. I had gotten cocky, thinking that I had the skills to re-create any dish. I had underestimated the art of cooking. Even with umeboshi, I didn't doubt for a moment that I would be able to do it. I'd had no idea how much work went into making them.

We were finally on the rooftop terrace. The rusty iron railing was still wet with rain.

I dropped my gaze, unable to face the reality. My legs refused to move.

Then I heard Hozumi say, "They're gone."

"What did you just say?"

"They aren't on the terrace. You put them there, didn't you?"

I turned in the direction Hozumi was pointing.

The umeboshi were nowhere to be seen. There must have been around eighty plums, divided equally between two large bamboo strainers. But everything had vanished without a trace. All I could see was the wet rubber covering on the ground.

"Did someone steal them?" I wondered out loud.

"Why would anyone want to steal two whole strainers worth of umeboshi?"

"True."

Calm down, I told myself. *With it being so hot, maybe I did something in a moment of madness.*

I scanned around.

Maybe I moved them somewhere without even realizing it, I thought to myself as I glanced behind the clutter of camping equipment.

At that moment, I locked eyes with the plumpest, sourest-looking umeboshi.

"They're . . . here. They're here! I found them!"

All eighty of them were nestling under the tent as if they'd been enshrined there.

With trembling fingers, I checked the condition of each plum one by one. They were fine. No sign of mold. They hadn't gotten wet at all!

It felt like I'd just been reunited with my lost children. A wave of relief washed over me, and I sank down to the ground.

"But . . . how?"

Had someone moved them here before it started to rain? It wasn't Iori or Hozumi, so who could it be?

Hozumi suddenly reached his arm out.

"Look at this, Momoko."

There was a piece of paper attached to the rim of one of the strainers. It was a sales slip, like the ones we saw in Kimura's house. Printed on it was the title of a recent bestseller. I flipped it open to find a short message inside:

I could smell the rain

I moved them inside

Kimura

It was written in a black marker with a rather scrawly hand. He'd probably come in a hurry and written the note spontaneously.

"Kimura!"

He smelled the rain? Wow. Never underestimate a man who's kept his business running in the shopping district for fifty years!

"Oh my God. How cool is he? No wonder Matsuko fell for him!"

I broke into full tears, holding nothing back.

Enveloped in the sweet and tangy scent of the plums, I felt like thanking the whole universe.

"Where did you get these . . . ?"

As I set down the bento box wrapped in indigo-colored furoshiki on the table, Kimura widened his eyes, as though he'd just seen something unworldly.

"It was all written in Matsuko's notebook, which we found and took the liberty of reading, hoping to get some clues. Your favorite color, the way you like your onigiri shaped, the type of bento box. She didn't miss a thing."

Thanks to her methodical personality, I was pretty confident that this was a faithful re-creation.

Kimura reached his hand out ever so slowly. Hesitating, he closed his bony hand into a tight ball, turning his worried gaze toward me. I gave him an enthusiastic nod to keep going. In response, he finally brought his hand to the knot tying the furoshiki.

The soothing whispers of the fabric drifted into my ears as he loosened the knot and opened up the square cloth. Kimura inhaled, filling up his lungs.

"She . . . Matsuko also—"

A pair of onigiri, wrapped in foil, sat atop the oval-shaped bento box made of wood.

"Matsuko also used these, err, silver things . . ."

"Do you mean the aluminum foil?"

"Yes, yes. Aluminum foil."

"That was in Matsuko's notes, too. Normally, I put Saran Wrap around them, but according to Matsuko, it has to be aluminum foil. Otherwise, the nori will get too soggy."

"Is that so? I had no idea . . ."

Starting from the edge, Kimura began to peel off the foil with his thumb. He seemed to struggle with the fingers on his right hand. He slowly removed the thin metal in stiff movements.

Finally, the white tip of the onigiri peeped out.

The onigiri, Matsuko wrote, should be shaped gently by hand into a triangle, once the freshly cooked white rice had cooled down. She had particular rules about how the rice should be pressed together, and I had followed her instructions as loyally as possible.

Kimura had said that he "had no idea" about Matsuko's efforts, but perhaps that was because she was so good at hiding them. Perhaps she didn't want her family to see the hard work she had put into her cooking. She didn't want them to know about the long journey that got her to the amazing chef she was. She had wanted to make it look easy.

At least, that was the feeling that I got. Why else would she go through the trouble of hiding her recipes so well?

"There's a magic spell," I said to Kimura. Apparently still nervous, he was holding the onigiri with both hands as he sat motionlessly.

"A magic spell?"

"There was a magic spell that Matsuko used to say every day when she made the onigiri. Did you ever hear it?"

Kimura, still in the same position, shook his head softly.

"It goes like this," I said, pressing together an invisible onigiri.

"God of Onigiri, please let Yasunari have another day of delicious meals."

"God of Onigiri? That's sweet." Iori chuckled.

"Well, there is that ancient belief that every grain of rice is inhabited by seven gods," Hozumi said.

If this were true, then it would mean that the onigiri is inhabited with enough gods to fill an entire concert hall. That sounded as though it could bring a lot of good fortune.

"Apparently, you chant this magic spell while pressing the rice together, and it makes the onigiri really tasty. I did it, too."

Kimura looked as though he had finally made up his mind. Slowly, he moved the onigiri to his mouth. I'd done everything I could do. I was sure of that. But the tiniest of differences can greatly influence the flavor of a dish. All I could do now was pray, pray to the God of Onigiri.

Gently, Kimura bit into the onigiri and chewed quietly. Then he took another nibble. And another.

And then, on his fourth bite, he ate a big mouthful, and scrunched up his face.

Kimura lowered his gaze to the half-eaten onigiri, surprised, watching the bright crimson umeboshi filling spill out. Just the sight of it made my mouth water and gave me a sore throat.

The more Kimura ate, the more scrunched up his face became, just like the wrinkly umeboshi.

"Oh," Kimura gasped, "that is sour."

The rest of us exchanged glances and burst into laughter.

I couldn't blame him. Matsuko's umeboshi was nothing like the store-bought ones, which are often sweetened with honey. Hers were done the proper old-fashioned way, making them thoroughly sour and salty. They were so sour that, when we each tried one earlier, our eyes squeezed shut and our lips puckered up like the mythical Hyottoko. It took a while for our usual faces to return.

It seemed as if Kimura was feeling the same effects. He squirmed in his seat, making gasping noises. He opened the oval lid of his bento box and reached for a piece of rolled omelet, probably in an attempt to neutralize his palate.

He wolfed down the rest of his onigiri, then peeled the foil off the second onigiri and bit into it. He ate some karaage, then, using his chopsticks, deftly carried the simmered hijiki seaweed and soybeans into his mouth before taking another bite of the onigiri.

Who knew he was capable of such a hearty appetite? I thought, watching him eat with surprising gusto.

Once he had eaten about half of his second onigiri, he suddenly stopped and lowered his gaze.

He sat seemingly paralyzed, still holding his chopsticks in his right hand, and the onigiri in his left hand.

"Oh, my, that is sour," he said.

A single teardrop fell on the umeboshi.

"This really takes me back." Kimura was laughing and crying as his face contorted. A waterway formed on his face, and tears slowly descended along the creases of his skin. A small cluster of rice fell from the side of his mouth and landed on the furoshiki.

"It's so sour, it's making me cry." He took another big bite of the onigiri, despite his wet eyes and drippy nose.

I was so relieved.

I brought out the extra onigiri I had made from the kitchen and put them down on the table.

"Shall we have some, too?"

"Yes, let's," Iori replied.

"I've worked up an appetite just from watching you eat, Kimura," said Hozumi.

Several bites into the fluffy rice, a burst of tanginess filled my mouth.

"Wow, that is sour. It's really, really sour," said Iori.

"My God, Matsuko is relentless," Kimura chortled.

Another day of delicious meals.

I felt that I understood how Matsuko felt. Being able to enjoy every meal of the day is something we take for granted, even though it's not always easy to do. There are days when you feel so down that you lose your appetite. Sometimes life gets so tough, everything you eat becomes tasteless.

"I'm going to make umeboshi next year," I said to Kimura. "I'll never stop making them." The words were tumbling out of my mouth.

"I'm going to make them every year just the way Matsuko intended, and serve them at Amayadori. You can come anytime if you ever feel like eating them."

Kimura looked at me intently, his eyes red with tears.

Then he crinkled his face up into a smile. "I'll hold you to that," he said. "I'm going to come here every day, then."

"I'll give you more coupons," Iori chimed in.

"Will you? You are really something, young man."

I interjected, "Not a chance! You have to pay!"

"Here we go again . . ." Hozumi said, rolling his eyes playfully.

Making sure that all meals are delicious. Enjoying meals with the people I love. Maybe this is what happiness means to me.

My mind wandered through these thoughts as we tucked into the onigiri.

It was so sour, even my heart squeezed inside my chest.

GRANDMA'S SECRET UMEBOSHI

- $4^1/_2$ pounds (2 kg) ripe ume plums
- $3^1/_2$ tablespoons (50 ml) Japanese white liquor*
- 12 ounces (360 g) coarse salt, for the ume (18% of the weight of the plums)
- 15 ounces (400 g) red shiso leaves (20% of the weight of the plums)
- 3 ounces (80 g) salt, for the shiso (20% of the weight of the shiso)

Bowls, lidded container, weights, bamboo strainer for drying (Should be as heavy as the ume if using ripened ones. If using underripe ones, should be twice the weight of the ume.)

* NOTE: White liquor is a type of flavorless spirit sold in Japan. This is preferred as it will not affect the flavor of the umeboshi. However, an alternative liquor can be used, as long as the alcohol content is more than 35%.

METHOD

PREPARING THE UME

Wipe off any moisture from the ume. Remove the stems, then wash in cold water.

Put the ume into a bowl and sprinkle with the white liquor. Layer the bottom of a container with salt, then layer the ume on top. Repeat, increasing the amount of salt for each layer, and then sprinkle the remaining salt on the final layer. Put the lid over it and weigh it down. Cover with paper and store in a cool and dry place for at least seven days. Once there is enough liquid (ume vinegar), remove half of the weight. Make sure the ume remains completely submerged in the liquid when doing so.

PREPARING THE RED SHISO LEAVES

Remove the stems from the red shiso leaves and wash the leaves in cold water, changing the water around three times. Thoroughly wipe the leaves dry.

Put the red shiso leaves into a large bowl (the larger the better) and add half of the salt. Mix with your hands, massaging the salt into the leaves, until a murky purple liquid is produced. Squeeze the leaves well, then drain the liquid. Return the leaves to the same bowl. Massage in the remaining salt, then drain the liquid again.

ADDING THE RED SHISO LEAVES TO THE UME

Open the ume container and transfer the liquid produced (ume vinegar) into another container, leaving enough liquid to keep the ume submerged. Put the red shiso leaves into a bowl and pour in enough ume vinegar to cover the leaves. Lightly massage and separate the leaves. A red-colored liquid will be produced.

Top the ume with the red shiso leaves, then pour over the red liquid. Put the inner lid on. Push in the shiso leaves if any are poking out from the rim. Put a light weight over it and leave for two weeks until the rainy season is over.

DOYO-BOSHI: SUN-DRYING FOR THREE DAYS AND THREE NIGHTS

Pick three consecutive sunny days for this step. First, remove the shiso leaves and squeeze out the liquid. Then place the ume into a strainer and drain the red ume vinegar back into the container. Lay out the shiso leaves and ume on a bamboo strainer (drying basket) and leave them in a sunny spot outdoors. Turn over the ume once during the day, so that both sides are exposed to the sun. Also expose the red ume vinegar remaining in the container to the sun.

On day one, return the ume to the container while the red ume vinegar is still warm, and bring the container indoors.

On day two, sun-dry the ume again. In the evening, bring the shiso leaves indoors. Leave the ume outdoors overnight and expose them to the humidity of the night air. Repeat the same process on day three. Pass the red ume vinegar through a sieve, store in a jar or a suitable container, and keep refrigerated to be used in cooking.

To test the umeboshi for readiness, lightly pinch the skin. If it feels soft and doesn't tear, they are ready. Put the umeboshi into a traditional ceramic jar and store in a cool, dark place.

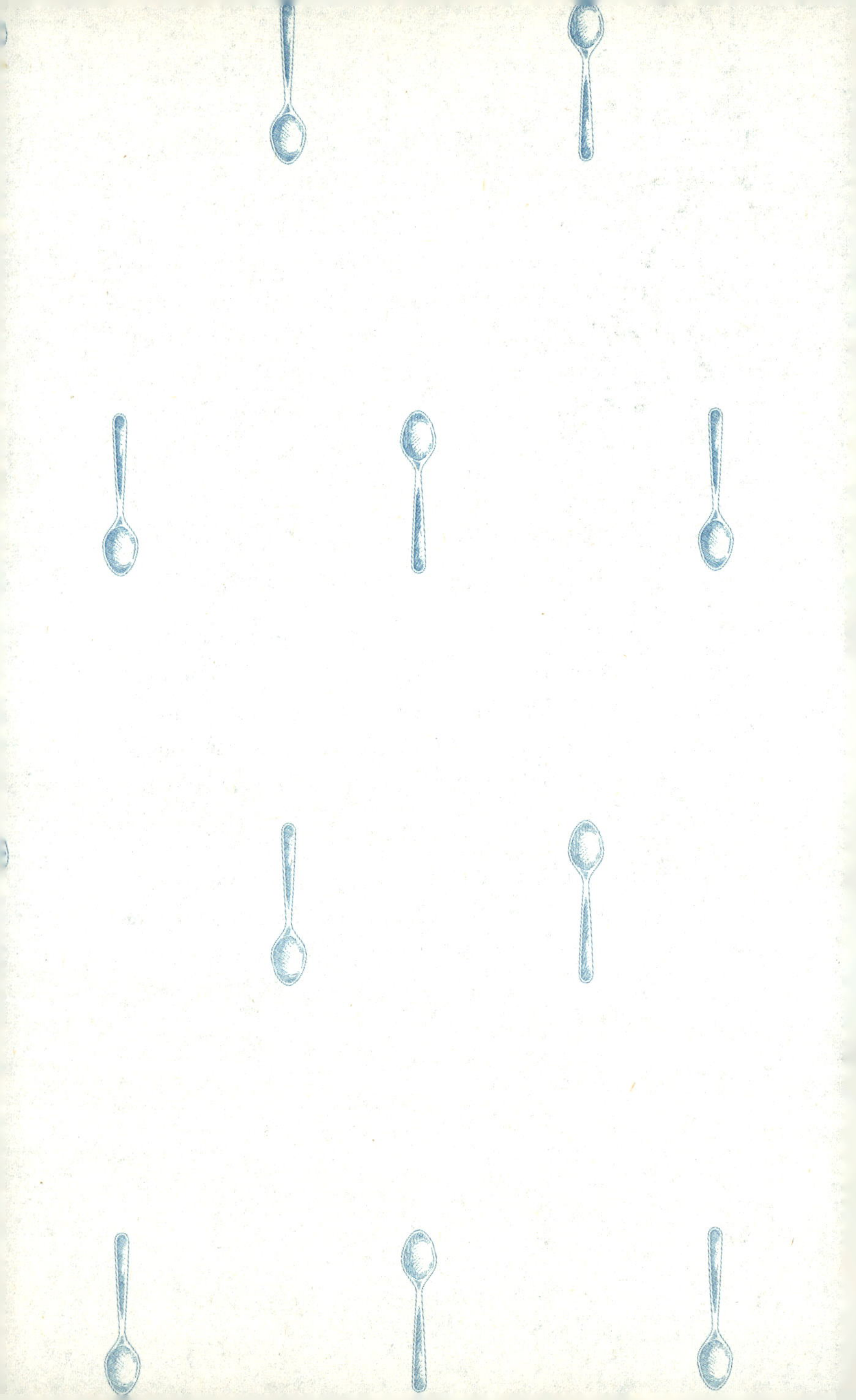

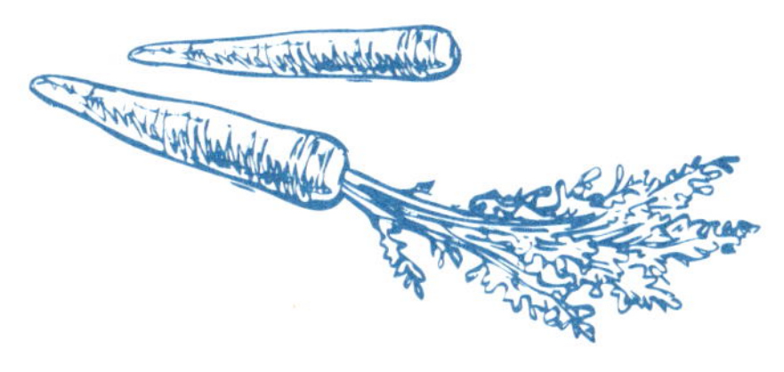

CHAPTER 5

THE VIEW BEYOND FRIENDSHIP CARROT CAKE

Again, Iori didn't pick up. It was the sixth time I'd called him.

"Still not answering?" Hozumi asked.

"The one time we really need him . . ." I bit my nails.

What are we going to do? Maybe we should contact the police.

I turned around to face the little girl, who was sitting on the sofa and idly gazing out the window. I sighed.

We had met her a few hours ago.

My dad had sent me a box full of fresh vegetables from home, and I had asked Hozumi to help me carry it to Amayadori. We staggered our way to the café, clumsily lugging the heavy box together. Upon arriving, we saw a small figure sitting curled up by the entrance. It was a young girl, probably in her third year of elementary school.

There was a somewhat ethereal quality to her. She wore her long hair in braids that hung below her shoulders. Judging from the T-shirt tan and sunburn that ran from her arms to the tips of her fingers, she probably got to play a lot over the summer vacation. Her face, on the other hand, was clear and pale, as though it had been edited using a filter app. She reminded me of an angel.

Clutched in her hands, unusually, was a snow globe. She kept shaking it back and forth, letting the glitter inside the glass sphere dance like confetti.

I squatted down next to her to meet her eyes. When I said hello, she opened her mouth slightly, but quickly pursed her thin lips and averted her eyes.

Hozumi and I tried every trick in the book to get her to speak, but none of it worked. She remained in the same position, staring into her snow globe.

"I'm worried she'll get sick from the heat," Hozumi said. "For now, let's just get her inside. When Iori comes in later, we can decide if we should call the police. He seems like the type who's good with children."

And so here I was, trying get ahold of Iori. I had texted him and called, but he wasn't answering. He had mentioned that he had some errand to run, although, per the rota, he was supposed to be working.

Why did he have to choose today of all days to be MIA?

The girl headed for the bathroom. She'd been before—she had been here that long. Outside, the sun had shifted. I looked toward the house opposite the café. A small tree peeking over its fence was now casting a shadow. Unable to wait any longer, I pulled out my phone, ready to call the police.

At that moment, the door flung open noisily.

"It's boiling! Let's hit the beach!"

In walked Iori.

Finally!

"Where have you been? We were waiting for—hey, why are you dressed like that?"

I had never seen Iori in a suit before. He wore a formal jacket in black and a starched shirt. His bangs, which normally hung loosely around his face, were neatly combed back, fully exposing his chiseled features.

"Oh, this? I was just running an errand. God, it's hot." Iori slipped his tie off and loosened his collar.

"How do I look? Not bad, right?" Iori continued, winking at Hozumi for no logical reason.

Hozumi waved him away annoyedly. Dismissing Iori's narcissistic comment, he cut to the chase. "Actually, something has happened. There's a little girl here and we don't know who she is or what to do."

"A girl?"

Iori pulled off his jacket and hung it over the backrest of a barstool, then rolled up his sleeves. I could see that his face had turned red, probably from the heat, so I poured him some water, filling the cup to the brim. He gulped it down and exhaled.

Hozumi and I gave him a summary of everything that had happened, explaining to him how we had found the girl sitting outside when we arrived at the café, and that she wouldn't reply to anything we said.

Having heard the story, Iori deliberated, placing a finger on his chin as he drank his second cup of water.

"I see. I hope we can find a way of helping her."

"Oh, I think she's coming."

Right on cue, we heard the tap shut off, and the girl reemerged from the back of the café. She walked toward us, drying her hands with a classy beige-colored handkerchief.

"Hi, sweetie," Iori said cheerfully, "my friends tell me you appeared out of nowhere . . ."

At this, the girl, who had been looking down at the floor, lifted her glance. She stopped short at the sight of Iori's face. Still gripping her handkerchief, she stared at Iori with eyes as clear as two amber marbles.

Iori sat paralyzed, his gaze fixed on the girl. It was as though the two of them were in their own world where time had stopped moving.

"What's going on, you two?" I asked.

"Shizuku . . . ?" Iori jumped out of his seat. He slowly approached her. "You *are* Shizuku, right?"

I had the feeling that something significant was happening before our eyes, though I didn't quite know what. I looked at Hozumi and gestured with my hands (*What the hell is going on?!*). He replied with a grim look (*How should I know?*).

The girl, who had been gazing at Iori with widened eyes, seemed to be finally convinced. Parting her small lips, she finally spoke.

"Daddy."

"Daddy?" Hozumi and I cried in unison.

What? Iori is a dad? This little girl is his daughter? It can't be!

How old is he again? I'm pretty sure he said he's thirty-three . . . I suppose he could have a daughter around the girl's age.

But still.

Iori lived in the apartment above Amayadori, which also doubled up as the café's office, so I'd been there a few times. It was a minimalist apartment, with no sign of someone else living with him. He only had one mug and one toothbrush (yes, I was looking).

"Shizuku, how did you know I would be here?"

Iori crouched down to meet the girl's level and gently took her hand—she softly brushed him away. Instead, she picked up the snow globe from the table.

"I didn't tell Mom. I didn't want her to get upset," said Shizuku.

"So you came on your own? It's a pretty long way."

"It was fine. It's not that far."

"All right. I'm proud of you for finding your way."

Iori lifted her hat and caressed her sweaty hair in a way that told me he had done it so many times before. I felt a little pang in my chest.

Iori had a world that belonged to him and only him—a world that I didn't have any part in.

Of course he did. Hozumi and I had our own worlds, too. Each of us was living our own life.

That's how things are, isn't it?

"Is this for me?" asked Iori.

Shizuku pushed the snow globe into Iori's hand.

"I wanted to give you something, since you've given me so many things."

"Isn't this—"

"I wanted to give you something for a change."

What a mature thing to say.

Shizuku quickly gathered her notebook and pencil case she had spread across the table and placed them into her backpack. While Iori stood there astonished, she promptly got herself ready. When she'd finished, she brushed the dust off her skirt and bowed deeply to us.

"Thank you for your hospitality."

Hozumi and I found ourselves bowing back. *Thank you for your hospitality?* I hadn't expected to hear such proper words from a little girl.

"Bye," Shizuku said, waving at Iori. She turned to head out the door in a manner that said *My business here is done.*

"Hey, wait! Shizuku!"

I watched as Iori hurried after her.

Turning to me, Hozumi dumbfoundedly said, "What just happened?" He spoke the exact thoughts that were going through my head.

A sense of tranquility had returned to Amayadori after Iori had run out, and it felt as if a weight had lifted off my shoulders. The two of us sat slumped over the counter. The whole conversation had lasted only a few minutes, but I was drained.

The hot afternoon sun poured in through the window, creating a parallelogram on the floor.

I searched my mind for the right word to describe what I had seen on Iori's face as the little girl walked out. *Sadness . . . ? Frustration . . . ?* Whatever you call it, it was the first time I had seen him look that way.

As if on cue, the gossip news program on TV started to give us the weather forecast:

"A low-pressure system is expected from this evening and overnight. If you're planning on going out tonight, be well prepared for rain."

"It always seems to rain on Funeral Committee nights." Crossing his arms, Hozumi spoke in an expressive tone, as though he were reciting a haiku.

"Didn't I tell you? No clients tonight. We don't have any bookings."

"Yes, we do. There's someone whose story we need to hear."

Someone whose story we need to hear . . .

Could he mean . . . ?

Now that I thought about it, I hardly knew anything about the man we called Iori Amamiya.

He is national-treasure-level hot and was hired as the manager of Amayadori a few years ago. There's someone else who owns the café, and he has a meeting with the owner a few times a month. If there is a story behind why he became manager, I've never heard it. Judging from the comments he makes during our Funeral Committee meetings, he never seems to have any problems finding romance, although currently he's not seeing anyone he would call his girlfriend (that I know of). Given how popular he is, there are probably plenty of women who would happily have a casual relationship with him, but he probably declines all offers.

That was what my (not so reliable) woman's instinct told me.

But do I know where he's from? No. Do I know anything about his past? No.

His hobby is . . . umm . . . coffee and . . . collecting coupons in the local shopping district?

What else do I know . . .

"Damn, I can't think of anything else," I said to myself.

After the incident, Iori returned to the café at around six o'clock, behaving as though nothing significant had happened. Although he acted in a nonchalant manner, he settled himself on the sofa at the back, where Shizuku had been sitting earlier, and kept toying with the snow globe she had given him. He stayed like that for hours. Even Adachi, who had come by to deliver our order of meats, asked worriedly, "He looks like he's turned into a ghost or something—is he all right?"

I was now alone in the café, staring off into the ceiling as I reflected on everything that had happened. It was almost ten o'clock, time for the Funeral Committee to gather.

That face. It wasn't the Iori I know.

The easygoing, nonchalant Iori who lived a carefree life had disappeared. The face he wore now was the face of a man who was worried about his daughter—it was the face of a father.

And that made me feel as though he had gone somewhere far away.

"How pathetic am I?" I mumbled to myself.

Hozumi's face suddenly came into my view.

"Why are you getting all melancholic?"

"Ahhh!"

I panicked, nearly falling off the sofa. I quickly straightened myself up.

"Don't sneak up on me like that!"

"I didn't? The door creaked as loudly as it usually does, *and* the bell rang out," Hozumi retorted, then plonked into the seat in front of me. "You seemed to be completely lost in thought."

"I was thinking maybe we shouldn't do this. Let's call Iori and tell him he doesn't need to come in, since there are no bookings."

"I'm sure he already knows what we're thinking about doing tonight. It was written all over your face."

"Seriously?" I touched my cheek instinctively.

"Besides," Hozumi said as he crossed his arms, "his daughter showed up, you know? I'm sure even he knows that he can't just *not* say anything."

"I don't want to make him talk about it if he doesn't want to. But maybe he does want to let it out. . . . Oh, I don't know."

As I groaned and cradled my head, Hozumi rose from his seat and disappeared into the kitchen. I heard him rummaging around for something, then he reemerged with two glasses filled with ice cubes and milky iced tea.

Without hesitation, he poured syrup into the glasses.

"Sugar is the best cure for an overworked brain."

He pushed one of the glasses toward me.

Although I wasn't thirsty, I brought my lips to the straw and sipped. It was nice and cold. The tip of my tongue tingled. The scent of tea and the sweetness of the sugar seeped into every corner of my tired body.

"You've known Iori much longer than I have, right?"

It seemed as if he and Iori had known each other a long time, but I had never asked.

"I don't know him that well, either," Hozumi said. "I've been a regular customer ever since this café opened its doors, but it's only recently that I started having proper conversations with him."

"Really?"

"Until we started doing the Funeral Committee, he was just the manager of a near-bankrupt café, and I was merely one of his local regulars. We said hello and made small talk, but that was about it."

Hozumi picked up the menu that was laid down on the table and flicked through it.

"Back then, there was hardly anything on the menu. It was just coffee, tea, ice cream soda. Not that it mattered to me—all I wanted was a quiet place to read."

I stirred my milky iced tea with my straw. The melting ice cubes shifted and clinked in my glass, emitting a soothing sound.

"You changed things," Hozumi said. "It was you who made this café a place where everyone belongs."

"What?" I was taken aback, unable to process his words.

"You wouldn't know, because you don't seem to have a problem with shouting out all your feelings to the world as you please, but there are a whole bunch of people out there who can't show their vulnerable side unless someone forces them to."

"Umm, is that a compliment?"

"Think about it," Hozumi went on. "Makiko, Nagi . . . remember how they were? Some people can't start talking about it—they're not able to realize what it is that is troubling them. Not until someone asks. Someone like you."

Now that he mentioned it, I realized that the clients of the Funeral

Committee came to us so that they could pour out the feelings that they'd been bottling up. Once we started to untangle those feelings, little by little, we would see the emotions buried deep within their hearts—emotions that hadn't been acknowledged, not just by others, but by the clients themselves.

People are inept at accepting pain and suffering.

They pretend to be grown-up. They pretend they're not needy. They pretend as though they can seamlessly switch between emotions. They don't know how else to live life.

"There are people who are in need of that somebody who will come in and track down the regret, loneliness, and insecurities they've long buried away," Hozumi said. "There are times when they need somebody like you, who can break into people's hearts with the vigor of a warrior brandishing a huge naginata sword."

"Wait—is that what people think of me?"

Hozumi leaned back in his chair and crossed his arms. "The point is, perhaps today is that day for Iori. And if so, you should be the one who listens to him."

Right.

Iori was the same.

Like the clients who had come to us, maybe he was hiding his true self. Maybe he was fighting through life pretending to be someone else.

"Don't you agree, President?"

It was the first time Hozumi had called me that.

"Sorry I'm late. The forecast said there were going to be light 'showers' today, but it doesn't look like this downpour rain is going to stop anytime soon."

Iori had changed his clothes, swapping his suit for his usual shirt and cotton pants. Brushing off the drops of rain on his shoulders, he lowered himself onto the sofa. "Who is our client again?"

"Oh, umm . . ."

Say it. Come on. Just be your usual bold self and tell him he's the client tonight.

But I couldn't. The words wouldn't come.

I lowered my gaze to find my hands trembling on my knees.

Maybe I was able to "break into people's hearts" before because I didn't know them that well. But Iori is different.

What if . . . what if Iori's feelings do become clear, and he decides to leave Amayadori and return to his family?

Then . . .

Where will I go?

"Momo-chan. Let me guess—I'm your client, right?"

Glancing up, I saw him grinning his usual smooth smile.

"I knew we didn't have any bookings today. I was just messing with you, sorry."

Iori's smile grew wider, trying to defuse the awkwardness in the air.

"Iori . . . if you don't want to talk about it—"

"I don't, to be honest."

The sound of rain, which at first was a light tapping, grew louder and louder. Soon it was pelting down.

"But," Iori continued after a beat, "if I hold on to this regret, it will continue to smolder in my heart, and life can get pretty hard when you have something like that trapped inside of you. It *has* been hard."

Iori shifted his eyes to the window.

"Maybe it's time I let the embers I'd kept going in my heart burn out."

Following Iori's gaze, Hozumi and I looked outside. Large drops of rain hit the concrete, making circular waves on the sidewalk over and over again.

"I didn't want to tell anyone about it, and didn't ever think I would. But I think now is the best time to talk, and the best people to talk to are you two."

Iori returned his gaze from the window and turned towards Hozumi and me.

"I will talk. I want to. I want you to hear it."

The grin had disappeared from his face.

"First of all, Shizuku isn't my biological daughter," Iori said in a tone that sounded as if he were confessing a crime. "But for a while I was something of a father figure to her. She's the daughter of Koharu . . . the person I love."

Biting his thin lips, Iori stared down at his palms. He seemed to be hoping that his next words would appear on the creases in his hands.

"Would you like something to drink?" I offered.

"Could you make me a coffee?"

Using Iori's favorite dark roasted beans, I made a hot cup of coffee and brought it to the table, along with additional servings of milky iced tea. Without saying anything, Iori drank the coffee in three sips.

"Koharu and I first met—let me see . . . seventeen years ago."

"That long ago?" I said in surprise. It would mean that they met when Iori was in high school. A thought crossed my mind.

"Was she your first love?"

Iori gave a tight-lipped smile, running his fingers over the handle of his cup.

"It's kind of a complicated story," Iori began. "I was raised by a single parent—my dad brought me up on his own. But when I was eight, he died in an accident while he was at work. Crushed by a forklift truck. After that, I went to live with my grandma."

My throat tightened. I swallowed drily.

"But then, just before I entered middle school, Grandma started to have problems with her memory. I also became her caregiver. I think this might be why I'm so good at getting others to help me. I learned from experience what kinds of things I needed to say in order for people to do me favors, and I *needed* those favors to survive. I hardly had the time to do my homework, you know? So I found the most efficient way of getting things done, like getting girls who liked me to take notes or do my homework for me."

"That's why . . ."

"Yeah. I'm good at swaying people, aren't I?"

Iori had a knack for negotiating with the people of the local shopping district. I once heard Adachi and his friends having a lively conversation about how they could never say no to Iori's requests. Without Iori's savvy networking skills, Amayadori may not have managed to stay afloat.

"Things were pretty bad. We were so broke. All we had was the money left over from my dad's insurance payout and my grandma's small pension, which was hardly enough to make ends meet. There was so much stuff to deal with every day, I once even reached my breaking point and briefly ran away from home."

Iori's tough upbringing came as a complete surprise to me.

"There came a point when I made a decision." Iori gently leaned his head against the window. "I decided to detach myself from all emotions. At home, and at my part-time job, I played the role of a sweet kid who adored his grandma. At school, I was the cheerful comic. To my girlfriend, a guy who had a sensitive and vulnerable side to him. Once I'd worked out the person that my counterpart wanted me to be, I chose the character I was going to play."

"Do you mean that you were switching back and forth between your true self and how you carried yourself in front of others?" Hozumi asked.

Iori crossed his arms and looked up. Leaning back against the sofa, he stared at the ceiling.

"It felt more like I was putting a lid over my true feelings—my true self. Whatever I did, I didn't want to feel the slightest bit of pain or suffering. I have really good looks, don't I? So I caught people's attention and was able to get what I wanted, even though it was exhausting. Eventually, I grew sick of it. I didn't want to do anything. I wanted people to leave me alone. I wanted to flee to a world where no one knew who I was."

A harsh coldness had developed in Iori's eyes.

"I wished that people would just say 'Is that so?' and end the conversation there. But as soon as I talked about my family, it was always 'that must have been tough' and 'you've had a hard life' and all that. That I didn't have a father, that I did all the housework at home, and that I looked after my grandma—these were just things that happened in my life. The idea that these were 'unfortunate events' had never even crossed my mind."

I tightened my grip on the glass I was holding. The back of my ears throbbed. Drips of condensation on my glass wet the base of my thumb.

"People wanted to see 'the heroic boy who puts on a brave face.' They would look at me expectantly, somewhat enjoying it. It gave them a kind of thrill. All the girls I went out with were the same. They would look into my eyes, wearing that face that says *Show me your vulnerable side. You can tell me anything.* And when I granted them their wish, they would squeeze my hand with a satisfied expression. They would stroke my head and say 'You've been so brave.' It gave them a rush, the feeling that they've been chosen as the person I've confided my painful experiences to, and they got a hell of a good cry out of it."

I had no words.

And that was because, at that moment, I was starting to feel a pounding in my chest. I was starting to feel the very thing he was describing.

I tried to repress my tears.

"I found it so repulsive I wanted to vomit. But even if I had said out loud everything I was thinking, what good would that have done? In the end, I realized that pretending like I would do anything for Grandma, and pretending like I was 'putting on a brave face' so that others wouldn't worry about me, was the easiest way to live."

Hozumi inhaled deeply, filling up his lungs.

Right. That's why. That's why Iori gets along with everyone.

"Sometimes I put on the face of a person who stayed positive no matter how tough life got."

There was something I'd always wondered about Iori, ever since we met.

Memories of Iori swept through my mind—

Iori having an animated discussion with the local ladies visiting the café about everything from asset management to illnesses.

Iori getting so absorbed in conversation with the middle-school boy minding his parents' dry cleaners that he didn't return to the café for hours.

I'd seen him exchanging favorite books with Kimura the bookseller and playing cards with the kids in the park. Everywhere he went, he found his way into everyone's hearts, as though he had been best friends with them for ages.

The reason he could do that was because . . .

"I don't have my own feelings. I'm an expert at faking my emotions depending on who I'm with. It's actually not that hard. All I do is behave in the way that the other person wants me to."

I felt goose bumps rising from my waist to my back.

Ever since joining Amayadori, I had seen Iori dozens—hundreds—of times.

And yet . . . who was this person sitting in front of me?

Coo-coo.

My shoulders flinched at the carefree sound of a cuckoo call. All of us glanced at the time. It was eleven. Pushed out of the door by a distorted iron spring, the wood-carved bird gave three cuckoo calls, then promptly returned to its home.

"My strategy worked wonders," Iori said. "Things became less tiring, and I had freed myself from unnecessary worries. My nimble mind had everyone fooled. Except for Koharu . . ."

Koharu—the second he said her name, Iori's eyes, which had grown completely cold, seemed to light up.

"What kind of person was she?" Hozumi asked.

"Let me see." Iori thought for a moment. "If she was in an all-female theater company like Takarazuka Revue, she would play the female parts. She was so elegant and feminine."

Hozumi and I let out a sigh; we knew exactly what he meant.

"She must have had porcelain skin," I said.

"She did."

"Her voice must have been crystal clear."

"It was."

"She must have looked like an angel."

"She really did . . ." Iori nodded melancholically. "The girls' uniform at our high school was a white sailor-style outfit. It suited her really well. It was a pretty good school, so there were lots of rich kids. They were a classy bunch, all brought up so well. The kind of kids who would innocently tell me that their family wasn't so rich because they *only* had four bedrooms in their apartment. Do you get what I mean? All the kids were like that."

"Ah. The kind that offend poor people without meaning to." I slurped through my straw although my glass was empty and it made a gurgling sound.

"I got into this high school through a scholarship. The kids there weren't rough like the ones I went to middle school with. I didn't have to worry about guys trying to beat me up because they thought I had stolen their girlfriends. I felt much more at ease. And if anyone ever tried to pry into my private life, I just dodged it by pretending to be like the person they wanted me to be. I was starting to feel like I was going to be okay."

Iori let his back sink into the sofa.

"That was when I met Koharu. I was in my second year of high school, and we were both on the student council. I was the president, and she was the secretary. She was in the year below me."

"Wait a second, you were the president of the student council? Really?"

I was so shocked that my hand holding the straw paused.

"Why? Is it weird?"

"I wouldn't say that . . ."

Actually, it was quite the opposite. It suited his image so well that it was almost scary.

"I was crazy popular. I felt more like an idol than a student council president." Iori combed his fingers through his hair, showing a playful smile. "I got really into the student council activities, too. Until then, I had hated the fact that I seemed to attract everyone's attention whatever I did. But now that I was president, that attention became my weapon."

As he spoke, Iori placed the empty coffee cup and glasses on a tray and carried them to the kitchen. Wanting to help, I started to get up from my seat, but he held his hand out in protest. He put the kettle on the stove. While waiting for it to boil, he perched himself on a barstool.

"When I started high school, I was on a roll. I knew exactly what to say in my speeches and presentations to motivate everyone. I hardly had any time to rest, what with the studying, the student council, and my part-time job, but that was a good thing, because it didn't give me any time to think. But then . . ."

For a second, he choked on his words. A shadow seemed to pass across his face.

"December came. It was a busy time, with the winter break just around the corner."

"Did something happen?"

"Grandma died. There was a call from her caretaker to the school. She'd had a heart attack."

As if on cue, the kettle blared off a high-pitched whistle.

Iori stepped back into the kitchen to turn off the stove.

"Sure, she was forgetful, but she was in good shape. She never missed a health checkup. All I could think at the funeral was, *Everyone I know is going to die suddenly.*"

Iori lined the coffee dripper with a filter, then ran his hand over the bags of different coffee beans arranged on the shelf, contemplating his options.

"Did everyone at school find out about your grandmother?" I ventured to ask.

"Of course. The whole school knew. It was an event worthy of a headline. *Student council president loses his only family and finds himself completely alone!* It was juicy gossip. But I tried my best not to pay attention. I did all my student council work as planned, and got good grades on my end-of-semester exams. And before I knew it, it was the last day of the year. I stood on the podium to deliver a speech. Everyone's eyes were pinned on me."

Iori put some dark roasted beans into the grinder and turned the handle. He transferred spoonfuls of the freshly ground coffee into the filter and slowly poured hot water from the kettle.

"So many eyes. The eyes of every student and teacher in the school. There were hundreds of them, all staring at me. Not that it was anything new—I had stood on that podium every time there was a school event, so I'd seen the same sight many times before. I could have played it safe. A few inspiring words would've been enough. The girls would've looked at me with a dreamy expression on their faces, and the younger students would've looked at me with admiration. I would've gotten a big round of applause, far bigger than what the headmaster would ever get. That was how it always went."

I swallowed hard. The sound of my gulp seemed louder than it should have.

"The air in the gymnasium, where we were assembled, was different that day. My mind went blank. I had a hard time breathing, and I felt nauseous. As I stood on the podium, I frantically searched my brain for an answer as to what made today feel off. Then I realized it was their eyes. They were looking at me with *those eyes*."

"Those eyes?" I asked.

Hozumi thought for a moment. "Do you mean . . ."

Seeing the expression on Hozumi's face, Iori nodded.

"Their eyes longed to see me as the 'person leading a tragic life.' They were expectant eyes, curious to see the face of a person who had just lost his family, to hear what he was going to talk about."

He set the kettle back on the stove and expelled a breath.

"I did wonder if I was being paranoid. So I cast a glance at this girl sitting in the fifth row, and guess what? She was gripping a handkerchief. She had come all prepared, ready to have a good cry. I hadn't even started talking yet! I got scared. I could have just ignored it. I could have just put the usual smile on my face and delivered a good speech. But then I realized I also wanted to control them. Isn't that why I'd been pretending to be the 'cool president of the student council'? I might as well see it through, and let the show go on."

"Iori . . ." I started.

"Before I knew it, I said, 'Recently, my grandmother passed away.' "

Iori placed both hands on the kitchen worktop and looked down. His hair draped over his face.

"The atmosphere shifted. I said, 'My grandmother was my only family. It happened so suddenly, I am still in shock. She was such a kind person.' With every word, their eyes brightened. As for the girl in the fifth row, her eyes turned red almost immediately, and she clung to the girl next to her as she listened. They all stared at me with pity in their eyes. The air that surrounded us was a cocktail of 'how tragic' and 'that feels good.' I despised those eyes. I wanted to run away. But I couldn't stop myself from playing the role of the tragic hero. Before I knew it, I had finished my speech. I don't remember much of it, but I'm sure it was a real tearjerker."

I wanted to say something, but I couldn't find the words. Hozumi and I sat in silence, waiting for him to continue.

"Before I knew it, everyone was clapping."

The coldness in his voice sent a chill down my spine.

His lips, wearing a contemptuous grin, peered through his bangs.

"The jerks. They were all crying and applauding me. At that moment, my vision dizzied, like I had just been punched in the face. I thought, *Why are you crying? Who gave you the right to cry? You're dirty rich. You have no idea what it's like to get your gas supply cut off. You get to do everything you want to do. When you get home, you don't have to eat dinner on your own, do you? You don't have a single reason to cry.* Then I thought, *Why wasn't* I *crying?* I was supposed to be 'suffering.' *What do I want? What makes me sad? What makes me happy?*

How do I feel? What am I? I really thought I was going to be sick, and I couldn't move."

Then the tone of his voice changed. It seemed that his eyes lit up a little underneath his bangs.

"Out of nowhere, a figure appeared, and I felt a strong grip on my wrist. It was Koharu. She pushed me aside and spoke into the mic. She said, 'The president has a fever of 102 degrees. But because he is so devoted, he is forcing himself to be here. We will ask him to finish things up now, out of consideration for his health. Thank you for your understanding."

I could see a vivid image of the heroic Koharu. A dignified woman, confidently approaching the podium. An angel dressed in a white sailor outfit.

"Then Koharu dragged me outside the gymnasium. Everyone was flabbergasted. I was in such a state of shock, I didn't even think to resist. We'd barely spoken to each other before. She wasn't a talkative person, and the whole school knew that she was the daughter of a prestigious family. Everyone considered her out of their league."

"Did you really have a fever?"

"Not at all. I couldn't understand why she would go through the trouble of telling a lie to pull me out of there. She had a surprisingly strong grip for someone so small. She took me through the school gates and didn't let go of my hand until we reached a nearby park. I asked her how she knew, and she said, 'Because it was like you were a different person.' She also said, 'They all looked like they couldn't wait to see the president cry. It was disgusting.' "

"She noticed it, too?" Hozumi asked.

"Yeah, I couldn't believe it." Iori smiled nostalgically.

He picked up the glass server jug filled with coffee.

"Then she looked straight at me and said, 'I'm sorry if I am mistaken.' I told her that she wasn't. That I hadn't wanted to say the things I said in front of everyone. I was honest with her. I also told her that I tend to do the opposite of what I want to do."

Iori poured fresh cups of coffee for everyone and brought them to the table. The café filled with the aroma, gradually mixing with the damp smell of rain.

"For a while we just sat on the park bench without saying anything. Then Koharu said quietly, 'President, there's something I've always thought about you. You try too hard to meet the needs of others. Your family just passed away, so of course you haven't been able to process your emotions yet. Just because your emotions are in a mess, it doesn't mean you need to put them back in order."

There's no need to put your emotions back in order.

It felt as if her words were tearing through my heart.

It was true. She was so right.

Not everything needs to be in order. There's no need to define everything.

Yet we try to comfort ourselves by giving a name to everything. We tend to think that labeling our emotions is better than having to carry undecipherable, unclear feelings. When our emotions are in a mess, instead of just leaving them that way, we try to process them and kick them out of our hearts, because it feels like that is the "correct" thing to do.

"When she said that, I suddenly found myself welling up. I couldn't stop the tears. I didn't know if I was sad or if I was suffering. I didn't know *why* the hell I was crying. But somehow, I felt really safe. I bawled my eyes out in front of her. And Koharu—she didn't do anything. She just sat by me. She didn't hold my hand or stroke my head. She didn't try to embrace me. She was just there. For the first time in my life, I experienced what it was like to have someone who would just be with me without expecting anything from me."

How many kids had asked the question, "Why don't you have a dad?" to the young Iori?

Iori Amamiya, your emotions are yours and only yours.

He had kept his emotions locked away inside his heart. The first person to tell him that he could keep them there, that he could leave his emotions in a mess, was Koharu.

"What? You didn't ask her out? You're not serious!"

The cookie in my hand snapped and fell on the table. In my shock, I had reflexively tightened my grip on the ginger cookie I had served with the coffee.

But who cared about the cookie? To my disbelief, Iori had just told us that he finished high school without ever telling Koharu how he felt about her. How could that be? Iori being Iori, I was so sure that they became high school sweethearts.

"It couldn't be helped. Koharu was in love with someone else," Iori said a little awkwardly, scratching the back of his neck.

"Is he Shizuku's father?" Hozumi asked.

"Good guess." Iori sighed. "You're right. He went to the same school as us. He and Koharu had been friends since they were small. Taiyo Okada was his name. Taiyo, as in the sun. It was the perfect name for him, because he was the warmest, sunniest guy I knew. I thought, *This is what a true hero looks like.* He was so genuine and pure. Koharu always said that she wanted to be like him."

Iori narrowed his eyes as he explained the next part.

"Koharu had loved him ever since she was little, so she had zero interest in other guys. From time to time, she would bring carrot cake to the student council meetings, mumbling something about how she baked it with her mom."

"C-carrot cake? A home-baked carrot cake?" I marveled.

Such classy girls really do exist, after all.

Iori chuckled at my response.

"Although she said she baked it with her mom, she kept asking things like, *How was it? Was it good? Are the spices too much?* She would take in everyone's feedback and improve her recipe. I had this gut feeling that she was making it for someone she liked. I subtly put the question to her, and she confessed that it was Taiyo's favorite food. That was when it hit me: She'd been getting me to taste-test something she was making for the guy she loved. It broke my heart."

Iori rested his cheeks on his hands and looked outside. It was as though he was seeing his past on the rainy window.

"Whenever Koharu brought the cake, I would know as soon as I stepped inside the student council room. The smell of carrots and spices wafted over everything."

Iori's gaze drifted toward the kitchen. Every time I mixed the spices for my chicken curry, did it make him think of Koharu?

I ventured, "If it were me, I would probably give her fake feedback to ruin the recipe. I'd tell her to put more spices in it or something."

Such an evil thought.

"I always told her it was delicious," Iori said with a wry grin. "How could I say anything else? I was in love with her."

My chest tightened at his words. Of course he wouldn't do something so unscrupulous. He wasn't like me, after all.

Iori stood up, the now-empty plate of cookies in his hand.

"Talking about cake has made me hungry. Momo-chan, do we have any more cookies?"

"Yeah, they're in the basket at the back."

"Thanks."

I could hear him rustling around in the kitchen.

When he reemerged, he was holding a J-shaped carrot.

"Momo-chan, what are these? There are loads in the kitchen."

"Oh, yeah, I forgot," I said.

Hozumi and I exchanged glances. I had forgotten that we had carried the box of vegetables to the back of the kitchen.

"My dad sent me a big box of them yesterday. He had a surplus of misshapen carrots. He was never going to get through all of them, so he sent them to me."

Iori stood frozen to the spot, his eyes pinned on the deformed carrot.

"Iori?"

"Are you hungry?" he asked Hozumi and me.

"I suppose I wouldn't be against eating . . . oh!"

Hozumi glanced meaningfully at me.

I was sure we were all thinking the same thing. We were going to re-create Iori's "ex-girlfriend" recipe.

I swiftly pulled my phone out and captured the aproned Iori on burst mode.

"So beautiful," I sighed, my inner monologue slipping out of my mouth.

To my left was Hozumi. I could sense him giving me an ice-cold glare, but frankly, I couldn't care less.

The veins on Iori's arms, stretching out from his casually rolled-up sleeves, mesmerized me. I noticed his hands—for the first time I was seeing how bony they were—and the tips of his long fingers as he ran his knife across the surface of the carrot, effortlessly peeling away its skin.

"We can sell these. We can definitely sell these pictures!"

I continued to hold the shutter button down, which meant that an inordinate number of images were being produced in my camera roll. Pictures of Iori peeling carrots were going to be the next big thing. I was *sure* of it.

"Cut it out," Iori said bashfully without stopping his work.

"We can turn them into merchandise! You know, print them on stuff," I said. "We can make them into mugs!"

"Who's going to want those mugs?" Hozumi said.

"Actually, if we're going to target the local ladies, maybe they'll prefer something more portable, like postcards. Or we could go all out and make T-shirts! We can display them by the till with a little slogan like: *Fill your days with Iori!* Good idea, huh?"

"Momo-chan." Iori's hands paused. A thin layer of carrot skin fell on the chopping board.

"Stop, please. *Now.*" Iori's deep voice boomed through the midnight café.

Oops. I had gotten a little carried away. I obediently returned to my seat next to Hozumi.

"Weren't you listening to him? He told us that he was doing the housework at home ever since he was little," Hozumi chided me.

"I was, but hearing it and seeing it are two different things," I reasoned.

The truth was, watching Iori work so confidently in the kitchen had made me feel a twinge of pain. He had told me before that he didn't know much about cooking, and I genuinely believed him, because he made that horrible curry on the day we met. But I now realized that, aside from the mistake that one time, he was a good chef. After I joined Amayadori, he pretended that he didn't have any cooking skills, because he knew that I would want to take the lead in the kitchen. He was probably paying far more attention to my needs than I could ever imagine, and this realization made me feel a pang of guilt.

Iori told us that although he and Koharu got along well, and thus became very close friends, their relationship never turned into anything else throughout their high school years.

Iori decided not to go to university. Instead, he juggled different jobs like modeling and working as a host in a club. At one point, he even became the top earner at the bar (not that this came as a surprise) and built up a healthy sum in his savings account. Deciding it was time to find a stable job, he earned a qualification in childcare and started to work in a preschool in Tokyo. That was where he was reunited with Koharu. Ten years had passed since they had seen each other last.

"I recognized her straightaway," Iori said, now grating a carrot. "Although the aura of sophistication she used to have had disappeared, she still had the air of a dignified woman, and her strong, honest gaze hadn't changed. If anything, she looked . . . livelier. The girl who used to giggle quietly with her hand over her mouth was now comfortably baring her white teeth as she burst into a hearty laugh. It was like witnessing an inanimate doll come to life."

"Did you not try to contact her before then?"

"I assumed she would marry Taiyo, so I stayed away. I wasn't about to fight a losing battle."

"I guess even *you* have these kinds of problems," I conceded.

"Of course I do. Everyone wants the person they love to love them back, right?" Iori said, letting out a small sigh. His words made my heart flutter. I pressed my hands on my flushing cheeks.

A deep scraping sound rang out as Iori rubbed the crooked carrot over the tiny blades of the oroshigane.

"But I wanted her to be happy more. Koharu was meant to have a good life—she was supposed to live in a fancy mansion that could fit a huge tree at Christmas. She was supposed to be eating carrot cake with a smile on her face! That's what I thought she deserved."

Iori tilted the oroshigane and scraped off the grated carrots into a bowl.

"So when I saw her again at the preschool where I worked, I was really surprised. The place where I worked was—well, let's just say it wasn't in an affluent area. I had it in my mind that she would send her child—if she ever had one—to a prestigious preschool, like one of those university-affiliated ones."

"Did something happen to her?"

Iori answered with a nod.

"Taiyo passed away. He had a rare type of stomach cancer—scirrhous carcinoma, to be exact. She said everything happened so fast."

"No . . ." I gasped, hanging on his every word.

"What made the whole ordeal that much more tragic was the timing of his death . . . it happened as she was giving birth to Shizuku. She went to his hospital room as soon as she could, but it was too late."

Iori slowly shook his head.

"All of a sudden, her husband was gone. She now had a tiny newborn to raise on her own. I can't imagine how that made her feel."

Their family was supposed to be growing. They must have had so much to look forward to. They must have been so excited for the future. And yet . . .

"So Shizuku hasn't met her father," Hozumi said, putting two and two together.

"That's right. Koharu has always raised her on her own. She didn't want to ask her parents for support, and she seemed to have her reasons for that. She chose to earn a living on her own as a single mom. We were reunited when Shizuku was three years old. I couldn't believe it when we ran into each other at that school, and she was in shock, too. Apparently, Taiyo had asked for a divorce before he passed. He had wanted her to find happiness through a new partner, but Koharu refused . . ."

I pictured Koharu by Taiyo's sickbed, firmly holding his hand.

"The look on Koharu's face when she told me that he had passed, I'll never forget it. Koharu was supposed to be happy. I *needed* her to be happy."

Iori stopped stirring the cake mixture.

"She also told me that she had taken his last name, Okada, and that she wanted to hold on to it, no matter what. She said, 'This might sound ridiculous, but it's the only thing that keeps me going. I know it's stupid . . . but right now, every time I see the name Koharu Okada on my documents, it gives me solace.' "

"This is unbearable!" I proclaimed.

"How's that for a heartbreak story?" Iori asked. "It's as sad as the ones we've heard so far, don't you think?"

Don't do that, Iori. Don't force yourself to smile like that.

Dark and deserted, the street was dead silent at night.

The rain had eased off. Now it was only light drops, sprinkling here and there sporadically, and our umbrellas weren't needed anymore.

After putting the carrot cake mixture into the oven, we realized that we didn't have any cream cheese, so the three of us went to the nearby supermarket to buy some. The plastic shopping bag swayed back and forth as we made our way back to Amayadori.

Iori continued his tale. "Our friendship rekindled. We talked a lot, just like the good times. The three of us—Koharu, Shizuku, and I—started hanging out together more and more. We went to parks, aquariums, amusement parks . . . all sorts of places. Being a single parent, it wasn't easy for Koharu to take Shizuku anywhere too far, so they were happy to explore with me."

I peered into Iori's face. "Did you not fall back in love with her?"

"Well, yeah."

At this, Iori seemed to remember something, and his cheeks turned red. He quickly averted his eyes.

"Wait, are you blushing right now? Oh my God, you so are!" I couldn't stop myself from grinning at his unexpected reaction.

"Stop being so loud . . ." Iori bashfully covered his face with his right arm. "The truth is, I had never stopped loving her. I couldn't get her out of my mind, even after becoming an adult."

He may have been covering his face, but his bright-red ears gave him away.

The sound of our sandals clacking across the concrete echoed through late-night Sangenjaya.

"And then what happened?" I prodded.

"Did you confess your feelings to her?" Hozumi asked.

"Did you tell her you love her this time?" I added.

Hozumi and I interrogated Iori, sandwiching him between us. At our relentless questioning, Iori's face started to redden again.

Iori had suddenly quickened his pace; he was marching three steps ahead of us.

Then he stopped, turned around, and said, "I told her."

"Oh my God!"

Hozumi and I clasped hands with each other in solidarity.

"So embarrassing . . ." Iori said. Squaring his shoulders, he walked briskly ahead.

Teaming up, Hozumi and I followed, once again sandwiching him in from both sides.

"No need to be shy now. Do tell us more. Here, allow me to hold that for you," I offered, referring to the bag containing the cream cheese.

"I think there might have been a lesson about how one's soul can be saved by telling people about your love life," Hozumi added.

"That is a load of crap. Karma will get you." Iori retorted.

I'd never seen Iori expose his emotions in this way. It was the first time I had seen him get angry or blush with embarrassment.

Maybe this is the "real" Iori. I gently shook my head to stop the thought. *It's not right to ask if this is his "real" self or not. Perhaps even he doesn't have a grasp of who he is yet.*

I pushed on anyway. "So? What did you say *exactly*? And where did you tell her?"

"I think it was . . ." Iori mumbled awkwardly, scratching at his ear lobes. "Inokashira Park."

Oh. My. God. The most romantic spot!

"I've never been there," Hozumi muttered.

"Are you the only Tokyoite who's never been there?" I exclaimed.

"I'm from Chiba."

"Well, I'm from Kagoshima, and from my perspective, Chiba is basically Tokyo," I said. "We should go there sometime! The place is massive. There's a pond with swan boats, and the park hosts different events, especially over the national holidays."

"Right," Hozumi said without even trying to feign interest.

We arrived back at Amayadori and gave our wet umbrellas a shake before sticking them in the stand outside.

As I groped in my bag for the keys, Iori reminisced, "Oh, yeah, we went on the swan boat. Shizuku absolutely loved it. That was fun . . ."

When I spun around, I found Iori staring idly into the night, his hands stuffed in his pockets. From time to time, I felt stray raindrops on my face.

"We had ice cream, and a balloon artist twisted a dog for Shizuku. We spent the whole day doing all sort of things. By the evening, Shizuku had grown cranky and fell asleep. She wouldn't wake up, so we went to one of the benches by the pond and laid her down while Koharu and I rested our feet."

A solitary drop of rain fell on the swirl of my head and streamed down.

"I was having such a good time. Having my loved ones next to me. Walking everywhere with them. Getting exhausted. Laughing our heads off. I thought, *Wow, such profound happiness really does exist.* I felt this from the bottom of my heart. That day made me realize that I didn't need to think that they'll disappear from my life unless I gave them exactly what they wanted; I could be entirely myself."

A raindrop fell on the tip of Iori's nose.

"Before I knew it, I had said the words."

The droplet descended to his lips and streamed down his chin.

"I love you. I always have."

He spoke as if he were talking to someone in the distance, far above the clouds.

" 'Although I'm scared of losing the relationship we have now,' " he said, looking straight ahead with unblinking eyes, " 'I want to see what the view beyond friendship looks like. Next time I see you, can it be a date?' "

His clear voice reverberated through the quiet night.

Iori expelled a breath. It was as though his emotional string had been pulled so tight that it finally snapped.

The view beyond friendship. How did he feel as he said those words?

"And then . . . ?" I asked. "What did she say?"

Iori quietly kicked a pebble across the concrete.

"She said no. She said that Taiyo was still her number one. That I was important to her, but she couldn't have a romantic relationship with me."

Hozumi sighed. Without meaning to, I followed with an even bigger sigh.

Not that I was surprised. I sort of guessed that would be the outcome. I'd gathered that Koharu was that kind of person, and that was the very reason Iori had fallen in love with her. I felt that I was starting to get to know her, little by little.

"I could never recover from that," Hozumi muttered, his head dropping in disappointment.

"Me either, I would probably regret falling in love."

I sighed yet again. The devastating reality of Iori's lost love hit Hozumi and me in a way that neither of us had anticipated. I was crestfallen, as if the whole thing had happened to me.

"But—" Iori said.

"But . . . ?" Hozumi and I both lifted our heads in surprise.

Iori kept his back turned as he muttered, "She told me that when she heard me say 'the view beyond friendship,' it also made her want to see a new world with me."

"Just to be clear—Koharu said that?"

"Yeah," Iori mumbled, his ears redder than ever.

"That is so . . . beautiful. It's like a waka poem."

I swung the bag with the cream cheese around and around. Iori kept his face turned away determinedly, probably because he could feel his face growing hot.

"She said that she wasn't ready for a relationship but asked me if we could still hang out as friends. That was enough for me. I was Shizuku's best playmate, and I wasn't ready to let go of the relationship we had either."

Perhaps Koharu hadn't finished processing her feelings yet. She probably saw him as a friend she could talk to and a person she felt a connection with. But up until then, she'd never even considered the possibility of having a romantic relationship with him.

Iori scratched at the back of his head, as if trying to cover up his embarrassment. "And that's the story of how Shizuku came to know me as 'Daddy,' even though in reality I was just a handsome neighbor who wanted to hang out with them."

Despite everything he had said about being good at behaving the way other people wanted him to, it turned out that when it came to Koharu, he was rather incompetent at hiding himself.

Having finished most of the cake-making, Iori sat down on the sofa as he wiped his hands. For now, all we had to do was wait for the cake to bake in the oven.

"The year the three of us spent together was the happiest time of my life. Truly, it was the best." Iori nodded as if acknowledging his own statement.

"We celebrated Christmas together. Me, celebrating Christmas in a traditional home setting! I couldn't believe it, but I guess there's a first time for everything. Koharu asked me to go and get a tree, but I had no idea how big it was supposed to be. I thought, *Surely there's no such thing as a tree being too big?* So I went to the home decor store and bought the biggest one they had. Koharu gave me a good scolding for that."

"I guess you thought better too big than too small," Hozumi said.

Narrowing his eyes, Iori smiled softly, as if his mind was traveling back in time.

"Shizuku loved it, though. She got all animated, saying no one else would own such a big tree. I even got a present from Koharu."

Iori got up and stepped toward the display shelf near the door. When he returned, he had something in his hand.

It was a snow globe. Inside the glass dome was a tiny Santa Claus and reindeer flying in the sky.

"Isn't that the snow globe that Shizuku gave you today—wait, no, it's always been on the shelf, hasn't it?"

"That's right. Shizuku didn't bring this to me today. It's the snow globe that Koharu gave me six years ago."

Iori had always kept the snow globe where he could see it, in a prime location on the shelf.

"That Christmas day was the best day of my life," Iori murmured, stroking the top of the glass dome. "I wish things could have stayed that way, but it didn't work out. We had been living together for about one year when Koharu told me she couldn't keep leaning on me. She said, 'If I stay with you, I feel like I'll become too dependent.' She was crying."

"What did she mean by that?"

"I think . . ."

Iori stared into the softly sparkling glass ball.

"Koharu wanted to be able to support someone, not the other way around. She was born into a wealthy family in Seijo and grew up in a huge house. Her father was an executive at a pharmaceutical company. As a child, she had access to everything: good education, friends from good families. A life everyone envied. Koharu's only misfortune was that she realized that she was born into fortunate circumstances," Iori said matter-of-factly.

"Her misfortune was that she was fortunate?" I asked.

Rubbing his bald head, Hozumi muttered as if he was speaking to himself, "Everyone wants to believe that they've built their lives through effort and talent. No one wants to admit that they had an advantage. That they only succeeded because they were lucky. Or because their parents invested a lot of money in them. Or because they were born into good circumstances."

Iori looked at Hozumi for a moment, then mumbled in agreement, "Yeah."

He continued, "From a pretty young age, Koharu was aware of the power of this 'advantage,' as Hozumi calls it. Which was why she wanted to do things on her own and why she struggled. Taiyo was the kind of person who could simply put all his heart into everything he did no matter what. I think that was why she was attracted to him."

It seemed that the unspoken ending to that was "and not me."

"Koharu had lived her whole life being handed things. Lots of things. Even things that should have been far out of her reach for her abilities. I think she was sick of that life."

Iori held his head, resting his elbows on the table. As he blinked his downcast eyes, his eyelashes fluttered.

"She told me something at the end."

"What did she say?"

" 'I am happy. I can make myself happy. I shouldn't need you, or someone else, to make me happy.' "

A waft of humid air drifted through the door and clung to my body. I pointlessly rubbed the back of my neck.

"When she said that, it felt like my heart was being ripped out. I had created a stupid fantasy in my head, where she was living a certain life and smiling in a certain way. I wanted her to be happy. I wanted to solve all of Koharu's problems and grant every one of Shizuku's wishes. I wanted to show them things. I wanted them to see things. I just wanted to see the looks on Koharu's and Shizuku's faces . . ."

At that moment, I noticed that Iori's shoulders were trembling.

Unable to do anything, I stared at Iori's hands, which were clasped together on the table.

"That was all I wanted. Really. It gave me pure joy. I was happy to be able to do something for the people I loved."

Right.

He knew. He remembered the pain of trying to live up to other people's expectations. Although those expectations were the complete opposite in this case, Koharu had suffered the same pain he felt.

"And I *did* see the view beyond friendship—I got to see what it was like to be a part of her family, even though we weren't lovers. It was bright and beautiful. I enjoyed every second of it."

A family of just a year.

Knowing Iori, he must have created an image of the kind of "Daddy" he wanted to be by observing all the fathers around him and gathering all of the knowledge he'd gained as a preschool teacher. He must have put his all into it.

"Argh!" I howled in frustration. "I wish I could trap Iori, Koharu, and Shizuku into a snow globe, so that you guys can be together forever!"

My eyes were wet with tears, and I frantically dabbed at them with the hem of my apron.

"Why are you crying?" Iori laughed.

I'm sure he was crying just a moment ago. Why would he laugh at my own tears?

"I—I can't help it."

"You're such a crybaby," Hozumi said.

"Sorry," I said sarcastically. "Coolheaded people like you will never understand—"

But just as I shot a glare at him, I found that Hozumi, to my disbelief, was gazing up at the ceiling. His neck was bent at an impossible angle.

No way. Is he crying?

"I'm not crying."

I sprang to my feet to peer into his face, but he leaned farther back, determined to hide his eyes.

"You're crying."

"I am not."

Although he said this, Hozumi walked over to the prime spot where he'd get the most air from the aircon.

"Ha! You're trying to buy time! Look at you, so desperate to dry your tears!"

As Hozumi and I continued to quarrel, Iori broke into peals of laughter. We laughed with him.

It was the break of dawn, and the sweet smell of carrots and spices spread through the room. Normally, I would have been fast asleep by now, but I didn't feel remotely tired.

The carrot cake had been baked in a rectangular loaf pan. The cake was filled with raisins and nuts, the creamy frosting on top garnished with pink peppercorns.

"I had no idea you could pull off such a showstopper," I said.

"She was always going on about this cake. Plus, I wanted to feel her close to me even after we separated." Iori answered.

The words that came out of his beautiful face suggested that Iori was the clingy type—he was as bad as me.

The first time I came to Amayadori, I cried my eyes out. Maybe he was so kind to me because he knew how I felt?

Iori told us that he explained to Shizuku that he was going to have to work somewhere far away for a while.

Although he thought it was a good idea to leave Shizuku before she got too attached, he knew from his own experience how lonely it was to have someone you cared about suddenly disappear. So he sent her presents from time to time. Though it meant he'd be cutting into his savings, he decided to go traveling around the world. He collected snow globes, picture books, and postcards abroad and sent them to Shizuku every Christmas.

My heart warmed at his unexpected devotion, and the tears came back. Seeing me with wet eyes, Iori started to laugh again.

"Shall we eat, then?"

Once Iori had settled on the sofa, I put my fork into the carrot-colored sponge. I gently carried the cake, along with the frosting, into my mouth.

"It's delicious! I didn't know carrot cake was so good!"

Whenever I found myself in a cake shop, I'd always been tempted by the classic ones, like strawberry shortcake, chocolate cake, or cheesecake. I had never thought of carrot cake as being very, well, cake-like. I don't know how I didn't realize this before, but for the first time, I was seeing that carrot cake was as satisfying as the classic cakes.

Sweet-toothed Hozumi spoke with uncharacteristic eloquence: "It's sweet, but I can really feel the zing of the spices. And the cream cheese gives it a tang that works wonderfully well together. It has the potential of being as delicious as ice cream soda."

He ate with unbelievable enthusiasm and in no time at all had started on his second slice. He continued to speak at the speed of a machine gun, saying something about which of the ingredients were key and so on, but he was getting so technical I couldn't understand half of it. He might as well have been speaking to me in a foreign language.

Doesn't he know any simple words?

Bringing his coffee to his lips, Iori said abruptly, "Right. Storytime is over. I'm going to forget Koharu. Because of you two, I can now rest my lost love in peace. I can finally move on from Koharu. Thank you."

I shifted my gaze toward the window. It was still drizzling.

Pressing my palms together, I started to speak, but something didn't feel right. I felt a subtle prickle at the back of my chest.

Something is off. Something is definitely off!

"You're lying about something." I narrowed my eyes at Iori.

"Huh?"

"Iori."

Half rising from my seat, I leaned forward, drawing my face close to his. His light brown eyes twitched.

"You're still in love with Koharu, aren't you?"

Iori blinked excessively. He was definitely hiding something.

"Err—I'm . . . not."

I've figured out the source of my suspicion.

"Iori, you haven't touched your cake."

Hozumi and I had long finished eating (in fact, Hozumi had devoured three slices), yet Iori hadn't had a single bite.

"Is it because you'll remember things if you eat the cake? Because you'll think, *Oh, that's Koharu's flavor,* and your memories will come flooding back, and you might fall right back in love with her? Is that why?"

It must have been his master plan to call it a night and pretend he was going to eat it up in his room.

Iori fell silent as his eyes darted around nervously. Clearly, he hadn't planned for the part where he got interrogated.

"Of course not. I can eat it."

Iori forced a smile and picked up his fork. He prodded it into the cake and brought it toward his mouth.

Just then, Hozumi grabbed his wrist.

"Where were you today, Iori?" he asked.

I turned to Hozumi. He had a point.

Why was Iori so late coming to work today?

"I could smell incense on you," Hozumi continued.

Iori averted his gaze from Hozumi, as if he was avoiding the awkwardness.

"You were visiting someone's grave, weren't you?"

Confronted by the evidence, our suspect finally let out a big sigh.

"You guys pay way too much attention to me. It's freaky. You must really love me," Iori said jokingly.

Why is that such a surprise to him?

Ever since we met, I'd felt that it was best not to get too close to him.

And it wasn't just Iori. I'd been like this since breaking up with Kyohei. I'd become afraid of telling people how I feel. Afraid of being told that I was too clingy. That I scared them because I was too serious.

But now is the time to be a warrior brandishing a naginata sword. Now is the time to be brave.

"Of course I love you!"

Iori lifted his head in surprise. "What?"

"Oh. I mean, not like *that,* of course. I mean, as a human! As my boss . . . no, as a member of Amayadori."

Now it looked as if I had confessed my love for Iori at the worst possible time. I desperately searched for the right words to fix the mishap.

"What I'm trying to say is that if something seems to be off with you, I can't help myself from worrying or looking at you closely. If a little girl shows up out of the blue and calls you 'Daddy,' then I'm going to want to know what the hell is going on."

I continued passionately.

"I mean, I really don't want you to go away! You're the reason that I have a job here. You're the reason I enjoy working for Amayadori as well as the Funeral Committee. Amayadori won't be Amayadori without you, Iori."

Silence filled the air.

Have I just said something really cringe?

"Iori, can you say something? I'm starting to feel embarrassed—"

"I went to see . . . Taiyo," Iori confessed with downcast eyes.

Hozumi pushed for more. "Do you go every year?"

"It's weird, right? I'm just an outsider, yet I keep visiting the husband of the person I love at his grave."

Iori expelled a short breath before continuing his confession.

"I couldn't explain why, but whenever I stand in front of Taiyo's grave, pressing my hands together, my honest feelings start to rise up from me. I'm sure Taiyo's thinking, *What do you want?* I was going to stop visiting him as soon as I had gotten over Koharu. I'd decided that today's visit would be the final one, this time for real. But then, when I got back, Shizuku was here."

No wonder he seemed to be completely out of it.

He must have tried so many times to give up, to lock away his feelings.

Ever since he was a young child, he pretended to be someone else, yet the one role he couldn't play was the guy who wasn't in love with Koharu. How painful must that be?

"Do you still love her?" I ventured.

Iori shut his eyes and thought for a while.

He opened his eyes and said, "I do. I love her so much it hurts. I want her to be by my side. Forever."

His words were loud and clear.

Okay.

That makes things simple.

I took Iori's plate and pulled the cake toward me.

"Okay. I guess we don't need to do a burial, then. I'll have your cake."

I started eating the slice.

Iori seemed to be at a loss for words. As I brought another bite to my mouth, I added, "Just because your emotions are in a mess, it doesn't mean you need to put them back in order."

Iori turned his gaze toward me.

"Koharu said so, too, didn't she?"

"She did, but . . ."

"Well, there you go. Who cares if your emotions are all over the place? You look pretty well put together on the outside."

"Whatever happens, we'll always be here for you," Hozumi said with uncharacteristic sincerity.

"Oh, Hozumi!" I said.

"No, wait, that was a mistake."

I started slapping his back in delight.

Hozumi tried to retract his words. "Actually, that was . . . a new Buddhist chant. I got the words confused."

"Thank you."

I heard relief in Iori's voice.

"Are you done yet?"

"Not yet."

"What are you going to put in it, Hozumi?"

"It's a secret."

"Show me. Just a little."

"No."

"Ooh, star-shaped beads? They're pretty. What do you think of mine? I can't seem to make up my mind."

"Quit talking. Focus on your own work!"

A week had passed.

We were gathered in Amayadori before opening time, diligently working on our snow globes. We had decided to make our own, filled with memorable items, as an homage to Iori's relationship, since a formal burial wasn't right.

"I have so much stuff, they're not all going to fit."

"I can't think why you would have so many things to put in a snow globe," Hozumi replied.

I'd planned on stuffing the things I had that were still bothering me into my snow globe: the receipt from the expensive pair of pumps I bought before my date with Kyohei, tickets from when we went to Disneyland together, a stray button Kyohei left behind. But I couldn't seem to get them to fit.

"Your snow globe is way too heavy. Only you would put this kind of stuff into it. Also, didn't you say you threw everything away?"

My shoulders tensed at Hozumi's probing question.

"I spent all that time helping you sort through the stuff," he continued.

"These are the only things that are left, I promise! I found them buried inside my desk. Plus, the instructions on the snow globe kit clearly state that 'you can fill it with anything you like.' See?"

I held the instructions to his face.

"Even so, this is crossing the—"

Cutting off Hozumi's mumbling, I turned to Iori.

"What about you?"

"I've finished."

"Already?"

Indeed, his snow globe was lidded and all ready to go.

Its contents were simple. Looking inside the glass ball, I saw the pink peppercorns he'd used to garnish the carrot cake and . . .

"Is that a key? What is it for?"

I could see a key floating inside the globe, slightly discolored and rusty.

"Here."

"Here?"

"Yeah. It's the key to Amayadori. The one the owner gave me when we first opened."

I was so surprised, I was unable to say anything. It was completely unexpected. I had assumed that he was going to fill it with something that Koharu or Shizuku had given him.

"This one is just a spare key, of course," Iori added. "I have my master key. Shizuku might need me for something in the future. Should that day come, it would be easy for her to come find me if Amayadori was still here. So . . ."

Iori picked up the snow globe again and firmly tightened its lid.

". . . this is my declaration that I will never close Amayadori. The day I break this snow globe to remove the key is the day Amayadori ceases to exist," Iori said, and pulled his lips into a smile. "Please stay by my side, Momo-chan and Hozumi."

I smiled. "And you stay by ours, too!"

The bluest midsummer sky spread across the windows.

I stood up and gave myself a good stretch. With my heavy snow globe complete, I felt a step closer to laying my resentment to rest.

"Maybe I'll put some protein powder in mine," Hozumi suggested out of nowhere.

"You want to put protein in your snow globe?"

"Yes."

"Seriously? Star-shaped beads and protein?"

"I thought we were allowed to put in anything we liked."

It seemed that Hozumi had a case of snow globe envy.

Iori arranged our snow globes on the display shelf.

Without needing words, the three of us gathered in front of them and pressed our hands together.

"Our condolences," we said together.

Catching the sunlight, the snow globes gave a sparkle of joy.

THE VIEW BEYOND FRIENDSHIP CARROT CAKE

Serves 5

2 tablespoons (20 g) raisins

Rum

MIXTURE

2 medium carrots, trimmed and peeled ($3^1/_2$ ounces / 150 g after prep)

2 eggs

Scant $^1/_3$ cup (60 g) cane sugar

$^1/_2$ cup (120 ml) cold-pressed sesame oil (such as Taihaku)

$^3/_4$ cup (100 g) rice flour

$1^1/_2$ teaspoons baking powder

$^1/_4$ teaspoon ground cinnamon

$^1/_4$ teaspoon ground cloves

$^1/_4$ teaspoon ground black pepper

$^1/_2$ ounce (15 g) walnuts, chopped

FROSTING

3 ounces (80 g) cream cheese

2 tablespoons (20 g) cane sugar

Ground cardamom

Fresh thyme

Pink peppercorns

METHOD

Soak the raisins in rum and leave in the fridge for at least 1 hour.

Finely grate a third of the carrots using an oroshigane (you can also pulse them in a food processor). Shred the remaining carrots.

Using a whisk, mix the eggs and the cane sugar.

Little by little, stir the Taihaku sesame oil into the egg mixture.

Add the finely grated/pulsed carrots to the mixture.

Add the flour, baking powder, cinnamon, cloves, and black pepper to the mixture.

Add the remaining shredded carrots, walnuts (chopped as desired), and rum-soaked raisins, and mix using a spatula.

Preheat the oven to 350°F.

Transfer the mixture to a 6-inch round cake pan.

Bake in the oven for 30 to 35 minutes.

Allow the cake to cool completely before leaving it in the fridge overnight.

To make the frosting, mix the cream cheese with the cane sugar and the cardamom and spread over the top of the cake. Garnish with the fresh thyme and pink peppercorns.

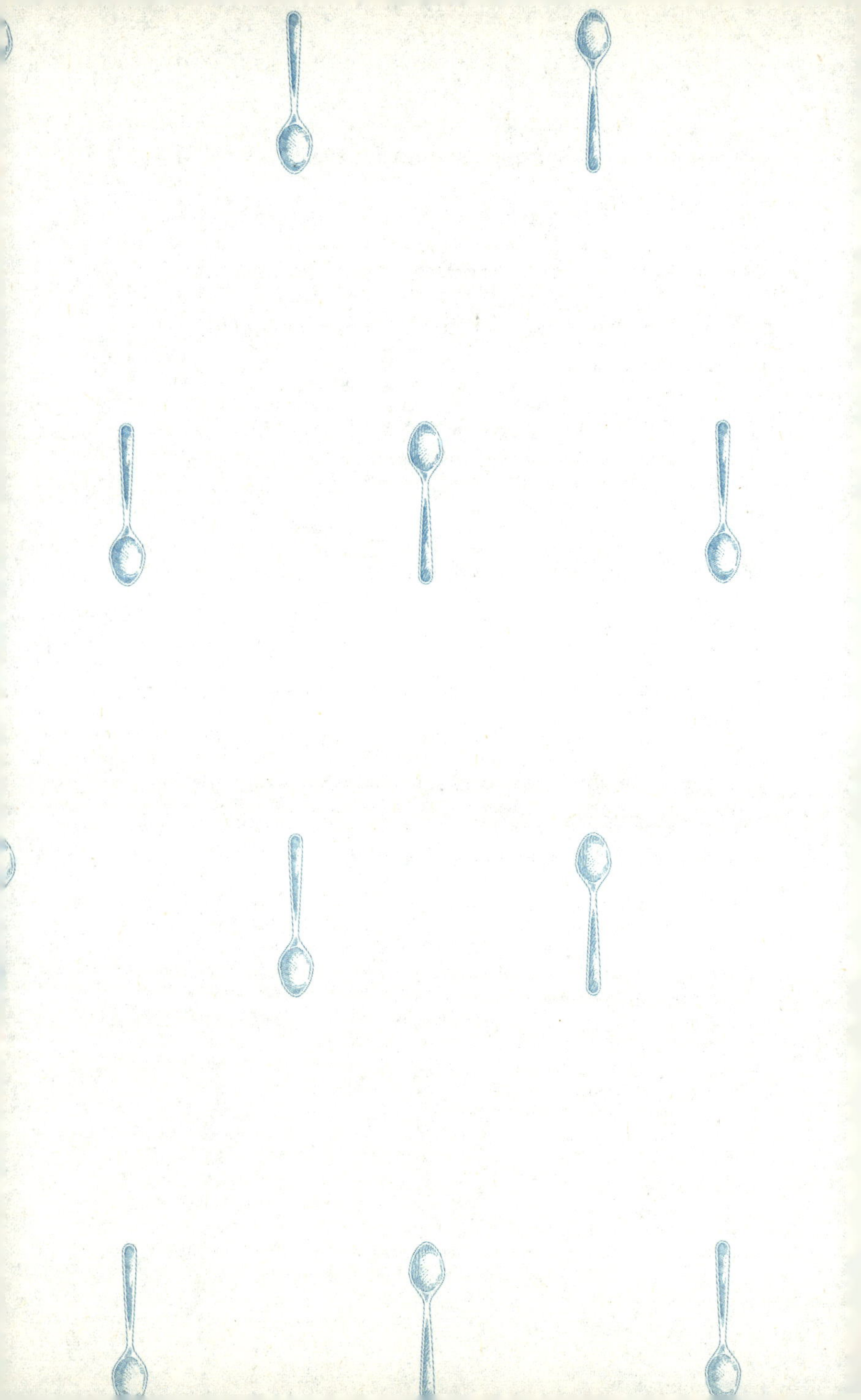

CHAPTER 6

IT'S ME OR YOUR WORK CHOCOLATES

"I'm not sure if I even want to know, but what exactly is going on with you two?" Iori, who'd returned from buying coffee beans, said in a mocking tone. Sitting at the counter, Hozumi and I were in the middle of a small conflict.

"Oh, hi," I said to Iori. "Hold on, I'll get started on the prep as soon as I'm done with this." Firmly gripping Hozumi's thumb with both my hands, I forcefully pushed it toward his phone. Shown on the screen was a review app.

"Come on, we can't keep Iori waiting. Please, Hozumi. Just do it. Just tap on it!"

"I will not! I will never give it five stars!"

"Why the hell not? The new dish is so good. It's worthy of five stars, isn't it?"

"Listen, my reviews are sacred. I put my heart and soul into them. I'm not going to ruin that with favoritism. Besides, I told you already that I have a policy of only reviewing sweet foods."

"Stop being so stubborn!"

"*I'm* the stubborn one?"

"Where do you guys get all your energy from?" Iori said coldly as he heaved a paper bag onto the counter.

But this was a matter of life and death! I'd finally managed to come up with a new dish to add to the menu. The ruthless saleswoman inside of me had awakened, and I wasn't about to give up on an opportunity for a good review.

I knew in my head that one little five-star review from Hozumi wasn't going to solve my problems. But still, I was so desperate, I couldn't help myself. October was here, and that meant we were now in a period I called "the Month of the Devil."

Generally speaking, the restaurant industry experiences a slowdown during the months of February and August. It even has a name for it: nippachi (*ni* as in two, and *pachi* as in eight). But for whatever reason, in every single branch that I was ever in charge of, October was the month where we saw the most decline in sales. I must have jinxed myself, because just as I feared, Amayadori was suffering from a huge drop in the number of customers. As a desperate measure to improve the situation, I had invented a new meal, the "Meat Feast," that Hozumi was now trying for the first time.

"I admit that it is delicious," Hozumi said, breaking free from my grip and pushing his phone back into his pocket.

"Of course it is. I begged Adachi to give us the highest-quality meats. It *has* to be good."

As the name suggested, my concept behind the Meat Feast was a meal that allowed customers to "indulge themselves in meat." The meal included a bowl of rice, miso soup, pickled vegetables, a rolled omelet, and fermented soybeans, as well as the meat dish of the day (although on most days, that dish was going to be grilled chicken with herbs, which was guaranteed to fill up people's stomachs despite its low cost). With many of our recent customers being office workers, I'd wanted to serve them a hearty meal they could tuck into during their lunch break quickly.

But glancing around the deserted café, I let out a sigh.

"The dish itself is pretty good, I think. What am I missing?"

Just as I was beginning to ponder this question, I heard the door creak. I felt a rush of cold air as the autumn breeze swept inside.

I jumped out of my seat, smoothed down my apron, and turned toward the door.

"I-ira . . . irasshaimase!" I was so startled, I stumbled over my words.

The woman standing before me was tall. Really tall.

I had to lift my head quite a bit to get to her level. She was almost a head taller than me, likely standing around six feet tall. She wore a simple blazer in light gray and white tapered pants. Her hair was tied back, and although she was dressed rather plainly in business casual attire, there was something about her that drew my gaze.

Her eyes darted around the café inquisitively. Before setting herself down on the sofa by the window, she said in a quiet voice, "Could I have the one written on the signboard outside? The Meat Feast."

"Oh, of course. Coming right up!"

Yes! Not only was she having the new dish, she was also a first-time customer.

I hurriedly prepared the grilled chicken with herbs.

She must be on her work break right now, I thought to myself as I ladled out the miso soup. I hoped that she would find the meal nourishing.

"Excuse me, I'm still waiting for the Meat Feast?" The woman raised her hand with a deadpan expression on her face.

Around forty minutes had passed since I had served the woman her meal, and I had been recounting the money in the cash register.

Huh?

I did serve her, didn't I?

I did. I'm sure of it.

I even remembered saying, "It's hot, so please take care," as well as the sound of the sauce sizzling on the hot plate.

"Umm . . . I believe I served you the grilled chicken earlier?" I said, pulling out the menu from my pocket and showing her a picture of the dish.

She took the menu from me with her slender fingers and spent some time staring intently at the image. She then looked me straight in the eyes, and sounding truly flabbergasted, she said, "*That* was the Meat Feast?"

What did she mean by that?

I stood there, an awkward smile affixed on my face. Turning around, I found Iori worriedly peering out of the kitchen.

Help me, I said to him silently. *I don't know what I've done wrong!*

The woman sat unmoving with her hand on her cheek, apparently deep in thought. Eventually, she mumbled to herself, "Ah, right, I understand."

Understand what?

She drained her glass of water and suddenly sprang to her feet.

"I'm sorry for saying something so odd. Thank you for the meal."

She pulled out her wallet, placed her money on the cash tray by the till, and dashed out of the café.

"Th-thank you! Hey, wait!"

I noticed that the money she had left was a ten-thousand-yen bill.

Ten thousand yen? But the meal was only 980 yen!

"You forgot your change!"

I tried to chase after her, but the tall woman had already disappeared.

Back inside, Iori and I looked at each other before casting a glance at the ten-thousand-yen bill in my hand.

"What just happened?"

"We'll start with the short ribs and the beef tongue. Oh, and we'd also like a plate of offal, please."

Before Funeral Committee night that week, we decided to have a meal at a popular yakiniku restaurant in the local shopping district. I could have easily whipped up some dishes using the leftovers in the fridge, but something had made me want to come here. Perhaps it was because what had happened with the customer earlier was still bothering me.

Maybe the customer was just a little bit weird. But I couldn't get her facial expression out of my mind when she said, "*That* was the Meat Feast?" Maybe I was imagining it, but it seemed that the look that slowly spread across her face was one of sheer devastation. As a chef, it hurt me—it really, really hurt.

And so here I was, doing a bit of research into what "good meat" truly entailed.

It was a small restaurant, but most of the seats were occupied. Plumes of smoke billowed from the meat sizzling on the gridiron. It was like sitting in an oven. I rolled up the sleeves of my sweater and quenched my thirst with cold oolong tea.

"By the way, Momo-chan, at the last Funeral Committee—" Iori suddenly stopped mid-sentence, open-mouthed.

"What is it, Iori? Are you okay?"

Iori was seemingly paralyzed. His eyes were riveted on a point to his right. He looked as though he'd been turned to stone by Medusa.

Hozumi and I followed Iori's gaze to find a woman tucking into her meal with such relish, I almost wanted to give her a round of applause for her sensational performance. Filling her cheeks with a chunky piece of skirt steak, she shoveled some rice into her mouth before washing everything down with seaweed soup. As she did so, she neatly laid out four thin slices of beef tongue on the hot gridiron. Turning them over almost immediately, she topped them with the accompanying green onion relish, leaving them to cook. In the meantime, she picked up a piece of prime rib that she had pre-dipped in a sauce-filled plate, wrapped it around some rice, and ate it in one bite. She then placed some meat on a piece of Korean lettuce and, using her fingers, shoved the whole thing into her mouth. She didn't bother wiping her greasy fingers off before sucking up more rice like a vacuum.

It was a brief moment, probably less than a minute, but it felt as though she was frozen in time—no, it was as though the world had come to a standstill and she was the only one moving. Her bangs were apparently now getting in her way. She combed her fingers through her hair and tied it back, revealing her large almond eyes and long pale-skinned neck.

The woman and I locked eyes.

"Oh," she said.

"Oh! It's you!" I proclaimed.

How did I not notice before?

"You're the Meat Feast girl! I still owe you your change. I wish I had it with me."

I owed her precisely 9,020 yen. I was glad to have run into her.

But she shook her head at my words.

"Actually, that was kind of . . . an apology. It's not the first time I've messed up like that."

"You messed up? What do you mean?"

"Not that I want you to get the wrong impression. I'm not some weirdo. I might not look like it right now, but I am the section head at a book publisher. I even have around ten people working under me!"

"Okay . . . what were *you* apologizing for?"

She took a sip of her beer.

"I probably shouldn't have made it so obvious that the 'Meat Feast' didn't live up to its name in any way."

Ah. So I hadn't imagined the look of devastation after all.

"You mean . . . it wasn't good?"

I rarely had the chance to receive such honest feedback from customers, so I wanted to seize this opportunity. Most customers kept their complaints to themselves. And if not, they posted a bad review online or mentioned their bad dining experience to a friend; it was never to my face.

"No, it was amazing. Absolutely delicious. The herbs gave it a refreshing flavor."

Huh?

My eyes flitted to Iori, wondering if he was as confused as I. Clearly no longer interested, he had moved on to cooking the short ribs with Hozumi. They were chatting excitedly about how tasty it looked.

"But it's not really a matter of flavor. The thing is, that was not meat, was it?" she said assuredly, holding a grilling tong and clacking it together.

"Not meat? Of course it was! That was absolutely meat!"

"Listen: Chicken meat is not meat."

"What?"

"You see this? *This* is what you call meat!" She held a gleaming piece of meat up as if showing off a trophy.

"If it's not red like this piece of meat here, then it's not meat," she said, displaying the raw slice of skirt steak.

I had to admit that, indeed, what she was holding *was* the quintessence of meat. Glistening with freshness, white streaks of fat ran through its crimson flesh.

Wait a second.

"Not all meats are red, though," I said. "Plus, you said 'chicken meat is not meat.' You even called it chicken *meat* yourself."

That was close. She seemed so convincing; I almost believed her.

"Chicken meat is quasi-meat."

Quasi-meat.

Quasi-meat?

"What?"

"It's quasi-meat. Meaning, it has qualities that resemble meat, though unfortunately it's not quite the real thing."

She shook her head regretfully, as though she were some sports commentator pointing out an athlete's error.

"So, are you saying that the grilled chicken I served you for lunch was not meat? You think it shouldn't be called 'Meat Feast'?"

"Frankly, no. I would say it was wrong to call that a Meat Feast."

"But you said it tasted good."

"I told you, this isn't a matter of whether it tastes good or not. For me, what is important is the experience of eating *real* meat. Chicken lacks that feeling."

The young woman drained her glass of beer and sighed with great satisfaction.

She spoke with such confidence, I started to wonder if I was the one who was mistaken here.

After wiping off the grease from her hands with a hot hand towel, she pulled out her business card holder.

"I do sales at a book publisher."

Drawing three business cards from it, she offered them to us.

Kikuno Yamada
Section Head—Sales
Seiran Publishing

"Today, I was out visiting clients and stopped by at Amayadori. But I couldn't have any *real* meat while there, which is why I'm here right now. Do you know what I mean?"

Not in the slightest.

"After all, my motto is 'one good meat a day.' "

Kikuno held her index finger up to my face.

"One . . . good . . . meat . . . a day?"

"As opposed to one good *deed* a day," Hozumi muttered before taking a sip of his egg drop soup.

" 'One good deed a day' means doing something good at least once a day, right? I'm definitely not cut out for something like that. Having meat at least once a day for my own benefit, that is much more important in my life."

"Right . . ."

"I'd planned on having my 'one meat' of the day at Amayadori, but then I was served *chicken*. So I had to make my way to this yakiniku restaurant with urgency. It was a close call."

"But chicken *is* meat!"

"Chicken is quasi-meat," Kikuno said adamantly. "This is a non-negotiable matter."

What is wrong with her? Why is she so stubborn?

"Ms. Yamada." Iori raised his hand as if he were in a classroom, suddenly interested. "What about pork? Is it meat, or is it quasi-meat?" He was clearly enjoying this.

"Good question. Pork *is* meat."

"But pork turns white when you cook it. Is that acceptable?"

"Well, that does make it inferior to beef, obviously. However, it's acceptable."

Which part of that is obvious?

With her speaking so matter-of-factly, and with Iori and Hozumi listening so amusedly, I was really starting to feel as if I was the crazy one.

"What about lamb?" I tested her.

"Above pork but below beef. It is meat, though."

"Hamburger steak?"

"Above chicken, below pork. It would be cutting it pretty close, but it's still meat."

I tried to trip her up. "What about chicken karaage?"

"I suppose that would be quasi-meat."

I guessed that no matter how hard it tried, chicken was never going to make the team.

"I kind of get what you mean." Iori chuckled. "I can relate to it, just a little. But why do you care so much about being able to eat meat?"

Kikuno looked as though she wanted to say, *Do you really wanna know?* and furrowed her brow as she reached for the menu. She ordered additional portions of meat, and we decided to do the same.

"I grew up on a farm," she began to tell us. Kikuno rolled her falling sleeves back up and turned the knob to adjust the flame on the grill.

"My family grows rice in Nagano. I lived with my grandparents, my parents, and my younger brothers—three hungry growing boys."

"So there were eight of you?" Hozumi said, counting on his fingers. "That's a big family."

"It was chaos. We weren't necessarily wealthy, and because we were farmers, we mostly ate our own produce, which meant our meals were normally vegetable-based. So on the rare occasions meat was served, it was like war. My brothers would go wild and dig right in, and I wanted to make sure my hardworking father got his share, too. Most of the time, there wasn't enough left for me to satisfy my hunger."

The waiter replaced our gridirons with clean ones. Like an inquisitive bird, Kikuno carefully inspected hers as she continued her story.

"Which is why I've always had this longing for meat. When I was a young child, I decided that when I grew up, I would move to Tokyo and eat as much meat as I could. But after I started working for a publisher, I became so busy that I forgot all about my hunger."

Iori chimed in thoughtfully, "I do get the impression that people in publishing are workaholics. The kind of people who work until three in the morning."

Kikuno nodded her head at Iori's words. "It's exactly that. We work to impossible schedules and targets, and we have to juggle so many different things. But I enjoyed it. When I first started, I wanted to be able to do the job on my own so badly that I spent most of my time outside of bed working. But then . . ."

Seemingly satisfied that the flame was now at the right strength, Kikuno laid the thick slices of marbled beef on the gridiron in a reverential manner.

"It was springtime, just after my twenty-seventh birthday. An executive at one of the companies I work with took me out to a fancy steakhouse. The experience was so . . . well, it's hard to explain. I didn't think it was *just* delicious."

Kikuno's eyes lit up as she looked at us. "The moment I bit off a chunk of that meat, it felt like every cell in my body came back to life. And I thought, *My body deserves nourishing foods. If I work hard, I can nourish myself with this kind of food.* From now on, I'm going to work for the sake of myself. Eating that steak made me go, *I'm alive!*"

Embracing Kikuno's motto, Iori stuffed his mouth with a piece of short rib. "That's where the 'one meat a day' motto comes from."

"Yes. At some point, I was able to just let go and think, *I'm going to work to eat meat, and eat meat to work*. It may be a simple way to live, but there's nothing wrong with that."

I felt a surge of emotion that I couldn't seem to suppress. Before I knew it, my vision had turned blurry. I had no idea that this was the reason she'd come to the café.

"It's too soon to cry, Momo-chan," Iori said.

"Just a moment ago, you were adamant that chicken was meat," Hozumi added.

Using the fresh hot hand towel that Hozumi requested for me, I mopped my eyes.

"I'm sorry that I failed to serve you meat, even though you had taken the time to come to Amayadori."

I knew I was being inconsistent. But until now, despite calling myself a chef, I had failed to see the direct connection between "eating" and "living." *That* was what I was missing.

Seeing my tear-filled eyes, Kikuno waved her hands concernedly.

"Oh, no, please don't apologize. The real reason I was there was because I'm interested in making an appointment with the Ex-Boyfriend's Favorite Recipe Funeral Committee. I thought I'd check out the café first."

"The Funeral Committee?"

My tears dried instantly.

"Then it was good that we ran into you here!" Iori said. "What type of meat do you use in your ex-boyfriend's recipe? Let me guess—

a cut of the prestigious Matsusaka beef?" he asked as he rubbed his sticky hands on a hot hand towel.

"Actually, it's chocolate."

"What?"

Out of nowhere, I felt a sharp coldness on the nape of my neck. Glancing up, I saw another droplet fall from the sky, this time hitting somewhere around my eyelid.

Not again.

"And of course it's raining—it's a Funeral Committee night," Hozumi mumbled as we made our way back from the yakiniku restaurant to the café.

"I'm starting to think that it rains because you always say that," I said.

"I'm only stating a fact."

We walked briskly toward Amayadori, hugging our bellies, which were filled to the brim with meat. Leading the pack was none other than Kikuno. Striding down the street with her long limbs, there was a lightness to her step that made it hard to believe that she had eaten the most.

She's a woman who makes you want to pursue her.

Watching the straight-backed figure in front of me, I felt the urge to catch up with her. I found myself going faster to keep myself from being left behind. Kikuno had this kind of mysterious charisma, though she probably didn't realize it herself. To be honest, she didn't look like the type of person who had relationship troubles. I didn't have the slightest idea what it was that she wanted to talk about.

Arriving at Amayadori, we hung up our wet jackets, and I led Kikuno to the sofa. Rubbing her hair with the towel around her neck, she took another long look around the café.

"May I ask you what you would like to discuss?" As I kicked off the conversation, Kikuno looked a little uncomfortable and scratched the back of her ears.

"Well . . ." she said.

"Yes?"

"What's more important—me or your work?"

Taken aback by the unexpected question, I found myself flinching.

She continued, "Have you ever asked that of someone you went out with?"

Yes. I definitely have.

My brain decided to recall unwanted images from the past and put them on autoplay.

Hozumi peered at me. "You've said that before, haven't you, Momoko?"

"Please, don't ask me that right now."

Evading Hozumi's gaze, I stirred my latte.

It's the classic relationship dilemma that never seems to get old despite being talked about over and over again. People are always saying, "Women who ask that question are the worst." So despite knowing that it's exactly the kind of question that destroys relationships, why do we keep saying it?

"Has anyone ever asked that to you?" Kikuno changed her question and directed it to Iori.

Hozumi and I turned to Iori at the same time.

"Oh, me?"

"Surely someone's said that to you before."

"Yes," Hozumi chimed in, "I bet this guy has been asked that a million times."

"I suppose so . . . okay, to be honest, I am constantly being asked that question."

"I knew it," Kikuno said. "Iori, what do you think is the right way to answer this?"

"I guess the classic reply is 'Sorry to have made you feel so lonely,'" Iori said. "Or, 'I didn't know that you were suffering so much. I'm so sorry I didn't realize.' I used to say that one a lot."

Used to say that a lot, eh?

He'd been asked it so many times, he seemed to have developed a variety of answers.

"Although only amateurs use words to solve a situation like that," Iori added.

"All right, let's hear what a *pro* would do," Hozumi said.

"You embrace them gently, of course. That's the best thing to do." Iori slid his fingers through his bangs, showing off his beautiful face.

"Maybe that only works because you have such a pretty face," replied Hozumi.

"You're really something," I said to Iori.

To Hozumi and me, it was just another typical chat with Iori. But while the two of us simply rolled our eyes at him, Kikuno seemed to take his words to heart. Letting her body sink into the sofa, she buried her head in her hands.

"Right. That's what I should have said. But I couldn't bring myself to say the words . . ."

Huh? She couldn't say the words?

"Hold on, you were the one being asked the question?" Hozumi said.

Kikuno gave a single nod.

Perhaps her partner saw how dedicated she was to her work and became insecure about their relationship.

"The second he asked the question, my mind went blank." Kikuno stared at the ceiling. "Before I knew it, I had told him that work was more important."

"Seriously?"

How many people in this world can give such a straight answer to this impossible question?

"Why? Didn't you love him?" Iori asked.

"I did . . ." Kikuno muttered, holding her hands behind her neck. "I thought I did."

The rain grew louder and heavier as the wind gathered force. The air inside the café had turned cold, and a shiver ran down my back.

"I met him when I was twenty-nine," Kikuno said, wrapping her hands on her cup and feeling its warmth with her cold fingers. "Which means this was six years ago. I was at that age when everyone around me was getting married. The majority of my friends were settling down or having babies, and my parents were pressuring me to do the same. I felt like I was running out of time."

I felt a pang in my chest, as if someone had scraped my heart with the bristles of a tawashi scrubber.

Twenty-nine. That's exactly my age.

"I wanted to find a husband as soon as possible. I signed up for every matchmaking app I could find, and went on God knows how many group blind dates. I met my ex-boyfriend at a matchmaking party in Roppongi."

Kikuno caressed the rim of her cup with her thumb.

"It was one of those large-scale parties. There were about two hundred attendees in total, a hundred men and a hundred women. It was perfect for someone like me, who wanted to find a partner in a cost-effective way. Of course there were all kinds of people there, but my ex was the one who really stood out. Within a minute of meeting me, he said, 'I'm looking for a partner to marry.' I thought, *He's perfect! I pick him!*"

She's a salesperson through and through, I thought. Once she'd set herself a goal, she mapped out the most efficient route to get there and followed it with confidence.

"So what kind of person was he? What were your first impressions of him?" Iori asked.

He had brought over a bottle of brandy at some point. A pleasant sound filled my ears as he glugged it into a balloon-shaped glass with a practiced hand. Kikuno accepted the glass with a slight bow and brought it to her lips without wavering. She took a long swig.

Isn't that a really strong drink?

I was impressed.

Staring at the ceiling, Kikuno considered Iori's question for a minute. She placed the glass back down on the table nonchalantly.

"He was gentle-natured. Not the chatty type. Time seemed to slow down around him. He was the complete opposite of me."

"What did he do for work?"

"He's an IT engineer at one of the big telecom companies."

"What about his face? Good-looking?"

"I'm not so bothered by looks."

"Could you at least try to describe him? What celebrity does he look like?"

"Okay . . . let me think." Again, Kikuno looked completely unfazed as she tilted her glass, generously pouring the amber liquid into her mouth. "If I had to choose . . ."

She turned toward me, giving a small gasp of revelation.

"If you had to choose?" I echoed her words.

"I guess he looked a bit like Orlando Bloom."

Oh. My. God.

This came as such a surprise that I spat out a bit of my latte. Dabbing my mouth with a hot hand towel, I took a moment to process the information.

"Orlando Bloom, as in the guy with the bleached-blond hair in *The Lord of the Rings?*"

An Orlando Bloom look-alike at a matchmaking party? Roppongi must be a fabulous place.

"I said if I *had* to choose. He wasn't actually Orlando Bloom."

"How many levels down from Orlando Bloom would you go to get to your ex's face?" I asked.

"Levels? Umm . . . maybe two?"

"That's pretty damn close to Orlando Bloom!"

Still maintaining a cool expression and now on her second glass of brandy, she mumbled something about how she didn't think Orlando Bloom was *that* good-looking, at least not as good-looking as Tom Hanks. I couldn't believe her indifference!

I was starting to get a little too excited, as it felt more like a night out with friends than a Funeral Committee meeting. I was beginning to wonder if someone like Kikuno really did have a past that she wanted to lay to rest, if this was truly a breakup story filled with any heartache for her.

"Anyway, what was I going to say . . ." Kikuno continued. "After the big matchmaking party, we went on about three dates. We became a couple on Christmas Day. I remember it being so cold."

"Christmas Day? So romantic!"

"Who asked who out?"

"He asked me to be his girlfriend."

"Where?"

"I think we were at Tokyo Tower."

"Wow, sounds perfect so far," I said, holding my blushing face. "Christmas Day, Tokyo Tower, Orlando the IT engineer. Talk about ticking all the boxes. It's like getting a straight flush in poker."

"From what we've heard so far, I can't think of a single reason why you would break up." Iori chortled.

"I don't see how anyone could go from that to an 'it's me or your work' situation."

After swallowing the cracker she'd been nibbling on, Kikuno spoke.

"It was nighttime. We saw the view from Tokyo Tower."

"Oh my God. A nighttime view of the city from Tokyo Tower!"

"Quiet, Momoko," Hozumi said.

"And then, as we were walking back to Hamamatsucho Station . . ."

"Wow, a station . . ."

"Why are you getting excited over a station?" Iori asked me.

"Right. Good point."

Oops. I had gotten so carried away, I had lost my sense of proportion. I relaxed my breath, inhaling deeply with my hand on my chest.

"Did you hold hands?" Hozumi asked.

"We did. We held hands as we walked, and that was when he asked me to be his girlfriend."

Hozumi gasped, clasping his big hand over his mouth, and I found myself doing the same. It seemed that neither of us had expected such a romantic story.

Oh, God, my heart is thumping!

Opening the window slightly for some fresh air, I felt a pleasant sensation as the cold rain touched the tips of my fingers.

"So, what did Orlando love about you?" Iori asked as he stabbed a toothpick into an olive.

"He didn't tell me. I never thought to ask him, either."

"Really?" I said. "I would've asked him all the time. Didn't you want to know?"

"Well, he was going out with me, so that means he loved me, doesn't it? He wouldn't have gone out with me if he didn't."

I felt a sense of déjà vu.

Where had I heard those words?

Ah, right. It was Kyohei.

Kyohei had said the exact same thing. "Why would you ask such an obvious question?" he would say. I was so insecure then that I would ask him over and over again if he loved me, and he would sigh at me and look annoyed.

Kikuno opened the window farther and leaned out of it. "But maybe that was the beginning of the end of our relationship. Since we're going out, he must love me, and he must want to marry me. Great, I've ticked that box! I've secured my future husband! Now, I have some work to do!"

Kikuno was looking up at the night. Every time she blinked, the streetlights reflecting in her eyes flickered.

"Thinking about it now, I did a horrible thing."

I started to disagree. "No . . ."

I couldn't blame Kikuno. For a twenty-nine-year-old woman, finding someone to marry is the heaviest, most suffocating task in life. When my relationship with Kyohei ended, it felt like the cruelest thing someone could ever do to me.

If only he had dumped me two years earlier, I thought, *at least I'd still be solidly in my twenties.*

Will I be alone for the rest of my life?

Thoughts like these echoed in my mind every time I saw my friends in their big white dresses. Is it so wrong to want to strike off that "task" as soon as possible? I couldn't say that it was.

"But he wasn't like that. He wanted to have a proper relationship. The kind where we would go out to places together and gradually build a connection with each other before getting married. It must have been hard for him."

Leaning on the edge of the window, Kikuno stared at her wrist, which was wet from the rain.

"There was a period where we couldn't see each other because I was so busy with work. I knew that he was growing more and more unhappy, but cutting back on my hours was just not an option for me. I'd just been promoted. I was finally doing what I'd aspired to do since I first joined the company. I'd worked so hard for that opportunity and couldn't stand the idea of losing that."

It takes a long time before you get to do the work you want to do. You have to build credibility for yourself. You need to prepare yourself with the right "weapons" to face the battle. But by the time we're armed with all the weapons needed to be allowed on the front line, we also reach the stage in life when we desperately want to get married.

"We rarely had the same days off. I kept having to turn him down when he tried to make plans. There were so many occasions where we'd make reservations at a nice restaurant, but I had to cancel at the last minute because I got held up at work. So when we did see each other, it was mostly at our homes."

"Did you cook for him at home?" Hozumi asked.

Kikuno straightened her back and retrieved her phone from her bag. She held the screen out to us. It was a picture of a beautifully plated stewed hamburger steak. A rich demi-glace sauce dotted on a floral-patterned plate, garnished with lettuce and cherry tomatoes.

"Yes, I did. I was even taking cooking lessons for a while."

"Seriously?" I asked.

Kikuno mentioned the name of a famous culinary school chain. When I was around twenty-five, I had once attended a trial lesson at the same school. They offered a "konkatsu course," classes specifically designed to prep people looking to get married with the necessary cooking skills. I told Kikuno this.

"That's the one! That's the course I took!" Kikuno exclaimed.

No wonder her cooking was presented in such a photogenic way. Kikuno showed us more pictures of the dishes she had made for him. Stew, nikujaga, omurice. The plating was beautiful, and the colors worked well together. Every dish looked as though it belonged on the cover of a cookbook.

"Come to think of it, I only ever made him dishes I learned in those cooking classes," Kikuno muttered under her breath as she scrolled listlessly on her phone. "I didn't want to risk making something that he didn't like, so I never cooked him any of my own recipes. I stuck to making dishes that men apparently go wild for, and followed the recipes that my teacher said would 'make your man happy.'"

Kikuno touched her now-empty glass. Iori responded silently by pouring her more brandy.

"The first dish I made him was this hamburger steak stewed in demi-glace sauce. He loved it, just as I'd hoped. My teacher was spot-on. So I kept serving him easy, foolproof recipes. But now that I think about it, they weren't really my kind of flavors. I was just applying the 'good wife template' to myself, because all I wanted was to get married."

She drained her glass, and Iori refilled it again.

"Did you really not make him a single dish that you liked?" I asked.

After deliberating for a moment, Kikuno shook her head.

"I didn't get to it in the end. I'm from Nagano, so when I cook for myself, I often make dishes using vegetables from back home. When I make shogayaki, for example, I add some grated apple to the soy sauce and mirin, and massage the marinade into the pork before frying it."

"That sounds so good, though!"

"But when I made shogayaki for *him*, I always followed the exact recipe I learned in class. The sugar content in apples makes it easy to burn, you see. Burnt meat doesn't look great. It was safer to use a classic recipe that everyone was familiar with. I was too scared to serve him flavors from home. But if I had . . ."

Maybe things would be different, I finished the thought for her.

She sipped her brandy as though she was trying to wash down the words that had made it to the tip of her tongue.

There are things in this world that are "right" according to everyone else. Then there are things that are "right" only to you. Sure, we all *know* that we should follow what feels right to you. But how many people can really say, "I'm right," when everyone else is shouting out a different answer?

Not me. I don't have that kind of courage.

I realized that my feet had turned completely cold. The heat on my face had also cooled off. And we were quite off track.

"So . . ." I said.

"Hmm?"

"About the recipe that you'd like to lay to rest . . ."

"Oh, right. The chocolate." Kikuno tapped her long, gel-manicured nails on the table. "The day we broke up was Valentine's Day. We met up in Akasaka and had dinner at a classy bistro. But I messed up. After we finished eating, the question of how we should spend the rest of the night came up. And I said . . ."

"Uh-oh . . ."

"I said, 'It's not too late, so I'm gonna go back to work.' "

I gazed at the glass in Kikuno's hand. That night, the two of them must have enjoyed a drink together like this. He must have been hopeful that they could spend the whole night together.

"That's when he asked me, 'Which is more important to you, me or work?' " Kikuno said. "He didn't look angry at all. He just looked very despondent and lonely. When I saw the expression on his face, I finally realized that my behavior had forced him to say such a thing."

Kikuno rubbed her nose with her index finger.

"But I couldn't bring myself to say, 'You're more important. I won't go to work.' I mean, I really did have to work! My team was on a deadline, and the project was impossible to complete without me."

I could picture the scene so vividly, it was almost as if an image of the bistro six years ago had appeared behind Kikuno, who sat staring into the stem of the glass in her hand.

"The moment he said those words, a million thoughts spiraled in my head. I did think of saying, 'I'm sorry I made you say something like that, let's spend more time together.' But in the end . . ."

"Why couldn't you say that, do you think?" Iori asked softly.

Kikuno scratched under her right eyelid with her index finger. "These were my initial thoughts: If I told him that work was more important, it would be the end of everything. Even *I* knew that—if I gave an honest answer, our relationship would be over. I needed to choose the right words to reassure him, at least for that moment. But then I had another thought, which was: Maybe he's asked me this because he *wants* to end things."

My heart thumped.

What's more important—me or your work? I know that feeling. That feeling of wanting someone to make that impossible choice. One's work and one's partner are two incommensurable things. I was fully aware of that. Even still, I found myself asking such a difficult question of the person I loved.

When Kyohei told me that he was trying to get me to break up with him, I was pained by the fact that he was being so dead honest with me. I thought, *This isn't the time to speak so candidly.*

Even though I longed for sincerity, there was also a part of me that wished he was better at lying.

Why can't you pretend to be a better guy? Why can't you try harder to be a good boyfriend and say something romantic to me, at least on my birthday?

Sometimes we just want to be inside a little romantic bubble. But maybe when two people are able to go in and out of that bubble with ease, that's what compatibility looks like.

"What happened after that?"

"So then . . ." Kikuno let out a small sigh and paused for a moment.

"He said, 'We're not quite right for each other, are we? I don't think we should keep seeing each other.' He told me that we should break up, and I said yes. The end."

An intense pain and sadness came over me, like a giant poison-tipped spear twisting inside my stomach.

Kikuno was tapping her nails on the table.

"Did you love him?" Iori asked.

"To be honest, I don't know. I still think about what it was that I felt. But . . ." Kikuno broke off then. As though she was trying to convince herself, she said, "One thing I know for sure is that I love working. I love myself when I'm working hard. This fact will never change. I think that I couldn't open my heart to him because he wished that I was capable of a textbook romance, and I just wasn't that person. I was so horrible to him."

"I don't think that you were horrible . . ." I said.

"I mean, it was me who kept pretending to be a woman capable of a textbook romance! I was the one who deliberately served him typical 'good wife' recipes that I learned in class, to try to get him to like my cooking."

Kikuno laughed bitterly, stroking her neck.

"But that's not me at all. I had set a dating criteria based on what I'd been told was 'right.' Like, he should have a certain type of job, and that he should be the youngest son, and so on. Maybe I couldn't be sure about my feelings because I had looked for someone that was 'husband material,' then tried to fall in love with him, in that order. Despite being well aware that I was out of step with everyone around me, for some reason I had made it a necessary condition for my partner to be regarded as 'desirable' by everyone else. It's strange, isn't it?"

I could relate to that.

"I know that feeling, Kikuno. I really do."

"Momo-chan—wait, you're not crying again, are you?" Iori said, then took a moment. "Actually, I don't blame you."

Kikuno's words resonated with me so deeply, my heart ached.

A romantic view from Tokyo Tower. A surprise present. Holding hands. Being asked to be his girlfriend on the third date. Cooking foolproof meals like hamburger steak and nikujaga to avoid disappointing him. A wedding in Omotesando. An engagement ring from Cartier, or Tiffany's at least. That's what we women have been taught to want!

We desire such things that "everyone else" wants, and yet as soon as someone falls in love with this version of us—a version that makes us an imitation of everyone else—we feel a sense of loneliness.

As I sat weeping, Kikuno stroked my head consolingly. "There's something I want to tell you, something that feels in contrast to everything else I have told you." she said. "That night, I had secretly brought chocolates with me."

"Huh?"

"I had turned him down so many times, I wanted to make it up to him. I'd prepared homemade chocolates for him. I really love chocolate, you know? I used to make them for myself every year on Valentine's. It's a nama chocolate that I have a special recipe for, and I wanted him to try some."

"Hold on a second."

In other words . . .

"You mean it wasn't one of the recipes from your cooking class?"

Kikuno gave a single nod.

"S-so . . ."

The day she finally brought her own cooking to him was the day they broke up? How can that be?

"That's what you meant earlier when you said that you didn't get to cook him your own recipe." Burying his shaved head in his hands, Hozumi slumped over the table.

"What did you do with the chocolates? Did you eat them yourself?" Iori asked.

"I put them in the trash at the breakup shrine."

"The breakup shrine?"

"There's a shrine near my workplace. It's famous for celebrating and honoring the breaking off of bad relationships. I put them in the trash can there, praying that we'd both find better relationships in the future."

"That is too sad, Kikuno!" I said.

Orlando has no idea that Kikuno planned on giving him homemade chocolates that night! And perhaps he still thinks that Kikuno immediately chose work over him when he confronted her with the question, that she didn't waver at all.

Where did it go wrong?

If only Orlando had waited a little longer. If only Kikuno had tried to meet him halfway just one day—no, just one hour earlier. Then maybe . . .

"Kikuno, you're off work tomorrow, right?" I asked impulsively.

"Technically speaking, I am."

"Let's make it, then. Let's eat it together."

"Make what?"

"The chocolates, of course! We can stay up making them and have a little party while they're cooling down. That can be the funeral recipe for your breakup!"

Kikuno widened her eyes in surprise. "W-wait a second. I couldn't ask you to do that for me."

She seemed to be taken aback by my unexpected suggestion, but my gut told me I needed to do this.

Kikuno must have been unable to let go of the fact that she couldn't give him those chocolates six years ago. Like a small fish bone caught at the back of her throat, the fact that she couldn't show him what *she* thought was "right" was still trapped inside of her.

So . . .

"Let us try your chocolates. We'll be sure to tell you what we think of them."

It's the only way we can bring this love to an end.

"Right . . . okay. Let's get this task checked off then, shall we?" Kikuno rolled up her sleeves, a grin rising to her lips.

When did it stop raining?

Under the first light of dawn, the business district of Minato was deserted apart from a few exceptions: a runner with impressive calves and his miniature pinscher; an izakaya worker cleaning up the remnants of Friday night; a hostess hugging her patron before getting into a taxi.

And . . . a handsome man with visible bags under his eyes, staggering his way down the street.

"Why do you look so drained? It was only an all-nighter," I said to Iori jokingly.

"Maybe you think it was *only* an all-nighter because you spent it sampling chocolates," Iori said before making a gagging sound.

"Hey, are you all right?" Hozumi put his arm around a pale and hungover Iori to assist him.

I supposed it was understandable that Iori was in such a state. Kikuno was quite something.

The chocolates were surprisingly quick to make, and we commenced our party in high spirits. But then Iori pushed his luck a little too far when he challenged Kikuno to a drinking contest. Despite having already drunk four glasses of brandy straight up, Kikuno maintained an air of nonchalance as she emptied drink after drink until Iori finally reached his limit and raised the white flag.

"There it is. That's the shrine."

Just like before, Kikuno took long strides as she walked along the street. Thrusting my hands inside the pockets of my trench coat, I trotted after her to find a small torii gate to a Shinto shrine, standing discreetly in a corner of the business district.

I say shrine, but it was a modest space that looked more like a tiny hut with a little box for offerings. There was a plastic trash can beside the entrance and next to the shrine was a park.

"Ah. This takes me back," Kikuno commented.

We decided to sample the chocolates on the bench inside the park. As the lid of the container opened, a bittersweet scent wafted through the air. I bit into a piece, letting the mellow sweetness of the chocolate spread into my mouth.

I heaved a sigh of delight.

"Hey," Kikuno said after swallowing her first piece of chocolate, "it's pretty good, isn't it?"

"It's absolutely delicious," I replied.

"You could sell these," Hozumi added.

"I am a genius, after all," Kikuno said, popping another piece into her mouth.

Kikuno pressed her eyes shut, savoring the sweetness.

She surely has a soft spot for chocolates, I thought to myself.

"Thank you, guys. I can finally have these after six years."

I was relieved. Kikuno had reclaimed her recipe.

"Hey, look." I suddenly noticed light spilling through from between the buildings. "The morning sun."

I glanced at my phone. It was 5:46, already time for the sunrise.

Kikuno and I moved to a spot where we could get a better view of the sunrise. We stood watching as the morning crept over the sky above the business district.

"Hey, Momo-chan." Kikuno squinted a little, the morning light on her face. "Do you ever want to get married?"

"Yeah, I do. Although . . ."

"Yeah?"

"There's a part of me that hates myself for feeling that way."

Kikuno chuckled.

"What?"

"It's just that I know what you mean."

How I wished I could say with certainty that I could be happy without ever getting married, that I had the confidence to say that I would be fine.

"I don't regret the choice I made that day," Kikuno said, her eyes fixed on the sun. "Work will always be important to me. Even if I were to go back to Valentine's Day six years ago, my answer would still be the same. Although sometimes—just sometimes—I find myself thinking that . . ." Kikuno turned to me and smiled bitterly. "I wish I was better at having a proper romance."

"Hey, should we go pay our respects to the shrine?" Iori called out. He had recovered a little after resting on the bench.

"Shall we?" Kikuno fixed her loosened hair into a tight ponytail and began walking toward Iori and Hozumi.

I felt a prickle at the back of my chest.

A proper romance . . . Perhaps she's right.

Even still . . .

"But, Kikuno . . ." The words were flying out of my mouth before I'd collected my thoughts. "You're somebody who can make yourself happy. You work hard, you always try your best, and you certainly know how to treat yourself to meat. You have the ability to trust what you believe is right."

Kikuno turned around. She kept her hands inside her pockets as she stared at me.

"I love my work, too," I continued. "I love myself working where I am. I'm proud of myself for being able to feel this way, for having worked hard to be able to feel this way. I wouldn't want to give up this version of me."

When I saw Kikuno last night and the way she devoured all that meat bought with her hard-earned money, the way everything made her think of work, the way her gel-manicured nails were all grown out, presumably because she'd been so absorbed by her work . . .

"Ultimately, you were able to accept your work-loving self. That makes you the most admirable, incredible woman in the world."

It made me admire her. That's how I'd like to live my life.

"I don't want you to forget that."

I dearly hoped that my words reached her heart.

The sky, just a moment ago a dim gray, had turned bright blue. The sun had transformed the cityscape entirely.

"Don't worry, I know," Kikuno said, a smile spreading across her face. "Thank you, Momo-chan."

Choosing your own path instead of following everyone else is a scary thing. The more we grow older, the more we feel like time is running out. That will probably never change.

Even still, I have the power to make myself happy.

At least that's what I want to believe.

After the four of us had paid a visit to the shrine and finished the chocolates, Kikuno made a startling statement.

"I feel so much better. Since I'm in the neighborhood, I might as well go to the office now."

"But you just pulled an all-nighter," I said.

"Oh, this is nothing. What do you think I eat all that meat for?"

Thanking us in a bright voice, she strutted off. The clack of her heels rang out as she walked briskly toward a glass skyscraper standing easily over thirty stories tall.

After all of that eating and drinking and chocolate-making? We even held a "funeral" at a shrine!

She's really something, I thought, and giggled to myself.

My eyes followed Kikuno as her figure receded into the distance. She took big confident strides. Producing her lanyard and employee ID from her bag, she exuded an air of pride as she headed off to work.

How amazing is she? She really does make you want to emulate her.

From the bottom of my heart, I thought that she was an incredible woman. So amazing, she could move you to tears.

"Please come back and have the Meat Feast again!" I shouted in her direction.

"I will if you don't give me any quasi-meat!"

Kikuno waved her right arm at us before she disappeared into the glass cuboid building.

The glare from the buildings filled my view with rays of transparent blue.

It was a crisp morning, and I had a feeling that I was going to have a fabulous day at work.

IT'S ME OR YOUR WORK CHOCOLATES

3½ ounces (100 g) milk chocolate

3½ ounces (100 g) 70% cacao dark chocolate

6 tablespoons (100 g) heavy cream

1 teaspoon Kirsch

1 teaspoon honey

Cocoa powder, for dusting

METHOD

Finely chop the chocolates.

Heat the heavy cream in a pan. Turn off the heat when small bubbles start to form around the edge of the pan.

Add the chopped chocolates to the heated cream and mix well.

Mix in the Kirsch and the honey.

Line a deep stainless steel baking tray with Saran Wrap and transfer the mixture into it.

Leave it in the fridge until it settles.

Line a clean baking tray with the cocoa powder and place the chocolate into it. Top the chocolate with more cocoa powder.

Cut into small squares.

Tip: Dust your knife with cocoa powder to prevent the chocolate from sticking.

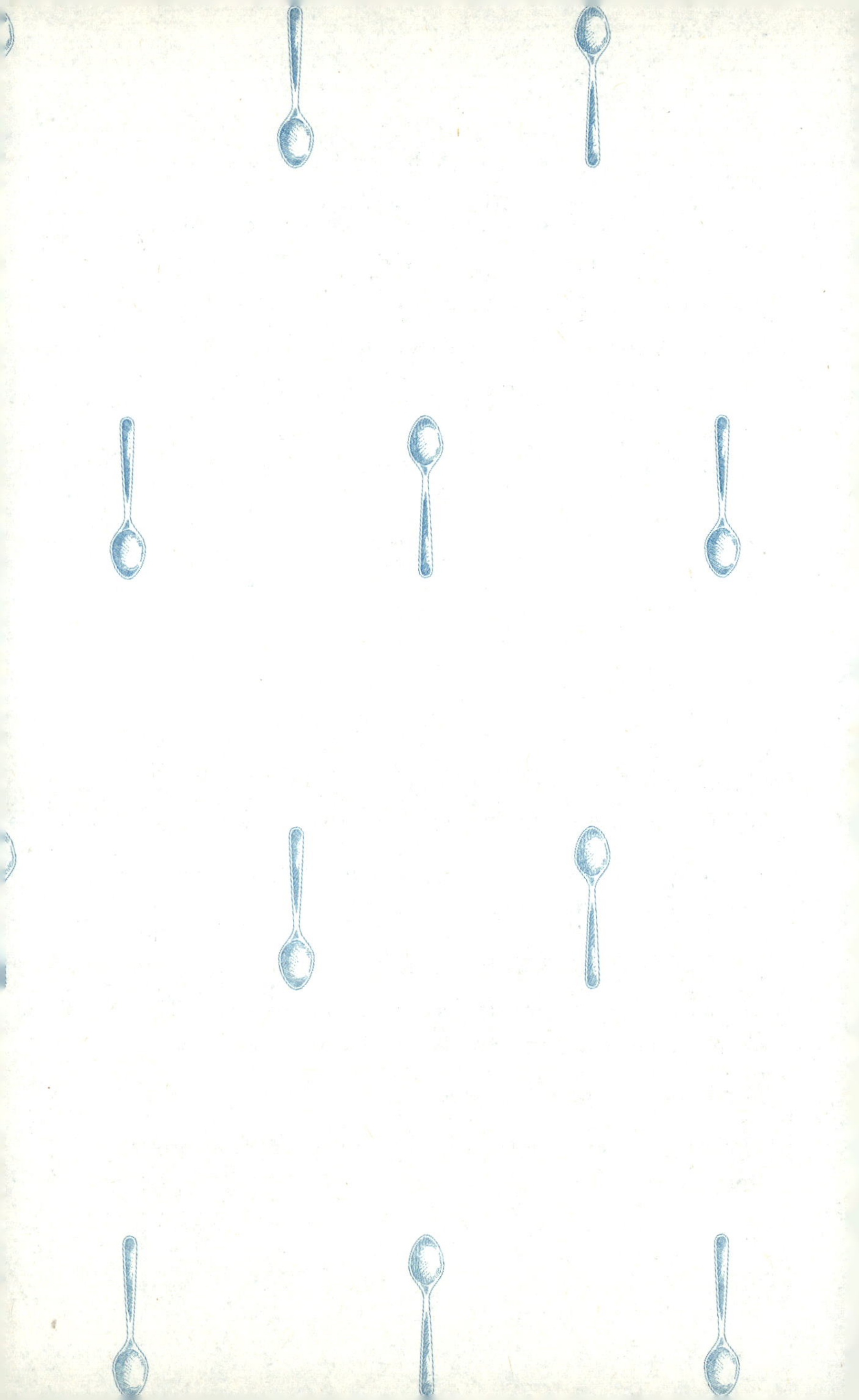

CHAPTER 7

PIZZA FOR THE RISING STAR

"Irasshaimase."

I turned around to greet our customer, and a soft shade of Wakakusa green suddenly came into my view. The café instantly filled with an air of sophistication, the bleakness of November seemingly dispelled.

"Do you have a table for one, please?"

"Oh, of course. Please follow me."

The elegant lady, dressed in a kimono, quietly closed the door behind her. Her demeanor was both gentle and authoritative. Taking her time, she stepped farther inside Amayadori.

She was beautiful.

Like an actress, I thought to myself.

Agewise, she was . . . maybe in her fifties? She had a distinct, chiseled jawline, and her gray-streaked hair was neatly pulled back into a tight bun.

The lady surveyed the café before taking a seat at the very end of the counter, where Hozumi normally liked to sit. Ordering a cup of Kilimanjaro coffee, she carefully folded her haori jacket and placed it over the back of her seat.

"She's a classy lady, isn't she?" Iori whispered as he prepared the coffee dripper. "Not the type we usually see in this neighborhood."

"Her style is more elegant. She must be from Ginza . . . No, maybe Kamakura? Or even Gion in Kyoto. One of those sorts of places."

"Wherever it is, it sure doesn't look very Taishido, Setagaya."

The lady emitted the kind of elegance that made me want to call her "Madame." While she waited for her coffee, she looked around the café curiously. I wondered if there was something that had caught her attention and made her come into our shop. It was a depressingly quiet Friday afternoon, and since the café was devoid of any other customers, I decided to try and strike up a conversation. Setting the cup of coffee down on the counter, I locked eyes with her. Madame gave me a graceful smile.

"It's your first time here, isn't it? Did you find us in a magazine?"

Crinkling the corners of her eyes, Madame drew a planner from her bag. She opened it up and removed from it a piece of paper folded in four.

"That's the flyer for the Ex-Boyfriend's Favorite Recipe Funeral Committee!"

It was undoubtedly one of the flyers we'd handed out when we launched. Thanks to word of mouth, we now had clients coming to us regularly and didn't need these ads as much. She must have held onto it for some time.

"Are you interested in booking a meeting with the Funeral Committee? You should have said so!"

She must have been too embarrassed to tell me.

"We don't have any bookings tonight, so we can have a nice long talk. Although it doesn't start until this evening, so we're still a long way away. You could of course wait here . . ."

"Actually, that's not it," she said. "There isn't anything I'd like to talk about." She flashed me a somewhat apologetic smile. Raising her cup and saucer to her chest, she drank her coffee with such grace, almost as if she was conducting a tea ceremony.

"I'd heard from an acquaintance of mine about this café and your initiative, that's all. I don't intend on booking an appointment. I'm sorry for the misunderstanding."

"Oh, not at all!"

I covered my blushing cheeks with the tray I was holding. *I* was embarrassed for misunderstanding.

"We're only happy to hear that the Funeral Committee caught your attention," I said, gesturing to Iori in the back. "We have another member, too; he's not here at the moment, but I'm sure he'll also be delighted when we tell him how far and wide word is spreading."

Though I couldn't be sure, she seemed to twitch her brow at the mention of Hozumi. And for a split second, I thought I saw a shadow creep over her face. But a moment later, that shadow had disappeared and a smile had returned to her eyes.

"By the way, I heard that a monk is part of the committee. Is that true?" she asked, sliding her finger along the text printed on the flyer.

"Yes. He trains at a temple nearby called Seizanji."

"Is that so? I heard he's very academic."

Hozumi's deadpan face floated into my mind.

"Ah, yes. He went to the University of Tokyo, and I think he worked in a corporate trading house for a while before he became a monk. He's a little different from ordinary monks, and that might be why. Not that I know much about him."

"Well, well. Is that so?" A triumphant look came over Madame as she nodded repeatedly and brought her cup to her lips.

She probed further. "What about his appearance? Does he look . . . healthy?"

"For sure! He's the epitome of health. He loves working out, so his body is ripped. He's always checking out his muscles in the bathroom here."

"His muscles? Right. . . . Well, I'm relieved to hear that. I really am."

What is she relieved about?

I began to make my way back to the kitchen. Just then, I heard the door creak.

I spun around and saw Hozumi. Speak of the devil.

"Could you make me an ice cream soda?" he said.

"Isn't it too cold for that? You really do love your ice cream sodas," Iori said, sounding impressed.

"I'll do as I like," Hozumi said under his breath.

He started to walk toward his usual seat, but quickly noticed that somebody was already there. Averting his gaze, he turned on his heel and settled on the sofa at the back of the café. He pulled out a paperback book. I remembered that he had mentioned something about finishing all the volumes of *Jean-Christophe* before the end of the year.

"Hozumi?"

It wasn't myself or Iori calling to him. It was the woman at the counter.

Hozumi, who had begun to flip through the pages of his paperback, stopped. As if in slow motion, he turned his face toward Madame.

"It's you, isn't it?" she said. "Long time no see."

It was as if time had stopped moving. Hozumi sat completely still as though he were paralyzed.

What the hell is going on?

Madame dismounted the barstool gracefully and slowly approached the sofa.

"May I sit?" she asked him timidly.

Subtly lowering his chin, Hozumi replied, "It's been a long time."

Leaving his paperback open, Hozumi placed it face down on the table. He removed his glasses and rubbed at his cheeks repeatedly, as though trying to confirm that the world before him was real. He put his glasses back on.

"Your name was mentioned on this." Seating herself opposite Hozumi, Madame opened up the same flyer from earlier and showed it to him.

"Right. The notice about the Funeral Committee."

"I'm glad that you seem well."

"Thank you."

"This is a nice café." She took another look at her surroundings.

"I guess," Hozumi mumbled, barely audible.

"Hozumi, aren't you going to come back home?" Madame peered into his face tentatively, as if she was trying to read it.

"I'll come back eventually."

"You always say that, but you never come home for the Obon holidays or New Year's. As your mother, I'm worried about you."

She's his mother?

"I'm not a child anymore."

"I'll always worry about my children, no matter how old they are. That's what parents do."

"I'm still in training."

"Training. . . . It seems to be taking you an awfully long time. When is it going to finish? Besides, you made a promise to your father. He set a time limit, remember?"

Time limit? What time limit?

Almost reflexively, I turned back to look at Iori. It seemed that this was all news to him, too.

"The promise with Father . . ." Hozumi muttered under his breath.

"Don't worry," Madame said. "Your father and brother aren't bothered by it anymore." She cupped Hozumi's hand with both of hers. Hozumi flinched slightly.

"Not bothered by it?"

"I know that you want to come home. I can see it. It's written all over your face. I'll try to convince him to forgive you, help you apologize. Please."

They were both struggling to keep their frustration under wraps.

I suddenly remembered something that Hozumi once mentioned. He had muttered to me that his family home was in Chiba and that he had decided to become a monk because he felt he was incompatible with the family business.

Madame tightened her grip. "Let's have a proper talk about it. I'm ready to listen. Why don't we go to that Italian restaurant again? You remember the excellent pizza there, don't you?"

Hozumi's face clouded over even more. He stared fixedly at a particular point in the air. It was as though he had forgotten that such a thing as blinking existed. Afraid of breaking the silence that now pervaded the room, I hesitated to breathe.

For some time, Hozumi sat with a pensive look on his face. Then he gently took his hand away from Madame.

"Okay. I'll contact you soon. But right now I need to get back to my training."

With those words, Hozumi bowed his head and reached for his shoulder bag. Flustered, Madame sprang to her feet.

"Hozumi."

But Hozumi kept walking and quickly headed out of the door, before even being served his ice cream soda.

Madame turned toward us and apologized profusely for asking questions about Hozumi without telling us that she was his mother, for bothering us with a family issue. Iori and I, still in a state of shock, told her that she didn't need to worry.

"I know it would be presumptuous of me to ask, especially given all the trouble I've caused already, but . . ."

Madame held out a paper bag tentatively. I saw something wrapped in a purple-colored furoshiki.

"My son . . . he loves this. Could you please give it to him?"

"Oh, umm . . ." I wasn't sure if it was right to accept it without consulting Hozumi.

"I'm worried about my boy. . . . Eating this should cheer him up."

Madame pressed the handle of the paper bag into my fingers. I was surprised to find her hands wrinkled and blotched with age spots, her fingertips dry and chapped.

Right. She's Hozumi's mother. Though she looks very young, she could be over sixty years old.

"Okay."

I wasn't brave enough to brush her away. The bag was heavy as I took it.

"Please be there for him."

With those words, Madame gave a deep bow and made her way out.

I undid the furoshiki to find a shiny, lacquered jubako. Inside the tiered boxes were long rolls of sushi, each wrapped neatly in Saran Wrap. They looked delicious. Normally, I would have been delighted, but under the circumstances, I found myself sighing.

". . . you made a promise to your father. He set a time limit, remember?"

Madame's words circled uncontrollably in my head, crashing through the walls of my brain. I felt a sense of unease.

Sensing my dismay, Iori tried to reassure me. "Try not to worry so much. We have the Funeral Committee meeting later, so we can ask him about it then."

I could see that he, too, had to force at least some of his smile.

I tried to find ways to keep my mind distracted for the rest of the afternoon, dusting the pendant lamp and rewriting the signboard outside. Before I knew it, I had scrubbed down every corner of the café. Feeling the breeze of late autumn on my face, I swept away the fallen leaves until the ground was spotless. Still, the unsettling feeling in my heart refused to go away. I couldn't help it; I needed to look up who his family was, try to uncover *something* about this glamorous woman who had graced our café.

As I looked up, the sky was completely overcast, the clouds huddling tightly so as not to let the slightest light break in.

"Hozumi . . ." I said to myself. I had a feeling that something bad was going to happen.

"It's only eight o'clock," Iori said.

"But normally he would already be here, and he's not answering his phone. I'm going to go see if he's okay."

I flung the door open, ignoring Iori's calls to wait. I couldn't shake the strange uneasiness I'd felt since the afternoon. My gut told me that I needed to find Hozumi and talk to him and—

"What are you doing here?"

"You sound disappointed."

Hozumi was standing right in front of me. He seemed rather fine.

Having missed his chance to have his ice cream soda earlier, he requested one as soon as he sat down in his usual seat. Once it was served to him, he dug his spoon into it as though he didn't have a care in the world. Making sure that the melted ice cream wasn't spilling over the sides, he gingerly pushed his straw through the soda, making a gurgling sound as he sipped.

He appeared to be his usual self. A little relieved, I lowered myself into the seat next to him.

Once he had finished his drink, I seized my chance and held out the jubako wrapped in the purple furoshiki.

"Here."

"Thanks," Hozumi said, accepting it without changing his expression.

"Aren't you going to open it?"

"I don't need to. It's rolled sushi, isn't it?"

Taken aback, I was at a loss for words. I hadn't expected him to be able to guess the contents so quickly.

"She never comes to Tokyo without them," Hozumi quickly added, probably sensing my astonishment. "In fact, I'm happy for *you* to have them. I've been eating these since I was a child."

"We can all share them later?" I stared at the wrapped jubako that was now in my hands again, desperately searching for my next words.

"Your mother is very nice," I added awkwardly, as if I were reading off some sort of script written for people who had just met their friend's parents.

"I really wasn't expecting any of that. Are you some kind of secret millionaire?" I blurted out.

I thought about how Hozumi had spoken to his own mother so formally and the way she acted as if it was the most natural thing. Of course, all families are different, I knew that. Still, there was something about their interaction that felt rather uncanny. I kept speaking, saying one wrong thing after another instead of asking him all the questions that were running through my mind.

Hozumi stared at me. Then suddenly he said teasingly, "Knowing you, I'm guessing you've looked my family up."

"What? N-no, of course not!"

"She's lying," Iori said, carrying a latte in his hand. "She spent the whole afternoon searching. She hardly got any work done."

He sat down, joining us at the counter.

"You weren't supposed to say anything, Iori."

I could feel my face growing red. It was true. I couldn't settle during my cleaning mania that afternoon, and when Iori said to me, "If you want to know so badly, why don't you look them up?" I couldn't resist the temptation.

It turned out that Hozumi was a member of a prestigious political family, the Kurodas—they were what we'd call "local dignitaries." On the website of the relevant prefectural assembly, I found the name Kosaku Kuroda under the tab listing its members. A picture of a man with his lips tightly pressed together was featured prominently. The man had to be Hozumi's father, they bore such a close resemblance to each other. The surname of Kosaku's predecessor was also Kuroda, probably Hozumi's grandfather. It seemed certain that the Kuroda family had been serving the constituency for several generations.

Although I didn't see the name Kazutoyo Kuroda—Hozumi's older brother—in the list of assembly members, I found some of his social media accounts. In his profile were the words *Secretary to assembly member, Protecting children's smiles*, and *Father of three*. His posts mainly consisted of information on local events.

"I'm sorry, I couldn't stop scrolling . . ."

When I confessed to him everything I'd researched, Hozumi snickered. "It's fine. You're not the type who can resist that sort of juicy gossip."

"I'm not an animal."

"You kind of are."

"Excuse me?"

I felt a little relieved that our usual squabbles had returned.

"Is your older brother your only sibling?" I asked.

"Yes, we're a family of four. My grandparents used to live with us, but they passed away a long time ago. I believe my older brother and his family—his wife and children—are now living there with my parents. It's a pretty common setup for politicians."

"I've heard some stories about politicians," Iori said. "Is it true that they have a funeral to attend almost every week?"

"Seriously? A funeral every week?" I said.

"Well . . . I wouldn't go as far as to say *every* week." Hozumi gave a bitter grin. "But we did go to many wakes; my family saw them as opportunities to stay acquainted with the local people. Plus, people would probably make snide remarks if we went to one and didn't show up to another."

"Sounds cutthroat."

"So you went alongside your father?" Iori asked.

"Of course. It was always the four of us—my father, mother, brother, and I." Hozumi dropped two sugar cubes into his latte and stirred.

"I remember them well," he continued. "My brother and I wore matching waistcoats and shorts. My mother would walk us from the car to the venue, taking my hand. For some reason, it seemed to rain whenever we attended a wake, so we always kept a black umbrella on hand. She would hold it over my brother and me, not letting a single drop of rain fall on us. Her kimono would get soaked."

I imagined Madame in her younger days.

The patter of the rain reached my ears. I faced toward the window impulsively. It had started to drizzle.

"I told her every time that I wanted to hold my own umbrella, but she never let me. She'd say, 'I can't let my future politicians catch a cold.'"

"That must have been hard to bear," Iori said.

Hozumi gave another bitter smile and rubbed his shaved head.

"But once we'd finished signing in at the reception desk, my father would take mine and my brother's hands. He would get more attention that way, to be seen walking us in. A loving father was his political brand, so I suppose it was a good tactic."

I felt a wave of nausea in my stomach.

What a horrible parent! I wanted to say, but I wasn't about to insult Hozumi's family. I forced my displeasure down with my latte.

Hozumi suddenly looked up as though he'd remembered something else. "That calls to mind another story. Guess what my mother and father always said to me growing up?"

Was he talking about a family motto? I'd heard of ones like "you must not lie" or "be kind to others." But I had no idea what sort of precepts a political family would teach.

"They told us to get along with everyone."

"Oh, I thought it was going to be something more unexpected."

"Yeah, that's more straightforward than I thought," Iori added.

Seeing our disappointment, Hozumi laughed self-deprecatingly. Then he added, "Because it's one more vote."

"Huh?"

"Because one person equals one vote. No matter how big of an asshole someone is, you need their vote. Even if you get bullied, just put a smile on your face and forgive them. If you get into a fight, just lower your head and apologize to them. Your anger will never be worth more than a vote. You should know how to get along with everyone."

My heart prickled at his words.

"When there was an incident at school, I was often blamed. Maybe it's because I have evil-looking eyes, but I was always the prime suspect. If a pencil case went missing, they would say, 'I saw Hozumi staring at it. He stole it, I can tell. It was definitely him, just look at those eyes.' There was no use in trying to defend myself."

Hozumi sighed softly. His hands clasped together.

"No one would believe me. . . . Actually, no one cared if they believed me or not."

"They didn't care?" I asked.

"When something like that happens, people need that one person they can blame. It doesn't matter who it is. They don't really care about whether that person really did it or not. All they want to do is create a certain atmosphere, one that says 'Hozumi's done it again.' "

Iori's voice quivered. "That pisses me off."

"Every time something like that happened, my father would tell me to go and apologize. I would tell him that it wasn't me. I really didn't do it. Please come with me and tell them so. Then he would say to me, 'Just take a moment to think about it. Does your anger outweigh the value of a vote? If you keep making a fuss about this, we're going to lose even more votes. Does that still make you want to express your anger?' "

Hozumi's tone was matter-of-fact as he spoke.

"I suppose he had a point. They weren't going to believe me no matter what I said. It would have only added fuel to the fire, and I didn't want to have to deal with that."

"That's messed up." Iori's face was uncharacteristically contorted. His cheeks had tensed up, unable to form his usual smile. "What value is there in a vote you've gained from becoming a dumping ground for the *shallow* emotions of *shallow* people?"

"Iori."

Hozumi quickly added, "Well, if you look at it another way, thanks to my parents, I was already learning to act calmly and forgive people when I was as young as five years old." It was as though he was trying to play down his story.

Iori ruffled his long hair agitatedly.

"Forgiving people is something you do *after* your rage pushes you to the breaking point." Iori spoke scornfully, and Hozumi widened his eyes. "If you have to forgive them right from the beginning, where are you supposed to put the anger you feel for these idiots? Where are *you* supposed to go, after being so humiliated, with no one standing up for you? Where are you now, Hozumi?"

"Stay calm, stay calm," Hozumi mumbled to himself repeatedly, as if he were casting a spell.

Is this why Hozumi is always so consistent and emotionless?

Is this why he always defends himself with theoretical arguments?

"Oops," Hozumi suddenly said, glancing at his watch. "I'm expecting a delivery. I completely forgot to tell them not to deliver on Fridays. I ordered some limited-edition fruit-filled daifuku rice cakes."

He's trying to run away. He was speaking so quickly that we couldn't cut in.

"It's unlikely since we don't have any bookings tonight, but if someone does request a Funeral Committee meeting, just let me know. I'll be on standby."

"Wait, Hozumi—"

"Good night."

The door opened, and I felt a gust of damp wind. Hozumi was being drawn into the bleak night.

No. Something isn't right.

I can't let him be alone right now.

"There are people who are in need of that somebody who will come in and track down the regret, loneliness, and insecurities they've long buried away. There are times when they need somebody like you, who can break into people's hearts with the vigor of a warrior brandishing a huge naginata sword."

Hozumi. When you said so . . .

You were trying to tell me something—

"Hozumi!"

Just as Hozumi was about to step outside, I was able to grab his wrist. He turned around with widened eyes.

I saw that Iori had also grabbed Hozumi by the hem of his samue.

"Hozumi," Iori said. "Whatever happens, we'll always be here for you. I promise. Besides . . ." Hozumi was still standing in the middle of the doorway, droplets of rain slowly dampening his shoulder. "It's raining. That *must* mean we're going to have a Funeral Committee meeting tonight."

They say that sometimes we need to give people some space.

But I'm sorry, Hozumi. We can't do that, not right now. Leaving you alone isn't an option.

For a long time, all the things that he'd been forced to "leave alone" had made Hozumi suffer. Buried deep in his heart was a suffering so great that he was afraid to even look at it. When someone has a strong fear, the simple act of asking for help can make them feel guilty. If I—if *we*—didn't break into his heart right now, perhaps he'd never let himself be vulnerable again. There was no way that I could let that happen.

I tightened my grip on Hozumi's large wrist.

"Umm . . ." Hozumi said. I had no idea how much time had passed. His voice sounded as though it had been squeezed out from the back of his throat.

"It's not really an ex's favorite recipe . . ." Hozumi's chest heaved. "But I'd like to do a funeral for it," he said in a tiny voice.

Just how long had he grappled with his inner turmoil before mustering up the strength to finally say those words?

We decided to gather at the counter, where Hozumi liked to sit. Hozumi sat at the very end with me next to him, with Iori behind the counter. I hadn't prepared anything to eat, so I had to resort to serving

Iori's supply of snacks—a packet of Pizza Potato Chips and some JagaRico sticks.

Little by little, Hozumi started to talk.

"All through my life, I think I've asked myself, *Why do I keep questioning things that no one else cares about?*"

Iori split open the bag of Pizza Potato Chips and laid it on the table so that we could share. The sinful smell of highly processed cheese and tomato wafted over us.

"I wanted to know things like *Why do people live? Where did I come from? What will happen after I die?*" Hozumi said. "I also had a habit of imagining things from the smallest details in people's gestures and behaviors. I would think, *Oh, that person said this, but maybe this is how they really feel.* I was curious about all these little things."

"Ever since you were a young child?" I asked.

"I don't remember too well, but every time I asked 'why,' my father would look at me annoyed. He always said to me, 'If you have time to worry about such nonsense, go and get some studying done.' I think I realized at a young age that I'd better stop asking those kinds of questions."

Hozumi ran his hand over his square jawline. Maybe because it was nighttime, I could see that a faint stubble had started to appear.

"My parents would take me to community meetings, but I was pretty slow at warming up to strangers. When people asked me things, I would go quiet. My mother would look at them apologetically and say, 'I'm sorry. He has a sensitive side to him.' I can't count the number of times she said that. In the end, my parents seemed to change their tactic. They started to only take my brother to those occasions."

"Your brother . . . Kazutoyo, right?"

I remembered his social media profile. He had dynamic swept-up bangs and an undercut trimmed short at the sides. Based on his hairstyle, which surely required a certain level of self-confidence, and the endless trail of selfies with his children, it was pretty easy to guess that he was the type of person who had little in common with Hozumi.

"My brother and I are like chalk and cheese. As a child, he was the energetic type—he'd run around the yard and get himself all muddy, then would come inside and dart across the tatami mats in his dirty clothes. Mother would shout at him, and everyone else would laugh. He's that sort of person. He genuinely believes that every single person in this world loves him with all their heart."

It felt as though everything Hozumi had felt over the years was being poured into these words.

"My father started saying to my brother, 'You're going to inherit the Kuroda family's political position.' He would say it every chance he got—during meals, when my brother did well on a test, when he came in first at a sprint on sports day. I remember my father stroking my brother's head as he said so. And my brother would cheerfully reply 'Yes!' without the slightest hesitation."

"What about you, Hozumi?" Iori asked. "You mentioned earlier that your mother treated you and your brother as 'future politicians.' "

Iori reached out his long arm and ate two sticks of JagaRico in one go.

"Seeing the way I was, I guess they gave up on me early on."

"Right. You had some shitty parents."

I was shocked. "I-Iori!"

"But it's true."

Iori seemed to have abandoned his filter for the night.

"Anyway," Hozumi said as he followed Iori's lead and stuck his hand into the tubular packaging of JagaRico, "my gloomy traits didn't change even after I became a high school student. And because I was the son of a politician, it felt like the other kids were always walking on eggshells around me. It's strange, isn't it? With my brother, the other students looked at him with envy. They would say, 'Wow, it's so cool that your father is a politician.' He often invited his friends over to our house. While people avoided me, my brother was like a people magnet."

Hozumi's brother was two years older than him. Being so close in age, people must have compared them a lot.

"I thought, *How can two people be so different from each other?* My brother had the ability to win a vote easily. But I wasn't like that. I couldn't get along with anyone."

Hozumi tapped the counter with the tip of a JagaRico stick.

"One day at school, we all needed to join one of the student committees."

"You seem like the Library Committee type," I said without thinking.

"How did you know?"

I could picture Hozumi quietly reading at the loan counter. When someone would approach him, wanting to borrow a book, I could see him turning to the computer, his fingers moving fluidly as he silently completed the checkout process. As soon as he finished, he would resume reading his book. It fit his image perfectly.

"Indeed, I thought the Library Committee would be perfect for me; I could just sit and read quietly. So I decided to make myself a candidate—members of the committees were selected from self-nominated candidates. Those who weren't given a position were assigned to committees that didn't have enough people, and I really didn't want that. I mean, I could have ended up on the Culture Festival Committee, and that would have been truly horrific."

"Really? Culture festivals are so much fun."

Hozumi gave me the side-eye.

"The allocation of members was dragging on, and the atmosphere in the homeroom turned languid. The students who failed to raise their hands for any of the committees started whispering to one another. I had nothing to do, so I waited for homeroom to finish while I read my book, as I always did. Then, from behind me, I heard the voices of some of the popular, outgoing boys. 'What about the Library Committee?' 'Who else is in that committee?' 'Kuroda? No way. I'll choose anything but the Library Committee, then.' "

An image of my own high school classroom flashed through me.

Hozumi paused and drank his oolong tea.

"It's strange how you can't forget certain things people say about you. Sometimes I still have dreams where I hear those voices coming from behind me."

With those words, Hozumi turned his body to his right, looking behind him. There was nothing but a blank wall. Hozumi's eyes were pinned on a single spot, as if he could see something else.

"They were all snickering. I could feel their gazes on my back. I was pretty sure that they were talking like that on purpose, half hoping that I could hear them. I'd overheard them bad-mouthing me before, so I thought, *They're making sure I can hear them again.*"

Hozumi removed his glasses and assessed the evenness of the frames.

"I tried my best to pretend like I was absorbed in my book. I kept telling myself that I couldn't hear anything. But it was no use. Even though I was reading the best part of an Agatha Christie book—the part where the culprit is exposed—I couldn't concentrate one bit. I kept worrying that I was sweating through my shirt."

Hozumi was pressing his hand over his underarm, perhaps almost unconsciously. The moment I saw this, a thought occurred to me.

He's still trapped inside the memory of that day. That day when he was stabbed over and over again by his classmates' hushed snickering.

"I made sure I turned the pages of my book at regular intervals so that they didn't know I was having a hard time concentrating. Their snickering continued. In the end, they all found committees to join, and since no one else wanted to be on the Library Committee, my teacher made an exception for me to do it on my own."

Hozumi put his glasses back on and gently cleared his throat.

"That's when it occurred to me. I was *incapable* of gaining their vote. The *only* thing I was capable of, in fact, was *losing* their vote."

"That's not true . . ."

Hozumi finished the rest of his drink in one gulp. The ice cubes clinked. Pouring from a large, wholesale-sized carton, Iori quickly replenished Hozumi's glass with oolong tea.

"I started to think that as long as I was part of the family, we'll keep losing votes. I knew from the beginning that I didn't have the ability to attract or lead people. But if people were going to decide *not* to vote because of me, then that was a different issue altogether. I could have lived with the fact that I was adding zero value to the family. But I realized that I was a *minus*."

He continued. "I reasoned that since I'm never going to be popular like my brother, I should at least do well in my studies. My brother wasn't as capable when it came to studying, so I thought that if I managed to get into a good university, maybe that would make up for my lack of popularity. And also, I thought that maybe, just a little . . ."

Hozumi broke off, pausing a moment before continuing.

"I had a bit of an ulterior motive. I thought that for once, maybe Mother would notice me."

The sound of a motorcycle hitting a puddle reminded me that it was raining. I belatedly noticed how cold it had become, and I switched on the electric heater.

"There was a dish that Mother only made when there was a special occasion."

"Special occasion?"

"Like my brother's birthday, or the night of his school entrance ceremony, or when he won first place in a tennis tournament—days when there was something to celebrate. On these sorts of days, there was always a star-shaped pizza on the table. She would stretch out the pizza dough, then make slits into it, forming a kind of five-pointed star before baking it. It had sausages, tomatoes, cheese, and—"

I'd seen round and square-shaped pizzas, but star-shaped ones? This was new to me. I tried searching for it on my phone.

"Ah, I see. Looks like you can pull it apart with your fingers—perfect for parties."

"I know it's childish. But ever since I was young, I really wanted to have one that wasn't made for my brother—I wanted one that was made for *me*. My brother always got to pick a piece first. Then it was Father. I was always last. I've only ever taken a piece from the left-overs."

"Did you not get one on your birthdays?" I asked.

"It was always sushi rolls on my birthday. I don't remember ever saying so, but for some reason, Mother is convinced that I love them."

"I guess it's one of those things where your parents think that a dish you liked as a child is going to be your favorite food forever."

My dad was the same. Every time I went home, he would always get sushi delivered. He would say, "You love these, don't you?" and order extra portions of salmon roe.

"Did you not ask her to make one for you?"

"I guess I didn't want her to make me one just because I asked her to. Besides, I barely knew how to communicate with my family, so it would've been a little weird if I suddenly requested a star-shaped pizza."

It was such a Hozumi-like thing to say. It wouldn't have been so bad if it were a classic dish like tonkatsu or grilled fish, but I could see why he felt awkward about requesting a cute dish like a star-shaped pizza.

"One day, I realized what the problem was. I hadn't done anything that was worth celebrating. My brother was sporty, and he took all sorts of extracurricular lessons, so he had plenty of opportunities to be commended. I, on the other hand, had spent most of my time holed up in my room reading books, I hadn't made any noteworthy accomplishments. *That* was why she hadn't made me the pizza."

"What did you do?" I asked.

"I got into the University of Tokyo."

"What?!"

"Just like that?" Iori was shocked.

I knew he had graduated from UTokyo, but I never expected *that* to be the reason.

"Well, I've always liked studying. All I did was draw up a schedule and complete the tasks one by one. I analyzed past entrance exams to predict the type of questions that were going to come up."

"You're really something . . ."

Iori and I laughed. We didn't know how else to react.

"What happened after you got accepted to UTokyo? How did your parents react?" Iori asked as he popped a wedge of lemon into a new glass.

"Even my parents could be happy about that. Father did a complete one-eighty. He started going around bragging to people, 'My youngest has been accepted to the University of Tokyo.' Until then, people saw me as 'that taciturn, sensitive, and gloomy son of Kuroda's,' but after that, I became 'the quiet, mature, and hardworking son.' They looked at me completely differently. It was shocking."

The "UTokyo student" label.

The "cute guy" label.

The "almost thirty" label.

We all carry labels. We judge people through labels, and people judge us through our labels. At some point, people stopped saying "you're still young" to me.

You need to experience everything; you're still young.

People used to say that to me all the time. I couldn't agree with them more. So I worked my butt off. I traveled. I joined study groups. I went to cross-industry networking events.

But then there came a point when I started hearing words like "already" and phrases like "it's about time." If I made a mistake, I could no longer get away with it.

Just when had I made that jump?

"So did you get to have your pizza then?"

Iori's voice snapped me back to my senses. Hozumi had wandered off to the sofa seats and was now staring idly out the window.

"My mother asked me what I wanted to have as my celebratory meal. I immediately said I wanted pizza. Having been accepted to UTokyo, I thought that I had finally earned the star-shaped pizza." Hozumi smiled wryly. "But instead, they took me to a famous Italian restaurant."

"They took you to a *restaurant*?"

"It was a really high-end restaurant. The four of us had a meal together in the private room that my parents arranged for the celebration. I had the most incredible pizza margherita there. The dough was so light and soft. But . . ."

Hozumi gently ran his fingers over the window. Drops of rain hitting the glass formed a pattern of abstract spots.

"But it wasn't . . . it wasn't what I wanted. I hadn't asked for a four-course meal in an expensive Italian restaurant. I didn't want anything like that. I longed to sit in our living room, in my brother's usual seat, and have Mother's . . ."

Hozumi was now clenching his fist against the window.

"Mother's star-shaped pizza."

There was a niggling pain in my chest, as if the back of my heart had been pricked by a needle.

Hozumi turned toward me and smiled self-deprecatingly.

"It's stupid, isn't it? That I'm so fixated on this."

No, it's not. It's not at all. There's nothing wrong with wanting a certain dish and saying so out loud. You're not doing anything wrong.

But perhaps Hozumi had been afraid of people and society for so long that he hesitated when it came time to ask for something as small as that. Perhaps he deliberately called it a "stupid" wish to safeguard himself in case he was rejected.

Iori was now tucking into a bowl of ice cream with whiskey poured over it, maybe because the snacks weren't enough to fill him up or because he needed to reset his mood. For someone so slim, he had a huge appetite. His stomach was so flat, I always wondered where all that alcohol and food was going.

Iori and I joined Hozumi on the sofa. Wrapped in blankets, we scraped at the rock-solid ice cream with our spoons.

"You spent about seven years working for a corporate trading house, right?" I asked, suddenly remembering him telling me how he worked nonstop in his twenties. "I get the impression that people in that industry are ruthless. It doesn't seem like that kind of work would have suited you . . ."

"It really didn't."

"I thought so. But you managed to stay for a while?"

"Well . . . I had made a promise to my father."

"A promise?"

"After I got into UTokyo, the tide started to turn. Before then, my parents saw my brother as the only successor to Father. But . . . how can I put this? It seemed like Father started to consider me as an option."

"What's that supposed to mean?"

"My guess is that other people told him that he shouldn't let a UTokyo student go to waste. Father was the one who decided where I should work. He gave me three choices: the civil service, a trading house, or a bank. He told me that since I had the brain for it, I might as well get one of those jobs so that I could get a 'learning experience.' I couldn't believe what he was saying. On impulse, I looked at my mother, who was sitting next to him. She held my hand and said, 'Your father has picked out these companies for you.' "

I remembered Madame holding Hozumi's hand. Come to think of it, we were now in the same spot where the two of them had sat earlier.

"Father showed me a list of around twenty companies. They were all big organizations that have been around forever."

"But this is about *you*. What makes your parents think that they can choose your future? It's *your* life!" I shouted, rising from my seat. "Didn't you fight back? Didn't you tell them that you had the right to pick your own path and that they should back off?"

"Momo-chan." Iori pulled my arm lightly and tried to get me to sit back down.

"But, Iori . . ."

"Sit down. Let him finish."

That was when I realized. *If Hozumi had been able to fight back, then he wouldn't be wearing that expression right now.*

Regretting my accusatory tone, I lowered myself back to my seat.

"I couldn't say the words."

With a blank expression on his face, Hozumi set his spoon down in the bowl next to his half-eaten ice cream.

"I wanted to. Inside, I was screaming in protest over and over again. All these emotions—rage, sadness, and loneliness—were coursing through my body. But for some reason, I couldn't say anything out loud. Not in front of my father. Not when my mother was holding my hand. I was too scared."

His tone was matter-of-fact. It was as though it was the only way he could keep his emotions from exploding.

"I mean, I had been causing the Kuroda family to lose votes. I didn't think I deserved to leave home without making amends."

Iori took a sip of his whiskey. A melting ice cube in his glass made an audible cracking sound.

"I couldn't muster the courage to go against my father, so I ended up joining the trading house that offered me a position. Father was proud. He started taking me around the neighborhood again. He made me bow my head to people as he bragged and laughed, 'At last, the time has come for my youngest to be of use. I suppose I'm reaping the harvest of my hard work!' "

"Why did you put up with that?" I couldn't relate.

I didn't know what it was like to be scared of your parents. I felt a wave of frustration at my inability to empathize.

"I'm not sure why. When I think calmly about it, I can see that the things my father said were unreasonable and terribly old-fashioned. I read everything from books on child education and emotional trauma to sociology, psychology, and philosophy. Every single book I read led me to one conclusion: It's my father who is wrong, not me. I know that. I really do. But still . . ."

Hozumi pounded his knee with his fist repeatedly.

"Whenever I face my father, my heart shrivels up like it's stuck inside a freezer and I can't breathe."

I had thought that a person's worries were something that could simply be solved through talking to someone. Once you vent, you need to hear someone say that they understand, that they can see how hard it was for you, and that you did your best. You need that bit of support. That's when you can finally start to feel that maybe you weren't wrong, that everything you felt was justified.

But in this moment, I can't do that for Hozumi. I can't tell him that I understand. Because I don't. If only I'd worked in a trading house. Then maybe I could have understood Hozumi's feelings, even a little.

Several cars passed through the alley. For a while, we sat and listened; the noise made me think of an enormous whale rising to the surface of the ocean.

"I had been working for seven years when I finally felt like I could leave home." Hozumi started his tale back up.

"It was the first birthday of my brother's child. Father and Mother were happily preparing for their first grandchild's big day. The walls were decorated with paper chains made of origami, and there was a huge balloon in the shape of the number one. Mother kept saying, 'It's a special day today,' as she carried numerous dishes to the table. That's when I saw it."

Hozumi pulled out a freshly pressed handkerchief and wiped the sweat off the back of his neck as well as his palms.

Iori gasped.

"You mean . . ."

I finished his question. "The star-shaped pizza?"

Hozumi gave a silent nod.

"Did she think that since it was my brother's favorite, his son would like it, too? But the child in front of us was a one year-old who was still eating baby food. So then I wondered, did she make it for my brother? It didn't make any sense. Then my brother said something."

Hozumi finally took a sip of his hot coffee, as though he'd just remembered that it was there. He hadn't put any milk or sugar in it, but he didn't seem to take notice of its bitter taste.

"He said, 'Please, Mother. How old do you think I am? I'm not a kid anymore.' Then he added in a sulky tone, 'Why don't I ever get a fancy meal in an Italian restaurant like he did?' and pointed his finger at me.' "

Slowly, Hozumi's face contorted.

"Mother replied, 'Don't be silly. The eldest son always gets the pizza, because you're our promising star, aren't you?' Then she poked at the plump cheeks of my brother's tiny son. She looked so happy."

A promising star.

"That's when I finally realized. That pizza was *only* for the promising star in the family. It was a star that only those who carried the *expectations* of the Kuroda family could have."

Hozumi laughed bitterly and leaned back into the sofa.

"I didn't know what I was feeling. I didn't know why I had worked so hard. It was just a stupid pizza. But I *longed* for that pizza. I wanted to find a reason, however small it might be, that made it okay for me to be here."

As if he was trying to hide his expression, Hozumi took another sip of his black coffee. His hand holding the cup trembled.

"The moment the star-shaped pizza that I wanted so badly was set down in front of a tiny human who'd only been born a year earlier, nothing mattered to me anymore. I realized that there was no use in making an effort, because everything had already been predetermined. I couldn't contend with that. Do you see what I mean?"

The rain beat hard and ceaselessly like bullets, large drops splashing and rippling on the concrete.

When I tried to open my mouth, I noticed that the back of my tongue wouldn't move, as though it had been numbed by an anesthetic.

Right.

"You, of all people, shouldn't have to say something like that . . ." I started to say.

I'm angry right now.

". . . there was no use in making an effort, because everything had already been predetermined. . . ."

These are not the words of someone as hardworking as Hozumi.

I pushed forward. "You're the most self-disciplined person I know, Hozumi. You put your all into everything you do, whether it's working out, sauna-sitting, eating desserts, or training as a monk. It's like working hard is your hobby. And yet they made you believe something like that."

I could feel my voice quivering. My eyes and nose suddenly flooded, as though my body had finally caught up with me. The backs of my eyelids were burning.

"Momoko," Hozumi said.

What exactly was I angry at? I didn't know myself.

But I couldn't stand it. I just couldn't.

It's not like I know much about Hozumi. I've only known him less than a year. But I know that despite training so hard, he's still full of worries, and that he's been fighting to overcome his defilements, or "bonno" in Buddhist terms.

"Your curiosity for the little things. Your sufferings. Your struggles. The way you're trying to change your awkward personality. All of these things make up who you are. Is the Buddha really watching you? Maybe he needs to get his eyes checked," I said.

"Th-that is not an appropriate thing to say," Hozumi stammered.

"I can't help it!"

I rubbed at my drippy nose and turned to yell outside the window. "Hozumi is trying so hard. He trains hard in front of you every single day. So what makes you think he deserves this kind of cruel treatment?"

I wasn't just ready to pick a fight with the Buddha. Unable to sit still, I picked up my vanilla ice cream and slid it into Hozumi's bowl. It was the only thing I could do for him.

"Here, have my ice cream!"

"Oh, uh, I don't need this much. Plus, it's melted."

The melting ice cream spilled over the side of his bowl and onto his fingers. Still sniffling, I started wiping him off with a hot hand towel. The sticky ice cream had run all the way down to his palm.

"I can do that my—"

"It frustrates me so much."

I tightened my grip, squeezing Hozumi's hand. His thick palm was like a rock, rough and hard and so different from mine.

"I want to be able to tell you that I understand, but I don't have the same scars that you do. I'm so frustrated with myself for not being able to empathize with you."

If only I could overwrite his memories.

If I couldn't understand him, then the least I could do was to paint over his painful memories. I wanted to paint them in fun, vibrant colors.

"If you find it hard to say no when your mother is holding your hand, let *me* be the one who holds your hand. When a memory that scares you comes back to you, think of the time when I held your hand, and come to Amayadori straightaway. I'll hold your hand for you. If you're too embarrassed for me to do that, then I'll make up an excuse for it. *I know,* how about we do a handshake event at Amayadori?"

Another hand joined me. Iori's squeeze was even stronger than mine.

"We could do a folk dance on the rooftop—how about the Oklahoma Mixer?" Iori said.

"Great idea! Let's do that!"

Behind his glasses, Hozumi's eyes flickered.

Was any of this actually comforting him in any way? Somewhere in the depths of my mind, a calm voice asked me. But this was the only way I knew.

Putting all my strength into my grip, I squeezed Hozumi's hand again.

The ceiling light by the counter flickered as though it was trying to signal something.

"People say that I'm a certain kind of person . . ." Hozumi eventually muttered under his breath. It was as though the words had just fallen out of his mouth.

"They say that they can tell, just from looking at my face. They say that they can see it in my eyes. People make their own decisions about who I am. They decide that I am a certain somebody, somebody who isn't me." Hozumi spoke with downcast eyes.

"Even if I want to say to them that I'm not the person they think I am, I don't have the confidence to do so, because I don't know myself either. I don't know what kind of person I should be. I don't know what kind of person I need to be, in order to be forgiven. What should I do?"

I met his wistful gaze. Hozumi's face contorted, as if pleading for help.

"What am I supposed to do? How can I be forgiven? I just want someone to tell me that it's okay for me to be in this world, for me to stay here as the confused person that I am."

"It's okay!" I said in the loudest voice I'd used all day. I was aware of the stream of tears on my cheeks and the mucus running down from my nose, but I couldn't care less.

"It's most definitely okay for you to be *you* in this world. Even if you're scared of your father. Even if you can't talk back at him. You can analyze every little detail about everything. You can be annoying. You can keep your sweet tooth. You can even admire your muscles in the mirror at Amayadori."

"Wait, you've noticed that?"

"What I mean is that you're fine the way you are!" I bellowed. "You remember what you said to me when we first met, right? You told me that I was fighting the four and eight sufferings. That I was doing something extraordinary because I had faced life. You told me that I didn't need to think that I was going around in circles like an idiot. That I didn't need to beat myself up like that."

As soon as I said those words, Hozumi's dark brown pupils grew smaller.

"Why don't we suffer together?" I said. "Let's do the thing we call living life. If rain reminds you of a bad memory, then we can paint over the rainy days with new memories. Like you always say, it rains every time we have a Funeral Committee meeting, right? We can do as many Funeral Committee meetings as you want. We can do dozens, no, hundreds of meetings!"

People expect you to be a certain somebody. You find yourself trying to fit into a mold that someone else created, and the next thing you know, you don't know who you are anymore.

"R-right . . ."

Don't worry, the three of us can be confused people together.

Hozumi flipped over his big hand and squeezed our hands back.

"Thank you."

One by one, drops of tears fell over the stack of three hands.

Click-clack-click-clack. The stairway reverberated with the sound of my heels against the steel surface of the steps.

Although it was already past two o'clock in the morning, my head was wide awake. Clutching a warm basket under my raincoat, I made my way up to the rooftop.

I turned my head toward the east to look at the sky. The rain hadn't let up yet, but the clouds seemed to have moved aside, bringing the waning moon into full view.

"Knock, knock!"

"Welcome, Momo-chan. Hey, Hozumi, scoot over a bit."

"There's no more space! Are we seriously going to do it here?"

Twisting my body, I squeezed myself into the tent—the same tent that looked after our umeboshi so well. We were cramped, for sure, but for me, it felt just right. The cozy little space was kind of exciting, as if we were in a secret hideaway.

"Now, the moment of truth . . ."

I opened the basket suspensefully. The tent filled with the sweet aroma of freshly baked pizza dough, tomatoes, and juicy pepperoni.

"Looks so good!" Iori said.

"What do you think, Hozumi?"

It seemed that Hozumi couldn't quite believe that the sight before him was real. Adjusting his glasses, he gently picked up the basket and stared at it pensively.

"The star-shaped pizza," he said.

The pointy crust, made by folding over the dough, was baked to a crispy golden brown. I was a little worried that I hadn't given the dough enough time to rise, but it had turned out beautifully.

"Come on, Hozumi. Try some."

Hozumi gingerly reached out. Hesitantly, he moved his hand toward the smallest piece. I turned the plate around and gave him a look that said *Take this one*. He finally seemed to summon up his resolve and tore off the biggest slice. The pizza drooped with the weight of the melted cheese and the topping started to slide off.

"It's gonna fall!" I said.

Hozumi quickly lowered himself, letting the pizza fall into his mouth.

"Excellent!" Iori said approvingly, popping the cap off his beer bottle.

Once Hozumi swallowed his mouthful, he widened his eyes and said, "It's . . . delicious. It really is."

"Sorry, it probably doesn't taste like your mother's pizza."

This time, I knew so little about the original recipe that I'd pretty much invented my own. Hozumi smiled sheepishly and shook his head. "Now that I've eaten this one, I've forgotten how the original one tasted."

"Right."

Still sitting in awkward positions, we munched on the pizza. The two kinds of cheeses, mozzarella and cheddar, melded together and softened on my tongue.

Nothing hits the spot like a late-night pizza.

I unzipped the tent to find the night adorned with stars.

"Oh, has it stopped raining?" I jumped out of the tent in delight. "Ah, that's cold!"

I felt a single drop of rain just above my right eyebrow.

"Someone got carried away," Hozumi said.

"I really thought it had stopped! Take the hint, sky!"

"Are you seriously talking to the sky?"

Actually, the rain wasn't so bad—not the kind of rain that called for an umbrella. Pulling up the hood of my raincoat, I leaned my body against the rooftop railing as I chewed my pizza and gazed up at the night sky.

"Hey, is that the Orion?"

"Really? Where?"

Iori and I were having a great time trying to spot constellations when Hozumi suddenly spoke.

"I'm going to call Mother tomorrow. I'm going to tell her that I'm sorry but I won't be coming home for a while yet."

Hozumi's breath showed white next to his profile as he looked up at the starry night.

"If I went home now, and if Father told me to become a politician, I don't think I could say no. I know it's cowardly."

"It's not cowardly. When you're afraid, you're afraid. It's completely normal." Lifting my chin, I followed Hozumi's gaze as I spoke. "You don't need to go home. You can be the unfilial son."

". . . Okay."

Hozumi let out a little laugh as he rubbed at his nose, which seemed to have turned red in the cold air.

I guess that means that Hozumi will be in Tokyo at the end of the year. How fun will it be if we all spend New Year's Eve at Amayadori?

"I know. I'll cook osechi for New Year's! Iori, you don't have any plans, do you? Let's spend New Year's Eve together." Suddenly, I was brimming with festive energy.

"Wait, why are you assuming that I have no plans?" Iori objected.

"Do you have plans?"

"I'm going to watch the New Year Ekiden."

"Watching a relay race on TV isn't a real plan."

"My plans involve staying inside the kotatsu blanket."

"You know, customers would love it if you wore a kimono for the three days of New Year, Iori. I'm sure sales will go through the roof."

"You're not serious."

Iori seemed genuinely unimpressed by my suggestions, but I didn't really care. The café had been practically empty all day every day since October, which obviously meant that sales were bad. Iori knew well that we were barely making enough to pay the rent these past two months. There was no way that we could afford to miss out on an opportunity that guaranteed good sales.

"Fine, fine. I'll do it."

"You'll help us out, won't you, Hozumi?" I asked.

Chuckling, he replied, "All right. I shall sell a hundred glasses of ice cream soda." There was a confident expression on his face.

"Oh, God, it's raining harder again."

"Retreat!" Iori shouted.

We jumped back into the tent and took our raincoats off.

"Maybe *you're* jinxed!" I said to Hozumi.

"I don't appreciate the accusatory tone!" he retorted.

"Children, no shouting in the tent!" Iori scolded us.

We joked and laughed out loud, and ate more pizza.

Someday . . .

Someday, when I'm about to die, I'll remember this day, I'll remember these moments.

PIZZA FOR THE RISING STAR

Serves 4

TOMATO SAUCE

2 tablespoons olive oil

1 clove garlic, finely chopped

One ($14^{1}/_{2}$-ounce / 400 g) can whole tomatoes

$^{1}/_{2}$ teaspoon salt

Coarsely ground black pepper to taste

BASE

$^{1}/_{2}$ cup (75 g) bread flour

$^{2}/_{3}$ cup (75 g) cake flour

$^{1}/_{2}$ teaspoon baking powder

$^{1}/_{2}$ teaspoon salt

1 teaspoon sugar

$1^{1}/_{2}$ tablespoons olive oil

$6^{1}/_{2}$ tablespoons (90 g) plain yogurt

1 tablespoon olive oil

TOPPINGS

3 ounces (80 g) grated mozzarella cheese

3 sun-dried tomatoes, sliced thin

Loads of grated cheddar cheese

Pinch of salt

Few slices of pepperoni

Pinch of ground nutmeg

4 basil leaves

1 tablespoon olive oil

METHOD

To make the tomato sauce: Put the olive oil into a frying pan and fry the finely chopped garlic on low heat. Once fragrant, add the whole tomatoes, squishing them as you stir. Turn the heat to medium and simmer for about 5 minutes. Season with the salt and coarsely ground pepper.

To make the crust: Sift the bread flour, cake flour, and baking powder into a bowl. Add the salt and sugar and mix. Make a well in the middle. Little by little, add the olive oil and plain yogurt. Stir with a rubber spatula.

Once fully combined, bring the dough together with your hands. When all the flour has blended, transfer the dough to a surface for kneading.

To knead, push your palm down into the dough and stretch it away from you. Then lift the far side of the dough and fold it back. Repeat until you get a smooth dough. Split into two balls and wrap each ball with Saran Wrap. Leave in the fridge for 15 to 20 minutes. Preheat the oven to 425°F.

To make the pizza: Put one of the balls on a lightly floured surface. Using your hands, stretch it out into a round of about 6 inches (15 cm). Then put it on a baking sheet and roll it out into a thin round of about 10 inches (25 cm).

Top the edges with some mozzarella cheese and sun-dried tomatoes. Using a pair of scissors, make 5 slits. Fold the two edges of each section over the toppings and seal.

Top the center of the dough with some tomato sauce (approx. 2 tablespoons), the remaining mozzarella cheese, cheddar cheese, a pinch of salt, pepperoni, nutmeg, and basil leaves. Then drizzle the 1 tablespoon of olive oil over the top.

Bake for approximately 10 minutes in the oven.

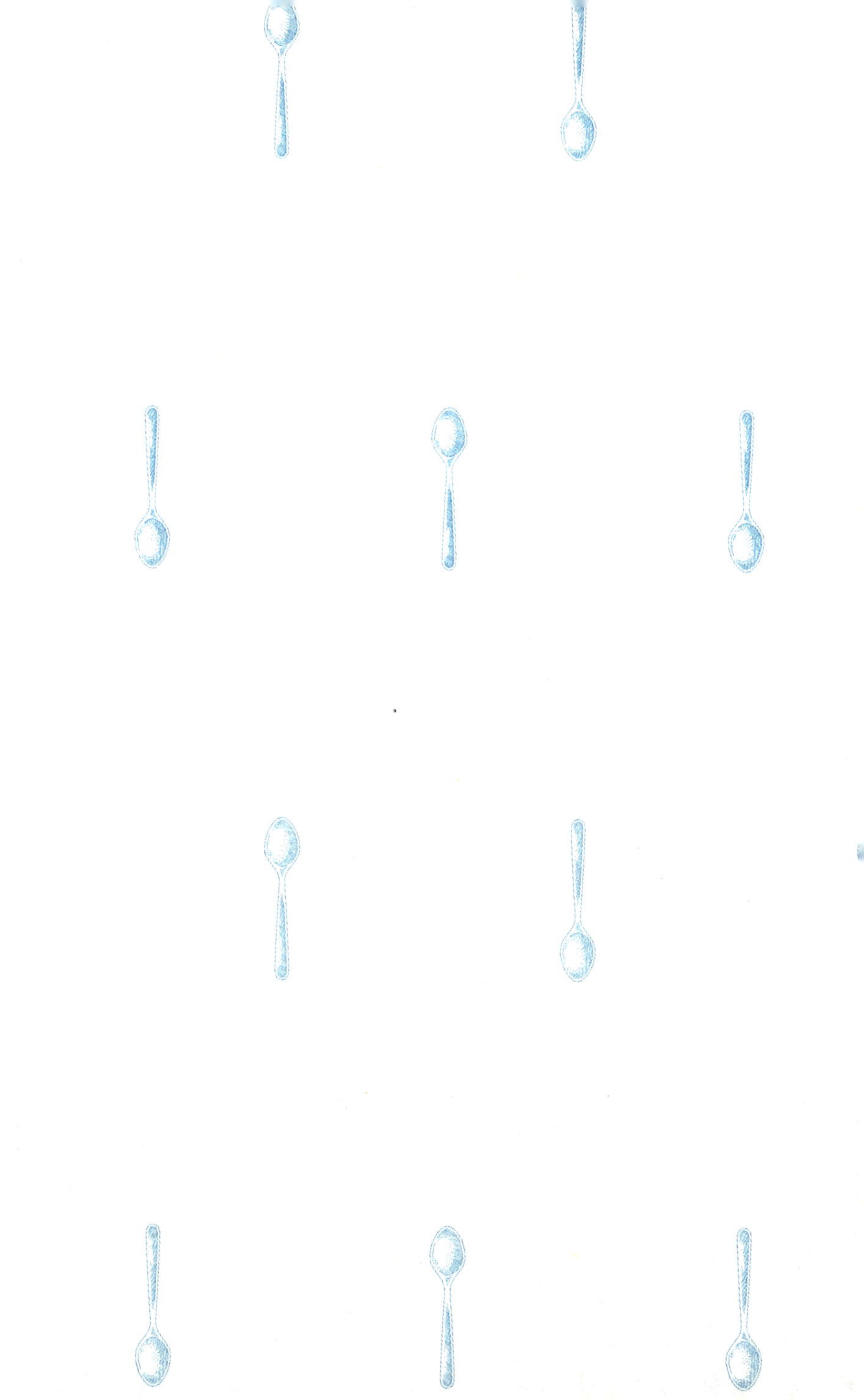

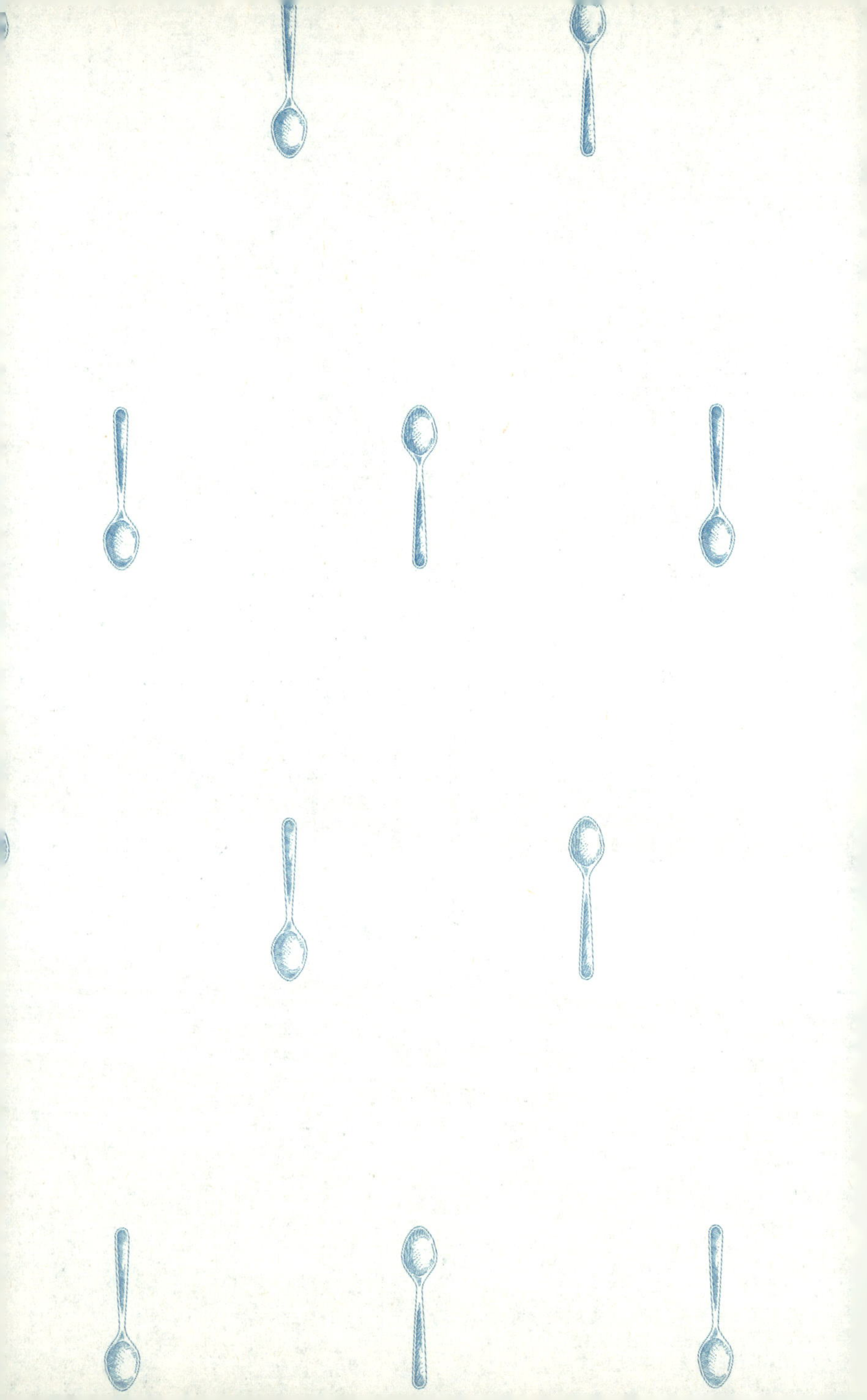

CHAPTER 8

THE MAN MAGNET'S OSECHI

Hey, God. Did you really have to break this news to me on my thirtieth birthday? Surely you could have picked another day to ruin.

Seriously. I've been working pretty damn hard, haven't I? I've been busting my ass every day. I've even drawn in more customers to Amayadori. I was supposed to have an amazing time on my birthday.

And yet . . .

Now I learn that Kyohei has gotten married.

Why? Why did I have to find out today of all days?

I had just attended a forget-the-year party with my girlfriends, and it was during this gathering that I had my unfortunate encounter with this shocking piece of information.

The story of my breakup with Kyohei had quickly established itself as the story of the night. Emboldened by my girlfriends' supportive remarks ("What a shitty guy!" "He's an asshole!"), I found myself reaching for my phone and saying, "Let's see what he's up to these days." And just like that, I had reopened the gate to the forbidden—I unmuted Kyohei's social media account.

At first, I couldn't quite believe that the photo in front of me was real. Kyohei dressed in a silver tuxedo.

How could this be? It's been less than a year since we broke up, hasn't it?

He was the one who dodged the conversation every time I dropped a hint about wanting to get married.

There was me, who, despite being with him for four years, couldn't even get him to *want* to marry me. And then there was "she," who, in a mere few months, had managed to make him tie the knot.

I knew it was a bad idea. I knew that it was only going to make me feel pathetic. But not comparing myself with the woman wearing the big white dress next to Kyohei was an impossibility.

She had round cheeks; they reminded me of daifuku rice cakes filled with strawberries and red bean. She had the kind of face that only good-natured people did. Her slender, pale upper arms caught my attention next. I was surprised. He'd told me that girls with big eyes and sculpted features had always been his type. So that I would fit his type better, I wore contact lenses that subtly enhanced my eyes. I got my lashes lifted. I mastered contouring to make my nose look sharper.

And yet the woman he chose had a flat, raccoon-like face. Her makeup was minimal, and she wasn't wearing colored contacts. (Trust me, we zoomed in to check.) Just the fact that she didn't feel the need to "go all out" on her wedding day, a day when her face would be captured in photos forever, made me feel incredibly inferior to her.

"At the end of the day, these are the kind of girls that guys go for."

Those words fell out of a friend's mouth as we gazed at the image.

I dragged my numbed feet forward one step at a time. Although it felt as if there were a big cloud over my head, my body was making its way to Amayadori almost mechanically. It had been snowing for several days, and a fresh layer had mixed wetly with the older hardened snow, turning the sidewalk into a gray sorbet.

I was crushed for feeling so crushed.

I thought that I'd moved on. Working at Amayadori, I've heard so many stories and witnessed so many people get over their breakups. I've met people who, despite the pain they carried, bravely got on with their lives. I've even given them encouragement, telling them that they'll be okay!

Out of nowhere, the smell of curry spread through my nostrils. *Someone's having curry tonight,* I thought as I walked through the residential neighborhood.

"My ex-boyfriend's favorite curry . . ." I mumbled to myself as I thrust my hands into my pockets. My breath formed a white cloud before being swept into the dark.

I'd been pretty resilient for the past year. But secretly, I had hoped that one day, he would find me and regret his choices. He'd chance upon my curry and recognize the flavor, and say, "This is Momoko's curry," and realize how lucky he was to have had me. I'd thought that if I could catch even a glimpse of regret on his face, then maybe I would be saved from this pain, just a little.

All this time, all I could think about was making Kyohei regret losing me. And yet he was way ahead of me. Not only was he completely over me, he'd also met someone and fell in love, and had *proposed* to her.

It wasn't as though I wanted us to get back together. Even if we had, it wouldn't have worked out, I knew that in my heart.

So why was I hurting so much?

I turned the corner into the silence of an alleyway. Taking off my headphones, I listened to the breeze.

Flakes of snow descended slowly and softly. A tiny cluster touched my wool coat and quickly vanished.

I looked up at the dark winter sky.

It felt as if the sky was telling me that it was finally my turn.

Deep in my heart, there was a "something" that I hadn't been able to lay to rest.

"Right."

I'm going to ask for a Funeral Committee meeting. I'm going to put an end to this love, this time for good.

"Pardon the intrusion!"

As I flung open the door to Amayadori with the fervor of a martial artist challenging a rival, I saw an unfamiliar young woman with light brown eyes standing in front of me.

"Oh, hello!" she said. "Hope you don't mind that I'm here."

Huh?

As far as I knew, we hadn't received any booking requests, and I wasn't expecting any walk-in customers so close to the end of the year.

"Wow, you're so pretty, Momoko. Just as I thought." Speaking in a voice that was as sweet as a jar of thick honey, she drew herself closer to me. Judging from her accent, she was likely from the Kansai region. She was a little shorter than me, and had to gaze up at me as she spoke.

"Oh, you're soaked. You're going to catch a cold. You don't mind if I borrow a towel, do you, Iori?"

Before Iori could reply, she darted behind the counter, grabbed a towel, and started to wipe my head, which was wet from snow.

What on earth . . . ?

Whoever she was, she seemed to know her way around the café. She was behaving as though she was the server and I was her customer.

"Welcome back, Momo-chan," she said. "Did you have a relaxing day?"

"Oh, Iori . . . ?"

"I hear it's your birthday today. Happy birthday! If I'd known earlier, I would have brought something better than this."

As she scratched her temples disappointedly, the young woman cast a glance at one of the tables, where Hozumi was eagerly preparing the chopsticks. I noticed three jubako boxes neatly arranged on the table.

"Is that osechi?" I asked.

Inside the boxes were classic osechi dishes: simmered black soy beans, kuri kinton, a herring roe and datemaki rolled omelet, as well as slices of roast beef and even braised pork belly. The ornamental carrots garnishing the dishes were expertly carved into elaborate three-dimensional flowers.

"You . . . made these?"

"This is my ex-boyfriend's recipe." The woman giggled bashfully.

Her name was Shiori Fukami. She had a chin-length blunt bob that suited her well. I learned that she was a freelance photographer, which explained the rather heavy-looking SLR hanging from her neck. She wore a chunky knit cardigan over a vintage-style printed dress that looked like it could be from a secondhand shop. On her feet were Doc Martens. When she smiled, you could see her pointed canine teeth, which made her seem almost childlike. Although she was twenty-seven and only three years younger than me, if I'm being honest, she looked as young as a university student.

It turned out that Shiori lived close by, on the other side of the station, and that she'd known about the Funeral Committee for some time.

"I didn't have any plans today, and I was so bored spending time on my own. So I thought, why not?"

Shiori mixed standard Japanese and the Kansai dialect as she spoke, and had a slight lisp. She seemed to connect with everyone instantly, and her level of friendliness was just right. When I arrived at Amayadori, the atmosphere had already been set. Even now, she was laughing and joking around with Iori and Hozumi as though they'd known one another forever.

I felt my lips tensing up. "People don't come to the Funeral Committee meeting because they're *bored*."

"Huh? What did you say?" Hozumi said.

Coming back to my senses, I realized I had mumbled the words almost unconsciously.

Oops.

I was in a rather foul mood and had to remind myself not to turn into a bitch.

"Since it's the last Funeral Committee meeting of the year, we're allowed to drink, right?"

Iori had emerged from the kitchen carrying a huge pile of food and drinks. Given how cold it was, he probably didn't want to have to leave the warmth of his seat again. Once we'd laid out the assortment of light dishes, we hardly had any room left on the table.

Shiori smiled. "This looks amazing. I'm a pretty good drinker, so I'll be excellent company."

With that, Shiori swiftly distributed the small plates and chopsticks and poured the beer into my glass, playing the hostess role.

Argh. Why did I choose the window seat? I can't reach anything.

"I'm sorry you're doing all the work," I said.

"Not at all. I can't let the birthday girl do it."

Distributing the chopsticks and hand towels. Pouring water for everyone. Livening up the atmosphere. I should have been the one responsible for these things, but Shiori had done them all.

I . . . I feel so . . . left out!

The worst part was that she looked like the girl Kyohei had married. Flat-faced, pale-skinned, round cheeks. She wore very little makeup, *if* she was wearing any.

At the end of the day, I can never compete with these girls . . .

I felt utterly miserable.

Get a grip, Momoko. Just snap out of it. She was a client, and I needed to treat her like one.

This is why I'm no good. Because I get jealous so easily . . .

"Momoko?" Shiori, who'd been eyeing the drinks, suddenly put her glass down and turned to me. She spun her body around to face me and stared into my eyes.

"Did something bad happen to you today, by any chance?"

Oh, no. Could she tell?

"N-no . . ."

Pull your chin up. Lift the corners of your mouth.

Despite my brain's desperate calls, the muscles on my face refused to cooperate. I tried to smile, but the sides of my lips had stiffened.

"You seem a little down. I could just be imagining it, though. I'm sorry if I am."

Why did you have to notice?

Why you and not Iori or Hozumi? Why did you have to notice first?

Now you've given me even more proof that you're a wonderful person. And that makes me feel even more miserable.

"The person that I love . . . that I loved. He got married." The tip of my nose burned. "I don't know why I feel so hurt. It's already . . . been . . . a year."

My voice was trembling. The uneasy feeling that I'd been fighting back came pouring out of me.

"I-I'm so—" I choked on my words. "I'm sorry. I'm supposed to be l-listening to *your* story."

"You poor thing. Come here." I'd broken into sobs, and without hesitating, Shiori pulled me in for a hug. A smooth and pleasant scent of milky roses enveloped me.

Right, I thought as she wrapped me in her warmth, *she's the type of person who doesn't hesitate to hug someone when she sees them crying.*

She knows how to connect with people instantly, to liven up the mood, to be attentive in a subtle way. If only I had been born that way, then . . .

"God, I'm so sorry. I'm sure you weren't expecting the president of the Funeral Committee to burst out crying like this."

Sniffling, I pulled away from her and bowed. Shiori handed me a tissue.

"It's totally understandable that you're upset about your ex-boyfriend getting married. You know, I was bawling my eyes out yesterday, so I really feel your pain."

"You were crying yesterday?"

"I broke up with the person I'd been in love with for five years. I've always felt like I should end the relationship, but I kept prolonging it."

"Oh, no. So you must be hurting so much right now."

"I'd made this osechi for New Year's, to have it with my boyfriend. But then we broke up, and I had all this food on my hands. I couldn't eat it all on my own, so I came here."

That . . . that was the reason? So when she said she was "bored," she must have meant that her plans suddenly changed because she broke up with her boyfriend.

I thought about all the emotions that she must have been carrying. She and her boyfriend were supposed to be together for New Year's. She'd put so much work into this osechi, yet she didn't get the chance to watch him eat it. Despite being so hurt, she was acting so cheerfully. Not only that, she had even looked after me, a stranger.

"Oh my God. I'm so sorry. I wish I'd known! Really, I am so sorry."

I can't believe I've been so bitchy about such a sweet girl!

I pleaded, "Please forgive me! You must think I'm crazy!"

"You *are* crazy," Hozumi said.

"You're funny, Momoko." Shiori laughed. "Honestly, don't worry about it. We can comfort each other!"

Shiori's face broke into a grin as she pulled at the tab of her can of beer.

And so we finally raised our glasses and belatedly commenced our meeting.

Shiori-chan's (she preferred to be called Shiori-chan rather than Shiori-san, which apparently made her feel awkward) ex-boyfriend was named Fujimoto-kun. They'd met at the photography agency she joined as an intern five years ago. Judging from the picture that Shiori-chan showed us, he was an attractive man, with long messy hair and a mustache that suited him well. There was a kind of gloominess to him, which gave him an air of maturity.

"I'd wanted to get married, but Fujimoto-kun didn't want the same things. Apparently I ruin the men I go out with."

I was surprised. She had such great communication skills, I expected her to be adept at navigating romantic relationships.

I took Shiori-chan's hands in mine. "I guess even girls like you can feel lost when it comes to romance. I know exactly how you feel."

Tears filled my eyes, this time for a different reason. *We're all fighting the struggles of life, aren't we?*

"I bet you ask him 'Do you really love me?' all the time because you needed constant validation."

"Oh, umm . . . yeah, totally. I always do that."

"And then the next thing you know, he's treating you like you're a clingy woman and telling you that he feels 'burdened' by you. Right?"

"Y-yeah, I . . . I can relate to that."

"Not only that, when you're over at his place, you secretly—"

"Stop right there!"

Clink-clink-clink-clink. Suddenly, a high-pitched sound rang out.

It was the sound of Iori tapping his chopsticks against a bottle of vodka. Hozumi covered his ears, annoyed.

"Momo-chan, just stop for a second," Iori said.

"Huh?"

"Hey, Shiori-chan, you don't need to hold back."

Hold back? What is he talking about?

"You attract a lot of guys, don't you?"

I could tell that Shiori-chan was astonished. The air between Iori and Shiori turned tense, as though they were trying to feel each other out.

"Oh, no. That's not true at all."

As Shiori-chan waved her hands around, Iori sighed briefly. "You're being kind and agreeing with Momo-chan because she's upset. But you're not being totally transparent with us, are you?" he said, looking straight at Shiori-chan unblinkingly. "If you really want your heartbreak to rest in peace, you need to put all your cards on the table. There's no point in disguising yourself in this meeting. This meeting is about removing the mask that you've been wearing."

Impulsively, I looked at Shiori-chan. She just sat there, glued to the spot.

"Sh-Shiori-chan? Are you all right?"

I put my hand on her shoulder, and Shiori-chan bowed down.

"I'm so sorry, Momoko! I'm actually a Man Magnet!"

"Wait, what?"

Iori was right?

"I've never *not* had a boyfriend. Even at school, I always went out with the hottest boy in class. I can get any man I want. The truth is, I can't keep them away. I'm so sorry I misled you!"

"What kind of apology is that?"

"One time, a ticks-all-the-boxes guy who had an excellent job at a foreign-owned consultation firm proposed to me, and I turned him down. To be honest, I've never needed validation from men. If anything, they're the ones who get insecure over *me*. I am a Man Magnet through and through."

"This does not sound like an apology," I insisted.

Is this what she meant when she said she "ruins" men?

"I get the impression that you and I are cut from the same cloth," Iori said. "Basically, you came to Amayadori to recover from your breakup, but once you met Momo-chan, the president of the Funeral Committee, you felt like you needed to get her to like you. Which is why you were talking so self-effacingly and were playing along with her."

Shiori-chan puffed out her cheeks and shot Iori a fierce glare.

"Y-you're a fine one to talk," Shiori-chan said. "You're the one who was pretending like you believed me. For the record, unlike you, I don't rely on a pretty face to win people's hearts. I worked hard to hone my skills to come this far."

"Oh, yeah? Show us what you got then—you must have excellent advice on how to make a guy fall in love with you."

It seemed that a rivalry had started between Iori, the Woman Magnet, and Shiori-chan, the Man Magnet. Sandwiched between the two, Hozumi looked at me, pleading to be rescued.

"So this is what happens when you pit two Magnets against each other," Hozumi said under his breath, as Iori and Shiori glared at each other. "It's rather dangerous."

"I agree. It's certainly put a stop to my tears, though. I don't even know why I was feeling so down anymore."

"I'm glad to hear that," Hozumi said.

The night grew darker, bringing more and more snow.

I gripped the bottle of vodka and picked up my chopsticks. The Woman Magnet and the Man Magnet seemed to be locked in an increasingly heated battle, and it was my turn to stop them.

"Now that I know who you really are, I expect you to tell me everything. I need to know how you get all the guys." I replenished Shiori-chan's glass with beer, filling it to the brim before placing it front of her. "Please?"

If Iori says she attracts a lot of guys, then she must be the real deal.

But there was something I still couldn't understand. To put it bluntly, Shiori-chan didn't strike me as the kind of girl that guys were attracted to. I mean, her style of clothes was what you would call thrift-store chic, and she wore Doc Martens, not heels. If anything, her appearance seemed to be the opposite of what I'd always believed guys liked.

"How to attract guys . . ." she said. "Well, I suppose it's lots of different things."

Shiori-chan gulped down her beer. She really was a good drinker. A thin layer of foam formed on her top lip, and she gave it a small, kitten-like lick.

"But for average-looking girls like me, there's really only one way to get the guy that we want," she continued.

"Wh-what is it? Tell me!"

Shiori-chan raised her index finger in front of her face. "The single most important thing you should do is *not* show your femininity."

"Huh?"

"Whatever you do, never be that girl the other girls hate. The second you become the enemy among girls, you stop being attractive to men."

"Seriously?"

"I couldn't be any more serious. It doesn't matter how beautiful you are or how big your boobs are. Girls who are a threat to other girls will never be the number-one choice for guys. At the end of the day, popular guys marry the girls who are good at flattering them, the sweet girls—you know, those girls that *everyone* says are nice."

My heart dropped. The picture of that woman in the wedding dress resurfaced in my head. I had to admit Shiori-chan's statements made sense. But a bigger part of me wished that it was untrue, and I desperately searched my brain for a counterargument.

"But what if you're group dating at a gokon? Unless you're drop-dead gorgeous, you have to make an effort to be noticed."

I noticed the bowl of Caesar salad on the table, one of the light dishes that Iori had prepared. I held the bowl out to Shiori-chan.

"Shiori-chan, are you that girl who dishes out the salad for everyone during a group date? The perfect, demure hostess, a trick to get the guys' attention?"

Let's see what she's got. I handed her a stack of small plates and a pair of salad tongs. For a moment, the Man Magnet sat in silence, examining the salad. Then suddenly, as though she'd flicked a switch on, she started to speak.

"Wow, this looks so good! Would you all like some? God, I'm starving."

With that, she began dishing out the salad in swift movements. I could have sworn that at that moment, I felt a spring breeze sweep past, filling the air with cherry blossom petals. I turned toward the window in spite of myself. Obviously, what I saw outside the window was a black-and-white view of a typical night in December. Just like that, Shiori-chan had captured my heart, drawing me right in.

In no time at all, she had finished distributing the plates of lettuce and croutons to all of us. She took a bite of her salad after saying, "Itadakimasu."

Then, slightly tilting her head, she said, "Delicious, isn't it?" and shot a big smile at Hozumi.

"Urgh . . ." Bending forward, Hozumi looked taken aback.

"Hey, you okay?" I said. "Did she get you? She got you, didn't she?"

"I . . . I feel like I can't breathe. She totally blew me away."

I couldn't blame him. I mean, the way she said, "Delicious, isn't it?" was so incredibly effective, it could have brought a tear to my eye. Her Kansai dialect, spoken in a soft tone, was pleasant to the ears, but not in a calculating way.

Shiori-chan expelled a breath and returned the salad tongs to the bowl.

"How was that? Did you think I was cute?" she asked, returning to her previous self.

I had no words. Before I knew it, my hands were clapping. A strange, exhilarating sensation coursed through me, as if I had just finished watching a theater performance.

"I have to hand it to you, you were amazing. It didn't seem like you were trying to score points, but you weren't being inattentive either."

Shiori-chan puffed her chest out with pride and reached for another can of beer.

"Master, let me pour that for you!" I seized the can and pulled the tab open. "So, specifically, how do you go from there to the relationship stage?"

We'd come this far already. I was now determined to find out just how it was that a true Man Magnet locked down a guy.

"Hmm . . . let me see."

With her thumb, Shiori-chan discreetly removed the lipstick mark from her glass. When it came to subtle movements like this, she was ever so elegant. So she hadn't completely abandoned her "femininity," after all. Why couldn't I be more like her? Why was I only capable of jumping back and forth between the "glamorous girl who is a threat to other girls" and the "ungraceful girl with zero womanly traits"? Why couldn't I find the midpoint and just be the "friendly and easygoing but subtly elegant girl"?

"First, you have to become best friends with the man you like. You have to be someone he can talk to despite being the opposite sex. Build a relationship that makes him say, 'I don't really feel like going to that party tonight, but I'll go if she's going.' Basically, you have to get inside him emotionally." Shiori-chan spoke passionately.

Get. Inside. Emotionally. I grabbed a sticky note and frantically noted down her words.

"But in doing so, you must remember not to act completely unwomanly. You shouldn't overdo it—flirting with physical touch, for example, is a strict no-no. However, laughing coarsely with your mouth wide open, or having really hairy knuckles, should be avoided at all costs. You shouldn't exude femininity, but you shouldn't abandon it either. Keeping that balance is the tricky part."

On impulse, I put my knuckles out of sight. *Crap. I haven't taken care of them recently.*

"If you're going to do something to get his attention, make it subtle, like simply turning your body in his direction. You could also try moving in an elegant manner and speaking in a soft tone."

"But wouldn't guys find it a little weird if a female friend suddenly started acting all girlie around them?"

"It would feel weird if you're forcing yourself to choose between super womanly or not at all. I'm talking about a slight touch of elegance and sophistication. Then it won't be weird at all. You have to strike a balance."

"But that's the part I struggle with—I can't stay at the midpoint. And it's not like I'm beautiful."

Gripping some dried squid with both her hands, Shiori-chan bit off a piece, making a snapping sound. "You seem to think that being beautiful is key, but I don't think men pay that much attention to appearance."

"Th-that can't be. You're joking . . . right?"

What is she talking about? Looks are so important to men. Everybody knows that.

"Actually, I think she has a point."

The Woman Magnet, who'd been quietly listening to our conversation, interjected. "Of course, men have certain 'types.' It's not like a man is attracted to a woman solely for their personality. But . . . how can I put it? A woman's view is ten times clearer than that of a man's when it comes to appearance. If a woman's vision is 20/20, a man's vision would be 10/20."

"That's exactly it!" Shiori-chan said.

What?

"In other words, although men do pay attention to looks, they don't see things as clearly as women do," Iori clearly stated.

"They . . . don't?"

"It's all a blur to them. That's why a lot of guys don't notice when women change their hair or their makeup. They don't really get women's clothes, either. All they see is that a woman is cute or beautiful in a really general way." Iori smiled slyly. "Unless they have a discerning eye like *I* do."

I can't believe this.

"Hozumi, this isn't true, is it? You notice the details, don't you? I had my bangs trimmed differently this morning—you must have noticed that."

I clutched at Hozumi. He was my only hope to prove them wrong.

"Err . . . now that you mention it, they do look a bit shorter?"

"I got straight bangs!"

Iori chimed in, "*I* noticed it, Momo-chan."

"That's because you have a 'discerning eye,'" Shiori-chan said.

I had thought that I had gotten a pretty big makeover, but Hozumi hadn't even noticed.

"Anyway, going back to my point," Shiori-chan said, patting me on my cheeks to snap me out of my stunned state. "Remember, they can't 'see' very well, so as long as you look after the easy-to-spot areas like your hair and your skin, you'll be fine. Once you've made it into the 'cute in general' zone, you just have to make sure that he feels comfortable with you."

"I have a question." Suddenly coming back to my senses, I raised my hand. "Once you're in the friend zone, doesn't it feel like you've been excluded from the girlfriend zone? These guys usually end up telling me that there's a girl that he likes—they even ask me for advice on their love life."

"And is that where you always give up? What a waste!"

I was taken aback by her unexpected reaction. I'd thought that she would be able to relate to that one.

"Of course. Why wouldn't I? I mean, the guy likes someone else."

"That's where you're wrong. Based on my statistics, you have an eighty percent chance of getting that guy." Shiori-chan gave her thigh a single slap.

"Surely that can't be true."

"It can."

"It cannot."

"It can! Listen to me, Momoko . . ." Shiori-chan squeezed my hand and looked straight at me with her light brown eyes. "Asking someone out takes courage, right? People are scared of getting rejected. When guys ask you for advice on their love life, it's because they want to see how you react. In other words, when they say that they like someone, it's basically the same as them saying, 'I'm thinking about asking you out. How do you feel about me?' "

No. That can't be.

I was so shocked, it was as if someone had hit me on the head with a huge hammer.

"The reason he loses interest in you is because the moment he tells you he likes someone, you become needlessly ungraceful, or you start self-sabotaging and act all differently. It's not game over as soon as he talks to you about his love life. The game is still on."

I almost forgot to breathe.

What did I do when a guy asked me for advice about his love life? Easy. I encouraged him with all my heart, telling him how much I hoped that it worked out. It was too painful to stay in love with him. Feeling foolish for still wanting to be in the "girlfriend zone" despite being permanently stuck in the "friend zone," I would start to wear Uniqlo instead of Snidel, and would drink beer instead of a cassis orange cocktail.

"Sh-Shiori-chan, I mean *Master* Shiori, what would you say to him in that situation?" I asked, summoning up the last bit of emotional strength left inside of me. Shiori-chan moved her eyes around inquisitively.

"I say, 'I get that you like this girl . . . but don't forget the one that's right in front of you.' Then I shoot him a bright smile." Shiori-chan pointed to herself, wearing a look of pure contentment. "That normally does the trick."

"Urgh . . ."

This time, she got me instead of Hozumi. I had to admit defeat.

"You seem to know a lot about how a man's mind works. So why didn't it work out with Fujimoto-kun?" I asked Shiori-chan, who was arranging the chikuzenni on the table after warming it up in the microwave. She had all this expertise about men. I was completely baffled as to why she couldn't make it work with this one guy.

"I'm not sure why. I hadn't even planned to fall for him in the first place. He wasn't my type at all. Normally, I have super-high dating standards, so I never imagined going for a twenty-seven-year-old chronic job-quitter chasing his dreams to become a photographer."

She told us that Fujimoto-kun was a perfectionist, and whenever they did a shoot together, he criticized every little thing, from how she used the equipment and how she communicated with the models, to her composition and lighting.

"God, I hated him. He kept saying stuff like my work was too repetitive and that I should give more posing instructions to models. I would be like, *Shut up! Let me do things my way!* You know? We were constantly at each other's throats."

"And yet you eventually fell for him." Iori snickered.

I was baffled. "Didn't you use your techniques on him?"

"That's the thing. I did, but it didn't work!" Shiori-chan said, as she dished out the osechi for all of us. "My techniques had no effect on him whatsoever. I'd never met anyone like him. I later found out that Fujimoto-kun had a difficult relationship with his family and he'd practically cut all ties with them. He'd been living a solitary life with no one to depend on. I guess he wasn't used to getting close with people."

She placed a beautifully plated selection of osechi in front of me.

"Oh, please help yourselves."

There was kuri kinton, datemaki rolled omelet, and herring roe, as well as braised pork belly. She must have had to work around the clock to make them.

A faint scent of ginger rose up from the braised pork belly, which was so tender it fell right apart inside my mouth. The succulent cubes of meat were soaked in the rich flavor of the sauce.

"So how did you go from hating him to falling in love with him?" I asked.

"Our mentor—the photographer I was interning for—decided to hold an exhibition. The two of us were put in charge of running it, forcing us to collaborate. We had to spend all day every day together as we prepared, and we gradually found ourselves working seamlessly with each other."

Shiori-chan sampled the herring roe after deftly using her chopsticks to cut off a small piece.

"I lived far from the office, so Fujimoto-kun let me store my things at his house. Plus, he owned lots of photography equipment, so I started stopping at his place to work quite regularly. We often practiced shooting together, too. I think that went on for about six months."

I took a sip of my beer to compose myself. I was starting to get butterflies in my stomach.

"Did you end up being . . . friends with benefits?" I asked tentatively.

Shiori-chan pulled a face and sighed. "The opposite of that."

"The opposite?"

"Nothing happened. For six whole months. Even though I was doing sleepovers at his place, nothing *ever* happened."

"What? Are you telling me that a man and a woman in their twenties did sleepovers for six months and nothing ever happened? Well . . . I guess it's possible if one of you was sleeping on the floor."

"We slept side by side on a single bed."

"No!"

The muscles in my cheeks were getting sore from sitting with my mouth wide open.

"After work, we'd have dinner together, then edit photos and do some file processing before sliding into bed and sleeping like logs. The next day, we'd go to the office again and work. Day after day, it was the same thing," Shiori-chan explained as she chewed on the decoratively cut shiitake mushroom.

"I didn't know what he was thinking. I was perplexed. As colleagues, we got along well—he was my comrade. I definitely felt comfortable in his company, and I was pretty sure that Fujimoto-kun trusted me, too. But he didn't make a single move. I started wondering if he didn't see me that way, and it outraged me. I mean, how could a guy be with *me,* Shiori Fukami, all day every day, and not fall for me?"

"If only I had half your confidence."

If I was in her situation, I would have been so disheartened.

"So I thought, *If I'm gonna do this, I gotta go all in.*" Swallowing her shiitake mushroom, Shiori-chan smiled mischievously.

"G-go all in? What did you do?"

"I jumped into his bed butt naked."

Hozumi started to cough violently.

"Are you okay?" I asked, quickly handing him a glass of water.

"Yes," Hozumi said, still coughing. "Sorry, I hadn't expected her tactic to be so . . . physical."

"What else was I supposed to do? It was my last resort. Every technique that had previously worked in my life as a Man Magnet had failed. I'd played all my cards. I thought, *This is my last chance. If this doesn't work, I'm going to give up.* So I literally threw myself at him naked."

Hozumi started coughing again.

"Was your tactic successful?" Iori swirled his now-empty can of beer.

"Well . . . kind of." Shiori-chan tilted her head ambiguously.

"What do you mean, 'kind of'?"

"Did you have sex?" Iori asked bluntly, and Shiori-chan gave a slightly awkward nod.

"But after that, nothing else changed. He didn't say he liked me or ask me to be his girlfriend. We carried on living as normal—we worked together, helped each other out during shoots. We had dinner together at least once every three days. It was the same old routine, except we were now having sex."

"So, then, you were . . ."

Were they lovers? Was it just sex? No, they were always together, like they were best friends, so it wasn't just sex.

I scanned the sumptuous assortment of osechi spread across the table. "You must have spent New Year's together every year."

"Yeah. The last three years have been the same. We would hike up a mountain overnight and get some shots of the first sunrise, then go home and pass out. We'd wake up around noon and have some osechi under the cozy kotatsu."

She continued, "I spent all the seasonal occasions with him. In the spring, we took our cameras to Shinjuku Gyoen for the cherry blossoms, and in the summer, we took shots of the sunset at sea. In the autumn, we traveled to Kyoto to catch the colored maple leaves. Although it wasn't all that romantic, to be honest. I mean, we were carrying loads of equipment with us. Tripod, strobe, umbrella . . . that stuff weighs a ton, you know? But even still . . ."

Shiori-chan looked a little lonesome as she gazed at the snowflakes quietly settling on the ground.

"It was fun. I had so much fun when I was with Fujimoto-kun."

She explained that although it was never explicitly mentioned that they were a couple, being together became the norm, and that relationship continued until yesterday. But she always felt there was some kind of barrier between her and Fujimoto-kun, like a thin layer of film that she couldn't seem to break no matter what.

Announcing that she couldn't carry the conversation any further in her sober state, Shiori-chan demanded that Iori bring her some tequila.

Iori and I agreed to join her in drinking shots, and I felt a wave of nausea at the glug of amber liquid poured in front of me. As I drew my nose to it, its heady smell rose up through my nostrils.

"Ready? Go!"

Throwing our heads back, we downed the shots and bit into the lemon slices in unison. My head was spinning. Shiori-chan screwed up her face and fanned at her warmed cheeks.

"I proposed to Fujimoto-kun, you know," Shiori-chan said. Her tone was so matter-of-fact that I almost missed what she'd said.

She didn't just say that, did she?

"You *proposed?*"

Shiori-chan chased her tequila with her whiskey highball now diluted with melting ice. I noticed that the skin around her eyelids had turned a little red.

"Once, we got a big cake for my birthday. Fujimoto-kun took a shot of me and the cake. Although the room was in a big mess and I didn't have makeup on, and I was wearing embarrassingly childish hair clips, the picture turned out great. We were like, *Look at that face!* and started laughing our heads off. And then . . ." Reminiscing, Shiori-chan chuckled. "I thought, *I love him so much!* and I just blurted out, 'Marry me!' "

Shiori-chan laughed to herself, scratching her head sheepishly. "Love makes you a bit crazy doesn't it?"

Iori leaned forward. "And what did he say?"

Shiori-chan's eyes dropped. "He told me he was scared. That he was scared to be with me." She stared idly at the table. "He said that he felt like he would be ruined if he were to stay with me. I didn't understand. We were having so much fun—how dare he say that he was scared? We ended up having a huge fight, and we didn't see each other for a while. Just thinking about it pisses me off," Shiori-chan said, and downed another shot of tequila. She bit into a slice of lemon and exhaled heavily.

"I was so pissed off, I even thought about dating other guys. But then I thought, *Why would I go out of my way to date other guys, when Fujimoto-kun was right there?* I was furious, yet I was already missing him. It was at that moment . . ."

Shiori-chan stopped speaking for a minute.

"It was at that moment that I realized I may never love someone the way I loved him. I thought, *I love Fujimoto-kun. I don't care if he's awkward and picky and oversensitive.* I don't care if he's 'desirable,' and I don't care what other people think. I just love him. I decided to simply keep loving him, and see how far that would take me."

"Wow," I said.

Have I ever felt that way about someone?

"So then I came up with the idea of making him osechi, in order to make up with him. Fujimoto-kun had told me that he'd never properly tried osechi before, because when he was growing up, there was usually no one home on New Year's. I wanted to make him his first homemade osechi."

"You're really something, Shiori-chan," I said. "Osechi takes a lot of time and effort."

"I had no choice. I mean, they say the way to a man's heart is through his stomach, right? But nothing that I cooked for him had worked, not even nikujaga, karaage, or beef stew. I thought that if I made him something as impressive as osechi, then he would be able to see a future with me. I desperately wanted to make him go, 'If it was with her, maybe I could give this being-a-family thing a try.' "

Shiori-chan tapped at the jubako with the tips of her nails. The osechi, once neatly packed inside the boxes, had now been reduced to a scatter of leftovers.

"From then onward, osechi became something of a magic cure for our relationship. Every November, on my birthday, I would get impatient and ask him if he was ever going to marry me. He would avoid answering properly, start saying that he was scared or whatever. I would get pissed off and leave. But then I'd start to miss him, and I'd show up at his place just before New Year's, my homemade osechi in hand. We'd enjoy the osechi together and make up. This whole routine has been our norm for the past three years."

Shiori-chan nonchalantly poured tequila for herself and drank it in one gulp. Her eyes had started to turn droopy.

"Yesterday, I was hoping to reset things by following that same routine: make osechi, go to Fujimoto-kun's house, have osechi together, and *poof!*—another year begins."

"I think you've had enough to drink." Iori seized the bottle of tequila from Shiori-chan. Protesting playfully, Shiori-chan laughed. Her blinking had slowed down.

"But as I was packing the datemaki into the jubako, a thought struck me. Didn't I do this last year? And the year before, and the year before that? It was like I was in one of those time-loop movies. He would allude to a future together by saying things like, 'Remind me next year that I've put away my winter clothes here. I'll forget.' He would talk to me as though we were going to be together in a year's time. It gave me hope that one day he would change. Do you see what I mean?"

Iori was about to pour his beer when, like a cat pouncing on its prey, Shiori-chan snatched the beer out of his hands and downed it. She let out another satisfied sigh and slumped over the table.

"She caught me off guard," Iori said, as an explanation for his weak reflexes.

We cleared the plates and glasses away from her hair.

"I wonder what Fujimoto-kun is doing right now . . ." Still slumped over on the table, Shiori-chan slurred her words. "He cried, you know. When I told him yesterday that I wanted to break up."

"He did?" I said. "He didn't want to break up with you?"

"Oh, I don't know . . . I don't get him. He said he was sorry. He told me that he would be ruined if he stayed with me. 'I'm scared. When I'm with you, it feels like a version of me that I never knew gets dragged out of me. It feels like I'm being stripped naked.' Imagine a brawny, bearded man crying his eyes out."

Her head still resting on the table, Shiori-chan shifted her glance to me.

"Hey, Momoko." She stared at me with sleepy eyes. Even her neck was red from drunkenness. "What was I supposed to do? I just couldn't do it anymore. I had done everything I could to convey my love to him. For five years, I was me. No games, no techniques. I confronted him as me and.I got hurt a lot. Even still, I really, really loved him. And now I've used up all of my love."

Tears pooled under her reddened eyes and dropped down the side of her face.

"I'm drained of love. I loved him to the last drop. I tried my best, but I'm at the end of my rope. How could he say that he didn't want to love me any more than he already did, when I've fallen this deeply in love with him? I couldn't fall deeper if I tried."

I could hear her sobs slowly building in her chest. Using the sleeve of her cardigan, Shiori-chan wiped at her face.

"Maybe I could have done more. If I had taken better care of him, or if I had been kinder to him, perhaps he would have wanted to be my family. But it's . . . it's too exhausting. It hurts that he didn't accept me, even though I showed him my naked self—literally. Had I been tactful, had I been showing him a different version of myself, then I could have lived with that. But I wasn't. I was just being me. I can't stand this, not anymore. How could he treat me this way?"

Overcome by emotion, I pulled her into a hug and held her tightly. A faint smell of alcohol mixed with the soft scent of roses.

"You did more than enough," I said. "You really gave it your all."

Shiori-chan was even smaller than I expected. I patted her slight and delicate back. Her chest heaved with sobs, her cries growing more and more audible.

"Fujimoto-kun. Please . . . please find happiness." Shiori-chan's voice trembled. "I need you to be happy, happier than anyone else. . . . Actually, no. Why—why couldn't it be me? I wanted to be the one who makes you happy, Fujimoto-kun. Why not me?"

Shiori-chan pressed her face against my left shoulder.

Truly, she's such a wonderful person.

This is what it means to love somebody.

Hiccuping, Shiori-chan gently pulled away. Her face was a mess from all the crying and the mucus dripping from her nose. Her bangs were stuck to her forehead.

"Momoko, I've done the right thing, haven't I? I know I'm embarrassing myself . . ." Shiori-chan said, still hiccupping.

"You've done everything right. I'm sure of it."

I've always wanted someone to love me for who I am. I wanted to meet that someone who loved the real me.

Perhaps I was the one who failed to face them as myself.

I was the one who was scared.

Pretending to be a woman with infinite patience.

Pretending to be a low-maintenance woman.

Pretending to be understanding.

Pretending to be the same as everyone else.

I was the one who couldn't live without pretending. I've been protecting myself so that I can make excuses. That way, I would never get hurt. I found a way to beat the system.

But Shiori faced him as herself, with all her heart. Her heart is shattered to pieces. Still, she puts a brave face on and says she's okay. But the next moment she's pining for him, bawling her eyes out. To the onlooker, she may come across as embarrassing. Maybe they'll think that she's stupid to have wasted five precious years of her twenties on a flaky jerk. That she should've locked down a desirable guy while she was still young and attractive.

I say they can go fuck themselves.

"It was a good love, Shiori-chan. You did something extraordinary. Maybe embarrassing yourself as much as you are right now is what it takes to truly love someone."

Shiori-chan's eyes widened.

"Fujimoto-kun will be okay. I mean, he's received so much love from you that you're drained of it."

"I—I guess you're right. I really gave him my all. He will find happiness, won't he?"

"He will. And so will you, Shiori-chan."

Sniffling, Shiori-chan nodded several times and laughed.

I had wanted to be absolutely sure that my ex-boyfriend regretted losing me.

But perhaps sometimes, wishing someone happiness is the best revenge.

I was so disappointed and so hurt, I made it all about myself.

I wasn't thinking about Kyohei at all.

I was protecting my own heart by making Kyohei the bad guy.

From now on, I will—
I will . . .

"God, my whole body aches!" was the first thing Shiori-chan said when she awoke on the café's sofa that morning. Despite her excessive drinking the night before, she acted as though nothing had happened.

Her face was unbelievably puffy, though, and the moment she emerged from the bathroom, she pointed to herself and said, "Oh my God, Momoko. Look at my face!" and burst out laughing.

"Oh, no, where are your eyes? Can you even see like that?"

"Actually, no. I can only see a tenth of what I normally see. By the way, your face is really bad, too, Momoko."

After that, we couldn't look at each other without laughing our heads off and we spent a good while snapping photos of our puffy faces as if they were the funniest things we'd ever seen in our lives. Agreeing that we couldn't let the boys see our faces, we decided that I would walk Shiori-chan home without waking Iori and Hozumi, who were still sleeping with their heads down on the table.

"I lied to you about something," Shiori-chan suddenly said as we made our way to her house.

"Huh?"

Shiori-chan grinned. Taking care not to slip, she moved her Doc Martens one step at a time. The snow reflected the morning sun, relentlessly attacking my swollen eyes.

"I've been to Amayadori once before."

"You have?"

"Yeah. The place was packed that day, so I guess you don't remember."

"I can't say that I do, sorry."

She'd probably come on that day we had long lines outside the café after we were featured on TV.

"I saw the Ex-Boyfriend's Favorite Curry on the menu, and I thought, who *does* that? So of course I had to try it. And when I saw you at the till as I was leaving, I told you that I enjoyed the curry. And guess what you said to me in reply?"

I couldn't remember it at all. I'd received compliments from other customers before, but what did I normally say to them? I'd never really thought about it. I had no idea what I'd said to her.

Watching me rack my brain at her question, Shiori-chan chortled.

"You said, 'I know! It's so delicious, isn't it? I love that curry!' "

I started coughing. I could feel my cheeks getting hot.

"How embarrassing! The appropriate thing to say would have been 'Thank you' or 'I'm glad that you liked it.' Knowing me, I probably got carried away because we had such a full house." I shook my head, a bit ashamed.

"But to me your words were like a ray of light. It felt like they gave me the encouragement I needed."

"Th-they were? How so?"

"Well, you made that curry yourself, yet you were talking as though someone else had made it. I realized that to you, the fact that you made it, and the fact that the curry tasted good, were two unrelated facts."

Shiori-chan buried her reddened nose in her scarf.

"Sometimes, when you're in love with someone, your feelings for that person gets buried under all this other stuff and you lose sight of it. Even when you simply loved someone at the beginning, you start thinking about whether that person makes you a better person. You start thinking about how you come across to others for being in love with that person. Which is why, if you're going to love someone, you want to choose someone that you can say you love without having to worry. Before you can declare that you love something, you find yourself prioritizing what other people will think. That's only normal."

The light turned red, and we stopped at the crossing. I slipped my cold fingers out of my pockets and pressed the pedestrian push button.

"When I went to Amayadori, I was uncertain about my feelings for Fujimoto-kun. But after speaking to you and seeing how honest you were with your feelings, with your love . . . well, that was when I told myself that I would give Fujimoto-kun all the love I had inside of me, until I was completely drained of it. And that's why I wanted to have a Funeral Committee meeting last night. I thought that if I saw you again, maybe something would change."

"Shiori-chan . . ."

I'd never imagined that anyone would look at me in such a way. Seeing that I was too surprised to speak, Shiori-chan thumped me on the back.

"My point is, you'll be fine, too, Momoko. Because you know how to protect your own love."

A voice rang out from the signal, along with a rhythmical sound. The light had turned green.

"We're nearly there, so I can walk on my own from here."

With that, Shiori-chan scurried across. Once she got to the other side of the road, she turned around and waved her arm.

I threw the finely grated ginger and garlic into the pan. The moment they met the melting butter, a wonderful smell exploded through the café. Once the pan was hot enough, I added the sliced onions and spices. I inhaled deeply, really taking in the aroma.

"Done," I said to myself.

Placing the lid over the pan, I extended my arms into a big stretch. It felt a little stuffy, so I opened the door, letting the crisp winter air fill up the café.

While the curry simmered, I idly sat at the counter and gazed at the interior of the café.

So much has happened . . .

My glance fell on the snow globes sitting on the display shelf—the ones that Iori, Hozumi, and I had made. Thanks to all the remnants of Kyohei I stuffed inside it, mine had discolored oddly.

"Hey, Momo-chan."

The bell made the usual dull sound as Iori and Hozumi appeared through the door. It seemed that they had just returned after showering at home. Probably still hungover, Iori stepped inside the kitchen and drank some water languidly.

"Urgh. My head hurts. Was Shiori-chan all right this morning?"

"Something smells good," Hozumi interrupted.

"You're right. I could do with some food," Iori agreed.

"You caught me," I said.

Although I had planned on having the curry on my own, the three of us ended up eating together.

I arranged the plates and spoons on the counter. Thinking about it, having curry for breakfast on New Year's Eve was kind of weird. But then again, we'd already had osechi on December 30, so it was too late to try to do things in the right order.

"Itadakimasu," I said.

Iori and Hozumi were ravenous. They gobbled down the curry as though they hadn't eaten in days.

"I swear, curry is the best hangover cure," Iori said.

"Well, it does contain turmeric," Hozumi pointed out.

"Smarty-pants."

Their voices sounded far away. With a trembling hand, I picked up the spoon. I'd made and sampled this curry hundreds of times, yet my heart was racing.

When we were still together, I had called it the Kyohei curry. It was a recipe I'd invented for Kyohei, a flavor that Kyohei loved. It was a dish infused with so many memories, I couldn't eat it without thinking of him. And that was why I agreed to put it on the menu—I turned it into material for a good story in the hope that it would alleviate my pain.

But none of that matters anymore.

I made this curry for me.

I can't leave it with Kyohei forever. I need to reclaim it.

I drank a glass of water to steady myself.

Then, plunging my spoon into the curry and rice, I scooped up half of each and thrust them into my mouth.

"Momoko?"

It wasn't anything fancy. It hadn't been slow-cooked over forty-eight hours, and it surely didn't have the depth of the famous curry at the Imperial Hotel.

But still . . .

"Yum."

I stuffed the curry and rice into my mouth, shoveling it all in, just as Iori and Hozumi had. The chicken, tenderized by the marinade of yogurt and spices, pulled apart effortlessly.

Devouring the dish in one go, I expelled a long breath. I dabbed at my mouth with a napkin.

"This curry," I said. "It's—"

—good, isn't it?

Just before the words spilled from my lips, I stopped myself.

I had grown so accustomed to worrying about what the person I loved thought and felt. I longed to become who the person I loved wanted me to be. It was as if everything had to pass the "Kyohei test" first—I couldn't say that I liked something unless I knew he liked it.

"Momoko? Is something wrong?"

I shook my head at Iori and Hozumi, who were looking at me, puzzled.

It's time for my love to rest in peace.

Do you love me? Do you like my cooking? Will I be able to remain the same person you fell in love with?

I won't be tempted to ask these questions anymore. It's time to say goodbye to that version of me. I'll be fine. I've given it my all. I've struggled and suffered. I've fought through life. I'm ready. I'm ready to say . . .

"This curry is *so* good. Seriously. It's out of this world!"

When I said those words in a slightly quivering voice, Iori and Hozumi looked at each other and chuckled.

"Indeed, it's good," Iori said.

"It's delicious," Hozumi agreed.

The three of us headed to the kitchen to have more helpings of the world's most delicious curry.

Under the morning light, a blanket of fresh snow shimmered ever so brightly.

THE MAN MAGNET'S OSECHI

Serves 2

- 5 snow peas
- One (5-inch / 12 cm) lotus root
- 1 medium carrot
- 6 dried shiitake mushrooms (rehydrate and keep the soaking liquid)
- 7 ounces (200 g) burdock roots, scrubbed
- 7 ounces (200 g) bamboo shoots
- 9 ounces (250 g) boneless, skinless chicken thighs
- 3 cups (700 ml) dashi stock (including the soaking liquid of shiitake mushrooms)
- $2^1/_2$ tablespoons soy sauce
- 3 tablespoons (40 g) sugar

METHOD

Blanch the snow peas and soak them in cold water.

Decoratively cut (kazari-giri) the lotus root, carrot, and shiitake mushrooms.

Chop up the burdock roots and bamboo shoots. Cut the chicken thighs into bite-sized pieces.

Heat a small amount of oil in a pot and fry the chicken thighs. When browned, add all the vegetables except for the snow peas.

Add the dashi stock and soaking liquid from the shiitake mushrooms and simmer. Add the soy sauce and sugar. Simmer for a short while until seasoned. Garnish with the snow peas and serve.

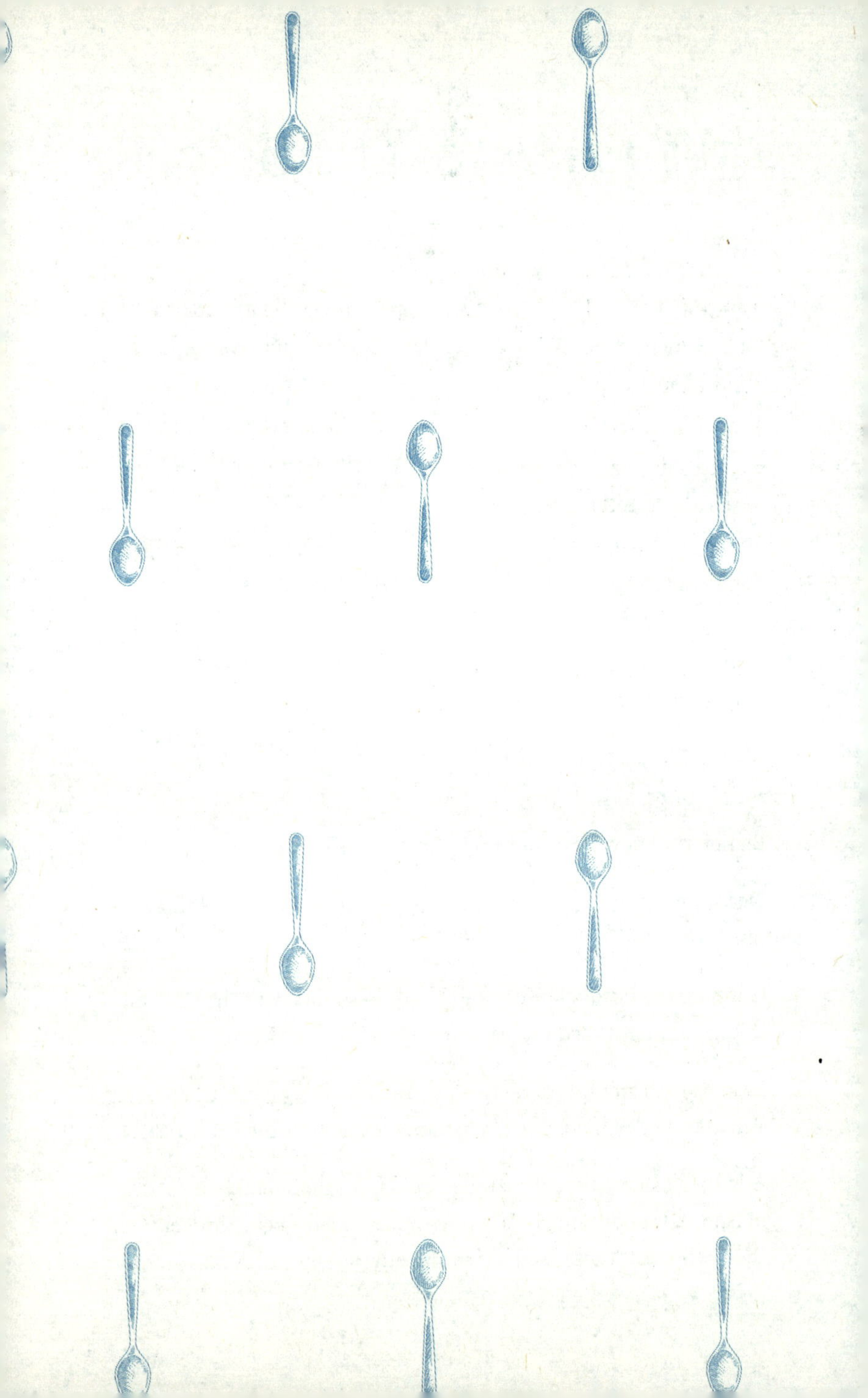

ACKNOWLEDGMENTS

This book was brought to life by countless heartfelt interviews, and by the generosity of those who shared not only their stories but also their recipes—each one a small, edible piece of a love once lived.

Special thanks to the unofficial members of *The Ex-Boyfriend's Favorite Recipe Funeral Committee*—you know who you are. Thank you for whispering secrets over coffee, digging through old cookbooks, and laughing (or crying) along the way. Your stories fed this novel in every sense of the word.

about the author

SAKI KAWASHIRO was born in Tokyo, Japan. An avid reader, after graduating from college she worked as a book-seller in Fukuoka, in southern Japan. While manager of the store's café, she invented a dish for the café menu—"My Ex-Boyfriend's Favorite Butter Chicken Curry"—that included a vignette about their breakup, which went viral. Author Toshikazu Kawaguchi (*Before the Coffee Gets Cold*) made an appearance at her bookstore, and Mr. Kawaguchi's editor inspired Saki to write a novel about her adventures, and she became Saki's editor. The result is *The Ex-Boyfriend's Favorite Recipe Funeral Committee*, Saki's first novel.